THE BASTARDS
OF PIZZOFALCONE

Maurizio de Giovanni

THE BASTARDS
OF PIZZOFALCONE

*Translated from the Italian
by Antony Shugaar*

Europa
editions

Europa Editions
214 West 29th Street
New York, N.Y. 10001
www.europaeditions.com
info@europaeditions.com

Library of Congress Cataloging in Publication Data is available
ISBN 978-1-60945-314-5

de Giovanni, Maurizio
The Bastards of Pizzofalcone

Book design by Emanuele Ragnisco
www.mekkanografici.com

Cover image:
detail from the 2014 Bicentennial edition of the Historical Calendar
of the Carabinieri.

Prepress by Grafica Punto Print – Rome

Printed in the USA

To Severino Cesari.
Brother of every word.

THE BASTARDS
OF PIZZOFALCONE

I

The sea.

The sea in the air. The sea in the street.

The sea in the sky, all the way up to the windows shut tight on the highest floors.

The sea in your ears, muffling the whistling of the wind.

The sea on the rocks, shattering itself against them and bellowing hoarsely.

The sea, drop by drop, flying. The sea whirling.

It's not unlike that damned snow of yours, you know. The way it kicks up, blurs your sight, and for a moment keeps you from seeing the landscape, only to settle again at the bottom.

Not always at the bottom, come to think of it. Sometimes, to one side. This time, to one side. Standing there, watching, as it settled slowly on the side. On the far side.

Only one person, on the street. Me. For that matter, at this time of night and in this weather, who'd be here? Who would risk being swept far away by the wind, onto who knows what island?

If only.

I can't believe it, that I actually did it. But it's true, I really did. I didn't want to, I wasn't planning it. I thought we'd talk. I thought we'd talk, and that you'd come around. That you'd say: all right, I understand. That you'd say: okay, you're right, you win. We'll end this, and then I'll leave.

I thought that maybe it wouldn't even be that hard, to make you see reason. But instead, instead: no. You're a stubborn woman.

Or you were.

God, all this sea in the air. All this noise. Deafening me. Confusing me.

I had to do it, you know that, right? It was necessary.

Because that's the way love is. You can hide it as long as you like, you can conceal it behind the gazes and gestures of everyday life. You can leave it in silence, tend to it like a plant; but the day you decide to bring it out into the light of day, from that day forward you're no longer in charge. Now love is in charge. It decides for you, it unfolds like a beautiful blossom, it wants to take up as much room as possible.

But you? Not a chance. You refused to make room for love. You were unwilling to take that step. Too bad for you.

You should have read what was there in my eyes. You ought to have understood. You had all the time you needed to figure out that I wouldn't take no for an answer. That I was bound to lose my head. It was there, clear as day, in my eyes.

The snow. Your goddamned fake snow. It's just like this sea, soaking me now like rain, filling my head with wind and water.

I don't see them, your closed windows. Too much wind, too much sea in the air.

Just like your snow, that you liked to watch as it whirled in the glass, concealing the landscape. Could you ever have imagined, that that very blizzard would be your last?

And it kicked up, in fact. For the last time, before starting to come back down. On the side opposite the blood.

By the time the snow settled, you were already a memory.

II

Giuseppe Lojacono was sitting in the squad car, in the passenger seat, back straight, hands motionless on his thighs. He really did look Chinese, which is why his colleagues had given him that nickname; not that they'd told him about it, of course: he wasn't the kind of guy you could kid around with. High cheekbones, almond-shaped eyes that, when he concentrated, narrowed until they were just a pair of slits; black hair, slick but rumpled; a bony physique, perennially tense, as if he might lunge forward at any second. A few creases at the corners of his mouth made it clear that he'd made it past forty, though not by much.

He was thinking. About how easy it had been to lose everything that, with dedication and hard work, he had managed to build. And he was thinking about how, back home, at that very moment, in late March, the almond trees were blossoming and the sun was already hot enough that you could lie on the beach and think as you looked out to sea; here, on the other hand, it might as well have been the middle of winter, with wind giving way to showers and women chasing tattered umbrellas down the sidewalk, while the stopped cars trumpeted their frustration with frequent blasts from irritated horns.

But home was far away, very far away in both space and time. Maybe it was actually impossible to reach, by now. And anyway, no one there wanted him back. He was too much trouble: trouble as a friend, as a relative, and as a colleague.

He thought back to his conversation with Commissario Di

Vincenzo, to whom he'd been assigned. Not that they'd ever liked each other, but after everything had happened with the Crocodile, it all had become too much to bear.

The Crocodile. The nondescript, grieving old man who had murdered four kids. And Lojacono, investigating even though he hadn't been assigned to the case, had tracked him down; he'd identified him and uncovered his motive. While the city's entire police force was rummaging through the usual closets— Camorra, corruption, drugs—and coming up empty-handed.

That case had worked to restore his reputation, at least in part, but it had made the other cops like him even less. A guy who doesn't know his way around, who isn't in contact with any informants, and who solves a complicated series of murders using nothing but logic. Pulling feet out of the fire at police headquarters, while his superiors struggled to cope with an increasingly angry press and public.

At that point, something had to be done with him. He couldn't be left manning the criminal complaints desk at a police station in a precinct seething with crime. No, now he needed a real post: otherwise some newspaper would wonder, as soon as they ran out of events to slap on the front page, what had become of the man who found the Crocodile.

For a while, Di Vincenzo had resisted, only to finally gave in and reluctantly assign Lojacono to cold cases, cases no one had made any progress on for years. No one, in any event, was going to tell the commissario what jobs he could or couldn't assign his men to.

Then Di Vincenzo had sent for him, just a few days ago.

And he'd told him about the precinct of Pizzofalcone.

This, Lojacono mused, might be the best solution, which is what you always think as you're tumbling out of the frying pan and into the fire.

The young officer driving had already tried twice to engage him in conversation, but his attempts at small talk had been met with silence. And so for the last few minutes he'd steered the car and kept his mouth shut, darting rapid glances at his passenger.

He found the Sicilian's profile unsettling. The driver, too, had heard all sorts of stories about the lieutenant, who'd been tossed off the Agrigento mobile squad because a state's witness had reported that Lojacono was passing information to the Mafia. From what the driver'd heard, no solid evidence had surfaced against him but, as always in these cases, it had been thought wise to station the suspect elsewhere.

The driver had already crossed paths with Lojacono a number of times when he found himself on duty at the police station's front desk, and of course he knew all about the Crocodile case. For a time, the city had talked of nothing else. And gone on talking for days and days, even after the case was over; until something new—more blood, more death—could take its place on the front pages of the newspapers and on TV. As for what had actually happened, he had no way of knowing. Still, sitting next to that man of so few words, he felt uneasy.

He asked: "Should I put on the siren, lieutenant? This traffic's locked up solid, as soon as there's a drop of rain in this city everyone hops in their cars."

Lojacono replied without taking his eyes off the line of cars ahead of them. "No, don't bother. We're in no hurry."

The traffic seemed to stir, but then it ground to a halt again: maybe a traffic light, a mile or so ahead of them, had just turned red again.

The wind was firing gusts of briny rain straight from the sea onto the windshield. A scirocco wind.

Without taking his eyes off his desk, Di Vincenzo pointed Lojacono to a chair.

"Please, come right in. Have a seat."

He rummaged through his papers. Then he took off his glasses and leaned back in his chair.

"Well, well, Lojacono: so you're going through some old files, are you? Who knows, with your instincts, we might be able to make some progress. Old stuff, I realize that. But if you're good, really good, you can see things that other men might miss."

The lieutenant said nothing, just sat there, expressionless.

Di Vincenzo drummed his fingers on his desktop, and then went on: "It's not that simple. People on the outside think the work we do is like some American TV show, that we leap from bridges onto rumbling motorcycles and have shoot-outs with criminals in the middle of the street. Instead, it's just paper, paper, and more paper. Aside from the occasional piece of sheer dumb luck, of course. That can happen too, sometimes."

The incompetent, Lojacono thought to himself, always attribute the success of others to luck. He wished he had a penny for every time he'd seen it happen.

"Commissario, did you need me? I'm at your service."

Di Vincenzo nodded, without bothering to conceal the dislike that shone through his gaze.

"No more beating about the bush, Loja': I'm pretty sure that the song and dance you've concocted, with this story of the Crocodile, is a mixture of playacting and good luck. Seasoned with the strange confidential relationship you seem to have established with Dottoressa Piras, which I'm not interested in delving into."

That vulgar reference to Piras, the prosecuting magistrate who had insisted on having Lojacono assigned to the Crocodile investigation, was meant to wound; but the lieutenant let it slide off his back. He could guess what was being said about him and Laura: attractive and not particularly interested in winning any popularity contents, she'd also made no secret of her fondness for him.

"Commissario, I don't like you and you don't like me. For both of our sakes, why don't we limit our conversation to what's strictly necessary. So let me ask again: was there something you needed?"

A muscle twitched in Di Vincenzo's jaw and a shadow of rage darkened his eyes, but he managed to keep a lid on it.

"You have a point, Lojacono: I don't like you. And that is exactly why I'm so happy to be able to tell you the following. I've been asked to reassign an investigative asset, for a period of time that remains at the moment indeterminate, to another precinct. I can prove that, of all my assets, the only one not currently committed to an investigation is, in fact, you."

Lojacono shrugged his shoulders; he didn't want to make this easy for him.

"Still, it's a voluntary reassignment, I would imagine. Which means you need my consent. My written consent. So if you want to get rid of me, you need to talk me into it. Is that about right?"

Di Vincenzo started to get to his feet, only to drop back into his chair, lips stretched taut.

"I had no doubt you'd be well briefed on procedures. Typical of good-for-nothings, to be intimately acquainted with union regulations. Yes, it's true. But it's also true that, if you don't accept, I can assign you to any task I please; and this special treatment that you're being given on account of the Crocodile won't last forever."

Lojacono let a moment pass, then he said:

"Then tell me more about this assignment. Who knows, I might even accept."

The commissario perked up at the idea of being able to free himself of that Sicilian with the inscrutable expression, whom he was afraid to really go after because he feared Piras's reaction; moreover, if Lojacono decided to get stubborn and refuse, he might be forced to give up some other man he trusted, and it was already hard enough keeping up with his work, given the limited resources at his disposal. He needed to convince him. He did his best to appear conciliatory.

"Well, it's a professional challenge, in a certain sense. Have you ever heard of the precinct of Pizzofalcone?"

Lojacono continued staring at the commissario, who finally decided to go on:

"The precinct isn't big, but it's crowded; it encompasses a part of the Spanish Quarter and stretches on down to the waterfront. Four different worlds, in other words: the lumpenproletariat, as we used to say in the old days; the white-collar middle class; the businessmen of the upper middle class; and the aristocracy. Everything except manufacturing, in an area barely three kilometers on a side. One of the oldest police districts in the city, small but strategic." Di Vincenzo furrowed his brow and his tone of voice changed: he must have remembered something unpleasant. "A year or so, give or take, there was a major drug raid. A shipment of uncut cocaine was confiscated, just after it arrived in the Spanish Quarter; a massive shipment, really huge. But well under half was officially logged in."

Lojacono asked, in a low voice: "Who?"

"It was discovered late. There were four partners, all of them detectives. A well-run operation, the information was cross-referenced, an ambush was set, and their timing was perfect: just moments after the delivery, not so early that they came up empty-handed, but not so late that the criminals had a chance to organize a defense. A clean, fast, bloodless raid. And of course, it was in everyone's interest to officially log much less product than was actually confiscated: in the interest of the gangsters, because it meant the sentences they would face would be sharply reduced, and also, unfortunately, in the interest of the cops, who proceeded to set themselves up in the cocaine business."

The lieutenant sat in silence, for once sharing the commissario's feelings. A nasty story. Truly nasty. For any honest cop.

Di Vincenzo went on: "One of them had a very sick son—cancer. Another was divorced, and his ex-wife had basically bled him dry. The third's father was a shopkeeper who had just been forced into bankruptcy, and the fourth gambled. They exchanged a glance, and that was that. I knew two of them, and I would have walked through fire for them. Go figure . . . In any case, when you alter the market equilibrium of the local narcotics trade with that much product, it becomes necessary to go out and get permission and authorization from the local dealers, and sooner or later word filters back. And their special investigations counterparts over at DIGOS figured it out. It took months of wiretaps, photography, surveillance videos. In they end, they took them down. All four of them."

A sudden gust of wind shook the window.

Lojacono said: "Got it. An ugly situation."

Di Vincenzo sighed.

"The commissario went down with them: Ruoppolo, a longtime colleague just about to retire, a great guy I knew very well. Honest, sure, no doubt about it: but certain areas of oversight fell to him. So he took his pension a little quicker than he would have otherwise. For a couple of months the police chief wondered whether he should just shut down the Pizzofalcone precinct entirely, and enlarge the jurisdictions of the surrounding precincts. Then he decided differently."

"And that's where we come in."

"Exactly. They need four investigators, and they've reached out to the four biggest precincts. The new commissario is Palma, a young guy on his way up. He comes from Vomero, you might remember having seen him at the meeting for the Crocodile. If I were him, I would never have accepted. There's no upside."

Lojacono made a face: "So you volunteered me."

Di Vincenzo raised an eyebrow: "That's what I would have done, if I'd been quick enough: in cases like this, you always take advantage of the opportunity to get rid of your bad apples. But Palma himself asked for you: apparently, you made quite an impression on him at that very same meeting. He's an idiot, I guessed it at the time. Obviously, I immediately agreed to the request. So, what do you think?"

The lieutenant sat silently for a good long time. Then he asked: "So what do I risk, if I accept? What could I be up against?"

Di Vincenzo snorted, losing control and slamming one hand down on his desk, scattering papers, pens, pencils, and eyeglasses: "That the attempt to keep this precinct operating fails. If worst comes to worst, they liquidate the station and the staff and send you all back where you came from. Or maybe they send you somewhere else, which is what I'm hoping, because in the meantime all four precincts will be busy trying to get replacements. And, of course, you'd be joining a group made up of people who aren't welcome where they are now, whose commanding officers are eager to get rid of them. Renegades, bastards, or screwups, every last one of them!"

Lojacono showed no visible reaction: "Commissario, I would have accepted a transfer to Patagonia in order to get out of here. But I wanted to keep you guessing. When do I report for duty in my new precinct?"

III

The woman enters, and slams the door behind her.

Before the door slams shut, he manages to glimpse astonishment on the faces of a couple of employees, fixed as if in some hyperrealistic painting meant to depict amazement, embarrassment, and terror, all in a single expression. One of them was actually halfway out of his chair, as if he meant to try to stop the intrusion. As if that was even possible.

The man heaves a sigh and tucks his head between his shoulders in order to absorb the loud banging of the door against the jamb; it sounds like its structural integrity is being tested.

"Well, what the fuck are you planning to do? Have you made up your mind? Don't I have a right to know?"

Hands on her hips, long legs braced, jaw clenched tight. Her red hair glows as if it's on fire, and so do her eyes. She's beautiful, the man thinks to himself. Beautiful, even when she's furious.

Which seems to be the case more often than not these days, truth be told.

"Lower your voice. Have you lost your mind? What are you trying to do now, air all our dirty laundry?"

She does lower the volume; but not by much.

"I need to know what you plan to do. Because enough is enough: I refuse to become that pathetic cliché—the poor idiot duped by the older professional. I'm a girl who'll knock you flat on your ass; that's exactly what I'll do, and you know it. I can't believe it, can't believe I've let this go on so long."

He knows perfectly well that if he starts whimpering now, she'll just get angrier. He does his best to think quickly.

"It's not a matter of anyone trying to dupe you. This is a complicated situation. A whole lifetime together . . . We own property together, a lot of it in her name, for tax purposes. And then it's a moral issue, it's not like I can just get up one morning and kick her out the door, not someone like . . . someone like her. And there are all our friends, our contacts, some of them politicians . . . It's not a simple matter."

"Friends? Politicians? I DON'T GIVE A FLYING FUCK about your contacts, do you get that? I will humiliate you in front of the whole world! Do you seriously think I don't know that everything you have comes to you from the curia? What do you think His Eminence would say, if he knew that . . . if he knew about me, about my condition? He'd send you straight to hell, that's where he'd send you!"

He shifts to get more comfortable in his chair, threading his fingers together in front of his face, his expression pensive. He needs to keep cool.

"Well done. That way we'll both lose everything. Is that what's in your best interest? And is that in . . . well, I mean, is that in our best interest? Wouldn't it be smarter to wait for the right time? Maybe we can get someone else to solve the whole problem for us. I'll talk to her, I told you. I'll do it. No matter what, I'll have to do it. She's reasonable, you know; she's certainly no fool."

She watches him, unblinking, with those green eyes of hers. Her breasts heave with her still rapid breaths. He can't help but stare at her in fascination.

"You'd better do it, and for real. Otherwise I'll do it for you, and I'll look her straight in the eye when I tell her. Maybe we women understand each other better, without a lot of fancy phrases. Maybe I'll bring her a present, and then I'll tell her: that it's not a very good idea to try to get in the way of someone like me."

He knows perfectly well that she would do it. That she's good, very good, at facing situations head-on.

"If you don't lower your voice, goddammit, you won't even need to go see her. Do you have any idea how many spies she has, here in this office? It wouldn't do you a bit of good, anyway. She'd never say yes to you. She'd just decide that there's a battle to be fought, and maybe she'd talk herself into believing that, since I wasn't the one who came to talk to her, I don't have the courage to leave her, and that therefore she might stand a chance of winning me back. God forbid. We'd get swallowed up in legal maneuverings that would never end. Her father is a retired judge who still has plenty of influence. No, I'm going to have to talk to her."

The woman walks closer to the desk, feline, like a tiger about to pounce on its prey. She places both hands flat on the desktop, long red fingernails pointing straight at him.

She hisses: "Well, then, do it. Talk to her, and soon. Otherwise, I swear to you that I'll go myself, and that'll put an end to it. One way or another."

IV

The entrance to the police station of Pizzofalcone was situated in the courtyard of an old palazzo, its façade covered with flaking plaster that had been patched in more than one place. The impression Lojacono got was of decay and neglect, which was so often the case in the city's older neighborhoods.

After a brisk wave goodbye to his driver, who roared off, tires squealing and siren wailing, he climbed a short flight of stairs that led into a small antechamber lit by fluorescent lights: even in the middle of the day, sunlight couldn't make its way into that room.

Behind the counter an officer sat sprawled in a swivel chair, deep in the pages of the sports section. There was the smell of coffee in the air, clearly emanating from a vending machine where two cops stood talking and laughing. The man behind the front desk didn't even bother to look up. Lojacono drew closer without a word and waited, staring at the uniformed officer.

After a while, the officer looked up from his paper and assumed a quizzical expression: "Yes?"

"I'm Lieutenant Lojacono. I believe the commissario is expecting me."

The man neither put down his paper nor shifted position.

"Second floor, room at the end of the hall."

Lojacono didn't move.

"On your feet," he murmured.

"What?" asked the policeman.

"Stand up on your own two feet, asshole. Give me your last name, first name, and rank. And do it fast, or I'll jump straight over this counter and kick your ass black and blue."

The lieutenant hadn't changed his tone of voice or his expression, but it was as if he had shouted. The two men drinking coffee exchanged a quick glance and then left the room, quickly and quietly.

The officer struggled out of the chair, displaying a jacket half unbuttoned over a prominent gut and a loosened belt. His collar was half undone, and the knot of his tie hung slack. He snapped to attention, his gaze fixed on the empty air before him.

"Officer Giovanni Guida, Pizzofalcone Police Precinct."

Lojacono continued to stare at him.

"Now you listen to me, Giovanni Guida of the Pizzofalcone police precinct. You're the first thing people see when they walk in here, so of course they'll assume that we're all filthy pigs, because you're a filthy pig. And I don't like it when people think that I'm a filthy pig."

The man said nothing, and his eyes remained expressionless. One of the two cops who had been drinking coffee stuck his head in for a moment, then vanished.

"If I see you looking like I found you just now ever again, I'll kick your ass for one solid hour out in the courtyard. Is that clear? And then you can write me up for it."

Officer Guida murmured softly: "Forgive me, lieutenant. It won't happen again. It's just that, these days, practically no one even comes in here anymore. People prefer . . . people go to the carabinieri, when they want to report something. They seem to prefer going there since . . . for a while now."

"I don't care about that," Lojacono replied. "Even if they turn this place into a cloistered monastery, you still need to present yourself looking the way you're supposed to look."

He went through the internal door as Guida was stuffing

his shirttails into his trousers, red-faced and swearing under his breath.

A short hallway led to the stairs. Out of the corner of his eye Lojacono took in sloppiness, disorder, and neglect. He felt distress rise within him, and he wondered if he'd ever again experience the excitement he used to feel for his profession.

The commissario's office was right at the top of the staircase. Behind the desk sat Palma, busy placing sheets of paper into a box file. Lojacono remembered him the minute he saw him, a man of about forty with a rumpled look, his shirtsleeves rolled up, a shadow of stubble on his face. More than sloppiness, however, the impression he gave was of someone who was constantly busy.

Commissario Palma noticed Lojacono and beamed a broad smile: "Ah, Lojacono, at last you're here! I was hoping to see you today. I would have called you, but the right thing to do was to let that old geezer Di Vincenzo talk to you first. Come right in, make yourself comfortable."

The lieutenant took a step forward. The window was closed, but through the panes of glass, wet from the gusts of rain, it was possible to see the stormy sea, engaged in its thousand-year effort to demolish the tufa-stone castle perched over the waves. That city never ceased to surprise him, treating him to sudden spectacular glimpses of deceptive beauty.

"Nice, eh? A magnificent view, but let's not let ourselves get distracted: we have work to do. Go ahead, have a seat. You want a coffee?"

"No, thanks, commissario. How's everything going, sir?"

Palma threw open his arms: "No, no, that's no way to get started, Loja'! We need to be on a first-name basis here. It's just the four of us here and we all need to be rowing in the same direction. And after all, we're practically all new; I got here last Monday, the others have come in over the past three days, you're the last. In fact, now that you're here we can have our first meeting, what do you say? Or would you prefer to get settled in instead?"

The lieutenant was overwhelmed by the commissario's enthusiasm.

"No, that's not a problem, if you'd like, sir . . . I mean if you want, sure, right away . . ."

"Perfect, there's no time to waste, I was just waiting for you. Ottavia! Ottavia!"

A side door opened up and a woman in a skirt suit stepped out.

"Yes, sir, commissa'?"

"No, what is this 'yes, sir'? Didn't we just say yesterday that we're all on a first-name basis around here? Come in, come in. This is Lieutenant Giuseppe Lojacono, the precinct's latest draft pick. Loja', allow me to introduce you to Deputy Sergeant Ottavia Calabrese, she was already here . . . she'll be an invaluable resource as we get ourselves situated."

Calabrese took a step forward and Lojacono, who had stood up in the meantime, shook her hand. A good-looking woman a little over forty, serious, weary-looking, her hair pulled back.

"Welcome, lieutenant. If there's anything you need, sir, just let me know."

Her voice, low and warm, was firm and nicely modulated. Lojacono liked to judge people based on first impressions, though he was always willing to change his mind if the facts seemed to warrant it. And he liked Deputy Sergeant Calabrese.

Palma laughed: "Well, there's no way around it, you can't seem to shake that formality, eh, Ottavia? Loja', Calabrese here is a computer genius. Anything you need on the Internet, she can find it for you. Ottavia, let's alert the others and have everyone gather in the meeting room, all right? Let's call down for some coffee and a bottle of mineral water, we're celebrating the new administration. Come on, Loja', let's head down and wait for the others."

V

The walls. The walls of this room.

They're six and a half paces long; actually, eight and three quarter paces, to be precise. And it's eight paces on the other side. I remember from school, to measure the area of a rectangle you have to multiply the long side by the short side. I liked that, going to school. But then, of course, once I reached seventh grade, I stopped going.

To measure the short side you have to take into account the dresser against the wall, so to take that step you have to move a little to one side, which lengthens the distance by almost a quarter pace. And on the long side, there's a tile that's slightly chipped, right where you place your foot after the third pace.

You learn lots of things, staying here. From the windows on the balcony, for instance, you can see five apartments in the building across the way. If I could go out onto the balcony, I'd be able to see others, I think, but I'd better not. One time, he stuck a piece of paper in the French windows, and he looked to see if it was still there. It was, because I hadn't even thought of trying to open the bedroom windows: but then if it had been gone, what would I have said to him? It was my good luck I didn't open that window.

It's been fifteen days now. He came yesterday, who knows when he can come back. He said: let's hope it's soon. Sure, let's hope it's soon.

Eight and three quarter paces, if you ask me, is almost thirty feet. An enormous room. All for me: and there's a bedroom, too, *and a kitchen, and a bathroom. Back home, in our* basso, *the hovel I lived in, a space that's half the size of this, there were five of us, and we thought we were doing fine. I'm really a lucky girl.*

But I am allowed to raise the shutters. Not all the way, he said I'd better not, even though there are curtains; but a little bit, I can. I like to look out the window, I pass my time watching what people do. For instance, on the fourth floor there's an old woman who likes to watch, same as I do. Once, I'm pretty sure she saw me.

Thirty feet long, twenty feet wide. More than 600 square feet, for just one room. Mamma mia, I really am a lucky girl.

And he left me all sorts of provisions, I have a refrigerator that's about to collapse with all the food in it, and who's ever seen such bounty? It doesn't seem possible.

There are times, I'll admit, when I miss fresh air. He had an air conditioner installed, he gave me the remote control, and how we laughed, I just couldn't figure out how to make it work.

I even have a washing machine that dries the clothes after it washes them, who would ever have believed it, it seems like a miracle. I told him I don't need such a thing, the few items of clothing I have I can hang over the bathtub, but he wouldn't listen to a word I said, he told me that I ought to have everything I need. Like a queen. That's exactly what he said, like a queen. And who would ever have said such a thing about me, that I was going to be a queen!

I keep everything clean in here, even if nothing gets dirty. When he comes here, I don't ever want him to think that I'm neglecting the cleaning. When I'm done, I sit down to watch TV; now that's a remote control I have no trouble using. But I keep the voices very low, he made a point of telling me to be quiet, even if the voice people would hear would be the TV's, not mine.

I wait for him, I always wait for him. Every so often he calls me, he's the only one who even knows the number here. The last time he called he even let me say hello to Mamma, what a pleasure it was to hear her voice! She was so happy! She told me that he had bought her lots of nice things, that he even gave Papà a job, and work to my two brothers, that everyone's fine. She told me: grazie, Mammà's little sweetheart. Grazie. *And I felt proud.*

I need to eat now. He said I can't waste away, that I'm too beautiful and I need to be careful not to lose my looks, if I do he'll kick me out. He said it with a laugh, but I was scared. He said that I'm eighteen years old, and that at my age girls get ugly if they eat too much or they don't eat enough: and so he brought me the things I need to eat, and he wrote down what I should cook every day, and at what time.

I put the sheet of paper on the fridge, with the magnet in the shape of a ladybug, and I read it slowly and I cook and I eat according to the schedule.

A little while ago I looked out the window, and there was that old lady, looking right in my direction.

I'm afraid of her, that old lady.

I wonder what she wants with me.

VI

N ow, then," said Palma, "here we are. Before holding this meeting, we waited for Lieutenant Lojacono, the last addition to the staff. Now that we're all here we can introduce ourselves."

Lojacono hoped that the commissario's cheerful and amiable demeanor was meant to encourage the staff; that it wasn't dictated by any real and, in his opinion, unjustified optimism. The group looked pretty thrown together and it was, as Di Vincenzo had maliciously pointed out, made up of rejects from the city's various precincts; and those rejects were here to replace dirty, disloyal cops, who had muddied their colleagues' reputations by getting their faces splashed onto the front pages of the national press.

For that matter, Lojacono mused, he too was one of those rejects; and people had also accused him of being a dirty, disloyal cop.

Palma was still talking: "I'm not going to pretend that it will be an easy task: people warned me against taking this position, and the police chief himself debated, up to the very last minute, dissolving the precinct entirely. But I like daunting challenges, and so I accepted. It if turns out well, it'll turn out well for all of us: if not, it'll be bad for me in particular, because I doubt that any of you, for one reason or another, are interested in going back to where you came from."

In the pause that followed, Lojacono shot a glance around the conference table, a long oval in light wood, coated with dust and scarred by cigarette burns. There were seven people, him included—all of various ages, genders, physical appearances, and expressions; he wondered what had brought them here, what stories haunted their pasts.

As if he'd read his mind, the commissario said: "I'd like you all to introduce yourselves, as if no one here knows anyone else. I'm Gigi Palma, the commissario of Pizzofalcone. I'm always available, I never close my office door, unless keeping it open is a problem for whoever is talking to me. I feel sure that if we work hard, and work honestly, in the end we'll see results, and they'll be good results. I try not to be prejudiced, and I don't give a damn about what the newspapers have said about any of you: I'm wiping the slate clean, starting today. Best of luck. I'd begin with those of you who were already here, if you want to tell us a little something . . ."

He gestured to the woman he'd introduced to Lojacono. She nodded and said, in a low, melodious voice: "Ottavia Calabrese, deputy sergeant. I'm in charge of computer research and the secreteriat, but also press relations, and recently that's been an especially nightmarish part of the job, believe me, even though some of the things . . . of the events that took place were handled by the police chief's spokesman. The station house has been gone over with a fine-tooth comb by the internal investigators, as you can imagine. We assumed they were just going to shut us down, so this reorganization came as a welcome surprise. Let's hope for the best."

A collective nervous giggle greeted the woman's closing sigh.

The next to speak was a bald, elderly-looking man with a raspy voice: "Giorgio Pisanelli, deputy captain. Before you ask, let me tell you: I'm only sixty-one."

There was another round of laughter, which the man accepted with calm detachment. He went on: "I've been here for fifteen years; I might have risen through the ranks, but my wife . . . well, I had some problems at home, and I decided to focus on other things. I'd say that I'm this place's institutional memory. I live in this neighborhood and I know more or less everyone. The internal investigators went over every single document that ever passed through my hands, to make sure I wasn't in cahoots with those who were here before you: I can therefore say that I am certainly an honest person, as I've just discovered."

He was satisfied to see that everyone, including Palma, was chuckling. Lojacono decided that Pisanelli must be a smart guy, to have figured out the atmosphere needed lightening.

Palma waved his hand toward the only other female present, a slender young woman, dressed in a neat, nondescript fashion.

"My name is Di Nardo. Alessandra Di Nardo. Officer first class. I come from the Decumano Maggiore precinct."

She'd spoken with her eyes straight ahead, addressing no one in particular and with no emotion in her voice.

Palma gestured toward Lojacono.

"Lieutenant Giuseppe Lojacono, from the San Gaetano precinct."

The commissario pointed to a young man sitting near the lieutenant.

As if operated by a remote control, he snapped to his feet. He was a short little man, with a strange Elvis hairstyle that concealed an incipient bald spot at the top of his head, and two long sideburns. He wore a shirt that gaped open over his neatly shaved chest. His skin was of a vaguely orange hue, the product of long sessions under a sunlamp. With studied deliberation, he took off a pair of blue-tinted aviators, a gesture which only accentuated his ridiculous appearance, and said: "I'm Marco. Corporal Marco Aragona. I come from police headquarters."

Lojacono decided that things were actually worse than he'd

assumed; it wasn't going to be easy to get that station house up and running at even a barely decent level. Palma sighed, and it was the first time that the lieutenant had seen him waver as he considered his real chances of success.

"Well, okay then," he said. "And what about you, down there at the end?"

At the far end of the table was a huge man, grim-faced, who hadn't joined in the comments or the laughter. He kept drumming the table softly with the fingers of his left hand, keeping his right hand in his lap. His hair was extremely short, his neck was thick, and his strongly marked jaw emphasized the dour expression in his eyes.

He spoke, with visible reluctance: "Francesco Romano, warrant officer. I come from the Posillipo precinct."

Palma nodded.

"All right, now we've all introduced ourselves. The one shortcoming that we have, compared to other investigative teams, is that here most of you are new to the precinct; that means we can't have that team spirit, that reciprocal familiarity that normally constitutes an advantage."

The suntanned young man snickered and said: "Maybe we should just say that they overdid it with the team spirit, the four cops who pulled that filthy move with the drugs."

Palma glared at him, and Lojacono caught a glimpse of what the commissario could be like, once he doffed the mask of jovial benevolence at all costs.

"Officer Aragona, one more comment like that and I'll kick your ass straight back to where you came from. And believe me, I can kick hard."

Aragona sank down into his chair as if he wanted to disappear. Palma resumed: "So we need to make a special effort to get to know each other as soon as possible. The investigations will be conducted, case by case, strictly by two-person teams. For now, so as to better coordinate things and offer support from here, Pisanelli and Calabrese, who know the precinct, will remain on desk duty. The rest of you will take turns working outside, relying on these two. Is that all clear?"

Having registered the general nod of assent, he proceeded, satisfied.

"Very good. I've had a large room set up for you, with six desks. You'll all be sitting together, so you can get to know each other. Break a leg."

And he stood up.

A few minutes later, alone in his office, Commissario Luigi Palma, better known as Gigi, reviewed for the umpteenth time the confidential personnel files HR at headquarters had sent to him.

There wasn't much to know about Pisanelli and Calabrese, the two who had been here when he arrived. As the deputy captain had said, their professional lives had been gone over with a fine-tooth comb, and if nothing had been found, that meant there was nothing there. But it was also true that they were both desk jockeys, and neither of them had much experience working in the field.

Di Nardo was young; she'd just recently turned twenty-eight; an aptitude for firearms, top scores on all her marksmanship tests, and it was this very enthusiasm that had proved her undoing, a shot discharged from her pistol in the police station where she worked, in circumstances that remained murky.

Romano was a hothead: he'd grabbed a suspect by the throat, and then proceeded to blacken the eye of a fellow cop who had tried—successfully—to keep him from making a real mess of things.

Palma let out a long sigh, and scratched his head. Aragona, the suntanned young man striking the ridiculous poses, was the product of nepotism, the grandson of the prefect of a city in Basilicata. He drove like a bat out of hell, and he'd been kicked off two bodyguard details, for two different magistrates. At police headquarters, they'd been only too delighted to be rid of him.

What about Lojacono? Well, he had that ugly episode on his record—the state's witness who'd fingered him as a corrupt cop back in Sicily. But Palma had seen him in action on the Crocodile case, and he'd liked what he'd seen. It was Palma who had wanted him, even more than his fellow commissario Di Vincenzo had wanted to wash his hands of him. He had a strong hunch that the man was a smart cop. And an honest one.

Commissario Luigi Palma, better known as Gigi, hoped he wasn't making a mistake.

He hoped it with all his heart.

VII

S eated on her throne, Donna Amalia kept her eyes focused on the fifth floor of the building across the way. On the balcony, to be precise: and Donna Amalia, everyone knew, was precise. Quite precise indeed.

She'd noticed something odd almost immediately, seventeen days ago. She'd paid close attention to the renovation work being done in the apartment, which had been done quickly but extremely well, at least as far as she could tell from her vantage point. They must have spent a considerable amount of money. Donna Amalia had even mentioned the fact to Irina, and as usual that slut had said sure, sure, but she'd actually been thinking about her own business: maybe about some wealthy old man she ducked in and serviced while she was out shopping for groceries, to make ends meet. She never seemed to have enough money, that slut. What with the money she spent here in the city and the money she sent home to her village, which was no doubt a complete shithole. Irina had showed her pictures, and even in photographs the place looked like a pigsty, in real life just imagine.

Donna Amalia was all but paralyzed, she couldn't stand up. She had osteoarthritis, a particularly grave form of osteoarthritis, she would declaim with tragic pride: the pain came in excruciating waves, and she could barely make it to the bathroom, but she wasn't going to let that slut bring her a bedpan; she'd make it if she had to crawl. To make a long story short, when she got up every morning she accepted the slut's help getting dressed, then she hobbled to her throne with the three-legged cane, and there she would sit. She'd spend the day with the television on, peering out the window.

Her son was in Milan, and these days he had an array of excuses to explain why he couldn't come see her, even on the holidays. He was dating some girl, no doubt another slut, who wouldn't even let him come see his *mamma* who'd made so many sacrifices for him. He thought he'd ease his conscience by sending her money, the piece of shit. As if money was enough.

Donna Amalia's legs might not work, but her head did. Her head was as fresh as the flowers in May, and all her cogs and gears were spinning merrily. She paid attention to the world, and when things changed she knew. Then she'd tell that slut Irina about it, and Irina would say sure, sure, but Irina didn't understand a thing, didn't know that it's the changes that tell you where the world is headed. All changes, from the smallest to the biggest, had a meaning in the larger picture.

Did that lady with a man's voice, on Channel 5, do a program with old people? That was a sign. Was the new pope an Argentine? That was a sign. Did a soldier murder his wife because he was having an affair with a lady soldier? That was a sign. The hard thing, my dear Ukrainian slut, was to put all those signs together. Interpretation, that was the key. To understand the system of signs, and therefore the changes.

The apartment in the building across the way, for instance, was a sign. An important sign. Very important.

A normal family used to live there. A horrible family, but a normal one. A father who was never at home. A mother, a vulgar tub of lard, who spent her days yacking on the phone; she could see her pacing back and forth in front of every window, gesticulating with the receiver cradled between her ear and her shoulder: how the woman managed not to develop curvature of the spine was more than Donna Amalia could figure out. Two kids in their teens, a girl who brought home boyfriends and locked herself in her room with them, and a boy who instead of doing his homework played the guitar and snuck cigarettes on the balcony.

Then they'd left, all of a sudden. They must have received an attractive offer, because Donna Amalia hadn't seen any of the usual warning signs of an impending move: a moving truck had shown up out of the blue, and in barely two days' time they had packed up and left, bag and baggage, headed who knows where. Donna Amalia certainly wouldn't miss them, there was never anything new to watch, by now she knew them too well.

The renovations had been done in a hurry because, from what she was able to see, there were a lot of workers in that apartment, for many hours every day. From her vantage point, she could see into nearly all the rooms, and the construction workers kept all the windows and balcony doors flung wide open. They'd even installed air conditioners in every room. Very fancy. She'd been asking that stingy son of hers to put air conditioners in every room for months now, but he'd only had one installed in the living room: according to him, they were bad for her bones. As if Donna Amalia's bones could possibly get any worse.

Then *she'd* arrived. A single person, a young woman.

She must have come during the night, because Donna Amalia hadn't noticed a thing, and Donna Amalia sat sentinel all day long, from sunup to late evening. First they'd moved in the furniture, every stick of it new; then a couple of crates of linen, and Donna Amalia had recognized the logo of a famous shop downtown. And suddenly, a few lights had come on and the pale blue glow of the television set could be seen.

One time, the window of what must have been the bedroom swung open, and a dark-haired guy had fiddled around with the handle; then it had swung shut, and since then, the curtains hadn't been pushed aside once. The curtains in the *whole apartment*. That wasn't right.

The guy at the window hadn't been seen since. She could only see a girl go by, behind the curtains. She recognized her silhouette. Another time the girl had poked her face up close to the glass of the French doors that gave onto the living room balcony, and Donna Amalia had been left breathless because she seemed pretty. Beautiful, in fact. Even Donna Amalia, who knew how to find even the smallest flaws in anyone, was forced to admit that the girl's face was perfect. But then she'd vanished, and never appeared again.

Donna Amalia, through that slut Irina, had arranged for a few discreet questions to be asked of the local shopkeepers. No one, absolutely no one, knew who lived in that apartment. No one supplied the place, no one delivered groceries, no one had a new customer who happened to be a stunningly beautiful young woman. No one.

As signs go, Donna Amalia thought to herself, this one was hard to interpret. Tremendously hard. Which meant there had to be something going on, something big, because when the signs didn't fit into a system, that meant she was missing some detail.

Donna Amalia waited. Then she waited some more. Everything else in the neighborhood went on as usual, but the apartment across the street continued not to fit into any known system. She even tried talking to her son about it, during the one weekly conversation she managed to pry out of him, but he said the same thing the slut Irina always said: sure, sure. And with some excuse, he ended the phone call.

It all seemed so strange that, in the end, Donna Amalia sent that slut Irina to buzz the intercom. She'd coached her to perfection: Irina was to say that she was looking for Signora Esposito, the one who lived on the second floor. And then, as soon as they answered, she was to say, very innocently: oh, I'm so sorry, I must have rung the wrong buzzer, and then, finally, she was to rush back to describe to Donna Amalia the voice that had answered. But no one had answered, even though that slut Irina claimed she'd rung twice. And yet the girl was home, because Donna Amalia had seen her go by behind the curtains. So she hadn't answered the buzzer—why? Maybe the buzzer was broken, that certainly wouldn't be anything new. Damned modern technology: years ago it would have been simple enough just to ask the doorman a few questions, but these days, doormen, with what they cost—well, no one had them anymore.

Behind the living room window, while the wind and the rain howled through the streets, driving the pedestrians into the shelter of the doorways, Donna Amalia narrowed her eyes: when a sign defied interpretion, then it didn't fit into the system. And someone had to be informed.

She called for the slut Irina, and told her to bring her the telephone.

VIII

Before going out for dinner at his usual place, Lojacono got the phone call from Marinella.

These days he talked to his daughter every day, ever since they'd reconciled after months of painful silence. It was still too soon for an actual visit, but there had been unmistakable progress: from a refusal to speak, to one-syllable answers, and then on to the occasional chilly report on the life the girl was leading, the progress of their conversations had been slow and difficult.

Lojacono loved his daughter dearly, and being apart from her had all but sent him over the edge; but in the aftermath of his trial and reassignment into exile, his wife hadn't hesitated in turning against him, not so much because she actually thought Lojacono was guilty of the charges that had been brought, but because of the social penalities that had come with them. To feel like a pariah, to see doors slammed in her face, to know that her friends were avoiding her: she wore a scarlet letter, and that meant no verdict could diminish her pain.

Even worse, Sonia and Marinella had been moved to Palermo as a precaution against any possible retaliation: Lojacono couldn't imagine why anyone would take revenge against his family for something he hadn't done, but everyone had to comply with the judge's decisions.

Marinella was fifteen years old, and along with the standard array of behavioral issues common to teenagers, she was an introvert, reluctant to try new things and meet new people; being uprooted from the life that was familiar to her, from a small city like Agrigento, where everyone had known everyone else for generations, had been like dropping an atomic bomb on a tropical atoll. Hearing her mother spew venom against her father and blame him for even the smallest of their new problems had done the rest, and Lojacono lost all contact with the girl.

But when he was confronted with the innocent blood of the Crocodile's victims, his daughter's absence from his life had suddenly seemed intolerable; and so, violating the terms of the divorce and his own good sense, he had phoned her, expecting her not to pick up.

Marinella had surprised him, not only taking his call but reestablishing regular phone conversations. Little by little, she had told him about the trouble she was having fitting into her new life, the challenges of getting along with her new classmates and teachers. Then Lojacono had listened as a few budding acquaintances blossomed into friendships: a girl her age who lived nearby and walked to school with her, another girl in their class who'd started walking with them. Now Marinella had a group of friends she went out with on a regular basis: to the movies, to get a pizza.

To avoid getting her in trouble with her mother, who demanded the right to monitor their slightest interactions, he never called her; he waited for Marinella to reach out. He was afraid of snapping the slender thread that he'd worked so hard to retie, and he was well aware that he himself wasn't much of a communicator. But even complete silence was a beautiful thing, if someone you dearly loved was on the other end of the line.

This time, the girl's voice was excited: "*Ciao*, Papi. What are you doing? Are you having dinner?"

"No, not yet. I'm running late, they trans . . . I have a new office."

"Really? Wow! Cool! It's a good thing to change every so often, right? And after all, it's not as if you really liked the old place. I could tell that from your voice."

From my voice, she could tell. Women have antennae, even when they're just teenagers.

"What about you? How do you think you did on your Latin test?"

"Good, I think I did good. I talked to Deborah about it, she's really good, and we had the same translation. But that's not the big news: tonight I'm going to a party! I was invited to a classmate's birthday, she's having a party in a club outside of Palermo!"

A party. Outside of Palermo.

"Oh, really? And how are you getting there? And with who?"

"Come on, Papi. What, are you worried about me? Nothing bad's going to happen, it's not like it's a rave. It's just a birthday party, this friend of mine was held back a year and she's turning eighteen. It was just nice of her to invite me, until just a few days ago she didn't even know I existed. And there'll be boys! And dancing, too!"

Be careful, Lojacono thought to himself. Try not to squelch her enthusiasm, or she won't tell you anything else.

"And does your mother know about it?"

"Oh sure, as if I'd tell her, she'd make my life miserable. Of course she doesn't know. I told her I was sleeping over at Enza's, and she had no problem with that, it just means she can go have her own fucking fun."

"Mari, don't talk like that. You know I don't like it. And I don't like hearing that you're lying to your mother. I'm far away, I can't help you if you need something, and . . ."

Her voice hardened.

"So, what are you saying, that I can't even tell you what I'm doing? Is that it?"

"No, that's not how it is. I trust you, you're intelligent and you're mature. But there are people in this world . . . if you only knew the kind of things I see every day, from sunup to sundown . . . Anyway, you go ahead. Just make sure you keep your phone charged and turned on, and if there's anything you need, anything at all, call me right away. All right?"

She was calm again now, but cautious.

"All right, Papi. Don't worry, I promise. And tomorrow I'll call you and tell you all about it. Okay?"

"Yes, sweetheart. I'll wait for your call. And don't forget . . ."

". . . phone charged and turned on, I swear. *Ciao ciao*, Papi. Till tomorrow."

And suddenly he was all alone again, with a silent phone in one hand and something new to worry about: he wouldn't be getting much sleep tonight.

As he was walking up the narrow lane, the *vicolo*, that led to Letizia's trattoria, he had time to ponder his total lack of emotion at hearing Marinella say: It just means she can have her own fucking fun.

There had been times, up until a few months ago, when that phrase would have gone straight to his gut and lodged in his intestine, making him twist in pain for hours. But now, nothing. A stranger, that's what Sonia was to him now. It seemed incredible that he had shared so many years with her, projects, plans for a future that would never come now. A stranger. He even hoped that she'd be able to form some lasting relationship, that she'd find a way to temper the resentment she felt for him; that he'd be able to be in touch with their daughter without having to sneak around, in the light of day.

Letizia saw him come in out of the corner of her eye; she was waiting for him, the way she did every night. All she needed was a rapid glance to sound out his mood: she wondered how that could be, since she had never been very good at reading men; and yet she was able to sense Lojacono's state of mind, even if those almond-shaped eyes never changed their expression. But the corners of his mouth, the way he carried himself, the way he moved his hands—these spoke loud and clear. Maybe it was just a matter of paying attention. Maybe it was because what he thought of as a fine, warm friendship meant something else to her, even though she would never have admitted it, even to herself.

Lojacono took a seat at the corner table that she held for him even when, as was so often the case, there was a waiting list a yard long. Letizia's trattoria was quite the hot spot, in part because of the proprietress's physical beauty and personal charm. Her customers loved the traditional cooking, and her full breasts and dazzling smile made a pleasing side dish.

Wives and girlfriends could count on the fact that she never overstepped the bounds of amiable professional courtesy, always keeping things on a cordial but not especially personal footing, and so they packed the restaurant hoping that the proprietress might sing the house a song, the way she sometimes did. They would even joke about her attitude toward the man with the Asian features, the only person in the restaurant who seemed to be unaware that Letizia was in love with him; it was like eating an excellent meal while enjoing a live telenovela. What could be better?

"What's wrong, you're worried, aren't you? Is it about Marinella?" she asked, sitting down at his table and wiping her hands on her apron.

He barely looked up from the bowl of rigatoni al ragù that he was rapidly polishing off.

"One of these days you're going to have to explain to me what it is you put in this ragù. I can't get enough, even when I'm not hungry. And as long as you're at it, you could tell me how you manage to read my mind. She's going to a party, a birthday party. Tonight, she's going."

"So what? What's wrong with that? A birthday party's hardly dangerous, as far as I know."

"That's what you think, that it isn't dangerous," Lojacono replied, his mouth full. "Anything can be dangerous if you're fifteen years old and you're a pretty girl. Do you know that the majority of drug users get started at exactly this sort of party?"

Letizia laughed: "Are you crazy? What drug users? Instead of being happy that she finally has some friends! And after all, it's just a birthday party . . . You ought to go to a party yourself. You're getting old and dreary, Peppuccio."

She was the only person who called Lojacono by the nickname his friends had used back home, when he was a kid.

"But if I wasn't old and dreary, do you think I'd come here for dinner?"

While Letizia was getting ready to fire back a sharp retort, Lojacono's cell phone rang. On the display the name "Laura" was blinking, perfectly visible to Letizia, too. The lieutenant apologized, picked up his phone, and headed outside, followed by the proprietress's suddenly black mood and the diners' curious gazes.

"*Ciao!* How did your first day of school go?"

The Sardinian accent and the cheerful voice immediately put Lojacono in a happier mood, in spite of the fact that the instant he set foot outside of the restaurant he was buffeted by a violent drenching gust of wind and rain; but for some obscure reason he didn't want to talk to her in front of Letizia.

"*Ciao.* You're well informed, as always, eh? Mind telling me how you know?"

The woman chuckled, and Lojacono felt as if he could see her, dimples and all.

"Don't forget, I'm a magistrate, and no one can hide anything from me. Especially when I'm interested in something, I always have a way of finding things out. Well, how did it go?"

"Well, what can I tell you? The commissario, Palma, strikes

me as a nice guy, and a smart one, too. The rest of them, well, they're pretty reserved, except for one, an overgrown kid, who seems like a bit of an asshole."

Piras thought it over: "Mmm, that must be Aragona. Looks like he spends a lot of time in a tanning bed and dresses like a TV detective?"

Amused, Lojacono asked: "What do you have, bugs and surveillance cameras in there? Yeah, that's the one. How did you know?"

"He used to work at headquarters, and they've tried to palm him off on everyone; they even tried to assign him to me as a bodyguard. I knew they'd unload him there. He's the grandson of a prefect, I don't know where, so there's nothing they can do to him. Be careful, don't let him drive because he's a lunatic behind the wheel; I came close to throttling him once. What about the others. Any women?"

There it is, thought Lojacono. The crucial question.

"Two. A woman who has been at the precinct house for years, and a strange girl, who won't look anyone in the eye and is something of a gun nut. Why do you ask?"

He imagined her, pensive, lost in who knows what fantasy. They hadn't seen each other recently, but they often talked on the phone. They were developing an odd friendship, taut as a violin string with the tacit, reciprocal knowledge that they liked each other—a lot.

"No reason. Just curious. Maybe you can find a girlfriend, right?"

Her tone was nonchalant, cheerful; but her intentions were something else altogether.

"I doubt it. At least not in there. Maybe I'll find one somewhere else."

Laura laughed and, for no particular reason, he imagined her breasts underneath her blouse.

"Or maybe she'll find you, one of these days. Let's talk

again soon, Lieutenant Lojacono. That way you can tell me how it's going at school."

Cold and drenched, the lieutenant went back into the trattoria; Letizia was sitting at another table now, laughing, with her back to him.

IX

Mayya opened the door, and noticed that today it wasn't locked the way it usually was.

The notary must have come home late, as he sometimes did, and maybe he'd forgotten to lock up. It had happened before, not all that often, truth be told, but it had happened. She put the grocery bags down by the front door, trying not to get everything wet. A driving wind was kicking up the surf and pushing it right across the street; it wasn't even clear whether it was actually raining, there was so much water in the air.

Mayya thought back to her hometown in Bulgaria, far from the sea, from waves of any kind, where when it rained it was raining, and when it was sunny the sun was shining; here it was never obvious just what the weather was.

She took off her coat and put it in the front hall closet. It was silent and there was no smell of coffee, which mean the signora hadn't woken up yet; strange, it was already eight o'clock: she should have been up and about for at least an hour. Perhaps she wasn't feeling well, or maybe she'd been out late last night.

For the past few days, Mayya had been worried about the signora. Mayya liked her: she was sweet and kind, she never raised her voice; compared with employers she'd had in the past, she was wonderful. And Mayya's girlfriends, whom she saw every Thursday in the piazza by the train station, made it clear with the stories they told that she really could consider herself lucky.

But her signora wasn't happy. Mayya was sure of that: something was bothering her, something big. Not that her signora ever confided in her, no: she was a very reserved person, and Mayya was anything but intrusive. Still, silences tell no lies, as they said back home: words do, but silences don't. And in the signora's silences, in her absent gaze as she stared into space, there was no happiness. There was something else. Maybe fear.

Maybe it was a good thing that she had decided to sleep in that morning, Mayya thought to herself; sometimes a good long sleep can put your heart at rest, and help you to see things more optimistically.

The young women moved through the darkness, noticing in passing that the windows and shutters, securely fastened, confirmed the fact that no one was up yet. She headed toward the kitchen: she'd make breakfast, a *caffe latte* and cookies. She wondered whether the notary was at home, and remembered that the man's overcoat hadn't been hanging on the rod in the front hall closet. Maybe he'd already gone out; or, more likely, he hadn't returned home.

She didn't see much of him, the notary. She left in the afternoon, long before he came home from the office. She'd run into him once or twice in the morning, when she was coming in and he was heading out, and another couple of times on the eve of major holidays, when she'd been asked to work a few hours extra. He was a good-looking man, tall and distinguished, with a thick head of gray hair and a fit physique; but Mayya had never liked him. She'd felt his cold eyes evaluating her, sizing up her body the way a farmer might look at cows at the market. She knew that kind of man all too well; the wrong kind of man to live with her signora.

While she was arranging the cookies on the tray and waiting for the coffee to be ready, she wondered to herself how such a badly mismatched couple could stay together for so many years, and without having children, either. Children bring a couple together, they constitute a topic of conversation that the parents never tire of. Children solidify the partnership between a husband and a wife, and when there's nothing else, at least they have them. But the signora and the notary didn't even have that.

It was understandable, at that point, Mayya thought to herself, that people would look around for something else to keep their minds occupied. And their bodies, too, she supposed. The notary who was never at home, what with his work and his card games and his who knows what else, and the signora with her charity drives, her tea parties with her girlfriends, and her social clubs. And her collection of glass snow globes.

The young woman shook her head as she poured out the coffee. Everyone has their obsessions. The signora collected those horrible glass spheres that, when you shook them, unleashed a fake blizzard over the landscapes and figures inside. She loved them so much, the signora did, that she wouldn't even let Mayya dust them: she would do it herself, slipping on latex gloves and devoting an entire morning every week to the job. It was the only time that she seemed truly happy, surrounded by hundreds of little glass globes that seemed like so many soap bubbles.

The signora's collection was famous. Whenever her friends traveled, they'd be sure to bring back at least one item to add to it. Once a journalist even came, to take pictures of her surrounded by her snow globes, and the signora had proudly displayed the magazine with her photograph to Mayya. She'd even told her that someday, she was going to have an exhibition somewhere, and that she'd donate the proceeds to charity. Truth be told, Mayya thought it was ridiculous that anyone would pay money to see those objects, but people, she knew, did all sorts of strange things.

Moving slowly with her tray through the partial darkness

for fear of falling, she went into the signora's bedroom; in the light that filtered through the shutters, she saw that the bed was still made and that there was no one in the bedroom.

Strange. Very strange.

If she'd had to leave suddenly for some reason, the signora would have called her: when she had any urgent news to communicate, the signora always used her phone; she always asked if she was bothering her. Why would she have forgotten to alert her, this time?

She headed toward the study with the snow globes. Maybe, she thought, the signora had fallen asleep in an armchair, with a book in her hand, in her favorite room. The wind was moaning in despair as it ran up against obstacles that hindered its blind gallop. The sea was hurling itself ferociously onto the street, doing its best to invade the space from which it had been barred.

The armchair was empty. A cloud hurried away from the face of the sun, and a beam of light illuminated the floor of the room, coming to rest on a shard of glass glittering under the chair.

Mayya realized that it was one of the glass globes with snow inside, and she wondered what it was doing on the floor.

Then she realized that there was something else on the floor: the signora's dead body, the back of her head shattered and a puddle of clotted blood around it.

The tray clattered to the floor with a crash of broken porcelain, scattering cookies and *caffe latte* everywhere.

Mayya brought both hands to her face and let out a scream.

X

Deputy Sergeant Ottavia Calabrese left the precinct house, shooting Guida, the officer standing guard at the entrance, a distracted nod. She almost failed to recognize him: his tie was knotted impeccably, his hair was brushed, his jacket was perfectly buttoned, and he was sitting up straight, his eyes trained firmly before him. She'd always seen him as a kind of funny ornament, a papier-mâché statue depicting a drunk in uniform reading the sports section; now he actually looked like a real policeman.

She had to admit that something in that place was changing. All credit to the commissario. A man out of the ordinary: she'd thought that from the very first time he appeared at her office door, asking permission to enter, smiling at her hesitantly like a little boy joining his class for the very first time at a new school.

Ottavia had liked Palma from the start. His rumpled appearance, his unkempt hair, his rolled-up sleeves. And the cheerful, youthful atmosphere that he ushered inside those cracked old walls. Moreover, there was no wedding ring on his finger: who knew why, who knew whether he was a bachelor or divorced, or maybe a widower. But widowers often continued to wear their wedding rings.

She wore a wedding ring. And she wasn't a widow.

Before boarding the funicular, she stopped in a *rosticceria*, a local takeout place. She wasn't up to cooking that night, and it was late already. She always seemed to leave the office late. Not that she minded: she did it on purpose. For so long now, work had been the best part of her day. A woman's work is never done; for policewomen, it's even worse.

In the crowded funicular car, with her purse on one side and the packet from the *rosticceria* on the other, she could find nowhere to sit. A kid, sprawled out on a seat, looked up at her defiantly and then turned up the volume in his headphones; then he turned to look out the window, chewing gum, his mouth wide open.

Ottavia felt someone move behind her, and an irritating pressure against her derriere. She sighed: every night it was the same thing. The crowd, stuffed into the car like sardines in a can, and some idiot ogling her and rubbing up against her. She was well aware that she had a generous figure and a healthy, taut body that she tried to conceal under sensible, unfashionable clothing, but there was nothing she could do: someone always noticed.

She didn't turn around, that would only make it worse. Instead, she looked down, identified the tip of a black loafer, took aim, and jammed her foot down. A single blow with her heel, smashing down on the man's big toe. A surprised gasp, a muttered curse; now Ottavia turned around, stared at the dirty old man behind her, and said: "I beg your pardon. Would you care to let me have your other foot, so I can finish the job and make it nice and symmetrical?" The man pushed away into the crowd, glaring at her, in search of other, more compliant, asses, less willing to defend themselves.

It was about a kilometer from the funicular to home. The shops were all closed, but Ottavia still took longer than necessary. My feet, she thought, give my heart away. She pulled her keys out of her purse with an exaggerated calm, imagining that she was moving underwater. Then, with a sigh, she opened the door.

"Is that you, my love?"

How the fuck he managed to be so cheerful, loving, and

affectionate, even after a hard day of work, Ottavia truly couldn't understand.

"Yes, who else would it be? It's me."

Her husband Gaetano appeared at the kitchen door with a cheerful expression on his face.

"*Ciao*! Have you seen the wind? The dish antenna is swinging around like a flag, we're only getting cable. You want an aperitif?"

As she was taking off her necklace and her earrings, Ottavia replied in a weary voice: "No, thanks. I'm shattered. I picked up something in the *rosticceria*; I just don't feel like cooking tonight."

"Cooking? Are you serious? I've already taken care of everything, my love. Just wait, it's delicious! Fettuccine with mushrooms and cream, and lemon chicken scaloppini. I got a bottle of red, too, an Aglianico, the kind you like. It'll be ready in five minutes, just relax until then."

Ottavia, standing in front of the bathroom mirror where she had gone to remove her makeup, thought to herself that being married to Superman was a curse greater than she could possibly bear. A highly respected and deeply educated engineer, he earned an enormous salary, had fifteen people reporting to him, and still found the time and energy to buy a bottle of Aglianico and cook *fettuccine ai funghi*. In any civilized country, she mused, he would have been executed by firing squad in the public square.

She went into the dining room and shot a look at the sofa. Riccardo was there, as usual. As usual, with a pen in hand. As usual, doodling on a sheet of graph paper. As usual, closed up in a world that excluded everyone else.

Gaetano walked in with a steaming tureen in his hands, and a fleck of cream on his cheek.

"Dinner's ready! To the table, family! Riccardo, sweetheart, did you see? Mamma's home!"

Slowly, the boy lifted his face from the sheet of paper and looked vacantly around the room; then his eyes stopped on Ottavia, and in a cavernous voice he said: *"Mamma. Mamma. Mamma. Mamma. Mammm . . ."*

From the corner of his mouth hung a streamer of drool. His hand went on methodically tracing circles on the sheet of graph paper, all of them concentric, all within the margins of the little squares, as if drawn with a compass. *Mamma.* The only word that he'd uttered in an intelligible manner in his thirteen years of life, amidst the indistinct murmurs he made as he watched his television shows. Nothing else. Nothing, ever. No window into the world of which he was the sole inhabitant.

Ottavia went over to the boy and caressed the face that so closely resembled her own. She helped him to his feet and walked him to the table where Gaetano, chattering on about his wonderful day, ladled into each bowl a quantity of fettuccine that would have sated an entire soccer team, second-string players, too. Ottavia wondered what Commissario Palma was having for dinner that night.

Mamma, mamma, said Riccardo. Gaetano looked at her lovingly.

Ottavia began eating, thinking how much she hated them both.

XI

Palma had turned the old precinct house cafeteria into their new joint office by knocking down a drywall partition that someone had put up to transform a nice big bright room into two small dark depressing ones.

The six desks had been arranged to as to allow each of them a certain degree of privacy if they spoke quietly on the phone; but each could easily attract the attention of the others. Lojacono, settling in by the window overlooking the castle jutting out into the sea, mentally recognized the commissario's strategic skill in the deployment of resources: the only way to create solidarity of any kind in such a diverse group of people was to keep them together for as much time as possible.

He noticed that the first to arrive had been Pisanelli, the deputy captain who was a veteran of Pizzofalcone. He'd hung a large corkboard behind his desk, and he was carefully pinning a series of photographs and newspaper clippings to it. Noticing his bewilderment, Calabrese, who was busy with the cables of two computers she was setting up on her desk, widened her eyes and whispered:

"It's an obsession of his. Those are all the suicides that have taken place in this neighborhood over the past ten years. He's convinced that they're actually murders, and he's been gathering material to prove it."

Pisanelli, from the back of the room, turned to look at them.

"I heard you, you know, Ottavia. I know that you're saying that I'm just a nutty old man."

He didn't seem upset. If anything, sad. Calabrese replied: "Why, no, I'm saying no such thing, Giorgio. I was just explaining to him what all those newspaper clippings and photographs are for. Otherwise, Lojacono will think it's to do with some complicated international plot."

The man spoke directly to the lieutenant, in a soft voice.

"The problem, my dear Lojacono, is that sometimes we can't see past the tips of our own noses. We just take the easiest route. If someone wants us to think that someone killed themselves, all they need to do is leave a suicide note and there you go. I don't think it's right that just because a person is alone in the world, and maybe depressed, you can throw him out like a dirty old rag. I think that everyone deserves an investigation, a little research. That's all."

Aragona, the suntanned young man, was carefully placing a silver paperweight, which wouldn't have looked out of place in the Italian president's office, on his desk; there, it simply made no sense. "As you can see," he commented acidly, "there's no real work for us to do here. If we're just going to investigate suicides and pretend that they're murders, then we might as well start playing contract bridge."

Pisanelli looked at him with unmistakable annoyance: "In that case, I hope that you live for a good many years, my friend. And that you turn into a lonely old man, like many of these here, on my bulletin board. And then, if someone 'suicides' you, you'll be filed away in a hurry and no one will ever think of you again."

Ottavia opened her mouth as if to intervene, then shut it again and went back to untangling the welter of cables.

The quiet girl, whom Lojacono remembered as Di Nardo, spoke in a low voice to Pisanelli: "And have any connections emerged to link the suicides? Have you found anything?"

She seemed to be genuinely interested. The man studied her for a moment, making sure that she wasn't just making fun of him. Then he said: "No, there aren't any direct connections so far. And anyway, this is something I work on outside office hours. I keep most of the material at home; still, there are some details that make you think. The repeated use of certain words, in the suicide notes. The fact that many of them were written on a typewriter or a computer, which is something a person would be unlikely to do at such a desperate moment. The disconnect between the ways that some of the people . . . well, the ways that they did it, with respect to their personalities, their psychological profiles. A series of things that . . ."

He was interrupted by Romano; the huge man had let himself flop down onto a chair and was now looking intently out the window: "If someone kills himself, then he kills himself. It's cowardice, it means they don't have the courage to go on living. You have to face life head-on, no matter how shitty it is."

His voice sounded like distant thunder. Aragona snickered.

"So you're saying that if someone jumps off a viaduct a hundred feet in the air, he's a coward. And so is someone who puts the barrel of a shotgun in his mouth and pulls the trigger, or drinks a bottle of acid. It seems to me that it takes more courage to die than to live."

As Romano was preparing a comeback, Palma ran in hastily, a sheet of paper in one hand: "Guys, we're in business. And this one's major: a woman was murdered on the waterfront, the wife of a notary. Lojacono and Aragona, you're up."

XII

L et's see: what time is it?

By now they'll have already found you.

It would have been the housekeeper, the Bulgarian woman. She must have searched the house for you—the kitchen, the bedroom. Maybe she tried the handle of the bathroom door, to see if you were in there. And the door would have swung open, into silence and darkness.

The apartment must have seemed deserted. Nothing, except for the wind shrieking outside. Not another sound.

Then she'd have walked down the hallway, uncertain. Maybe she assumed you'd left.

I wonder what it would be like, if emotions hung in the air like a smell. If the scent of your sad smile, the last time I saw your face, was still suspended in the room. What sort of a scent would it have had, your smile?

She must have gone looking for you, the Bulgarian house-keeper. Moving circumspectly among the furniture and the carpets, taking care not to knock anything over in the dark. Maybe she wouldn't have even turned on the lights, for fear you might be fast asleep somewhere and she'd wake you up.

But there's no real risk of that, is there? As far as waking you up goes, no one on earth can do that.

Who can say what she did, when she finally came face-to-face with you. Or face-to-face with what was left of you, to be exact. A bundle lying in the semidarkness of the windows, shuttered to preserve the last scraps of night.

I look outside. The wind is still blowing, and big black clouds are being shoved across the sky. It's not raining, now.

Instead, just a few dozen yards from your dead body, the sea spray is still whirling through the air, covering the walls of apartment buildings and the balconies with salt. But all around you, everything is inert. Motionless.

Your snow globes, for instance. Hundreds of them, maybe thousands. Shelves filled with them, arranged according to that odd system you seemed to prefer. With fake snow, lying nicely and obediently at the bottom of the globe, just waiting to be shaken up. What will become of them now, of your snow globes? We'll have to think about what to do with them.

With all of them, except for one. That one, I think, will follow a different path. It will go on its way through crime labs and courtrooms; it'll wind up in a big cardboard evidence box, archived on some forgotten shelf. And there it will sit for years and years, until it's finally thrown away. That snow globe is special. Unique. The one with the girl playing the little guitar. The one with your blood smeared on its surface.

The one that ripped away your last truly happy smile, and then ripped away your life.

I wonder what she'll do, the housekeeper, when she finally understands. When she realizes that it's you, or that it used to be you, now lying there in a pool of blood with your head bashed in. She'll scream, I think. Or maybe not. Bulgarians are tough.

Now starts the hard part. For me, for those of us who are still here.

Not for you.

For you, it's all over.

Too bad. If only you'd been reasonable.

If only you hadn't turned your back on me.

XIII

As soon as Palma finished, Aragona sprang to his feet, ready for action. Lojacono, on the other hand, turned a gaze of mute supplication in the commissario's direction; his commanding officer took great care not to meet his eyes, studiously looking elsewhere.

"I'll drive, I know exactly where that is," the young man had said, grabbing for the sheet of paper with the directions.

Palma had shrugged: "Do as you like, there's no hurry; two squad cars are already on the scene, and the medical examiner and the forensic team are on their way. This time of day there's a lot of traffic."

Lojacono, putting on his coat, replied sardonically: "Oh, there is? When you have a minute, could you draw up a chart for me of the times when there isn't a lot of traffic in this city? Maybe on August 15th, when the whole city's at the beach?"

They'd taken a compact, unmarked car that had been parked in the courtyard. Aragona had the engine running before Lojacono got in the car, and he screeched out of the parking spot before the lieutenant's feet were in the car.

"Aragona, have you lost your mind? Are you trying to run someone over? The way you're driving, our first official act in this precinct will be to run over a few locals, and you know how much they love us already."

The young man drove as if the streets were empty, causing the pedestrians in their path to bolt. Out of the corner of his eye, Lojacono saw a little old lady darting to one side just in the nick of time, with a leap worthy of a classical ballerina; he agreed wholeheartedly with the stream of angry dialect she showered in the driver's direction, even if he couldn't understand a single word.

"Calm down, Loja', don't worry. I took a course in performance driving, I know exactly what I'm doing."

"Just where did you take this course, in prison? You heard him say there's no hurry, didn't you? Why the fuck are you going so fast?"

Aragona kept his foot on the accelerator.

"It's quite an honor to work with you. Fuck, the man who nailed the Crocodile! For weeks, no one in this city talked about anything but you and how you made all the other precincts working on the case look like pieces of shit. You're a legend!"

Clutching the door handle, Lojacono said through clenched teeth: "Not that it did me a lot of good, though. It's not as if they let me go home."

"Eh, well, that's a horse of a different color. From what I've heard, someone back home thinks that, even if there's no evidence against you, you must have been in touch with those people somehow. But don't give up hope, if you do a good job, maybe they really will send you back home."

Lojacono looked over at his colleague's profile, watching him as he did his best to kill anyone who threatened to hinder his rapid progress.

"What do you know about my me and business, Arago'?"

"Ah, I know plenty, actually. I told you before, I used to work at police headquarters. That's where all the documents wind up, and if you have the right connections, you can find out anything you want to know. For instance, when this opportunity opened up in Pizzofalcone, I read the files on all the characters the various precincts had volunteered in the hopes of getting rid of them. A fine assortment of losers."

"In that case, why on earth did *you* volunteer? From what I've heard, you could have found yourself a much more comfortable berth somewhere else, no?"

"No, for me this place is perfect, believe me. Just think: a very serious crime took place here, which ruined the whole department's reputation. They wanted to shut this precinct down, and sure enough, they sent us the worst cops they could lay their hands on. Are you with me so far?"

Lojacono had noticed that, when Aragona spoke, he slowed down ever so slightly; he decided he could stand the kid's ravings if it meant saving the life of some innocent pedestrian.

"I'm with you. Keep talking."

"You know what they call the people who work here, the other cops in this city? They call us the Bastards of Pizzofalcone. Don't you think that's great?"

Lojacono shrugged his shoulders: "I don't think it's anything, personally. What's so great about it?"

The young man looked hard at Lojacono and just missed a bicyclist, who veered sharply away and rode right up onto the sidewalk.

"What's great about it is that if we do something good, then we become heroes; and if we don't do anything at all, then things remain as they were."

"Listen, Aragona, don't you care anything about doing a good job? What if someone wanted to be a cop just so he could be a cop?"

The officer put on an offended expression: "Why on earth would you say that? Of course that's the most important thing. It's just that a person has to think about his career too, doesn't he? Certainly, if you're someone they've put out with the trash—someone like the four of us—it's harder to prove that you know how to do your job right. But that's exactly why it's so exciting."

"Put out with the trash? That's overstating things, isn't it?"

Aragona turned serious.

"Listen to me, I've seen the files. I can tell you for sure, every one of us is tarred by some black mark. Take Di Nardo: the quiet girl, the one who loves guns. You know you're not supposed to carry loaded weapons with the safety off inside the station house: that's against the rules. Well, she actually discharged her firearm inside the building. And she came *that* close to killing another cop. Can you imagine?"

As he was being tossed between car door and seat, Lojacono was forced to admit: "Just think, that little girl. I would never have taken her for a pistolero. And the other guy, what's his name . . ."

"Romano, Francesco Romano. You know what his fellow cops used to call him? They called him Hulk. Behind his back, though, or he'd rip their heads off. He can't control his own strength, much less his anger. The third time he grabbed a suspect by the throat, they suspended him. When he went back on duty, they sent him straight here."

Lojacono nodded.

"Mmm, he did seem a little on edge, that's true. And we know everything about me. But what about you, Aragona? Do we know everything about you?"

The young man turned defensive.

"Well, my good Lojacono, in my case, the fact that I'm . . . that I have a certain name seems to have created overblown expectations. And when everyone's looking over your shoulder, you wind up doing something stupid. Or other people make you do something stupid. But I don't give a damn, and sooner or later I'm going to show everyone just how wrong they were. Maybe with your help. Well, here we are, this is the place. You see what I mean? It only took a couple of minutes."

Lojacono catapulted himself out of the car.

"One of these days I'll have to remember how you're

supposed to thank God for still being alive. Let's make one thing perfectly clear: next time, I'm driving. Come on, let's go."

And they got out of the car, battered by the wind and the spray from the sea that reached all the way onto the street.

XIV

In spite of the blustery weather, a small crowd had gathered outside the entrance to the building. The door was on the side of the building, not along the façade that overlooked the sea, and you reached it by walking through the piazza that opened out away from the waterfront, its other side adjoining the large park that was the Villa Comunale.

Lojacono, raising his voice to be heard over the wind, asked Aragona:

"This is a wealthy part of town, isn't it?"

The officer nodded his head, clutching his raincoat closed at the neck: "Hell, yes, it's wealthy. The richest neighborhood in the city, as far as that goes. And on the waterfront? Forget about it. These buildings are priceless; they're monuments."

Outside the entrance were a pair of squad cars and an ambulance with its flashers on. Lojacono identified himself and asked one of the two uniformed officers how long they'd been there.

"Twenty minutes or so, lieutenant. And ten minutes ago the medical examiner got here. In any case, it's up on the fifth floor."

"That means they waited to call us," Aragona commented. "Before calling us, they took some time to think it over. They still don't trust us, that much is clear."

On their way in, Lojacono stopped to take a look at the front door, which showed no signs of forced entry. Then he started up the wide marble staircase.

Aragona, who had headed over to the elevator, followed him: "Hey, it's up on the fifth floor! Why are you taking the stairs?"

The lieutenant went on walking, his eyes fixed on the low, shiny marble steps.

"Because if you've just murdered someone, you don't take the elevator when you leave. At least, not always. And if you're trying to get away, you might just drop something. Or you might trip and fall. Listen, Aragona: I'm here to do my job, not to tutor you. Watch what I do, try to understand why I'm doing it, and quit busting my chops. If you really can't figure it out, even through deductive reasoning, then you can ask and I'll answer. Fair enough?"

The officer looked offended: "I'm an investigator too, you know. And I've been to school, I know things. It's just that I want to see them in the field, because I've never had the opportunity."

"Anyway, as far as I can tell, there's nothing on these stairs. Either the murderer was very careful, or else you were right and he took the elevator. Or maybe he flew away on a gust of wind."

On the fifth-floor landing, there was just one dark, wooden door, without a nameplate; a red doorbell in the mouth of a small bronze lion was fastened to the doorjamb. Aragona made quite a show of inspecting the side of the door to make sure there was no sign of a break-in. Lojacono smiled, despite himself. After a second, inner door, at the center of which was a pane of frosted glass decorated with what seemed to be a monogram, there was a front hall; daylight came through yet another door, and with it, the sound of an agitated conversation. Lojacono and Aragona continued inside, following the voices.

"Jesus, do I have to keep telling you the same things over and over again? If I've told you once, I've told you a hundred times, a thousand times. You touch nothing, do you get that or not? Nothing, not until I'm here with the forensic squad. Fucking Christ, these are the ABCs! Don't they teach you anything at all at the academy?"

The man who was talking was about forty, solidly built with very close-cropped hair. He was wearing a sweater and a pair of jeans.

A uniformed cop was objecting weakly: "Hey, dotto', what did I do wrong? I opened the window to let in a little fresh air, it's stale and it stinks. Plus you couldn't see a thing, we could have knocked something over. Anyway, I closed the window right away . . ."

The medical examiner was having none of it: "Aside from the fact that there's no stink in here, because this is a relatively fresh corpse, didn't it occur to you that there's a stiff breeze blowing? And we're up on the fifth floor, after all. If there had been documents and papers, by now you would have ruined everything."

Lojacono decided it was time for him to speak up.

"Right. The doctor has a good point. I'm sorry we got here late, we could have secured the crime scene ourselves." He walked over to the man, who was putting on a lab coat and a pair of gloves. "Hello, doctor. I'm Lieutenant Giuseppe Lojacono, and this is Corporal Aragona, from the Pizzofalcone precinct house."

The doctor looked them up and down, still frowning.

"Pizzofalcone, eh? New blood. Well, let's hope it works. Certainly, you'd be hard put to do worse than the guys you're replacing. I'm Lucio Marchitelli, medical examiner. I'm the lucky guy who usually gets called in this part of town."

Lojacono looked around. It was a strange place: the room was enormous, with two balconies—one whose shutters were open—and two entrances. A table, four chairs. An olive-green leather armchair. A long wall adorned with a single piece of furniture made of dark wood, a built-in cabinet with five deep shelves filled, in row after row, by just one kind of object: glass spheres, with fake snow inside.

The uniformed cop who had been talking to the doctor came over, giving Lojacano something that half-resembled a military salute: "Officer Gennaro Cuomo, lieutenant. We were the first to arrive, from police headquarters. At your orders."

Lojacono was looking at the floor. The body, facedown, was that of a middle-aged woman, her pink dressing gown hiked up slightly on her legs. A pair of socks, a slipper on one foot, another slipper a few inches away. The face was gray, and it rested on one cheek. The eye that was visible, half-open to the panorama of life's end, was expressionless. The mouth gaped partly open. A face with regular features, Lojacono thought; but her body was plump, the ankles swollen, the legs stout.

Not far from the body was an overturned tray, *caffe latte*, cookies. A broken mug.

He turned back to look at the corpse: on the back of the head, a dark stain, a patch of blood. The carpet the woman was lying on was stained as well, near the head.

"Who found the body?"

Cuomo quickly replied: "The Bulgarian housekeeper, and her name is . . ." he consulted a sheet of paper, carefully sounding out the words: "Ivanova Nikolaeva, Mayya; her Christian name is the last one. A girl, really, she's in the next room crying, she says she doesn't want to see. The victim was named Cecilia De Santis, married name Festa; her husband is Arturo Festa, a notary. The housekeeper says that he's not home and she has no idea where he is."

Lojacono spoke to Aragona.

"Talk to the housekeeper. Get her to give you the notary's office number, a cell phone, some way of getting in touch with him. I want to know where he is."

The officer headed toward the apartment's interior, glad to

have a specific job to do. Lojacono focused on the doctor, who had, in the meanwhile, been joined by an assistant who was jotting down notes on a pad while the medical examiner danced his minuet about the corpse.

"Now then, Matte', first of all, tell the city morgue attendants, when they get here, that they'll have to wait a while, because we're going to log clothing and everything else as evidence here, that way we can avoid contamination during transport. Are you ready? Okay: start writing."

Extracting instruments from a leather bag he'd set on the floor, he began reciting his litany. His hands moved strips of cloth, inserted thermometers, pushed limbs aside with slight movements; the dead woman cooperated with docility, like a doll, like a mannequin. Lojacono listened, carefully registering the information: he knew how important these first facts could be.

"Room temperature taken in proximity to the cadaver: 20° C. The radiators are on, but they're turned down low. The cadaver is prone, with the head rotated to the left, the right hemiface pressed against the surface of the floor, right arm semiflexed, and left arm extended along the torso. Lower limbs extended and parallel. The feet present as intrarotated . . . just put down 'in opisthotonos,' Matte', I'll know what it means. She's wearing a dressing gown, satin, rose-colored, the sash in place, a nightdress, antique white with lace trim, flesh-colored panty hose, a pair of panties the same color, also lace. Around the neck we note the presence of a white cord. Upon turning over the corpse, we note that the extremities of the cord are attached to a pair of eyeglasses, with burgundy frames, for reading; the right lens appears to be broken at the level of the nosepiece on that side. We herewith note that the garments have been removed for the purpose of being produced individually as evidence, for whatever potential subsequent biological investigations might be considered useful. Length of the cadaver, 169 centimeters, with gynecoid adipose tissue distribution."

The doctor crouched down near the face, sighing: "Eyelids open. Corneas slightly opaque and the presence, at the corners of the eyes, of Sommer's sclerotic patches. Oozing from the rima oris is a rivulet of pinkish liquid. Discharge of hematic material from the left ear, which has gathered partly on the floor and partly around the pavilion of the ear and the homolateral cheek, soiling them. Upon a preliminary external examination, tissues of a pasty consistency were found in the left occipital region, as per subgaleal collection. Despite the presence of dense scalp hair, it is nonetheless possible to perceive that the dermis of the occipital region appears to be affected with a shift in hue toward the reddish-blue range. Further inspection also reveals, at the center of the dyschromic area in question, a small wound, roughly 1.5 centimeters long, which, upon preliminary inspection and delicate manual divarication of the margins of the wound, allows glimpses of connective tissue strands as in a lacerocontusion, with modest blood loss. The remaining skin surfaces are free of traumatic lesions."

He turned the body over, gently pulled open the dressing gown, and lifted the nightdress.

"We note the presence, in the paraumbilical region, of an old scar, with an axis of roughly one centimeter. Two other scars, each with an axis of more than 0.5 centimeter, are located on the line of the anterior superior iliac spine, 5 centimeters to the right and left, respectively, of the median line. This scar cluster can be attributed, with high probability, to a laparoscopic surgical procedure. The body is negative for the presence of extraneous material beneath the fingernails, which moreover appear to be intact, with white nail polish normally applied. Cadaverous rigor mortis is underway in all regions. Presence of hypostasis at anterior site, as produced by prone posture, with the exception of the decubitus areas, already immune to probing via digital pressure. Rectal temperature of the cadaver is 26.5° C. The inspection is concluded at 9 A.M. And also write, Matte', that the window was locked."

Beyond a contrite Cuomo who stood looking down at the tips of his shoes, Lojacono took in the panoramic view offered by the open window. An extraordinary spectacle composed of wind, sea, and sky, with the peninsula enclosing the bay as distant backdrop. He decided that if he ever had the good luck to live in such a place, he'd just sit and stare out the window all day long; he wouldn't get himself killed, wouldn't let himself get bonked on the head while he was wearing a dressing gown.

"Doctor, do you have any idea of when it might have happened?"

The medical examiner got to his feet with some effort, removing his latex gloves.

"Lieutenant, for now we can state that this woman died between nine and eleven hours ago. She suffered a violent cranial trauma at the nuchal site. More than that I can't tell you. There don't appear to be any signs of struggle. Now we're going to transport her to the morgue, where we'll perform an autopsy."

With a curt nod he left the room, just as the men from the forensic squad arrived in their white overalls. Soon a different performance would unfold: cameras would flash and dust would be scattered over all the surfaces, as the team searched for tracks and prints. But something fundamental was missing, and the lieutenant hoped it hadn't been carried off by the murderer: he knew very well how greatly their chances of identifying the guilty party depended on the immediate discovery of that something.

Lojacono crouched down.

Right under the leather armchair he found himself eye to eye with a Hawaiian ukulele player, who was smiling at him from inside a glass globe.

The globe was smeared with blood.

XV

Warrant Officer Francesco Romano is thinking back to the night before. To his return home, to be exact. He's thinking as he sits at his desk, looking out the window at the wind pushing the clouds, while these new coworkers bustle busily around their useless desks, as if they're moving in. Who gives a damn about a new desk, he thinks. What am I, an office clerk? An accountant, a bookkeeper? I'm a policeman. Or at least I would be, if they'd let me do my job.

He drums on the desktop with the fingers of his left hand and he keeps his right hand stuffed in his pocket. He always keeps his right hand in his pocket. To keep it in line. To keep it out of sight. He thinks of that hand as if it were an undomesticated animal, a dangerous dog, not strictly legal, that you can't take anywhere except on a very short leash, with a good stout muzzle. The problem is that Warrant Officer Romano can't seem to put a muzzle on that hand. Even yesterday he couldn't do it.

He had been in an especially bad mood yesterday. His first day on his new job had been the final blow, and he'd plunged into a true depression. They'd sent him to work with a crew of lost men in a station house famous throughout the region for the lawlessness and incompetence of those who had worked there before. He was one of the Bastards of Pizzofalcone. Him of all people, the man who had solved dozens of cases. Him of all people, the most honest and incorruptible policeman who had ever lived. Him of all people.

And you had to see them, his new colleagues. They looked like the contents of a junkman's cart. The policeman's dump, is what this place looked like. One of them might be a Mafioso; then there's a green kid, the hapless product of nepotism, a kid who plays at being a cop; a psychopathic girl who's obsessed with weapons; a good-natured mother and housewife; an old man who looks at a bunch of suicides and sees visions of murderers. And then there's the commissario himself: a door-to-door vacuum cleaner salesman, with all that fake enthusiasm.

How did he wind up there, surrounded by this mess? Why is he, too, sitting there with all the others, in that dump?

Blame it on the hand, he thinks to himself. Blame it on that damned right hand, which is now shut up in his trouser pocket. Until it comes out again, to do more damage.

He remembers the last time, the time that resulted in his suspension. He remembers that little piece of shit, that two-bit idiot Camorrista: you can't touch me, he said over and over, laughing in his face. You can't touch me, you can't do a thing. I know it and you know it too, that I had the drugs on my person; that I was the one who emptied my pistol into that stinking shithead. But since I was careful to toss it down the sewer, after polishing it thoroughly, you can't touch me. And I've got a good lawyer, a first-rate lawyer. You just wait and see, I guarantee you that I'll be out of here tonight before either of you two. And it was true, Romano knew it was true. And his hand had shot out and seized that little asshole by the throat, and there was nothing he could do to stop it.

Ten days' suspension. And that idiot of a commissario who kept saying to him, foaming like a pig at the corners of his mouth: Roma', you're through in this precinct. Clean out your desk, you're not coming back here. And that's the way it was.

Ten days shut up at home. With nothing to do. He's a guy who doesn't read, doesn't listen to music, doesn't watch TV. What would he watch TV for? To watch stupid movies, with cops who are faker than Aragona, that sunlamped kid who's a parody of himself, only now he's his coworker. Of course a guy would lose his mind, Romano thinks to himself. Of course a guy would do things he wouldn't do normally.

Giorgia. No one but her, to keep him company. And irritate him even more, with those sidelong glances, the way she watched him secretly all the time. How long had they been married now? Eight years. No children, the kids never came, and it was no one's fault: tests, hopeful journeys, figuring out when she would be most fertile, hearing her weep into her pillow at night while she was pretending to sleep soundly. And then silence. Lots and lots of silence. Tons of silence, hanging in the air like some foul stench, like some intolerable miasma.

You cling to your work, in cases like this. Especially if you're good at it, capable. Above all if that work is something you care about passionately, the work you've wanted to do ever since you were a little boy. And then all of a sudden his job goes to hell in a handbasket. Even his job.

The night before, Romano came home but Giorgia wasn't there. She'd gone out. Maybe she'd gone for a walk, or to see that idiot father of hers, her sweet loving daddykins, so she could cry her heart out about her miserable fate.

The apartment was empty and dark. Cold. After his first day spent in the dump, after becoming a Bastard of Pizzofalcone.

When she got back, not even half an hour later, he was sitting in the dark, sunk in silence. She'd come over to him, murmuring some excuse or another; to him, who'd expected to have her support at such a difficult and complicated moment. If she hadn't looked at him, if she hadn't spoken to him, it would have been better. Instead, with that fucking whiny voice of hers, so full of sympathy, she'd murmured: forgive me, I'm sorry. I'm sorry.

Do you feel sorry for me, Giorgia? Do you think I'm pathetic?

His hand had spoken for him. Before he could think, before

he could even begin to imagine how to construct a reply, his hand-animal had lashed out. And he'd hit her, with a back-handed smack, straight on those lips pursed in compassion. Now, the morning after, sitting at his new, useless desk, Warrant Officer Francesco Romano, whom his old coworkers had secretly called Hulk, felt the little cut on the back of his hand inside his pocket. The little cut made by his wife Giorgia's left incisor, which, luckily the smack he'd given her hadn't broken.

He hadn't budged off the sofa all night long. He'd heard her sob and sob, in their bed. He'd waited, absurdly, for her to tell him: it's okay, come back, nothing's happened. Come to bed. Let's forget about it. But she hadn't told him any such thing.

When the first light of dawn had become visible through the window, he'd gotten up and gone into the bedroom. She'd finally fallen asleep, a handkerchief knotted around her fingers, wrinkles around her eyes. Her upper lip was swollen where he'd hit her.

God, how much he loved her.

God, how much he hated her.

The door-to-door vacuum cleaner salesman stuck his head into the joint office, with that disgusting enthusiasm of his:

"Romano and Di Nardo, come see me. We have a complaint for you to go check out."

XVI

Lojacono caught up with Aragona in the kitchen, after telling the forensic squad that under the leather armchair was a glass snow globe that had enjoyed a brilliant career, becoming the murder weapon.

The corporal was on his feet with a notepad in his hand; facing him, slumped on a chair with a handkerchief jammed against her mouth, was a lovely blonde, her eyes red from crying. Aragona reported that this was the Bulgarian housekeeper, Mayya Ivanova Nikolaeva, and that she was upset.

The lieutenant joined in the questioning, and discovered that the young woman had been very fond of the late Cecilia De Santis, who was practically a saint, good, kind, generous, etc, etc, that the signora had never found fault with her, that they'd respected and admired each other, etc, etc, that the deceased had been completely satisfied with the work she'd done for her, etc, etc. No, there was no one else working in the apartment: no one lived there but the late signora and her husband, the absent notary. And that said husband frequently didn't even come home at night, he was an important professional and he often had to go out, etc, etc. That the signora on the other hand for the most part stayed at home all day, passionately obsessed as she was with her collection of snow globes, did you happen to notice the snow globes? Which she cleaned and dusted on her own, which she kept neat all by herself. That that day, like every day, she had come in early and fixed breakfast for the signora. That . . .

"*Mamma mia*, I drop tray in signora's living room! I must clean, now all dirty!"

Mayya started to stand up, but Lojacono stopped her with a hand on her shoulder:

"I wouldn't worry about the living room, Signorina. My colleagues are in there investigating the crime scene. But tell me: did you ever hear anything about any threats made against the signora? Or about anyone who, for whatever reason, had it in for her?"

The Bulgarian opened her eyes wide: "No, signora kind, signora good to everyone. Everyone love signora, no one have it in for her!"

Certainly, thought Lojacono. Of course. No one have it in for signora.

"We need the husband's phone number, we need to track him down immediately."

Mayya shook her head no: "I don't have notary's phone number, I never talk to him, signora talks to him. But office number, written on little blackboard."

She tilted her head to indicate a small blackboard hanging on the kitchen wall, upon which, in neat handwriting, was a phone number next to the words: Arturo's office. Lojacono pondered whether it was best to warn the notary, thus preventing him from perhaps being given the news by one of his employees, which would allow him to more easily control his reaction. As he mulled these thoughts over he realized that, as always, the husband was the prime suspect.

Aragona surprised him: "We could look for the signora's cell phone. Maybe we'd find her husband's phone number."

Lojacono agreed: "Right. Maybe it's in the bedroom, since we know it's not in the living room. One more thing: take a turn around the apartment with the signorina, look around as carefully as you can. I want to know if anything is missing, especially any of the valuables."

As if pursuing a single thought, Lojacono pulled out his cell and dialed the number of the station house. Guida, the officer at the front desk, picked up on the first ring. When Lojacono said his name, the man's voice became clear and alert: the lieutenant almost thought he could see him sit up a little straighter in his chair. Lojacono asked for Ottavia Calabrese.

"*Ciao*, Lojacono, what's up?"

"Are you done setting up your computers?" asked Lojacono.

"I'm ready. How's it going there? What do you need?"

"Everything seems to be more or less under control. The forensic squad is in there now, and the corpse has already been taken to the morgue. Listen, would you do a broad sweep of the Internet for me?"

"Sure. What am I looking for?"

"The dead woman is the wife of a notary, a rather prominent one, I believe, because the apartment is like something out of the Arabian Nights. Her name was Cecilia De Santis, he is the notary Festa, Arturo Festa."

"Is there anything in particular you're looking for?"

"No, not for now. Just anything interesting you can come up with. Call me on my cell phone as soon as you have a general picture."

Ottavia spoke distractedly.

"There, the search engine tells me that the notary's office isn't far from where you are: Via dei Mille 32. You could walk there in no more than five minutes. I'll call you in a little while with everything else. Do you want me to say anything to the commissario?"

Lojacono thought it over for a second or two.

"Maybe tell him to get in touch with the investigating magistrate, and alert him that we're on the move."

"Is Aragona coming with you?"

Lojacono thought he could detect an ironical note in his colleague's voice.

"I'm afraid so. But this time we're going to be on foot. Let me give you a piece of advice: never, and I mean never, get in a car with him. Understood?"

Calabrese burst into laughter.

"Yes, I'd already heard that from a few of my colleagues at police headquarters. Talk to you later."

Aragona came back into the kitchen, followed by the girl, brandishing a cell phone he held carefully with a handkerchief.

"Hey, I heard you! You're safer in a car with me, going 125 mph, than sitting in this kitchen with a phone in your hand, take it from me. In any case, here it is, the signora's cell phone. It was on the nightstand, turned off and charging. I didn't touch it; that was right, wasn't it?"

The lieutenant sighed: "You watch too much TV, Arago'. In any case, yes, better to be too careful than not careful enough. Now go and see if anything's missing."

He turned on the phone and waited until it had picked up a signal. Lojacono checked the most recent calls up through the night before, remembering that the doctor had placed the woman's death at the very most eleven hours earlier. There were a couple of "Unknown Callers," an "Adele," two "Monicas," and an "Arturo," the last one, at 10:10 P.M.

The lieutenant wondered whether it might be a good idea to use that same cell phone to call the notary, but he decided it would be best not to alter the contents of the device's memory. He took down the information in his notebook and handed the cell phone over to his colleagues from forensics so they could check for fingerprints and then send it on for electronic analysis.

Now it was time to head over to the notary's office, at the address Ottavia had given him, hoping someone was already there. He liked to be able to look people in the eye when he gave them news of a murder. People's faces told you a lot of things.

While he was heading for the door he practically ran straight into an excited Aragona: "Lojacono, you were right. A few pieces of silver are missing, things they kept on the living room table, where the corpse was, in the hallway, and near the entrance."

"Is that all?"

Aragona nodded.

"Yes, in the woman's bedroom everything's still there: the jewel box on the dresser, with all the jewelry still inside, and on the nightstand we found the jewelry that she'd taken off to go to sleep. And in the husband's study, whose door was closed, there was a gold paperweight—that, if you ask me, is worth as much as my entire apartment with all the furniture in it—and a collection of coins in a glass display case that's just spectacular. Everything's there, except for these silver pieces. The girl says that there was a vase, a centerpiece, a couple of framed photographs, and a statuette."

Lojacono was doing his best to think on the fly. He called Cuomo, the uniformed policeman who had come over from headquarters.

"Take a witness statement from Signorina Nikolaeva, with a list of the objects that she remembers and that are now missing. Make sure, above all, that the list is precise. Then take down her details and her home address, make a copy of her ID, and get the number to her cell phone: we have to be able to get back in touch with her when needed. Signorina, you can't leave the city for the time being. And we have to be able to contact you at any time. Aragona, let's go. We have work to do."

XVII

On the way, the conversation was monosyllabic. Both of them were lost in thought; and for that matter, what did they have in common? What would they have had to talk about?

As things stood, Officer First Class Alessandra Di Nardo and Warrant Officer Francesco Romano had nothing in common except for their recent assignment to the same precinct, which had been dubbed—with little affection—the station house of the Bastards of Pizzofalcone in the city's law enforcement circles. Not much of a basis for a close acquaintance. Not the best foundation for a frank friendship, one might safely say.

And so they walked along, in silence and against the wind, on their way to ascertain the reasons for a dismal, dubious telephone complaint. A goddamned telephone complaint. Taken down by a rumpled police officer in a catatonic state sitting at the front desk—a front desk that, in any other precinct house would have been mobbed, but here was as empty as the Gobi Desert.

A woman had made the call, apparently; and despite the customs of the city, she had not chosen to remain anonymous; in fact, she had been very exacting and generous with her details, repeating her first and last name—Amalia Guardascione—several times, spelling out the address and carefully enunciating her phone number. A crazy mythomaniac, Romano had thought to himself, no doubt about it. But since responding scrupulously to every report was policy as far as the vacuum cleaner salesman that he had as a commissario went, there they were, in the street, chasing down what were almost certainly the deranged fantasies of a woman who was probably crazy.

And anyway, this was still better than sitting with his feet up on his desk watching the clouds go by and thinking about Giorgia's swollen upper lip.

Di Nardo felt the reassuring heft of the modified Beretta 92SB that she carried in the pocket of her baggy trousers. She had purchased this weapon on a specialized website and had then registered it; it had a number of polymer components, which made it far easier to handle than its all-metal counterparts. This, as she'd had the opportunity to confirm over the course of her interminable sessions at the firing range, shortened considerably the time needed to draw the gun. No doubt, it required a much firmer hand to avoid any loss in accuracy: but that wasn't a danger that Alex, as the very few friends she kept in touch with called her, stood any chance of running.

Because Alex was herself only when she was firing a gun. Whether it was a rifle, pistol, or submachine gun, Alex was only happy and fulfilled when an extension of her upper limb was ejecting small, lethal chunks of metal. When she was pounding a target to shreds, when she was tattering a silhouette.

Alex practiced shooting constantly. When she was forced to take vacation days, she'd go out to the old farmhouse her family still owned in the countryside, take up a stance behind a window—which had a very narrow firing range—and shoot at targets that she'd carefully prepared in advance.

She'd been taught to shoot by her father, a general in the Italian army, now retired. Captain, later Colonel, and later still General Di Nardo had wanted a son, but destiny and that incompetent wife of his had conspired to give him only that scrawny daughter—not someone who deserved his attention.

But once he had taken her to shoot at the firing range, and the little girl had shown such an incredible talent: all things considered, the two of them might actually have something to talk about.

Since that day, Alex had been a shooter. As soon as possible, in whatever circumstances, she shot. In order to be able to talk to her father, to whom she displayed a doglike devotion, she shot. It was the only way she could get him to smile at her. And almost the only pastime she cultivated.

Almost.

They'd reached the address that Officer Guida had taken down. It was one of those working-class neighborhoods that had become fashionable ten years ago, raising prices and ambitions, but the gentrification had stopped well short of completion; the resulting effect was one of arrested development, with a mix of high-end boutiques and middle- to low-end shops, and newly constructed buildings alongside tumbledown relics. The apartment building in which Signora—or Signorina—Amalia Guardascione resided was, all things considered, nice enough, with a clean front entrance and a working elevator.

A young foreign woman came to open the door, either a housekeeper or a caregiver; she had a bony physique and small, light-colored eyes. A strong smell of fried garlic filled the air. The young woman led the two cops into a living room furnished with old but well-kept pieces of furniture, and with embroidered doilies everywhere: on the table, on the backrests of the sofa and armchairs, on the counter of the credenza. Beneath the smell of fried garlic, a pungent smell of urine could be detected, betraying the presence of an elderly person with incontinence problems; sure enough, seated in an armchair by the window was a monumental old woman with a grim expression on her face and a blanket over her legs. Romano was surprised not to see an embroidered doily there, too.

"*Buongiorno*, I'm Warrant Officer Romano and this is Officer

First Class Di Nardo, from the Pizzofalcone police station. Are you Signora Amalia Guardascione?"

The woman scrutinized them in silence. She oozed wariness from every pore. Finally she spoke, in a deep voice: "Yes. That's me. Show me your badges. And you," she added, addressing the foreign girl, "get out of here, all this is none of your business." While the two police officers were producing their official IDs, she hissed: "Gossipy slut."

After performing a thorough verification though a pair of eyeglasses perched on the tip of her nose, and allowing that she was at least temporarily satisfied, she handed back the two IDs and said: "Out of uniform, eh? So we're saving money on uniforms too, these days. I like cops who look like cops. And then, a girl cop. Well, we'll have to make do."

Romano and Di Nardo exchanged a baffled glance. Then the policeman spoke up: "Signora, you filed a report claiming that a crime may have been committed. Could you tell us what this is about? That way we can keep from taking up too much of your time and leave you to your more urgent pursuits."

The unmistakable irony fell flat, because Donna Amalia nodded in satisfaction: "Excellent. Let's not waste time. Now then, from this window, where I spend a fair part of my day, it sometimes happens that I find myself watching the windows across the way."

Alex decided that she would never want to live anywhere that had windows within eyeshot of that old woman.

"One of those windows, you see it? On the fifth floor of that building."

Romano took a casual look across the street. He was confirming inwardly that this was a spectacular waste of time.

"It's an apartment that was just renovated; they completed the work about twenty days ago. Then someone moved in."

She shifted to get more comfortable. The chair groaned beneath her.

After a long silence, during which the two police officers

looked at each other with a growing uneasiness, Di Nardo finally asked: "So who moved in?"

Donna Amalia nodded contentedly, like a schoolteacher when a student shows that she's paid attention to the lesson.

"Exactly. Who moved in?"

Romano started losing his patience.

"Signo', let me repeat: we don't have time to waste. If you have something to say, go on and say it. If not, we can leave with our apologies for having disturbed you."

The woman looked at him with disgust.

"The point, my dear . . . what did you say your rank was? Warrant officer? That's exactly the point. Someone lives there, in that apartment. And that someone is being held prisoner."

"What do you mean, being held prisoner?"

Donna Amalia clasped her hands together.

"Oooh, Jesus! What do you think being held prisoner means? This person, or these people, who live in there, never leave the apartment. They never look out the window. They never open the windows. They don't answer the buzzer. They're prisoners, I'm telling you. And you need to ascertain the why and the wherefore, which is why I called you."

Romano sighed.

"Signo', the fact that someone doesn't leave an apartment and doesn't look out the window doesn't mean that person is a prisoner. Even if we accept, for argument's sake, that that's what's going on. Maybe the inhabitants of that apartment are leaving and returning, but they're doing it at moments that, shall we say, elude your surveillance. And maybe they look out windows, who can say, on the other side of the building, where you can't see them."

The woman shook her head firmly.

"No. I can assure you that that's not the way it is. I can't walk, you know. I depend entirely and for everything on that Ukrainian slut who opened the door for you, and it isn't easy.

But my head still works perfectly, I spend my whole day here, and I assure you that something strange, something very strange, is going on in that apartment. I've been here for years and years. My sole pastime is looking out that window, and I've never, let me repeat never, focused on something that later proved not to be true. Once, just once, a woman peeked her head around the curtain: I saw her face, a young woman's face, a beautiful face. The face of a madonna, she had. And there was fear in her eyes. I'm telling you, someone is holding that girl prisoner; and maybe there are other people in there, I wouldn't be able to say. Now, if you want to check it out, check it out; if you don't want to, go on back to your office. I'm at peace with my conscience, you two can do as you like as far as yours are concerned."

After her lengthy tirade, the woman heaved a sigh and picked up an embroidery frame that lay on a table near the armchair; she set to work, a gesture which explained the presence of all those doilies and also made it clear that the conversation was over.

Romano looked at Di Nardo again, then said: "Signo', a criminal complaint is a serious matter. You shouldn't make them lightly and we certainly don't take them lightly. You've filed one, and I hope that you thought carefully before calling 911; we have received it and we're going to check it out. Thanks, and have a good day."

Without looking up from her work, the woman shouted in a shrill voice: "Irinaaa! See these gentlemen to the door, get moving!"

XVIII

They'll come.

They'll come and they'll start asking questions.

They'll delve into the words, into the expressions. They'll try to understand the color of the feelings; they'll sniff like dogs after the scent of a reason for hatred.

Perhaps they'll do a bad job of searching, because they won't search for love. But in fact it is love, in many cases, that puts an end to life. Love is a powerful current, I would tell them; love is like a river, which flows along nice and calm, and then, around a bend that seems no different from any of the others, that seems no different from any of the other bends along the course a river follows from its source all the way to the sea, suddenly, there's a cliff, and the river turns into a violent and terrible waterfall.

You can live for love, I'd tell them. Love is a force that takes you by the hand and leads you to the end of the day, of the month, of the year, of the night. Love is a dream, a mere illusion: but you can treasure it and foster it, that illusion, you can make it grow until it's big enough for you to live in.

They'll come, and maybe they'll delve into the documents, in search of some foul-smelling trace made up of money and vested interests. And maybe they will find traces, and they'll think they're on the right trail.

I would tell them to look elsewhere, to delve into caresses. Into sighs and flesh—that's where I'd say to look. Because maybe the reason for everything is there, in an old acquaintance, in a gaze held for an extra fraction of a second. Because that is how *an illusion is born, with a gaze and a fraction of a second. And you imagine something, and you cradle it in your arms like a newborn baby, helping it to grow, feeding it until it becomes so big that it takes up every bit of room there is.*

I would tell them that love is to blame for everything. That those who get in love's way always run a terrible risk. Because love is powerful, and when it rushes down to the sea it doesn't recognize obstacles, it uproots, it overturns, it undermines, it crushes; and then it carries away the pieces.

I would tell them not to search for money, because the logic of love is much stronger than any mere pecuniary interest. And I would tell them that I tried to make her understand how absurd it is to try to stand in love's way. I explained to her, speaking with my heart in my hand, that right around that last bend that resembles all the others, lies the abyss. That this wasn't like the times before, that we were all now faced with real decisions. But she wouldn't listen to what I said.

We'll watch them delve into the usual motivations, but they'll be searching in the wrong direction. Because they won't think of love, and all its reasons.

I would tell them, if they only asked the right questions. I'd explain it to them, because it happened.

Because I did it.

But I won't tell them, because they won't search in the right direction. And the one who'll pay is the one who ought to.

Love will pay.

XIX

They really did take five minutes to reach the address that Ottavia Calabrese had given Lojacono. A shiny brass plate next to the front door of the luxurious building announced: "Arturo Festa, Notary."

It was early, not yet ten o'clock. The lieutenant wondered whether anyone was already in the office. He couldn't reasonably linger to give the husband the news in person. He had his cell phone number: he could try to call him. But what he really wanted was to observe the reactions of the people who knew the notary well, when they heard the news of the murder.

They went over to the doorman, a diminutive, middle-aged fellow who was sorting catalogues into the various mailboxes. Without even turning around, the man gestured to the foot of a flight of stairs with his head: "Mezzanine, Staircase A," he said.

Which meant that someone was already there.

Aragona rang the doorbell, and from inside someone hit a button to open the door automatically. They walked into a small waiting room, and a young woman, short, pudgy, and wearing glasses, came toward them; her manner was businesslike: "Hi there. Can I help you?"

Lojacono saluted and said: "Perhaps. *Buongiorno*, signorina. My name is Lojacono and this is Officer Aragona, from the Pizzofalcone police station. We'd like to speak with the notary Arturo Festa."

The young woman seemed unsurprised. It couldn't have been unusual for the police to show up at this office.

"I'm sorry, the notary isn't in just now. Could you tell me what this is about? Did you have an appointment, have you spoken to him directly?"

"When do you think that we could talk with him? This is a confidential matter, and it's quite urgent. You are . . ."

"I'm sorry, I haven't introduced myself. My name is Imma, Imma Arace. I'm in charge of bills of exchange and promissory notes, the only part of the office that is open for business at this hour. The other employees come in later on; now it's only me and the preparer, Rino. I'm sorry, but I really wouldn't know how to help you."

"How many other people work in this office, signorina? And what time do they come in?"

"There are two other employees, both women, and they get here by 10:30. We leave earlier, so their shift is staggered with respect to ours. You'd just have to wait . . ." she glanced at the clock, "half an hour, more or less, for the entire staff."

Lojacono and Aragona exchanged a glance.

"Perhaps we could speak with the two of you, in that case. While we wait for the other office employees to come in, and for the notary himself. And, signorina, you really ought to tell me where the notary is."

Signorina Arace noticed the change in Lojacono's tone of voice, now more emphatic and urgent. And she realized that these two police officers weren't here to handle some confidential bureaucratic procedure: this must be something far more serious.

"Please, come right this way."

She led them into a large room with wood-paneled walls, which contained six desks. Only one desk was occupied, by a stout bespectacled man with thick lenses who was sorting an array of promissory notes into separate little piles.

The man narrowed his eyes when he heard the trio enter the room. The woman spoke to him in a worried voice.

"Rino, these two gentleman are from the police and they'd like to talk with us. They were looking for the notary."

The man put down the promissory notes he was still holding and walked around the desk, coming to stand next to Imma. Side by side like that, they seemed like relatives: both of them tubby, both bespectacled, both frightened and surprised.

"They were looking for the notary. The notary isn't here, he's out of town. Did you tell them that?"

The young woman nodded, looking insulted: "Of course I told them, what kind of fool do you take me for? But they still want to talk with us."

"Still want to talk with us. But what can we tell them, if the notary isn't here? They'll just have to come back, is what they'll have to do."

The girl had lost her patience. Clearly, Rino wasn't the brightest bulb.

"Then you try talking to them. I already told them, and I'll tell you again. They said that they would wait."

"They would wait."

Aragona glanced at Lojacono: it seemed like a farce. The man's habit of repeating the last few words that the young woman said was like an old-fashioned comedy routine straight out of the commedia dell'arte.

The lieutenant broke the spell: "We need to speak with the notary, whom you certainly know how to get in touch with. We need to speak to him now."

The man ran a trembling hand over the comb-over that spread what little hair remained to him across the top of an otherwise bald head, as if checking to make sure every hair was in order.

"Speak to him now. The notary is on Capri, for a conference. He ought to have been back yesterday, but with the choppy seas the hydrofoils weren't running. So he's stuck there and we don't know when he'll be able to get back. If there's anything we can do to help . . ."

He looked over at his colleague uncertainly, and she dropped her eyes. Something isn't right, thought Lojacono. He tried bluffing.

"Okay, then we can get in touch with the police station there on the island. You must certainly be able to tell me the name and phone number of the hotel. I would imagine that for you the notary must always be available, isn't that right, Signor . . ."

The man opened and shut his mouth a few times, as if he couldn't think of what to say. The young woman threw him a lifeline: "De Lucia, Salvatore De Lucia. As I informed you, he prepares the promissory notes, he's in charge of . . ."

Aragona interrupted her, raising one hand: "You can explain all that later, signorina. Right now we just need to know where we can find the notary. And fast."

The officer's abrasive tone further frightened the fat man, who stammered: "Actually . . . that's classified information, where the notary is. Top secret."

He shot Imma a sidelong glance.

Lojacono said: "Not anymore, it isn't. Now you'd better tell me. You have to."

De Lucia looked down at the floor and murmured: "He's in Sorrento, with . . . on vacation. He'll be back today, later this morning. But please, I beg you, this can't get out. No one can know, especially not his . . . his family."

He had blushed to a pathetic degree. His coworker glared at him in disgust, and Lojacono wondered whether her reaction was due to the fact that the man had revealed a secret or just that he'd tried to cover up the notary's affair.

"You can rest assured that this information will remain confidential," Aragona told the two employees. "The notary's wife, Signora Cecilia De Santis, was found dead this morning, in their apartment."

It was as if someone had unexpectedly fired a gun. The man

stared at Aragona in disbelief, as if he'd just heard a very unfunny joke. The woman was the picture of surprise, eyes and mouth wide open like three capital O's. Then she began to tremble, and finally she burst into sobs. De Lucia hesitantly raised his arm and put it around his coworker's shoulders. Lojacono felt sorry for them both.

"I'm sorry to have had to break the news to you like this, but it was to make you understand the urgency of the situation. Now, would you please tell me how to get in touch with the notary?"

XX

There seemed to be no way to reach the notary. His cell phone was turned off, and the two employees said they didn't know the name of the hotel where he'd stayed that night and the night before because, according to the answers the police officers managed to wring out of the pair—grudging and monosyllabic though they were—the notary had left Saturday morning, that is, two days ago.

Nothing, clearly, about who was traveling with him: but Lojacono got the impression that the two employees knew perfectly well who it was.

There was nothing to do but wait. In the next hour, the other two employees came in, and they were immediately brought up-to-date on what had happened.

The first was well over fifty years old, a wiry woman with thin lips and a pragmatic air; her name, which she reeled out as if it were some elaborate honorific, was Raffaela Rea, nicknamed Lina, and she ensured legal compliance after a deed had been drafted. After learning that Signora Festa was dead, she turned pale, sank into a chair, and stayed there. She stated that she had no idea of where the notary might be, and when she learned that De Lucia had revealed the truth, she shot him a glare that ought to have incinerated him on the spot.

The second one, who showed up out of breath, was a petite, attractive, hyperactive blonde named Marina; she was in charge, as she explained immediately, of all electronic registrations—by now a major chunk of the work done by every notary office in Italy—and also of certifications. When she learned of the murder, she reacted with absolute astonishment and bewilderment; she shook her head back and forth, with a terribly sad expression, and went to sit gloomily at her desk. She was the first to emerge from her trance, and offered the two police officers a cup of coffee, which she made on a hot plate tucked away in a nook in the office.

Lojacono wanted to keep an eye on them all, to keep anyone from secretly alerting the notary. While he waited, he called the precinct house, to report in and learn what Ottavia had found online.

Calabrese herself answered the phone.

"Oh, *ciao*, Lojacono. I was just about to call you. Palma spoke to the magistrate and let him know that you're there; maybe he'll swing by. The forensic squad is finishing its work and we left a squad car on site; if the notary decides to swing by his apartment before heading for the office, they'll alert us and we'll alert you."

"Did you find anything interesting online?"

"Characters decidedly out of the ordinary, the signora and the notary. She's mentioned on a huge number of sites—charitable work, involvement in drives, social programs. A true benefactress. From a few references I gathered that she's from money—a lot of money. The notary, on the other hand, is a bit of a social butterfly; he's always on the guest list: party here, party there, inaugurations, receptions. The odd thing is that the two of them are never—and I mean never—mentioned together; he goes his way, and she goes—or used to go—hers. Separate lives, in short. At least as far as I can tell from the Web. And one more thing: on a gossip site, in a fairly recent post, there was mention of the notary's 'new flame,' and he, I might add, appears to be a very handsome man, at least based on the photos. Now, a new flame presupposes old flames: if you ask me, he's a guy who leapfrogs around."

Lojacono was pleased with his colleague's efficiency: as a member of the support staff, she was really quite useful.

"Thanks, Ottavia. Will you take care of letting Palma know? We're here, waiting for the notary."

"Sure, I'll take care of it. Ah, Lojacono, a piece of advice: make sure nobody starts fooling around with the notary's computer, even though we'll have to wait for the magistrate to affix the official seals. We might find something interesting in it."

"Got it."

"Ah, did you know that Romano and Di Nardo went out to investigate a complaint? Fingers crossed, the idea of those two together scares me. Take care, see you later."

Lojacono allowed normal office work to proceed, as long as no one left. A few people came in to pay off promissory notes and checks, which Imma took care of; and De Lucia went on arranging his stacks of bills of exchange, but his hands were shaking and every so often he stopped to look off into the distance.

The other two women didn't even try to pretend to work. Lina, the older employee, stared insistently out the window that overlooked the courtyard, expecting to see the notary arrive; the other one, Marina, sat with downcast eyes, her fingers knit on the desktop before her.

Arturo Festa arrived after about an hour, toward eleven o'clock. He seemed to be in an excellent mood. He was a handsome man, just short of sixty, tall, gray-haired, dressed in an elegant, sporty suit, a healthy, natural tan glowing on his face and neck, which had been left uncovered by the open collar of his shirt. The shoulder bag he carried could have contained everything he'd need for a couple of days away. He was alone.

He sensed something was wrong the minute he walked in. Lina started toward him, but Aragona stepped quickly between them.

Lojacono stepped forward and said: "Notary Festa? I'm Lieutenant Lojacono from the Pizzofalcone precinct house, and this is Corporal Aragona. We need to speak to you; can we step into your office?"

The notary furrowed his brow, catching the eyes of his employees. Imma once again burst into tears.

"Certainly. Please, come right this way."

A large door at the far end of the room led into the notary's office; a single, multipart bookshelf covered the walls floor to ceiling, which gave the place the warm and reassuring ambiance of a library. The desk was large and old; a slab of glass protected the elaborately carved desktop, clearly a valuable antique. Sitting in front of it were two leather chairs. On the other side of the office, an oval table, with eight chairs.

The notary pointed to the chairs with one hand, but neither Lojacono nor Aragona sat down, so he too remained on his feet.

Then Lojacono said: "I'm sorry to have to tell you, but it's my duty to inform you that your wife, Cecilia De Santis, was found dead this morning, in your home, by the housekeeper. It seems that her death was the result of a violent act."

His words fell into silence. Festa turned pale and staggered, propping himself up against the surface of the desk. He went on staring at the two police officers, as if he were expecting them to tell him that it had all been an absurd, macabre joke. He raised a trembling hand to his throat, then said: "No. No. You've got it all wrong, no. That can't be. It isn't her. I . . . we spoke just last night. No. No, I tell you."

Lojacono sighed.

"I'm afraid not, notary. There's no mistake. And the death can be timed to late last night."

Festa turned to look at the closed door. He really was overwrought, thought Lojacono, or else he was a remarkable actor.

"I . . . I need to go to her. I have to see with my own eyes. I need to go home."

"That would serve no purpose, Notary Festa. Your wife has been taken away. Later, you can identify her body at the morgue, but the young woman, the housekeeper, confirmed that it was her. I'm sorry."

The man walked around the desk, dragging his feet. Suddenly, he looked like an old man. He let himself drop into the chair and covered his face with his hands. A few seconds went by, then he showed his face again. It seemed filled with an immense grief.

"Who . . . who could have done this? And what kind of violent . . . I mean, what exactly happened?"

Lojacono tried to understand the nature of the notary's reaction. Experience had taught him that no grief seems more real than counterfeit grief.

"Apparently several valuable objects are missing, pieces of fine silver. Neither the apartment door nor the downstairs entrance were forced open, which means that your wife allowed her attacker to come in, or else he had a set of keys. Your wife . . . received a blow to the back of her head, possibly with an object that was found on the floor, stained with blood. We don't believe that she suffered."

The notary nodded, and his lower lip began to tremble. He was doing his best to keep from crying, but the tears poured out in spite of him, streaking his cheeks.

"Objects, you say. So it was a burglary, is that right? Cecilia was killed during a burglary? And where, in which room? And with what object?"

Lojacono didn't want to reveal too many details, because you could never tell: perhaps the notary might betray knowledge of some detail that he wouldn't otherwise have been able to possess.

"Your wife was found on the floor, in the room where she kept all those snow globes. And as for the object used as the murder weapon, until we've heard back from the forensic squad, we can't really say."

Festa nodded again, continuing to weep in that strange, silent way. Then he spoke to Lojacono again.

"I'm at your service. How can I help you find out how . . . who did this?"

Lojacono sighed. This was going to be the hard part.

"Before anything else, I have to ask you where you were last night, between 8 PM and midnight. And if there's anyone who can vouch for it."

The notary shot a glance toward the door that led to the open-plan office where the employees worked. Lojacono did his best to guess what he was thinking: perhaps he was wondering if someone had already revealed to the police that the Capri story was nonsense.

"My wife thought I was on Capri for a conference, and that the reason I didn't return was that the seas were too choppy. Actually, I was in Sorrento."

Aragona asked: "And just why would you have told this lie?"

The notary looked at him without expression, then answered Lojacono: "I was with . . . with a person. And I didn't want Cecilia to know it."

Lojacono pulled out his notebook and asked: "In what hotel were you staying? Did you register in the normal fashion?"

"No, we were staying at the home of friends of mine. They're away, and they gave me the keys to their villa."

"The person you were staying with, notary, you'll have to give me her name. We need to check your story out."

The notary seemed to awaken from a state of unconsciousness, as if he'd just now noticed that he was in his office.

"I believe I need to talk to a lawyer. Yes, yes: I definitely need to talk to a lawyer. I don't think I ought to answer any more of your questions, lieutenant. I'm going have to ask you to excuse me, but right now I'd prefer to be alone."

Lojacono tried to regain lost ground: "Notary Festa, our questions are meant strictly to ascertain the direction in which we ought to investigate, nothing more. If you have nothing to worry about . . ."

Festa interrupted him in a low but determined voice: "I understand you, lieutenant. But I need to take my own precautions, precisely because I'm not the one who did it. And I don't want . . . people who had nothing to do with it to be dragged into this."

"In that case, will you allow us to talk to your employees and check your computer system?"

The notary stood up. He was still grieving, but he was recovering quickly.

"Let me repeat, lieutenant: first I want to talk to my lawyer. I think it's necessary. Now, if you don't mind, I'd like to go see what's happened at my home. So . . ."

As he was pointing to the office door to invite the police officers to leave, it opened, allowing a young, very beautiful woman to enter. She spoke in a strong Sardinian accent: "*Buongiorno*. I'm Laura Piras, a magistrate from the district attorney's office, and from this point on I'll be supervising this investigation."

XXI

Having left Donna Amalia's apartment, Romano and Di Nardo lingered on the sidewalk, not sure what to do next. They both thought the old lady was a pathological liar, but what the warrant officer had said about the seriousness of criminal complaints had been true.

After a long silence, Di Nardo, in her usual deep tone of voice, suggested: "I'd go by and ring the doorbell. Just so we can say that we checked it out. The odds are 99.99 percent that they'll open the door and invite us in for a cup of coffee, and then we can go back to the old lady and tell her to calm down and stop making crank calls."

Romano agreed. "Right, we're already here, what's the worst that could happen? Even though I feel like a fool, chasing after the hallucinations of a crazy woman."

They went over to the intercom. There were two apartments per floor, and the only buzzer without a name was on the fifth floor. Romano pushed the button, waited, and then pressed it again, but there was no answer.

The two cops looked at each other, uncertain. Then Di Nardo, on impulse, pushed the button for the other fifth-floor apartment, which was marked "Casa Sprint Srl, Real Estate." There was a buzz and the street door swung open with a click.

The elevator left them at a silent landing. There were two doors, one on either side of the hallway. One was shut tight, and one was open wide; inside was a desk behind which sat a young woman with dark hair. They realized that this was a real estate agency. The young woman greeted them politely.

"Hi there! Come on in. What kind of apartment are you looking for?"

Romano told her the real reason they were there: "No, thanks, signorina. We just need some information. Is the other apartment on this landing occupied?"

"It was recently renovated, and it's already occupied. I'm afraid they didn't use our agency, it was a private transaction."

"And do you know who lives there? Have you ever seen anyone go in, or come out, or . . ."

The young woman sat pondering for a moment.

"No, now that you mention it, I've never run into anyone or seen people come in or leave. But I'm only here for a couple of hours every morning; then I take people around to view apartments. So I couldn't really say. But why are you interested? Who are you?"

Romano identified himself, flashing his badge: "Routine verification, you understand, for our files."

Vague references to bureaucracy always reassure people, and the girl was no exception. She took a phone call. The two police officers took advantage of the opportunity to wave goodbye and leave.

They came to a halt outside the door of the other apartment on the landing. Romano rang the doorbell, and the sound echoed inside. Silence. They rang again. Silence. Romano threw his arms wide and turned to head for the elevator, but someone, inside the apartment, uttered a faint: "Who is it?"

At first, they both thought that they'd had some kind of auditory hallucination; then each realized that the other had heard it, too. A woman's voice, very faint. Romano brought his face close to the door.

"*Buongiorno*, signora. Could you please open the door? We need to verify a few details."

A long pause. Then:

"You need to verify? What do you need to verify? Who are you?"

Di Nardo stepped in at this point, thinking that a woman's voice might reassure whoever was inside.

"We're from the police, signora. Go ahead and open the door, there's no danger."

"The police? Why? What's happened?"

Romano replied: "No, signora. Nothing serious. We're just doing a routine check. Could you open the door, please?"

Another pause. Then: "No, I can't."

"You can't?"

Absolute silence, not a sound. The woman on the other side of the door said nothing for a long time, then: "I don't want to. I don't want to open the door. I don't know who you are, and I don't want to open the door."

"You said that you can't. What do you mean?"

"I made a mistake. I said that I didn't want to. Go away, thank you, I don't need anything."

"Signora, who lives with you? Is someone there? Signora?"

After another silence, the answer: "No. There's no one here. I'm alone. I don't need anything. I have to go now."

They heard footsteps moving away from the door, then the sound of music coming from a radio or the television. They knocked again, and the music got louder. They turned and headed for the elevator.

Once they were back in the street, Di Nardo asked: "Now what do we do?"

Romano thought it over. "Technically we checked it out, didn't we? That is, we went to the place in question, we had a conversation with whoever lives in the apartment, and we heard the actual voice of the supposed victim of the crime tell us that no crime has taken place. Which means we don't have to investigate any further."

The young woman was having none of it: "Well, so what? If it's true what Guardascione claims, that is, that this woman is being held prisoner, that maybe she's being threatened, she would have responded precisely the way she did. Do you think that having quote-unquote checked it out is enough?"

"Explain to me then, what do you want to do now? At what point would you consider yourself satisfied?"

Alex had no doubts: "I want to see what's going in that apartment, that's what I want. If the police come and knock on your door in broad daylight and you don't have anything to hide, you open the door and you let them in and you offer them a cup of coffee. You joke around with them, you rhetorically wave bye-bye to the nosy old bat, and that night you tell your friends the story down at the bar."

Romano resisted, but without much conviction: "Maybe she thought we weren't really cops—these days it's dangerous to open the door to strangers, even if they identify themselves; or she's an illegal immigrant, or something like that, and she's afraid of getting in trouble; or else she's living in someone else's apartment and doesn't have permission to open the door to anyone."

"Don't you think all of these hypotheses deserve to be investigated? Plus there's this: first she said, 'I can't open the door,' and then she said, 'I don't want to open the door.' A telltale slip of the tongue, as far as I'm concerned. Come on, Romano, this smells fishy to you, too. I agree with you, maybe it's nothing; but maybe there is something going on. And violence against women is unfortunately all too common a phenomenon. Please, let's get a warrant to go in there, so we can put our minds at rest."

Romano saw Giorgia, fast asleep, her brow furrowed and her lip swollen; a muscle twitched in his jaw.

"All right then. Let's go back to the station and talk it over with Palma. We'll ask the magistrate for a warrant and then we'll come back and see what's going on."

XXII

I t was that damned old woman. I know it was her.
That evil gaze, the minute I saw it, I knew it could only
bring trouble.

What am I going to do, what am I going to do, now what am
I going to do . . .

Police, they said. Maybe it wasn't true, maybe they were just
trying to sell something, trying to rob me, maybe they wanted to
do one of those interviews, how would I know . . . Or else they
really were two police officers. That's what I think, that they
were two police officers, and the old woman sent them here, the
old woman who always watches my windows, from dawn till
dark, what the fuck does she want from me? Why doesn't she
just mind her own business, and let me live my own life?

And now what am I going to do, what am I going to do, what
am I going to do . . .

He gave me that number, but he told me never to call it. Then
why are you even giving it to me? I asked. And he told me: only
if something really serious happens, something very, very serious.
It's not my number, he told me. Someone else will answer, you
tell him your name, and he'll let me know. He knows how to get
in touch with me.

Now, is this or isn't this something serious? How would I
know?

I can't afford to lose everything. If for one reason or another
he decides that I'm more trouble than I'm worth, that I'm not
what he says I am, something beautiful and that's it, he'll just

trade me in. He'll get another girl; can you imagine how many girls much better than me he could find? And I'll be plunged back into the shit, and my family will be ruined, and my brothers won't have work anymore. It wouldn't take much. If I call, maybe he'll send me away and replace me with another girl.

But what if I don't call and those two come back? And what if it's like in the movies on TV, and they come back and knock down the door? What would I tell them—who I am and why I'm here?

What am I going to do, what am I going to do, what am I going to do . . .

If they come back and force open the door, they might arrest me, and that would certainly be worse, even though I'd never tell them his name.

But if they arrest me, then he'll definitely find another girl to take my place.

No, I'm sure: I have to warn him.

Where is that slip of paper with the number? Here it is. He told me: the only number you can call is this one. No other number. Just this one.

So I'm going to call this number. In a hurry.

Damned old woman, I hope you burn in the fires of hell.

XXIII

Leaving Aragona to keep an eye on the notary's office, Piras and Lojacono walked out of the building and into the wind that continued to lash the streets.

The magistrate had taken the situation in hand with energy and expertise, sparing the policeman the sad embarrassment of having to put the investigative machinery into reverse in order to get them all out of a bind. The bureaucratic process would take a few more hours, and the notary would have the chance to consult a lawyer, but at least the computer had been seized and, in the meanwhile, they'd be able to proceed with the questioning of anyone they felt it necessary to talk to, first and foremost the employees in that office.

"You see, Laura: from the attitudes I observed, the glances, the expressions, I'm convinced that they know a lot about the notary's private life. If we leave them alone, they'll come up with a single, agreed-upon version and we won't be able to get a thing out of them. That's why your arrival was so crucial and timely. Thanks."

"If I waited around for you to show up," the woman retorted mischievously, "I'd be an old woman. Thank your commissario, who reached out to us as soon as he guessed what was going on. And you can also thank your lucky stars that I was on duty; if one of my colleagues had heard 'Pizzofalcone,' he might have just decided to hand the whole thing off to the Carabinieri. For that matter, good old Palma had the good sense not to come here himself. He just let you do your job;

that's not what everybody would have done, you know, there are those who would have hurried over to grab the credit for themselves."

Lojacono had to admit that she had a point.

"True. You know, all things considered, this Palma isn't a bad guy. Compared with that asshole Di Vincenzo he's certainly a cut above; but tell me the truth, this thing in Pizzofalcone . . . is it a sort of punishment, internal exile, or what? Aragona told me a little something about why the others are here, and I have to say that what he said really struck me."

The woman wrinkled her nose. She was, Lojacono thought to himself, irresistible.

"Aragona is out of his mind, I'm pondering whether or not to take his driver's license away entirely; when he was my body-guard and driver he almost killed me, and I don't like the idea of you sitting in his passenger seat. Pizzofalcone has a bad rep-utation, and it's understandable that they're not exactly lining up for a shot at a job here; and it's equally understandable that the other precincts should have sent over people that, for one reason or another, they wanted to get rid of. But that doesn't mean anything. You just do the kind of work I know you can do, and everything will turn out fine."

For a while, Lojacono watched her as she clutched the col-lar of her coat to her neck, the wind tousling her hair. He wished he'd met her in another life, a life in which he wasn't afraid, in which he believed in himself so completely that he could imagine a woman like her being interested in him.

Piras in turn was thinking that Lojacono was the first man she'd found at all interesting since the death of Carlo, the only man she'd ever had, so many years ago. And that her work was no longer enough to fill her life, as it had always been able to. She stared at him for a while, his almond-shaped eyes, his high cheekbones, his sleek black hair; he was a good eight inches taller than her, even in heels. Her imagination filled her mind with filthy fantasies, and she struggled to control them.

Lojacono was struck by the rapt expression on her face.

"What are you thinking about?"

"I'm thinking that you're back in the field. And that maybe you have a chance to revive a career you'd assumed was dead."

"That's bullshit. And you know I don't give a damn about my career, and I didn't give a damn about it before all that happened. I like doing this work, which by the way is the only kind of work I know how to do; I mean, I'm not someone who belongs behind a desk."

"I don't believe you. Another thing you like is not having bosses over you telling you what to do, and so, the fact is, you need to rise in the ranks so you can do what you want. And after all, didn't you want to go back home a winner? Aren't you happy to be able to show that the things that were said about you weren't true?"

It seemed to Lojacono that her reference to the fact that he might eventually return home was more than merely professional; or maybe that was just something he hoped.

"That's not home to me anymore. I wouldn't fit in, now that I know the way everyone acted toward me. And after all, the only thing I care about is my daughter, and we're finally on speaking terms again. In fact, I'm going to give her a call right now. She went to a party last night, and I'm a little worried about her."

Laura laughed.

"How sweet, the doting father worrying over his little girl. Make the phone call, and then get back to work: there are four employees waiting to be questioned. I'm heading back to my office; we'll talk later. And remember one thing: don't do anything too risky. This notary Festa has all sorts of connections, and if he decides he wants to stop us, he knows how. If he gets in your way, call me and I'll step in. Take care of yourself, lieutenant."

She turned to leave. As usual, her overcoat, her severely

tailored skirt suit, and that fact that she wore practically no makeup had done nothing to conceal the shapely figure that had made Piras the subject of endless wisecracks among the city's lawyers, cops, and magistrates. Lojacono sighed and pulled out his phone.

"Hello, Marinella? What are you doing?"

"*Ciao*, Papi. I'm still sleeping . . ."

"What do you mean, you're still sleeping? It's practically noon! Didn't you go to school?"

"No, Papi. I stayed here, at . . . at Enza's, we stayed out so late last night, and . . ."

"What are you talking about—you stayed at Enza's? Just how late did you stay out?"

"Come on, Papi, don't you get started, too. That idiot mother of mine has already called a hundred times this morning . . ."

"I'm not trying to start anything but . . . still, didn't you say you wouldn't stay out super-late, and . . ."

". . . and instead I stayed out super-late. What's the matter, don't you trust me?"

Her voice had turned hard and mistrustful. Sleepiness had given way to anger and disappointment.

"No, no, of course I trust you. I just wanted to make sure you were okay, that's all. Sorry to wake you up."

"Ah, that's better. I'm fine, don't worry. I just need to get some sleep. We had fun last night, but we did stay out late, later than anyone expected. And that's all. Now, if you don't mind . . ."

"Certainly, certainly. Go back to sleep, sweetheart. Can we talk later?"

"*Ciao*, Papi. I'll call you, no worries."

No worries, thought Lojacono as he went back into the notary's office.

No worries, my ass.

XXIV

Deputy Captain Giorgio Pisanelli briefly rings the doorbell, as always, before unlocking the door. Honey, I'm home, he calls.

A rush to the bathroom, just in the nick of time, belt, zipper, he heaves a sigh of relief; but the trickling spray dies out almost immediately, it felt like ten gallons, he thought he wouldn't make it. Instead, barely as much as a single shot of vending-machine espresso, maybe less.

He washes his hands. Today, at the office, he must have gone to the bathroom twenty times. He wonders if anyone noticed. But in there everyone's busy minding their own business. Just as well.

You know, my love, he says, the new guys arrived today. They're not bad. Certainly, we knew that the Bastards were going to be replaced with discards from the other precincts; people that, for one reason or another, nobody wanted anymore. But I expected worse. I really expected worse.

He moves without turning on the lights, in an apartment he knows by heart.

Now he's in the kitchen, making a light cup of tea. He ought to eat dinner, but he isn't hungry. He speaks in a low voice, toward the bedroom.

One of them, my love, actually comes from Sicily. Do you remember, that time we went to see the tragedies performed in Siracusa? It was Aeschylus. You were very critical, but actually the actors weren't bad at all. But he's not from Siracusa, I think he's from Agrigento. He looks Asian, he has almond-shaped eyes and his expression never changes: one of his ancestors must be Chinese. But I think he's good at his job.

He takes off his jacket. He arranges it on the back of a chair, what's the point of hanging it in the closet, he's just going to put it on again tomorrow. He loosens his tie.

Two of them are similar, a man and a woman. They don't talk much, they look around, disoriented. Maybe they're afraid. Maybe they're afraid of themselves, who knows. You know, sweetheart, that's the way it works; as soon as you get one thing wrong, you know it can happen again. And you don't appreciate the fact that you have another opportunity. That's the main thing: having another opportunity. If I'd only had another opportunity.

A new, stabbing need to urinate. Not even five minutes, this time. Damn it. From the bathroom he goes on talking, in a higher-pitched voice.

The other one is a kid, a bit of a blowhard, and you should see the way he dresses. If you ask me, he thinks he's a cop on TV. He's cheerful, though. Maybe something good can be made of him.

He washes his hands again. The fact I have to pee constantly is making me look like one of those hygiene freaks, he thinks, the ones who wash their hands every two minutes.

He goes back to the kitchen. The tea is ready. He pours in milk, opens a packet of cookies. Chocolate-flavored, why not? Let's live a little.

You know I talked to Lorenzo today, sweetheart. He's fine. He was in a hurry, he had class. I know, it's true: he always has class. He's a university professor, after all, not a mechanic or a lawyer who can always find five minutes to talk to his father; he has to follow other people's schedules. Plus the schools up north aren't like the ones we have down here, which are so much more relaxed. They're sticklers up there. No, we didn't really say that much. He's fine, that's the main thing. I think he's still seeing the same girl, I didn't really ask, truth be told. You know, men don't talk to each other about certain things; if he wants to tell me about it, he will, if he doesn't, he won't.

He takes the tray with the tea and cookies into his den, and he turns on the lamp. The light illuminates a wall covered with newspaper clippings and photographs, and a bookshelf packed with file boxes and manila folders, organized under a series of labels bearing names. *Mamma mia*, what a mess. I'm going to have to refile all of this one of these days.

He unbuttons his shirt as he walks into the bedroom.

My love, you know, I'm just not sleepy. Would you mind very much if I work in here? You don't mind, right? You've always been so sweet and understanding.

He takes off his shirt, lays it on the bed, and grabs the old sweatshirt he wears around the house. His back aches from the night before, when he fell asleep at his desk with his head on his papers. It's a good thing I have to wake up to pee, he says to himself.

He looks at the bed. It's empty. And he sighs: we just have to be patient, my love. I know that sooner or later I'll get my hands on him. It's just a matter of time.

And he goes back to his study where, among the photographs tacked to the wall, there's one of a woman who smiles at him tenderly.

Ciao, my love.

XXV

...a *nyway, the lawyer was very clear. We can't see or talk to each other. Just for a little while."*

"You're crazy. And why? It makes no sense. Why don't you just tell me that you want to take advantage of this situation to get rid of me. But not me, I'm not going to let you get away with it, you hear me? I'm not going to let you!"

"No, that's not the way it is! In fact, it's the exact opposite! If we want to stay together, the two of us, if we want to . . ."

"Nonsense. This lawyer of yours is an asshole, or else you're just using him for purposes of your own. The fact is that you want to break up with me, and that you already wanted to do it before . . . before this happened. There, that's the truth."

"You don't understand. You don't want to understand. Can't you see that I'm calling you from another number? Don't you realize . . . don't you understand what's happened? The lawyer was clear, I can't answer any questions. And you know why not? Because I have no proof. We have no proof. We didn't register in a hotel; we have no witnesses; no one ever saw us. There's not a fucking shred of evidence, not one shred, that we were ever even there, much less that we stayed there the whole time."

"Oh, sure, because usually when someone goes somewhere to fuck, they call a bunch of witnesses: please, everyone, hurry on down and leave your first and last names, your social security numbers if you have them handy, that way you'll save us the time and effort of tracking you down. And after all, it's your

fault, you and your damned obsession with secrecy. Hide and hide, and here's what happens."

"In any case, I'll tell you again, the lawyer was very clear on this point: no contact, if you want to be kept out of this mess. It's the only way."

"What about those shitheads who work for you? They've always hated me. How are you going to keep them from saying anything about us? You know they'll start shoveling shit in my direction the minute they have the chance."

"No, no, calm down. I pay their salaries, they'd never do anything to hurt me. You're the one I worry about; do you think you can manage to be good?"

"You're talking to me as if I were a little girl. Quite a difference, compared to . . . compared to the other times. I guess I wasn't exactly a little girl when that was what you needed. I can be good if I think that I should be, but as you know I can also be very, very bad. I'm not like the other little sluts you've had: I'm a woman, a woman with balls, and my balls are bigger than yours, I've shown you that that's true."

"That's not what I'm saying, darling. That's not what I'm saying at all. I'm just saying that we're in danger now, so much so that I have to use a phone card in someone else's name, which I'll destroy when I'm done, to talk to you. The lawyer says that . . ."

"I've had enough of this fucking lawyer! Tell that lawyer that you won't be able to keep me a secret much longer. That everything is going to have to come out into the light of day, one way or another, or else I might be capable of anything!"

"Help me understand: what does that mean, that you're capable of anything? I'm sick and tired of your goddamned threats! Don't you know what's happened? Don't you understand? She's . . . God, I can't even bring myself to say it. Don't you have a heart?"

"So what? People die all the time, lots of them, all over the

world. And after all, didn't you say it yourself? 'How I wish she wasn't around anymore.' Don't you remember? That's what you said to me, while I was lying naked in your arms. And not just once! So really, you ought to be happy right now, no? Have the courage, if nothing else, to be consistent."

"I . . . I feel guilty. I feel like I'm dying myself. Just to have had that thought, to have . . . my God, my God . . ."

"You're crying, aren't you? Go ahead and cry. You're useless, I don't know how I ever got tangled up with you. But now there's no going back. There's no going back, you understand? Now we have to go all the way. The last thing we need is for you to get thrown in jail."

"It's a real danger, don't you get that? It could really happen. That's why you need to be careful, why we both need to be careful, if for no other reason. Do it for us. Do it for . . ."

". . . for him, that's right. I'll do it for him. But remember: you have to get everything taken care of very, very quickly. As quickly as possible. Because if you don't get everything taken care of, then I'll talk. I'm not going to wait long."

"I'll do the best I can. I promise you, but please, please, don't do anything crazy. Listen to me."

"There we go, good boy. Do the best you can."

XXVI

The notary left his office and headed for home. His face was marked by grief, worry, and a sudden, all-encompassing weariness; he was light-years away from the youthful, cheerful, suntanned man who, just an hour before, showed up here after a weekend he had evidently found satisfying.

Lojacono and Aragona watched him go, careful to catch—per Piras's instructions—any warning glances he might send in the direction of his employees, who still needed to be questioned. The notary, however, kept his sad eyes fixed straight ahead; he met no one else's gaze. The oldest employee, Rea, took a step forward as if to intercept him, but she stopped when it became clear to her that the notary had no intention of talking to anyone.

Before leaving, Festa murmured: "The office is closed for business. Advise the clients who had appointments to contact Mr. Dal Canto if they need a notary right away. I'll be back in touch; in the meantime, I don't want to be disturbed."

The door swung shut behind him with a dull thud. Lojacono and Aragona went into a small, unoccupied office, where they would be asking the employees, one by one, a few questions. The lieutenant knew that these were strictly informal sessions, which wouldn't hold up in court; but what they needed now was a lead, and you could only make out a trail if the tracks were still fresh.

The first to come in was in fact Rea, the employee who had

been with the notary longer than anyone else: "Ever since he started the office, lieutenant, more than thirty years ago. We were young, full of passion; and the work was so different then, every document had a story behind it, we weren't working with all these damned thingies, these computers, that make everything seem the same. Tell you about the notary, you ask? The notary is a wonderful person. Intelligent, impassioned, ironic, and kind. He confronts life head-on, never taking the easy way out. We didn't see much of his wife, not much at all. I remember that she used to come to the office every day, years and years ago. Then, little by little, she started to live a life of her own. And the notary . . . the notary isn't the kind of man who can be left on his own. Who will remain alone. No, that's not what I said: I don't know if he had affairs, and it's none of my business if he did. But you can't possibly think he was the one who hurt his wife. He's too straight of an arrow, keeps his nose too clean, the notary does."

Lojacono, observing the tightly compressed lips, the small eyes behind the thick lenses, and the harsh creases at the corners of the mouth, perceived—above and beyond the words that she spoke—the woman's slavish devotion to Festa. He knew that he'd never get anything out of her that might prove even slightly damaging to the notary.

He decided to see if he could use jealousy for leverage.

"Sometimes, a man with energy, full of life and passion, can feel alone if those who share his life neglect him. It happens. And when it does, that man might go looking for company, so to speak."

Lina snorted: "Company for the passing moment. That's not what counts: what counts is who's there for the long run, lieutenant. And asks for nothing in return."

"Like his wife, no?"

"Yes, like the signora. Poor, poor signora."

"Where was the notary, late last night? And where were you?"

Her eyes flashed from behind her lenses.

"Not together, lieutenant. I was at home, with my mother and my sister, watching TV. You can check that with them whenever you like. The notary . . . you'd have to ask him."

"But where do you think he was?"

"He's a man who's full of life, lieutenant. But he'd never hurt anyone. Least of all his wife. I'm sure of that."

Before ushering in the next person, Aragona spoke to Lojacono. Aragona's irritating habit of slowly taking off and then putting back on his blue-tinted aviators, a move no doubt perfected thanks to hours of study before American cop shows, had reached new heights of implausibility.

"This one, if you ask me, is an old maid who, in the middle of the night, in her single bed, fills her mind with filthy fantasies, all of them involving the notary. I doubt we're going to pry any information out of her about where he was last night, or who he was with."

"Yes, she strikes me as a tough nut. Anyway, you take notes on everything, that way we can check out the alibis afterward. Now send in the next one."

Imma Arace, the young woman who had met them when they first entered the office, still hadn't stopped crying. In one hand she clutched a damp handkerchief, and her eyes were bloodshot and puffy. She sniffled continuously, and from time to time she blew her nose loudly.

Aragona looked at her in disgust: "Signori', you need to quit your crying. Were you that fond of the signora?"

"No, what gives you that idea? I only ever saw her once, at a surprise party we threw for the notary's birthday, two years ago. I didn't even know her!"

The officer looked at her, puzzled: "Well, in that case, why are you crying like this?"

"I just get emotional when I hear these things. Plus, I feel sorry for the notary, poor thing. Even though . . ."

Lojacono perked up. "Even though?"

The woman made a face. "The notary, well, he's a man. And men always are quick to console themselves."

Aragona swept his glasses off with a broad gesture, and focused his untanned eye sockets on Imma's face; he looked like the negative of a photo of a panda, but the woman seemed quite struck by him.

"Are you trying to say: with another woman?"

Arace blinked rapidly, surprised: "What do you think, with another man? Let me tell you, the notary definitely wasn't playing for the other team."

"And how would you know that?"

"How would I know that . . . I know. I can see. I mean, if a guy is gay, you can tell, can't you? From the way he moves, the way he talks . . ."

Lojacono decided to put an end to that droll skirmish out of a comic opera: "Signorina, do you know of any relations the notary might have had with other women?"

The question was greeted with total silence. After a lengthy hesitation, the young woman replied: "No. Honestly, I have no idea if he's been having an affair. But that he likes women, yes, that I can tell you."

She refused to say more. When she left, Aragona whispered: "This is another one who knows something, Loja'. But she's not talking either, is she?"

"In fact, I don't expect us to get anything from these sessions. Still, we've got to do our best, because by the time the notary gets himself organized no one's going to be talking anymore, and that's a fact."

Aragona called in Rino De Lucia.

The man in charge of promissory notes was the only male in the office save for the notary himself, but he couldn't have been any more unlike his boss. He kept nervously fussing with the few strands of hair that remained atop his bald, gleaming head, arranging them in a pathetic comb-over, and the lenses of his Coke-bottle glasses magnified his myopic eyes.

"I can't think about her, lieutenant, the poor signora. And the poor notary, his heart is bound to break. They've been married for so many years . . ."

Lojacono nodded wearily.

"Tell me, De Lucia, did you know her, the notary's wife?"

"Know the notary's wife? Of course I did, lieutenant. I've been working here for more than twenty years, plus the notary used me as his driver: I'm in charge of promissory notes and bills of exchange, and there's never much to do in the afternoon. The signora doesn't drive . . . didn't drive, so I sometimes took the notary's car out and drove her when she went shopping or to one of her charity events. A wonderful woman, lieutenant. A saint! And always so kind to everyone."

Aragona did his little act with the sunglasses: "Did she ever tell you about anyone who might have it in for her for any reason? Did she seem to have any problems, any worries, recently?"

"Any worries, recently? No, none. We didn't talk much, to tell the truth. I'd wait for her in front of the building, she'd get in, she'd say good morning or good evening and then tell me where she wanted to go, and I'd drive her there. That's all."

In fact, Lojacono decided, no one would have confided in someone with the terrible habit of repeating the last phrase spoken to him.

"When we first came, you knew that the notary was in Sorrento and not on Capri, as he had told his wife. How did you know?"

"How did I know? I knew because, no matter what, we always have to be able to get in touch with the notary, because he has to be available to sign any certificates of protest. These documents must be filed by a certain date, and there has to be someone who's responsible. Since I'm in charge, I have to know how to reach him wherever he is."

"So then you also knew who he was with?"

The man started sweating; beads of perspiration were forming across his broad forehead.

"Knew who he was with? No, I didn't know who he was with, lieutenant. I said that I had to know how to reach him, not that I went to see him. There was no need."

"De Lucia, you know that you're endangering yourself by withholding information. Perhaps some day in the not too distant future, if we find that you've covered up for the notary, and that he's committed a crime, you, too, could find yourself in very hot water."

"Find myself in very hot water. Why, the very idea that I wouldn't tell you if I knew something that important, lieutenant. I was very fond of the signora, and to think that, poor woman, she was . . . I don't even want to say it, all alone in that apartment, the windows and doors shut tight against this windstorm, her husband gone . . . I really don't know anything about it. Not a thing."

Aragona looked at Lojacono disconsolately, before putting his glasses back on.

The only one left was the little blonde with the efficient demeanor who was in charge of the computer system, Marina Lanza. She was the most recent hire; the notary, as she explained to the two policemen, had finally admitted to himself that Signora Rea was entirely incapable of learning how to manage the office's computers.

"And it's not as if it would take a computer engineer, let's be clear. All it takes is a little logic and an open mind, which the good woman simply lacks."

Lojacono noted the clear fault line running through the notary's office. Maybe there was a ray of hope, after all.

"Tell me, signora: can you guess where the notary was last night, and with whom?"

The woman smirked sarcastically.

"He was in Sorrento, or someplace like that. He certainly wasn't at home."

Lojacono nodded.

"Yes, so we've been told. But I was actually interested in hearing your opinion."

"My opinion, you say. Well, my opinion is that the notary is someone who enjoys life, lieutenant. But this is where I work and where I want to keep on working: it's a good job and, all in all, the pay is good considering how much effort I'm required to put in. Sure, the work environment isn't ideal, but I mind my own business and, since nobody understands a thing about the work I do, they pretty much leave me alone."

Aragona broke in, brandishing his aviators: "No one's going to repeat a word of what you say, let me assure you. You can speak freely, signorina. It *is signorina*, right?"

From Aragona's moronic expression, Lojacono realized that his partner was actually courting the young blonde, and he feared the young woman was about to flee; instead, to his surprise, she seemed to be flattered, and actually blushed.

"That's right, *signorina*. And I'm not afraid of anyone, least of all that old harridan, Rea; and the other two don't matter at all, they're both idiots. But, if you can assure me of your utmost discretion, especially where the notary is concerned . . ."

Aragona tilted his head theatrically to one side; he looked at Lojacono and placed one of the arms of his glasses between his lips. The lieutenant had to struggle to keep from laughing out loud, but he nodded conspiratorially.

"My dear, go right ahead," Aragona—who was by this point doing the questioning—said reassuringly. "As I told you, none of this leaves the room."

Marina said: "Last week a very pretty young woman strode into the office like a Greek fury; she didn't say a word to anyone and went straight to the notary's office, slamming the door behind her. You could hear her shouting, but not clearly enough to make out the words. The others exchanged glances as if they knew who she was, but I'd never seen her in my time here. Then she emerged and left the same way she'd arrived, without a word to anyone."

Aragona and Lojacono waited, but as far as they could tell, the girl had nothing more to say. The lieutenant asked: "And no one commented on what had happened? Did any of the other employees say anything?"

The young woman looked at Aragona, as if awaiting his authorization to answer. After the officer nodded, she looked toward the door and whispered: "That old maid, Rea, said: 'That bitch.' Under her breath, as if to herself. And Arace started laughing. De Lucia, as usual, just hunkered down over his promissory notes and said nothing at all."

Lojacono asked: "And you don't have any idea what this woman's name might be?"

"Of course I do. Her name is Russo, Iolanda Russo. Arace told me so, that same day. She told me that she's an accountant, and that the notary met her when they were working for the same client, once, on a deed. And that they'd been dating for the past year. She said that at first she was always here in the office, but that no one had seen her for a few months."

"And you think that the notary was with this Iolanda Russo, last night?"

Marina nodded with conviction.

"Yes. After she'd left, the notary came out of his office, pale as a sheet, and said that he'd be gone that weekend, but that we should tell everyone that he was going to be on Capri for a conference."

Aragona and Lojacono pondered that piece of information.

Then the lieutenant asked: "How does the office computer network operate, signorina? Does everyone have his own, independent computer, his own email, or . . ."

"The computers are on a network. There's an office email account and the notary has a personal account as well. Rea and De Lucia, who might have urgent work to attend to while the notary is away, have permission to use his computer. But not to go into his personal email, at least I don't think so."

"So, if the notary had had any private correspondence, it would only be accessible from his computer, right?"

"Definitely. Certainly not from any one else's. And he's not much good when it comes to computers, he once told me that at home he doesn't even have a computer, much less a laptop."

Lojacono made a mental note to have the technician from police headquarters remove the notary's computer; he was curious to see what they could find. He said farewell to the young blonde, thanking her.

Aragona, putting his glasses back on, asked: "Could I have your phone number, signorina? Just in case we need to ask you more questions . . ."

XXVII

Alessandra Di Nardo, better known as Alex, would have liked to eat dinner with the television off.

Not that she really cared about dinner-table conversation, but at that volume—too low to hear anything clearly and too loud to be ignored—the television bothered her. Not that there was anything that could be done about it, if that's the way the general wanted it.

Ever since he'd retired, Alex's father had noticeably reinforced his already intrusive status as the absolute center of familial life. His needs and his demands had always been of fundamental importance, but now that he necessarily spent a much larger portion of his time at home, he was, whatever the topic, almost inevitably consulted. And when the general was consulted, there was only ever one possible conclusion: he was right.

Alex, eating in silence, shot a glance at her mother, a neat, quiet woman, who looked over at her husband at least once every minute, in order to anticipate any eventual wishes or needs. Her entire life had been spent serving that man. It was sad.

For his part, the general, though he showed absolutely no appreciation for the food, was shoveling forkful after forkful into his mouth; this would continue until his plate was clean. Alex couldn't say how many times she'd heard his accounts of epic hardships in distant lands, drills or secret missions during which there was nothing to eat for days, and how important it was, therefore, to respect the fact that there was a plate of hot food on the table. What a pain in the ass.

Not that she'd ever even hinted that she was tired of listening to him. When her father spoke, the clocks in the house stopped, and objects and people both held their breaths, awaiting the oracle's pronouncement. Suddenly she couldn't breathe.

"*Mamma*, I'm going out after dinner. My new coworkers and I are having a get-together."

"Good, so you're already all friends? It's a fine new initiative, isn't it?"

The second question was directed at the general, who merely grunted, not taking his eyes off the screen. Alex replied: "No, it's just that the commissario is interested in getting us to bond as a group. That's it. To get together outside the office, you know, there aren't many of us, so it's easy to arrange."

"And are there any unmarried men?"

The general's question had come promptly; he hadn't so much as tried an indirect approach. The general always came straight to the point.

"I don't know. Maybe."

Twenty-eight years old, and not even a boyfriend. The only topic of conversation Alex had with her father, aside from guns and shooting ranges.

Her mother tried to steer the conversation elsewhere.

"Maybe the atmosphere will be better than it was at the other precinct, right? And you won't have the same . . . you won't have problems."

Problems. In a very real sense, she'd *caused* the problems, she hadn't *had* them.

"I'm done eating. I'm going to go get ready."

There were evenings that Alex couldn't stand to spend at home. Something would start to howl inside her, and she'd have to go out. She'd always been that way, she thought to her herself as she drove through traffic, heading out of town. There were two Alexes: one that resembled her mother, quiet and submissive, and the other one, the one she kept hidden in the room at the bottom of her soul, but that sometimes cried so hard that even she couldn't help but hear.

Two. Two natures, two people. Light and shadow. Maybe, she mused, everyone's like that. Maybe there's no real difference, between me and *Mamma*, between me and the general. We're all the same, with a dark side and a bright side.

She thought back to Romano, the colleague she'd spent the morning with, chasing down what might prove to be merely an old woman's fantasy, or perhaps something more. He, too, silent as he was, might have his good sides; maybe he was a good father, or maybe when he was with his friends, drinking a beer, he lost the dolorous expression that seemed to be stamped on his face.

Not that she was all that different, she thought to herself as the lights of the city center faded away, to be replaced by the semidarkness of the outskirts. Silence, the closed door. Perhaps the last time that the side in shadow and the side in light had fit together was at boarding school, twelve years previous. That wonderful summer when she was sixteen. So long ago. Maybe too long ago.

Alex was driving slowly; her compact car was calmly tooling along nearly deserted roads. A weekday evening, in the middle of an economic downturn. People went out less and less, these days. Certainly, they weren't as bad as the woman who'd answered through the locked door that morning; according to the old woman, she never went out at all.

Alex had detected indecision, in that voice. And also, from behind the wood of the door and the steel of the lock, a hint of fear. Fear of what? Of losing something? Of someone's anger? Fear is always the daughter of violence, thought Alex. It's just that there are so many different kinds of violence. And therefore so many different kinds of fear.

She thought about the general as she passed a half-empty bus. My fear. Or maybe I'm his fear. Now that he's old, now that he knows he'll get nothing more from his life, I've become his chief fear: fear that at my age I'm not thinking about a husband, about kids. You sneak looks at me, general. I know that you look at me. But now it's my turn to give you a blank wall, to block any attempts you might make to get to know me. Too late, general. Now it's too late.

She couldn't say why, but she thought of Palma, the commissario. A strange boss, cheerful and sociable. Perhaps it was because they were just starting out, and he wanted to motivate them. What would it have been like to have him as a father, instead of the general? Maybe it would have been exactly the same. Or maybe not. No point in thinking about it, anyway.

One thing she knew was that Palma was different from that asshole Rigoni, the commissario of Decumano Maggiore. An old man who was afraid even of his own shadow. She thought back to the look on his face when he'd emerged from his office, after hearing the shot. The expression of terror, of uncertainty. And then the anger, at her.

I didn't lose a thing, thought Alex, switching on her turn signal before pulling into the nondescript courtyard. Not a thing. One place is as good as another. The important thing is to be able to do my job.

She got out of the car after pulling into a stall that hid it from view. Discretion, she thought, feeling reassured. Discretion was the first thing about this place, which meant it had the finest clientele.

She took the elevator from the garage straight up to the coat check. From her purse she pulled a bandanna, which she used to tie back her short hair, as well as a small black mask. She handed the girl her raincoat, her jacket, and her bag; the black top and tight pants she was wearing had struck her as a perfect compromise between the one Alex and the other.

The warm, welcoming jazz enveloped her as her eyes grew accustomed to the darkness, which was only slightly attenuated by dim, colored lights. She went up to the bar and ordered a drink. She no longer needed to screw up her courage, the way she'd had to the first few times; but she'd grown fond of the heat of the alcohol as it sank into her body, and by now she associated it with this setting.

A man came over, no mask, salt-and-pepper hair; his eyes were confident, his smile artificial. Someone who was pretty sure of himself. He asked if he could buy her a drink, and she said no. His gaze cooled instantly, and he sank away into the darkness without a farewell. Alex hadn't come here for someone like him.

With her glass in hand she ventured further into the club. She knew exactly where to go, but she liked to take her time getting there, as if arriving by chance. She enjoyed pretending that she'd stumbled upon the place, without making any kind of specific effort. As if it hadn't been an acute, urgent drive that had impelled her to come.

She continued through several rooms, all of them immersed in the semidarkness, with music piped in discreetly, low enough that you could talk, but loud enough to guarantee that any conversation was absolutely confidential. Many were masked, as she was, but others felt no need. Alex knew that for some people, the pleasure lay precisely in displaying themselves and their identities. Not for her.

There were times when she'd fantasized about meeting someone she knew. She couldn't help laughing at the thought. She wouldn't have been recognizable, and she'd have enjoyed seeing people's true nature; maybe even the general's. She thought about how unlikely that would be; in all his life, the most reckless thing the general had ever done was smoke in the boys' bathroom at school.

She saw two masked men walk past, holding hands. Further on, a man introduced the woman he was with to another woman, who kissed her on the lips.

It was starting to warm up in there. Alex took a drink.

She reached a larger room, where people were dancing languidly to the lazy rhythm of the music. She stopped and took in the scene. At the edge of the room, she saw a woman standing alone. She was tall, with long red hair, a glittery mask covering her eyes and nose. Bare shoulders over a wide, low neckline; large breasts, just barely starting to sag, hung free beneath the fabric of her short black dress. Long legs, bare, and shoes that glittered with sequins. Aggressive clothing and a shy, awkward demeanor: typical for someone who was there for the first time.

Alex went over, her manner reassuring. She whispered a few words in her ear and the girl smiled, tense. After a short while she held out her hand and starting moving her hips in time to the music. They danced like that for a while, not touching, eyes locked through the masks, while around them everything faded and vanished, leaving room only for the saxophone and the scent of the faint sheen of sweat exuding from their bodies. After a few minutes, there was nothing and no one but the two of them: the slender, lithe girl in pants and a shirt, and the soft, feminine redhead with long, bare legs. They moved closer, imperceptibly, and the tips of their breasts brushed, sparking an electric charge that made both of them shiver.

Alex pressed her lips against the young woman's, and the redhead tasted alcohol, lipstick, and mystery. Her green eyes grew lazy, losing all awkwardness.

They kissed, tongues intertwining, as desire took shape, sweeping away every barrier until it dominated their thoughts. One song gave seamless way to the next, accompanying the movement of their bodies. Alex placed one hand behind the redhead's neck, and she in turn placed her hands on Alex's hips. Then their lips parted, leaving their eyes to gaze levelly, saying to each other what the flesh already knew.

Alex took the woman by the hand and walked her to the door that led to the private rooms, where the guests could finally be themselves.

And the side of her usually left in shadow was suddenly beaming.

XXVIII

The night before, once he was done questioning the notary's employees, Lojacono had phoned in to the precinct to update the team on their findings.

Ottavia had taken careful note: "Iolanda Russo, accountant. I'll see what I can do. Listen, the commissario said that tomorrow morning we're all supposed to be here for an operations meeting. Pisanelli is asking around about the victim, and we ought to receive a preliminary report from forensics. The notary's apartment house is thronged with reporters. Word has gotten out."

The lieutenant thought those meetings were a waste of time, and anyway he preferred to work alone: he found Aragona's presence irritating, even if he had to admit that the corporal had served his purpose, casting, incredibly, a certain spell on Lanza.

He got to the office early, and was surprised to see Ottavia and Pisanelli already at their desks.

"Hey, don't either one of you ever go home?"

The woman chuckled: "Oh, we go, we go. But you know what this job is like, it worms its way into a corner of your mind and you keep chewing it over. I have some news for you. But I'll tell you about it later, in the meeting."

Pisanelli, who was reading the paper, piped up: "I have some news for you myself. We're on the front page again, the eyes of the whole city upon on us. But what else is new?"

In the meantime, Romano had come in too, his face weary from what looked like a sleepless night. He'd had a long argument with his wife, after trying to apologize for hitting her; she'd cried the whole time, and the cop had been forced to go sleep on the couch again, for the sake of her peace of mind.

"Early birds, eh? Well, so much the better. What time does the boss come in? I need to get a warrant to enter an apartment."

"He should be here any minute now," Ottavia replied. "It's about the complaint that came in yesterday, that phone call, isn't it?"

Alex came in too, wearing a pair of dark glasses: "That's the one, yes. Good morning, everyone. There's something strange about that place."

Pisanelli studied her: "Hard night, eh, partner? Well, at your age . . . In any case, I checked the archives, we don't have any previous calls from Amalia Guardascione; she's not one of those people who call 911 and invent some complaint just so they have someone to talk to."

Romano nodded: "I don't know, at first I thought it sounded pretty fanciful. But then, in fact, the young woman wouldn't let us in."

Alex chimed in: "And that's not all: there were strange hesitations in the way she talked. And no one we spoke to seems to have seen anyone go in or come out of that apartment."

Palma walked into the group office and was pleased by what he saw: "That's great, you're all here first thing in the morning. Clearly, we're starting to get into gear. So, Di Nardo and Romano, you're interested in following up on the complaint from Guardascione."

Before either of the two had a chance to answer, Aragona walked in, whistling. As soon as he noticed that everyone was already there, he abruptly broke off the tune, checked the clock on the wall and then his wristwatch to make sure they matched up, and said, bewildered: "Wait, excuse me, but it's eight . . . was there an early meeting this morning I wasn't told about?"

Palma laughed: "No, Aragona, don't you worry. It's just that evidently we're all early birds, and I think that's a good sign."

Di Nardo did her best to bring the group's attention back to the issue of the locked apartment and the mysterious woman: "We were hoping to ask for a warrant, commissario. There's something in there we've got to figure out."

Romano tried to chart a more cautious path, worried that if the bubble that was their operation burst, they might be seen as overzealous: "We don't have all the evidence, that's true. It's more of a . . . sensation, I guess you'd say. But yes, we both agree that this bears looking into. Just to be absolutely sure."

Palma made a quick note: "All right, then. I trust your sensations. Ottavia, let's ask for a warrant from whatever magistrate's on duty; Di Nardo, give us all the necessary information: street address, time of the complaint, any evidence you have, etc. Let's see if we can get this taken care of this morning. Now, since we're all here, let's move on to the next topic."

He pulled a bundle of newspapers from his bag and spread them out on Ottavia's desk.

"Now then, the De Santis murder is on the front page of every newspaper in the city. Some idiot, one of the officers from headquarters who arrived in squad cars, or maybe the Bulgarian housekeeper, let slip that there are pieces of fine silver missing: as a result we have an avalanche of commentary on public safety, on the fact that burglars no longer show any restraint, etc. As you know, a crime of passion is one thing; a burglary that results in murder is quite another."

"No one's worried about the fact that a woman was murdered," Lojacono commented bitterly, "whoever it is that did it. Instead everyone's just wondering whether the same thing could happen to them, or whether this all happened because of an affair. Just as usual."

Palma conceded the point: "Unfortunately, we not only have to be mindful of public opinion, but also of our superior officers. Yesterday the chief of police himself called me up, asking whether we thought we were up to it, whether we needed some help, or whether, believe it or not, we wanted to hand the case over to headquarters."

Lojacono looked at him, his face expressionless: "So what did you tell him, commissario?"

"What do you think I told him? That the situation was under control, that we don't need any help, and that we'll be able to handle it all on our own. That's what I told him. But now we know that we don't have much time to work."

Aragona broke in: "Still, the fact remains that the silver is gone. Not many items, according to the housekeeper, but definitely a few."

"Are there any signs of forced entry on the downstairs door or on any of the windows?" Romano asked. "Broken glass, a hinge unscrewed . . ."

The corporal began his routine: slowly, he removed the blue-tinted aviators; then, just to change things up, he furrowed his brow and dropped his voice by an octave: "No, nothing. Evidently the woman knew whoever killed her and opened the door to him herself."

Ottavia and Pisanelli concealed their laughter behind, respectively, a hand and a newspaper. "Or else the murderer had a key. Which takes us back to the notary: where he was, who he was with, etc. The silver might be nothing more than a red herring."

Di Nardo asked a question: "What kind of woman was she, the notary's wife? Could someone have had it in for her?"

Palma was pleased: the fact that everyone was absorbed in the discussion was an excellent sign. "Pisanelli, you know everyone in the neighborhood, can you answer the question?"

"Thanks for the compliment, Palma; I do know a lot of people around here, that's true, and over the years I've also figured out where to go to find things out. I asked around, supplementing that information with what I already knew and remembered." He sorted through a few sheets of paper, put on his glasses, and began: "All right: Cecilia De Santis, fifty-seven. She comes from a prominent family of builders and hoteliers, very wealthy and highly respected: Rotary Club, other associations, everything you need to be at the center of society's upper crust. Cecilia, well educated and wealthy, wasn't beautiful: average height, a bit plump; but she was well read and very intelligent, though not especially outgoing. She fell in love with the notary when they were in university together—they're the same age; he's from Luca, his family's humble, he even worked as a waiter to support himself while he was studying."

As he put his glasses back on, Aragona commented: "I can just picture him as a waiter—he's so arrogant. I'll bet they ran him ragged."

"Maybe he wasn't so arrogant back then. Long story short, they meet and they fall in love. Her family, I'm told, was opposed: it took him time to bring them around, and apparently it was ten or so years before a couple of cousins would even invite him into their homes. She practically supported him until he passed the civil service exam. But he was a sharp young man, and he passed the test with flying colors the first time he took it."

Romano snickered: "Without any help from on high, I imagine."

Pisanelli shrugged: "That I couldn't say. The fact is, that same year, the two of them got married. And little by little he became one of the most prominent members of his profession in the city; he was in charge of a couple of very significant mergers and incorporations. She, on the other hand, gives up all professional aspirations, not that she seems ever to have really had any, and starts weaving her web to procure contacts for her husband."

Di Nardo's curiosity was aroused: "And how was their marriage going?"

"They had their ups and downs, from what I hear. They couldn't seem to have children, and that might have driven a wedge between them. Aragona and Lojacono saw for themselves: he's a good-looking man, athletic, youthful—plus he's powerful, and that's the best cosmetic a man can hope for. She, on the other hand, looked every bit her age. From what various sources have told me, at least three separate times over the years, he had affairs that he didn't bother to conceal. She, however, has always led a very private life."

Calabrese asked: "And how did she handle her husband's escapades?"

"They were rarely seen together, only on truly important occasions. And there are no reports of outraged reactions— tantrums and scenes and things like that just weren't her style. In any case, for the past four or five years, everything seemed to have gone back to normal. Until a few months ago, when he once again began frequenting certain social circles in the company of a much younger woman."

Ottavia took a sheet of paper from the printer: "Iolanda Russo, up-and-coming accountant and tax consultant, just twenty-eight years old but already quite well known; she's in charge of major debt rescheduling plans, and she mostly works with banks. They met on the job, working a couple of real estate deals. At first, they did their best to keep it under wraps, but then they started to be seen out and about as a more or less official couple. She's a redhead, quite striking, an elegant dresser, obsessed with shoes: she likes to wear wedges and five-inch heels."

Everyone looked at her, confused; she suddenly found herself on the defensive: "Well, what's wrong with that? Gossip websites have all sorts of news, so . . ."

Pisanelli resumed: "In short, our victim is a character in need of some deciphering. I did a little informal asking around, and an old friend of mine who knew her very well, the Baroness Ruffolo, told me that if we promised to be extremely discreet and to keep everything she said strictly to ourselves, she'd be willing to tell us something about what kind of person she was and what kind of life she led."

Lojacono heard the news with pleasure. "Well, now, that's an interesting development. Still, we shouldn't overlook the theory that this was a robbery gone wrong, even though the fact that there are no marks to indicate forced entry seems very strange. Where can we talk to this baroness?"

"At the La Vela yacht club, where the ladies of the upper crust gather. They play canasta, fill their lungs with tar and their livers with alcohol, and spew venom all over each other. Let me know when you can go, and I'll make a phone call; generally speaking, she's there every afternoon from four o'clock on."

Aragona put in his two cents: "Maybe, before we go, we might go poke around in the notary's neighborhood. I don't know, talk to the concierge, a few of the shopkeepers around there."

"If I were you," Romano added, "I'd check up on how the housekeeper lives . . . she's Bulgarian, if I understand correctly. Not that I'm prejudiced, but I've heard of plenty of cases where burglars take advantage of the help to get into private homes. After all, she did have the keys, didn't she? That could explain why there are no signs of a break-in."

Di Nardo puffed out her cheeks in annoyance: "The same old story. Find the woman and there's your guilty party. Plus the housekeeper certainly knew where the signora kept her really precious possessions, didn't she? It's not as if she'd be satisfied with carrying off a few trinkets."

Aragona thought this over. "If you ask me," he said, "the

Bulgarian girl was sincerely shaken up. But maybe the signora surprised the burglar, and he killed her with the first thing he could lay his hands on, and it happened to be one of those glass snow globes; and then, as he made his escape, he was only able to grab the things he found on his way out of the apartment, that is, along the hallway and near the front entrance. If it was the Bulgarian girl, why would she have come back, given that she risked being seen?"

Romano defended himself: "I didn't mean to say that the girl was in on it or that she's the murderer. Someone could have taken her keys and duplicated them, for example. It was just an idea."

Palma, pragmatically, tried to establish a plan of action: "All right then, first go talk to the concierge and the people who live and work near the notary's building, and see if you can get any sense of whether the housekeeper has anything to do with it or not; then take a walk over to the yacht club. In the meantime, we'll see if we can get the results of the autopsy and the forensic report, and we'll also examine the newly widowed notary's computer to see if that produces any leads."

Lojacono nodded: "What remains is the hardest part of the investigation: figuring out where the notary was when his wife was killed. And the same thing for our young accountant who, according to Aragona's new friend, threw quite a tantrum in the notary's office last week. It would be nice to know what they said to each other and what they decided to do over the weekend."

Ottavia jumped in: "I have a friend who works in the computer lab; I can give him a call and ask him to fast-track an analysis of the notary's computer; if anything useful emerges, I'll tell him to let me know in advance."

Palma was delighted: "Good work, Ottavia. Your friend can't possibly say no to someone like you."

The woman blushed, but luckily no one else noticed.

The commissario went on: "For my part, I'll talk to Piras and bring her up to speed on the investigation, even though she's already told me that she has utter confidence in Lojacono. Anything you need, call us immediately. We may be Bastards, but we can still show them that we know how to do our jobs."

XXIX

Ottavia Calabrese took her son to the swimming pool day one day a week.

Riccardo went to the pool three times a week, but since Ottavia's husband was so sensitive, so dedicated—Gaetano took care of nearly everything that had to do with their son—Ottavia was only responsible for one visit. And even that one visit was a burden.

It wasn't a matter of having to move her shifts around so she could get the time off; or even having to drive in the city, which she loathed. It wasn't having to spend an hour and a half in a damp building that recked of chlorine and sweat, nor being subjected to the swim instructor's coarse attempts at flirtation. She didn't want to admit it, but she couldn't stand being alone with her son.

She couldn't say when that feeling had first come to her. For many years, after it had become clear that Riccardo lived in a world all his own, a world from which he would never emerge in order to interact with the rest of mankind, she had been a loving mother, wholeheartedly devoted to her child's needs. She'd accepted that there were no wounds that could be treated, no operations that might give Riccardo—and his family—a shot at a normal life. She had understood that her son was going to stay that way, with only a few, almost imperceptible improvements, for as long as he lived.

And she certainly couldn't have asked for a better husband. Gaetano had become, if anything, even sweeter, more loving, more affectionate. He lived for his wife and son, he devoted every ounce of himself to them, taking on the vast majority of the tasks and responsibilities. Riccardo's care demanded spending hours and hours with the boy; and yet Riccardo seemed hardly to notice him. For Riccardo, there was no one but Ottavia, his *mamma*, the only word that he'd ever pronounced intelligibly since he'd been born.

As she waited for the two of them to be alone in the locker room so she could undress him and put on his swimsuit, Ottavia thought back, attempting to determine when she had first begun to think of her home as a prison cell. If it had been from the very beginning, that might have been easier to understand: not everyone has the strength to take on such a burden. But that's not how it had been.

She had loved her husband. They'd been together for years and years. She'd supported him as he pursued his career and he'd done the same for her, well aware that ever since she'd been a little girl, she had wanted to be a policewoman. They'd been through so much together, and Riccardo had come along when they were strong enough as a couple to survive even that. And in fact they'd been exemplary, held up as examples by all the parents' associations they belonged to.

She made sure that they were finally alone. Riccardo didn't want her to help him put on his swimsuit when other children were present. He'd shake his head vigorously back and forth and moan, attracting everyone's attention. It was better to wait.

He let her slip off his sweatshirt and jeans. Once again, Ottavia noticed how much he'd grown, maybe even more than the other kids his age. The hair on his face, chest, and pubic area was getting thicker, standing out against the whiteness of his flesh. *Mamma, Mamma*, he said in a deep voice.

Ottavia didn't bother to answer. She knew that it was nothing but a refrain, a mere confirmation of the fact that she was there, close to him. She slipped on his swimsuit, first one leg, then the other; she wondered what would happen now that Riccardo was visibly beginning to enter puberty. At work she had seen terrible things: atrocious acts of violence perpetrated by the intellectually disabled who experienced the explosive sexual development natural to their age, but had no way to control it; she hoped with all her heart that such a thing never happened to her son.

In another way, too, the thought of sex made her cringe. That night, Gaetano had reached out for her, and she had pretended to be asleep. Again. She wondered how long she could tough it out with little excuses and postponements.

As she walked to the edge of the pool, holding Riccardo's hand, she thought back to the day, months ago, when she had finally decided to be straight with herself and admit it: she could no longer stand being around her husband and son. At first it had been a relief, in fact, it had even been amusing: to speak in the same tone of voice as ever, to say the usual things; but to know that she wished she were a thousand miles away.

Then her awareness had become keener, and she'd started to think of their home as a prison cell, even the hope of an end to her sentence. And the more her husband lavished kindnesses upon her, the more her son uttered her name, pressing his head against her shoulder, the stronger grew the urge to run, to run far away.

The instructor took Riccardo from her, greeting him fondly and shooting her a long, lingering glance.

Ottavia was one of those full, mature beauties, who might not strike you at first glance but then, the more you see them, become ever more alluring; wavy chestnut hair, cheerful, intelligently ironic eyes of the same color, a sullen mouth, and a soft but lithe body that never failed to attract men, who increased the attention they paid to Riccardo in hopes of getting to know his mother. It had happened with doctors, male nurses, and schoolteachers. She almost didn't notice it anymore, and she'd never felt any urge for another man: all she wanted was freedom, also from that vague sense of guilt that followed her everywhere.

The attraction she felt for Palma, the new commissario, was entirely unprecedented, and she didn't know what to do about it. She kept the feeling to herself, without encouraging it except as a fantasy, and for the moment she preferred to believe that it was nothing more than evidence that she actually was still alive.

Riccardo stepped into the water while she went to sit on the bleachers, along with the other parents. The swim lesson had been recommended by the boy's pediatrician, who'd said that regular physical activity was a necessity. Riccardo was happy to do it, was always eager to go to the pool, and aside from the problems in the locker room, Ottavia thought it did him good. Moreover, her son had liked the water ever since he'd been a little boy; once immersed, his mood improved perceptibly.

She watched him as he launched into a breaststroke, in the lane set aside for his lesson. Next to her, two mothers chatted about their hairdressers, mine is good and yours is good, mine is cute and yours is cute, mine does feet, too, mine works really fast. It was hot, the smell of chlorine made her vaguely nauseous. Fifteen minutes passed.

At a certain point the rhythm of Riccardo's breathing changed so that it was no longer in sync with his strokes, and he breathed in a mouthful of water. She noticed it immediately, glimpsing for an instant an expression of terror in her son's eyes, though he made no noise and didn't call for help. It lasted no longer than a couple of seconds, but it seemed like an eternity. The instructor was showing a little girl in the next lane over how to kick her feet, while the other boy swimming in Riccardo's lane was a good half a lap behind him and wouldn't get there in time to realize that the boy was in trouble. The women beside her went on chatting about shopping.

For a brief moment the image of a life free of commitment

and suffering, of interminable and useless visits to doctors, of fruitless conversations with special ed teachers, went through Ottavia's mind. For a moment, the image of the end of the only reason she and Gaetano were still together and so then the image of her rebirth as a woman went through Ottavia's mind. For a moment, the image of a new world, in which she would be free of that vague sense of guilt at not being a good mother, a sense of guilt that was with her every single instant of her life, went through Ottavia's mind.

Then, for a moment, the image of a nurse placing in her arms that tiny fragment of life that was her son went through Ottavia's mind.

And so she rose to her feet and let out a hoarse shout.

"Signora, believe me, I have no idea how it could have happened. As you know, Adelia wasn't here today . . ."

"Don't worry about it, really, these are things that . . ."

"No, signora, it worries me and then some, you know that we're always very careful about watching the kids."

"I insist, it's not important, the only thing that matters is that I noticed in time."

"I'll say it again, Riccardo, as you know, is one of our dearest boys. Just the thought that we might have somehow failed to pay adequate attention, especially to him . . ."

"Look, forget about it. As you can see, it all ended for the best. He only drank a little water. You saw—he didn't even want to get out of the pool, he's always so happy when he's here."

"Then I can count on the fact that . . . in other words, we won't give it another thought, right? I can assure you that, starting next time, once Adelia is back, I myself am going to work right next to this little man; and maybe I can teach him to do the butterfly. He's such a good swimmer . . . I can't believe it happened to him of all the kids . . ."

"On the contrary, I should thank you, you went straight to him. You're always so kind."

"Really, I can't offer you anything? A cup of coffee, a glass of juice, nothing? What can I do to earn your forgiveness?"

"Nothing at all, thanks. Listen, let's just not say anything about this to my husband, when he brings Riccardo on Wednesday. You know, he's very anxious, it might occur to him that this is somehow dangerous, he might decide to stop bringing him. But Riccardo is always so happy to come. I mean, you know, of course that he doesn't talk, but I see it."

"Don't worry, signora. No one will know a thing, that's the last thing I want, it's hardly in my own interest. Thank you. Thank you so much."

In the car, during the drive home, feeling the pressure of Riccardo's head on her shoulder, Ottavia wept.

She wept the whole way.

XXX

When Lojacono and Aragona reached the area near the apartment building, which sat at the intersection of Piazza Vittoria and Via Caracciolo, the wind had died down; the waves were no longer crashing onto the street and sea spray had stopped whirling through the air above the rocks, but heavy black clouds were still gathering in the sky.

Aragona sniffed the air like a bloodhound and said: "Loja', I think we're in for a good drenching. We should have taken the car."

"I'd prefer wet and alive to dry and dead, thanks, I'm happy to walk. The obsession you have with driving everywhere in this city is incomprehensible: it must be three quarters of a mile to the station house, maybe not even. And after all, you're just a kid."

The officer nodded his head with conviction: "And I'd like to live to be an old man. Let me remind you that those three quarters of a mile are all uphill. Anyway, here's the concierge: a dying breed, with what they cost."

In the building's atrium was a concierge's booth in dark wood, which clearly dated back to before the war; but these were deluxe accommodations, and had been since their construction, in the late eighteenth century—no economic crisis had ever affected this apartment building. Inside the booth was a counter, behind which a door led into the concierge's residence, into the kitchen to be exact, where they could see a man busy making a pot of espresso.

In the street, a squad car from headquarters was still parked, with two bored cops sitting inside. No sign of journalists; they'd clearly realized that there would be no more footage to shoot and no more information to gather at that address about the murder of Signora Festa.

They tapped on the glass window of the booth. The man inside turned around and gestured for them to wait, pointing to the espresso pot as if to explain the delay.

Aragona and Lojacono exchanged a disconsolate glance. The concierge stuck his head out: "Gentlemen, can I offer you a cup of espresso? Since this morning it's been a nightmare here, what with the police and the press; I don't know if you heard, there's been a terrible accident . . ."

Aragona grinned, sweeping off his glasses—as usual—as if he were on TV: "And you're still not done, because we are in fact two cops: Corporal Marco Aragona, and Lieutenant Lojacono, here, from the Pizzofalcone precinct house. And you would be Signor . . ."

"Mascolo, Pasquale Mascolo, at your service. Forgive me, I certainly didn't mean to suggest that you've been causing an inconvenience, it's just that it's been sheer mayhem since this morning."

Lojacono nodded: "I can easily imagine. And in any case, it wasn't an accident, it was a murder. Which is why, Signor Mascolo, we need to ask you a few questions, if you don't mind."

The man, reassured by the lieutenant's jovial tone, said: "I just made a cup of coffee, as I was telling you. Why don't you come on in and I'll pour you a cup so we don't have to stand out there in the wind."

Mascolo's kitchen was little more than a cubbyhole, but it was clean and welcoming; the aroma of fresh-brewed coffee and the light that slanted in from the front entrance, illuminating the few well-loved pieces of furniture, gave the room an air of times gone by. Mascolo himself fit in perfectly: an elderly man, well over seventy, with short white hair, a pair of suspenders holding up a pair of dark pinstripe trousers, a white shirt with a black tie, and a navy blue jacket. He looked as if he'd walked out of a play by Eduardo De Filippo, so much so that Lojacono, who had been an impassioned fan of De Filippo in his youth and had watched all his plays and movies on TV, felt a kind of déjà vu.

"Poor signora, I still can't believe it. I knew her for all those years, from when my wife was still alive; I saw her move into this building as a newlywed, and now I've seen her leave in a casket. So sad. How much sugar?"

Aragona had pulled out his notebook.

"Two and a half, thank you. When do you go on and off duty, Signor Mascolo?"

"I open the doors at seven in the morning and I lock them at eight at night. Between three and four in the afternoon I take a little rest, but I don't close the front doors, just this door that opens into the booth."

Lojacono shot Aragona a look: "You like your coffee bitter, eh? Just one spoonful for me, thanks. And the day before yesterday, did you see the signora go out, Signor Mascolo?"

"No, I didn't. Oh lord, she could have gone out and come back at some point when I wasn't here, I do the mail, the garbage—I mean I have chores to do, some of the time. And then, like I told you, from three to four I'm not watching the door. But I certainly didn't see her, I would have noticed."

Aragona sipped his coffee with a slurp so annoying that Lojacono thought it might be criminally actionable. He shot him a glare, which the young man missed entirely.

"Why do you say you would have noticed?"

"The signora didn't go out often. Let's even say she almost never went out. Occasionally the notary's car would come to pick her up, but it always brought her back early. She was always kind, if reserved; perhaps she just didn't like being out in the world."

Aragona had poured himself another demitasse of espresso, and he was mixing three teaspoons of sugar into the black liquid.

"One more thing: what about the notary? Did he stay home with her?"

Mascolo gave a small laugh: "No, the notary leads, let's say, a very different life. He leaves early in the morning, and I almost never see him come home while I'm still at my post, even if I lock up later than usual for some reason. Altogether, in the last year, I've seen maybe him a couple of times. At the most."

Lojacono forced himself to think, distracted though he was by Aragona, who was slurping his espresso with gusto.

"Let's go back to the day before yesterday. Did someone come looking for Signora Festa? Did anyone, I don't know, ring the buzzer, ask about her . . ."

"No, Dotto'. At least, not while I was here. And then, the day before yesterday there was that windstorm, the water washed up right to the lobby, I broke my back getting the place dry. There was practically no one out on the street. That's just what I was saying to poor Signora Festa, that we hadn't seen weather like this in years. The seasons are changing, the climate . . ."

Lojacono interrupted, raising one hand: "Hold on, didn't you say that you hadn't seen the signora the day before yesterday? When did you talk to her?"

"You asked me if I'd seen her go out," Mascolo clarified, his mien serious, "and I'll say it again: no, I didn't see her go out. But I did see her in her apartment, that morning. She had called me, the way all the tenants do if they need little repairs or have problems in their apartments. The roller blinds in the smaller bathroom were stuck because the clasp of the hoist strap was rusted. I cleaned it, I oiled it, and I closed the shutter, like the signora asked me to."

Aragona asked: "And how did she seem to you? Was she on edge, worried about anything, angry, sad . . ."

"No, no. She was in her dressing gown, she had a cloth in her hand, she was cleaning those glass balls with the snow inside that she collected, *mamma mia*, she had so many. She actually apologized for bothering me, she apologized to *me*, if you can believe it. She said that she was afraid that such strong winds might push some window open, and she wanted to keep the blinds closed. She gave me a twenty-euro tip. She was so generous, poor signora. She seemed untroubled, as usual. Ah, the housekeeper, Mayya, was there, and she said to me: be careful, don't get the floor messy. As if I was going in the bathroom to take a shower."

Aragona kept pushing: "And while you were there, did anyone else come in? Did she get any phone calls? How long were you there, and what time was it? Try to remember, this is important."

Mascolo thought it over, then said: "No. No one came, no one phoned. I was there for ten minutes or so, and it was around eleven o'clock. I went up because it's always slow then, so I can step away."

Lojacono broke in: "I noticed the door to the notary's apartment is the only one on that landing. Who lives one floor up? And one floor down?"

"It's an old building, and there's just one apartment per floor; well, actually, some of them have been subdivided, but that's all interior—you still enter through that one door and then there's a sort of partition. Downstairs and upstairs, on the fourth and sixth floors, there are offices: an investment bank and a tax lawyer's office. Obviously they're closed Saturday and Sunday, and there's no one there."

Without much conviction, Aragona asked: "And this weekend, no one came into either of those offices, right?"

"No, no one came in."

Lojacono stood up: "One last thing: did you see the notary after what happened? When he came home, was he alone?"

A solemn expression appeared on Mascolo's face: "Certainly, he came home late yesterday morning. Your men were still upstairs, the ones in white jumpsuits. He was alone. He waited until they had finished their work, then I saw him leave, carrying a suitcase. I went up to him to express my condolences, and there was a look on his face that frightened me: he looked like he'd aged a hundred years. He told me that he was checking in at the Grand Hotel Vesuvio, right around the corner and also on the waterfront, and that if I needed him I'd be able to get in touch with him there. Poor man, he must have so many regrets now: he always left her by herself, the signora."

XXXI

As they were about to leave, Lojacono felt the impulse to go back upstairs to the apartment.

Over the years, he had learned that to follow one's instinct was nothing more than to listen to a part of the mind that continued to work away, beneath the threshold of consciousness. And frequently, for that very reason, it was the best part of the mind, the part that could focus without all the distractions of the outside world.

Aragona followed him without objections; he knew that he had a lot to learn, and despite his shortcomings, he did recognize—to his credit—that his partner had a great deal more experience. And so he went along without asking for too many explanations.

At the apartment door they found a man standing guard, sent there by Palma. Lojacono appreciated the commissario's style; he didn't meddle with his investigators in the field, but at the same time he provided plenty of support. The officer opened the door and let them in.

The atmosphere in the deserted apartment was grim; Lojacono sensed with a shiver that this was now a place without a soul, that it would take an enormous amount of time for it to become a home again—and perhaps only if occupied by another family. More than twenty years of practicing his profession had taught him that when there is a violent death, the air becomes the vector for immense sorrow; it can't be purified again, except by the presence of someone who knows nothing of that pain. Gray light from the rain-heavy sky filtered in through the living room window, the only one left open. Clearly, when the notary came back to get the few things he needed to bring to a hotel, he'd preferred his presence be limited to the strictly necessary; he hadn't even turned on the lights. Understandable, Lojacono decided.

They wandered silently through the rooms. The apartment was immense, but cold. It was clear that most of the rooms—the office, the drawing room, the guest rooms—though they were clean and extremely neat, hadn't been used in years. They lingered in one of the guest bathrooms where, presumably, Mascolo had repaired the blinds; Aragona checked to see that they closed properly, making sure that the strap and lifting mechanism were clean and well oiled. He nodded in Lojacono's direction, confirming that the concierge's story had in fact checked out.

As if by tacit understanding, they saved the room where the murder had taken place for last. Ironic twist of fate, thought the lieutenant: the room bathed in sunlight was the one in which a murder had taken place.

The gray bay could be seen through the glass of the balcony windows, the waters still very choppy and clouds scudding across the sky. An oil tanker offshore, black and red and immense, looked like a passing whale. The peninsula, on the far side of the water, was a dark silhouette pointing a finger into the gray murk, as if trying to call attention to the profile of the island nearby. Lojacono thought about just how beautiful the city could be. If admired from afar.

He walked over to the spot on the carpet marred by the dark stain. He wondered what the signora might have been thinking right before she died. That would have been useful to know: the last, fleeting thought before the darkness of night. Who could say whether she'd thought of love, if she'd remembered something, someone. If she'd been surprised.

He looked up toward the wall filled with shelves crowded with glass spheres of every shape and size. Each containing an object, a landscape, a monument, a celebrity. He noticed that their sizes varied considerably, and he wondered what order they'd been arranged in.

Backlit, the shelves were spotless, the dark wood had not yet been invaded by the uniform veil of dust that would, with the passing of the hours, settle over the room. He went closer to get a better look.

Nearest the dark bloodstain, the snow globes enclosed European monuments and panoramas. Lojacono walked the length of the shelves and soon realized that the snow globes were arranged by nation and continent. From left to right, the globes depicted first the nearest vistas, gradually moving to more distant ones, all carefully and methodically sorted. This was the case on the two lowermost shelves. Higher up were the holidays—Christmas and Easter globes with religious vignettes of various kinds: from Buddha to Christ crucified; from Mohammed to the Hanukah menorah. Lojacono wondered how it had ever occurred to her to collect objects of this kind.

Aragona said: "It makes me wonder why anyone would collect these things. They gross me out, if you want to know the truth."

"A person has to do something. From what I understand, the signora lived a pretty solitary life."

The officer snorted: "I've never been able to understand people with money who are depressed. I mean, in Africa, where they have nothing to eat, are they all depressed? And anorexic? Or bulimic? This kind of loneliness is a disease that comes with money, take it from me."

Lojacono, displaying a certain indifference to the profound social issues Aragona was exploring, was visually sketching a hypothetical trajectory of events. Finally, he said: "Here's what I want to know: if you hear a noise, walk into the room, and find a burglar, what do you do?"

"Sorry, I'm not following you."

"So the signora walks in here, sees someone with her silver in his hands, someone who, by the way, got in without forcing the doors or windows—but for now let's leave that detail aside. If you were in her shoes, what would you do?"

Aragona was bewildered. He tried to picture the scene.

"I don't know: maybe I scream? I try to stop him?"

"Right. Or else you try to run, to get away. And in that case, which way do you go?"

Aragona pointed hesitantly toward the door that opened onto the front entranceway.

"I'd go that way, and try to reach the stairs."

Lojacono nodded, lost in thought. When he was concentrating this hard, his Asian features made him look like a Buddhist monk meditating.

"But instead she went toward the other door, as if trying to escape toward the interior of the apartment. Where there was no way out. And there's no doubt about this, because she was clubbed in the back of the head, so she had her back to the murderer."

"Maybe she hadn't seen him, and was simply passing through this room on her way to bed, after wishing those horrible snow globes a good night's sleep. Or maybe she was going to lock herself in her room and call someone."

Lojacono agreed, reluctantly. "Certainly, that's a possibility. Maybe the murderer, who really could have been anywhere, was standing between her and the door, though that doesn't add up either, because in that case he'd have hit her in the temple, not the back of the head. Plus, the victim would have been between the murderer and the shelves with the snow globes: where would he have grabbed the murder weapon?"

The officer listened to the analysis, interested: "Maybe it was actually something valuable. After all, what do we know? Maybe he'd come to steal that specific object. Maybe someone hired him to take it. Maybe we should start looking into collectors of shitty objects."

Lojacono didn't agree: "No, that strikes me as implausible. Though maybe we should take a closer look at the murder weapon. One thing is certain: the murderer didn't come here intending to kill. He would have done it with a weapon he'd brought for that purpose, or even barehanded—but certainly not by striking the signora with an object that he just happened to find."

"Well, what do you think happened? Where was the signora headed? And most important of all, how did the murderer get in?"

The lieutenant thought it over for a while. Then he said: "We don't have enough information. We need to gather more evidence. In my opinion, either she didn't see who was in the room or else she knew him and felt secure enough to turn her back on him. There were no signs of a struggle, the signora was neat and fully dressed; the medical examiner saw no traces of violence on her body."

"There's still the fact that the door was opened without being forced. It's true, it could have been someone who stole the housekeeper's key, or else the signora's, or even the notary's: but in that case, he would have had to have known the victim's routines, and if he had he wouldn't have entered the apartment then, knowing that she was there."

"Or else it was someone she knew," Lojacono added, "and she opened the door to him. Then they had an argument and, once she thought the conversation was over, she turned her back on him to leave. Only the murderer didn't think their conversation was over—and he ended it in his own way."

"What about the silver?"

"That could be a deliberate red herring. Or a way of paying back an insult, a souvenir he took away. I've seen it happen before. In any case, the key to it all is figuring out who the victim really was: it's the only way we'll be able to explain her behavior."

Aragona scratched his head, baffled. "We don't know much about her, that's true. Maybe we'll get a little more information, like you say, from the Baroness Whatshername, the one that feeble old geezer Pisanelli arranged for us to interview at the yacht club."

Lojacono replied brusquely: "I'd call you feeble sooner than I would Pisanelli. While we're here, let's put in a call to the station house and see if there's any news."

Ottavia answered the phone, her voice much more somber than usual.

"Everything okay?" Lojacono asked. "You don't sound like yourself."

"Just a headache, nothing important. Listen, I have some news for you: they've found the stolen silver. In a dumpster, a few hundred yards from the scene. The forensic squad has it, and if you want to take a look, you can swing by. Maybe you could do it before your appointment with the Baroness Ruffolo at the yacht club."

XXXII

Pizzeria Il Gobbo was a happy exception to the rule. In the midst of the neighborhood's most well-to-do quarter, surrounded by designer boutiques and elegant florists' shops, there was a steep uphill *vicolo* so narrow that cars couldn't enter it; a few yards up the *vicolo* was the entrance to the pizzeria, marked with a tiny sign, and inside a narrow staircase leading up to the dining room, with fewer than ten tables and a small balcony.

Il Gobbo—the Hunchback—himself had been dead for many years, but he appeared in a yellowed photo, dressed in a pizza chef's white smock and cap, short and twisted as a question mark, between two mustachioed gentlemen identified as Di Giacomo and Scarfoglio by the scribbled names below. The pizzeria was run these days by his grandson, a big gruff man who, despite his perfectly erect spinal column, had still inherited the nickname; this new Gobbo also possessed a substantial gut that confined him to the front of the restaurant, between the cash register and the oven: the stair leading up to the dining room was too narrow for him. A slender and agile young Polish woman named Yula took care of the waitressing; her appearance was yet another of the place's attractions.

Twice a week, Giorgio Pisanelli went to have lunch at Il Gobbo with the only friend left to him; the only one he kept no secrets from, and the only one from whom he was willing to accept good-natured ribbing for his elaborate theories.

Yula greeted him as usual, as if she had been waiting for him all her life: "*Ciao*, Dottore! Monacello wait you at table."

Pisanelli climbed up the stairs. Brother Leonardo Calisi, known as 'o Munaciello—the little monk—was a Franciscan from the monastery of Maria Annunziata. And what else were people going to call him: he stood four feet eleven inches, he dressed in a cassock and sandals even in the winter, was white-haired and blue-eyed, and his mischievous expression was ever present. If that poltergeist of pranks and jibes and minor acts of charity, that regular protagonist of Neopolitan legends known as 'o Munaciello, were ever to take living form, it could only be as Brother Leonardo Calisi.

Pisanelli found him at the table by the balcony, patiently waiting.

"How long, exactly, were you planning to make me wait? You do realize that I have a parish to run? Ten minutes to walk over here, ten minutes to walk back, and then a full hour before you decide to show up!"

Pisanelli, raised both hands, defending himself against the monk's tirade. "Come on, we agreed on one o'clock and it's only 1:10! And everyone in the neighborhood knows that no one's set foot in that parish church for years now. You could just lock up and go home and no one would even notice."

Brother Leonardo made a show of feigning offense: "How dare you, you disbeliever! It certainly is true that each judges others according to his own heart's intentions, just like the proverb says. You never come to church so you think no one else does either. In fact, Maria Annunziata is the only church downtown that's becoming more popular—both in terms of worshippers and as a location for religious ceremonies. My brothers and I have more work than we can hope to handle, and here you are, staining my conscience with the knowledge that I'm idling over lunch in a restaurant, instead of working with my fellow monks."

Pisanelli had taken a seat with a small grimace of pain: "A criminal conspiracy, that's what you are, you and your brother monks. One of these days I'll ask one of our racketeering experts to look into the lot of you; I'm pretty sure we'll dig up a nice case of fraud. My bet is that you're laundering money for the Camorra."

The monk nodded: "It's true, but I know you're a friend and you'd never tell a soul. But listen, let me ask: are you in pain? I saw you grimace just now . . ."

The policeman waved his hand distractedly: "Forget about it, let's not ruin our meal. Just a little pain, now and then."

"I don't understand this nonchalance of yours. If I wore hiking boots instead of sandals, I'd kick your ass black and blue. You're telling me that you have a disease that's now perfectly treatable, and instead of going to see a doctor, you try to hide it? Have you lost your mind?"

"Leona', I don't know how many times I've told you: I don't want to talk about it. We're living in strange times—they declare you unfit for active duty at the drop of a hat, and next thing you know you're sitting at home, alone with your thoughts and your ghosts. These days, now that Lorenzo's gone, all I have is my work, and you know it. If it weren't for my job, I'd already be dead, ever since . . . well, let's just say I'd be dead. So I'm not telling anyone, and I expect you to keep it to yourself as well—if you don't, you'll be violating the secrecy of the confessional."

The monk was trying to catch Yula's attention so they could order.

"Aside from the fact that you didn't tell me in confession, so technically I have no obligation to keep your secrets, I wouldn't even know who to go tell, you big-headed cop. Ah, here you are, my lovely Yula, two margherita pizzas with extra mozzarella and two potato croquettes, the usual. In a hurry, I've got someplace to be. So what else is new?"

Again, Pisanelli waved vaguely.

"Well, you know, the last one was six months ago, that man who hanged himself in the bathroom. I managed to speak to his daughter, in Canada; she didn't even come back for the funeral because she didn't have enough money for a plane ticket, or so she said."

"And what did she tell you?"

"What do you think she told me . . . that she didn't understand why I was calling her, that her father ought to be left to rest in peace, that he'd made his own decision, reprehensible but understandable. That he was eighty years old, that in twenty years, he'd never managed to come to terms with her mother's death. And that the note he'd left explained it all. Nonsense, in other words. That's what she told me. And then she hung up on me."

"And doesn't that tell you something?" Brother Leonardo asked sadly. "Why do you have this obsession, that's what I'd like to know. It's a terrible thing, a mortal sin, a crime against life, to commit suicide. Still, people do it, they've always done it, and, I'm sorry to tell you, they're always going to."

Pisanelli furrowed his brow: "There's suicide and then there's suicide, Leona'. Some of them are plausible, the circumstances are explanation enough: young men dumped by their sweethearts, drug addicts unable to get a fix, and, in this slowdown, businessmen being throttled by debts and organized crime. But you're going to have to explain to me why a man would kill himself because his wife died twenty years ago. And just how he managed to hang himself from the overhead light fixture in the bathroom after balancing precariously on the rim of the toilet—even though he's eighty years old and practically crippled by arthritis. Why he left a note written in all caps: 'I just can't go on.' No signature, no advance warning. He's just like all the other cases: elderly, lonely, depressed. This has been happening over and over again for the past ten years;

all have been in the same neighborhood, all have left very brief notes, written in caps or on a computer, never in their own handwriting. You have to admit it's odd, don't you?"

The monk rolled his blue eyes heavenward as if in despair: "Lord God, maybe You can help him. Would you mind telling me just what is it that you're trying to prove? That the despair that comes with feeling old, alone, and useless isn't a powerful enough motive to drive someone to end it all? You know, out there, right in the middle of these crowded streets, there's more loneliness than you can imagine. Take it from me, I spend my time in the confessional listening to people tell me about the specters that overwhelm their hearts. Many of them lack the sheer physical courage, but trust me, there are plenty out there right now who'd be happy to have done with all this. Sometimes it's hard to convince them it's worth it to go on living despite that fact."

The policeman waited until Yula had served them their food and the monk had crossed himself before answering: "I already know everything you're telling me. And I know that you work hard to bring comfort to the people of this neighborhood, as if you really were 'o Munaciello himself. Still, it doesn't add up, you know? I just see too many elements in common, too many peculiar details."

Leonardo was devouring his pizza with unmistakable delight: "Mmm, you tell me how anyone can doubt the existence of God after eating a margherita pizza. Bless Il Gobbo, and bless you, too, since you're so kind as to treat me to lunch, given my vow of poverty. But to get back to what we were saying, don't you think that this theory of yours, that a serial killer is murdering depressed old people, smacks a little too much of an American TV show? Here in our country, these things—these particular kind of things at least—just don't happen. And then I don't understand what the alleged killer could possibly gain."

Pisanelli turned defensive: "I never said that there's definitely a serial killer. I'm just saying that these cases were filed away far too quickly, that's all. These dead people deserved a little attention, before being disposed of with a rubber stamp at the bottom of a death certificate and an awkward funeral. And I'm also saying that silence in the aftermath of such an act is convenient for everyone, even the family."

"My poor friend. You're transferring your grief onto other people, that's what you're doing. Ever since we lost poor Carmen, you can't seem to accept it. It's very common, you know. If you only knew how often I've seen it happen . . ."

The policeman answered coldly: "Carmen has nothing to do with this, Leona'. Carmen was a very sick woman, and she simply couldn't bring herself to face the terminal phase of her illness. And she took advantage of the fact that Lorenzo and I were both away to swallow a bottle of pills. She really did kill herself. These suicides are different."

"I was the last one to see Carmen alive, do you remember that? We have her to thank for the fact that you and I even know each other; in her search for some relief from her depression, she turned to faith. And I'll tell you now what I said to you at the time, that talking to her was like looking into an abyss. She was in despair, psychologically, she'd gone past the point of no return. But I'm convinced that she found her faith, in the end. And that the Lord took her in, even though the thing she did to herself was terrible. She just was too afraid of the pain the cancer was going to subject her to, before the end. Her brain was flooded with fear, and that's why she did it; not because she had stopped loving you."

Pisanelli looked out the window to conceal his tears. Just a few yards away, on the balcony across the narrow *vicolo*, sheets on a clothesline flapped in the wind like white flags.

"I talk to her, you know, Leona'. I still talk to her, as if she were alive. I'll come home, and I talk to her. Sometimes, all night long. Do you think I'm losing my mind?"

The monk patted his friend's hand, gently.

"No, my dear brother. You're not losing your mind. You talk to her because Carmen really is with you, close to you. She watches you, and she follows you, and she hopes that you can free yourself from your obsessions. And that you take care of yourself, so you can live a long life. Because you do want to go on living, don't you?"

Pisanelli met his friend's gaze with his own tear-reddened eyes: "Yes, Leonardo. I want to live. I want to live so I can know for certain whether these dead people left this world willingly, or if they were forced to. That's why I want to go on living. And that's why I keep my prostate cancer to myself and tell no one else about it. First let me crack this case, and then I'll be glad to die, too."

XXXIII

The offices and laboratories of the forensic team's inter-regional division, housed inside an old military barracks in the city center, were a cell of efficiency and modernity: to step inside was to travel to a different planet.

The building itself was austere and gray, built a hundred and fifty years ago for military purposes: a large courtyard, a colonnade, a handsome stone staircase. Then, inside, clean hallways and strong, diffuse lighting, men and women in white lab coats striding briskly out one door and in another, focused on what they were doing, no one loitering or killing time by the vending machines.

Lojacono and Aragona were received by a guard at the entrance who, after taking their names, pointed them to a small waiting room. A few minutes later, a slender man with a receding hairline came in. His white lab coat was unbuttoned over a light blue shirt and a bow tie festooned with butterflies; a pair of reading glasses dangled from a strap around his neck while a pair for distance perched on the bridge of his nose.

"I'm Superintendent Bistrocchi, *buongiorno*. And you are . . ."

The two policemen introduced themselves. When they mentioned Pizzofalcone, the expression of cordial welcome vanished instantly from the superintendent's face, replaced by a scowl of mistrust.

"Ah, Pizzofalcone. So they didn't shut it down after all. What do you need?"

Aragona attempted his famous dramatic gesture with the glasses, hoping to regain a shred of credibility.

"We need information about the murder of Cecilia De Santis, on Via Caracciolo, which we presume occurred between Sunday night and Monday morning. You investigated the crime scene, and from what we've heard . . ."

Bistrocchi interrupted him with a sharp gesture: "We can't say anything; you'll receive an official report in due course."

Lojacono, who hadn't yet spoken, broke in: "We know that we'll receive the report. It's just that, as you know very well, sir, the first few hours are fundamental. And since we know, as Aragona was just saying, that the stolen objects have been found and are now here on the premises, under examination, we thought that . . ."

Bistrocchi didn't even let him finish: "There's nothing for you to think, sir. We work always and exclusively through official channels; this is a laboratory, we don't do things by halves. When we're done running the tests we need to run, we'll inform you of our results. And not a minute before."

Aragona ground his teeth and spoke to Lojacono: "Because we're from Pizzofalcone, you get that, Loja'? If we'd come from anywhere else, we would already have been given an informal look at the information."

The superintendent didn't bat an eye: "Think whatever you like. I'm not authorized to preview our reports for anyone."

Lojacono said to his partner: "You know what I think, Aragona? That this would a good time to go get a cup of coffee. Someplace nearby."

As soon as they stepped out of the barracks and back onto the street, Lojacono pulled out his cell phone. Aragona was seething: "What a ridiculous asshole! And this whole Bastards of Pizzofalcone thing is a real pain in the ass! You tell me: why are we being shamed for what those four idiotic criminals did a year ago, miserable feebleminded . . ."

Lojacono raised a hand to stem the tide of complaints.

"Hello? *Ciao*, Laura. It's me. Am I bothering you?"

The pleasant, Sardinian-accented voice replied: "Oh, what a lovely surprise! You know, I was about to call you to ask, off the record, just how things are going. I'm in regular contact with Palma, but I wanted to hear it from someone in the field."

"And here I am, calling you from the field. You know I try not to bother you, if I can possibly help it."

Piras's laughter poured out of the phone.

"As far as that goes, you actually do your best not to call at all, not just to avoid bothering me. What's up?"

Lojacono told her that he was standing with his partner outside the offices of the forensic squad and summarized what had just happened with Bistrocchi.

". . . and we really need to get the information immediately. You know very well that the first few days after a murder that might turn out to be a crime of passion are fundamental; the more time passes, the easier it is for the murderer or murderers to get themselves organized, and the harder it is for us."

"Let me see if I understand, are you saying that you think this was a crime of passion? Not a robbery, or a burglary gone wrong?"

"I don't know. There are pieces that don't match up, the fact that the door wasn't forced open, the fact that the corpse was pointed toward the rear of the apartment . . . Which is exactly why we need to know what the forensic squad knows. As soon as possible."

Piras thought it over for a moment, then said: "All right. Wait a couple of minutes, then go back in. You'll see, you'll be given a different welcome."

They went to a café and had the cup of coffee, as announced, along with a couple of slices of pizza, which they ate standing at the counter. Aragona commented on how depressing their lunch was. When they walked back into the

barracks, fifteen minutes had passed, and they found a mortified Bistrocchi awaiting them, alongside a woman in a lab coat.
She was young, very attractive, and clearly in command; she
immediately introduced herself: "Lieutenant Lojacono, is that
right? Hi, I'm the chief administrator, Rosaria Martone. I
supervise this investigative squad. I apologize for the earlier
misunderstanding: Bistrocchi here hadn't been informed of
the importance and urgency of your investigation. We've
brought all the documentation with us," she said, pointing to
the file that Bistrocchi held in one hand. "Would you care to
come to my office?"

She led the way down a corridor, followed by Bistrocchi; as
they walked, Aragona shot sweet darts of mental vengeance at
the man. The office was a large, clean, tidy room, lit by a window overlooking the interior courtyard. Martone pointed
them to two armchairs and a small couch in a corner of the
room opposite a large desk cluttered with documents and file
folders.

"Let's sit down here, we'll be more comfortable. All right,
Bistrocchi, bring us up to speed."

The superintendent, who had remained standing, gazed in
embarrassment at his fingertips.

"My apologies, I hadn't realized that this case was a prior-
ity. We've completed our examination of the apartment, but
the report still hasn't been drafted . . ."

Martone waved one hand impatiently. Lojacono though to
himself that behind the woman's delicate features and petite
stature must lurk a formidable personality: "Bistrocchi, let's
not waste any more time—ours or our colleagues'—with
bureaucratic excuses. Summarize the crucial points for us; the
precinct will receive the report in due time."

The man took a deep breath, switched to a pair of reading
glasses, and opened the file.

"Now then, first of all the points of access to the apartment:

there are no signs of forced entry, either on the building's main door, which is wood on the exterior and metal on the interior, nor on the front door—which is made of wood and is single-paneled—that gives onto the landing, or the second, internal door, which is glass. The apartment appeared to be in excellent condition, both structurally and in terms of plumbing, with . . ."

"Bistrocchi," the woman roared. "Get to the point!"

The man blinked rapidly.

"Certainly, boss. The only room here described, because it was in a state of disorder, is the living room, which is where the corpse was found. All of the surfaces were carefully analyzed, dusted with hygroscopic and magnetic powders, but no latent fingerprints were found. Likewise, two buccal swabs were performed on the cadaver, and fingernail clippings from both hands were taken as well; here, too, negative results from the analyses performed by the laboratory we operate that specializes in the examination of organic and biological material."

Now it was Aragona's turn to blink rapidly. "Which means?"

"Nothing," the director explained. "No prints other than those belonging to people whose prints ought to have been there, I'd imagine."

Bistrocchi nodded, turning to the next page. "Exactly. Only the prints of the dead woman, the housekeeper, and two prints belonging to the notary on both the handles of the door leading to the rear of the apartment."

"And nothing on the corpse," Lojacono added, speaking more to himself than anyone else. "No flesh under the nails, no bite marks. She didn't put up a struggle."

Martone nodded. "So it would appear."

There was a moment of silence. Then Lojacono asked: "What about the alleged murder weapon? The glass ball, in other words."

Bistrocchi flipped through his papers.

"Here we are then: glass sphere with wooden base, found beneath the armchair, etc, on carpet, etc . . . intact, free of abrasions or cracks, etc . . . at the top of sphere we found traces of organic, hematic material, as mentioned in analysis attached . . . and hair . . . here's the analysis. Blood and hair matching those of Cecilia De Santis. The marks are compatible with the wound on the back of the neck of the cadaver. In all likelihood, then, this was the murder weapon."

Martone puffed out her cheeks and ran a hand over her face. "Bistrocchi, please. I think what Lieutenant Lojacono wants to know is whether there were any foreign prints on the object. Can you tell us, or are you going to keep us in suspense for a few more hours?"

The man's ears reddened, and he said hastily: "A partial print was detected. Made by a glove. That's all."

Nothing. No fingerprints. Never once did things turn out to be simple, thought Lojacono. Never once did they luck out.

He addressed the director: "At the station house they told us that you were given several articles that might turn out to be the items stolen from the apartment, pieces of fine silver, I believe. Could you tell us something about them?"

Martone was happy to oblige: "Yes, we received those this morning. They were in a plastic bag, which had been abandoned in a dumpster. There was nothing on the bag or on the objects themselves: two small vases, two picture frames, a centerpiece, and a statuette of a lady dressed in nineteenth-century attire. Not even the housekeeper's fingerprints; evidently they had recently been cleaned. The thief or thieves wore gloves and didn't remove them. There are no marks of any kind."

Aragona scratched his forehead: "I don't get it. Why steal a couple of pieces of silver in an apartment overflowing with extremely valuable objects, and then toss them into the first dumpster you see?"

"Sometimes these things happen," Lojacono answered. "It

might suddenly have dawned on them what they'd done, and they panicked and dumped the loot. Or else they realized that we might be able to trace them through their fence, or whoever eventually bought the pieces. Or else, again, the burglary might have been nothing more than a crude attempt to cover up the real motive. Dottoressa, may I ask a favor? Could I see the murder weapon?"

XXXIV

What were you thinking? What was in your mind when you did it?

Lojacono was sitting in the little anteroom of the forensic squad's laboratory, his head resting on his hands, which were on the table, fingers intertwined. His almond-shaped eyes had narrowed to slits, and there was no discernible expression on his Asian features. As if he were sleeping. But he wasn't: he was looking.

He was looking at the glass sphere, its top smeared with a dark stain. The only object on the spotless laminate counter-top, white against the white floor, between white walls, illuminated by the white light from the ceiling fixture. The white ceiling.

A faint reflection gleamed off the curved surface of the glass.

Aragona, the only dark patch in the room, except for Lojacono himself, shifted his weight from one foot to the other, uncomfortably. He would have liked to know what was going through his colleague's mind.

What was going through Lojacono's mind? Death.

He was trying to receive a message from that innocent object, a piece of kitsch that had ended the life of a woman he'd never met. He was trying to intuit why that glass sphere, created to—best case scenario—make children smile, had ultimately become the instrument of an act as irrevocable as murder.

Don't you know that murder is a serious matter, Glass Ball? Lojacono mused. Murder is a very serious matter, that touches lots of people. You see this place, Glass Ball? People rushing to and fro, in white lab coats, serious and efficient; instruments, test tubes, microscopes. And parked outside are armored cars, and there are phones ringing, uniforms, handguns, tears, and laughter. All propelled by the murder.

Murder ought to have the right, since it's such a serious matter, to be executed via gunshot or, at the very least, via sharp blade. Murder deserves to be repaid with a complicated piece of machinery, such as an electric chair, or a sophisticated device such as the ones used to administer lethal injections. Murder calls out for historical tools of execution: the garrote, or the guillotine, or the gallows. Murder is a serious matter, not a joke.

From inside the globe, a woman's smiling face stared back at him. Inside the sphere was a sort of dancer, from the Caribbean or Hawaii, with a flower wreath, her probably bare chest covered by a tiny guitar and, underneath, a skirt made of long green leaves.

A ukulele. It came to him in a flash, the name for that little guitar. Ukulele. Marilyn Monroe played one in *Some Like It Hot*, that movie with Jack Lemmon and Tony Curtis; he'd probably seen it ten times. She was so beautiful, Marilyn Monroe was.

De Santis, on the other hand, wasn't beautiful. That is, even aside from the fact that she was now dead.

Aragona coughed softly. Lojacono didn't blink.

She wasn't beatiful, okay. So what? Did she deserve to die in such an absurd way for the crime of not being beautiful? Clubbed in the back of head with a glass ball?

Glass ball, glass ball. Not one of those crystal balls that fortune-tellers use to see into the future. There's no future inside this glass ball. Maybe just a little of the recent past.

Lojacono thought to himself that the globe must have traveled several yards before doing its dirty work to the back of De Santis's head. Because the corpse was sprawled out at the end of the wall that led to the door that gave onto the interior of the apartment, and that part of the room was closest to the globes depicting Europe, globes containing the Eiffel Tower and the Cologne cathedral, London's Tower Bridge, and the Little Mermaid of Copenhagen; this little hula dancer with a ukulele smiling at him from under the glass, therefore, should have been located in another part of the room, next to the golden sands and palm trees of the tropics, the cliffs of Acapulco and the stone heads of Easter Island. What were you doing there, little dancer? Why were you under the armchair, maybe five yards away from your proper place on the shelf?

Because the gloved hand took you and brought you down onto the back of your doting mistress's head?

Lojacono lifted his head to free his own hand and picked up the object. The director of the forensic squad had told him that they'd need to hold onto it, but that since they were done with their examinations, he was free to touch it.

The lieutenant shook the base, hefting its weight. It was a ball of medium size, heavy because of the liquid inside and thanks to the block of wood that formed its base. He turned it upside down and then turned it back right side up.

Inside the globe, there was now a tiny blizzard. Snowflakes—entirely out of keeping with the climate of the place depicted and with the little dancer's garb—whirled, covering everything in a glittering flicker. Aragona coughed again.

Slowly the flakes settled to the bottom and, indifferent to the cold, the dancer once again stared at Lojacono, blithely unaware of the dark stain of organic origin smearing the top of her spherical abode.

What were you thinking? Lojacono wondered again. You, with your gloved hand, with the silver from the front hall and living room in that plastic bag, what did you have in mind? Why take such an innocent object and hurl it or smash it against that woman's head? Why kill her in *this* way? If she'd screamed, if she'd called for help, maybe you'd have suffocated or strangled her. If she'd been closer to you, instead of four or five yards away, you'd have killed her with your hands, instead of using the first object you came across.

If that's the way it went, of course. Because maybe things went very differently. Maybe you'd had an argument, and maybe Signora Cecilia De Santis, Festa by marriage, hadn't been as malleable as you expected.

And so, in a burst of fury, you killed her, perhaps while she was heading back to her bedroom, thinking the discussion was at an end. Calmly turning her back on you, never dreaming you might react like that, never dreaming she was in danger.

Never dreaming that you'd kill her—much less with one of her beloved glass balls.

The dancer smiled at him. He stared at her for another minute, in silence.

Then he stood up and left the room, followed by a perplexed Aragona.

XXXV

The warrant had been faxed in midmorning, and Di Nardo and Romano had left immediately.

This time, threatening black clouds had forced them to take the car. Alex was at the wheel and she hadn't removed her sunglasses, even though there was no sun.

As they tried to make their way through the tangled traffic, Romano had tried repeatedly to get through to Giorgia; when for the umpteenth time he reached a recorded voice informing him that the phone was turned off or out of range, the man swore under his breath and hurled the phone into the backseat.

"If you break your own phone," Alex commented, without taking her eyes off the road, "I can guarantee no one will ever answer you."

"And that might be better," Francesco replied, gravely. "That way we can just stop worrying about it once and for all."

Di Nardo drove in silence for a while, then said: "You know I'm really curious to look this mysterious tenant in the face. And to know why she's locked herself up in that apartment."

"If you ask me, we're chasing our tails. If a woman chooses not to go out and wants to spend her time sitting indoors, she has every right, doesn't she? We shouldn't be at the beck and call of some delirious old gossip who, by the way, never leaves her apartment either. Tomorrow morning our mystery woman could call us up and report that the old paraplegic is a recluse: and there we'd be, running back and forth across the *vicolo*, from one place to the other, asking them both why they never go out."

Di Nardo burst out laughing, and her infectious laughter soon had her partner Romano chuckling too: the image of the two of them, barraged by criminal complaints, scampering from one apartment to the other, was surreal.

"Just as well we came out for a little fresh air since there isn't that much to do in the office"

The man grimaced in disgust: "Sure, I get it. We're the new Bastards of Pizzofalcone, aren't we? Other policemen have inherited the right to turn their noses up at us; and because we're still police officers, criminals do too; ordinary civilians do the same, a little bit by right of inheritance and a little because we're still police officers. We turn our own noses up because each of us feels that we've been sent here—with the other rejects—unjustly."

Alex shot him a glance. "You think? Personally, I hated the place where I was before more. Here at least no one looks down on you when you make a dumb mistake."

Before Romano had a chance to reply, they'd reached their destination. They left the car in a no parking zone, their police insignia in plain view on the dashboard, and headed for the street entrance. A peal of thunder rumbled past overhead, causing a few pedestrians to turn a worried gaze up to the sky. Before stepping through the large door, which stood ajar, the warrant officer shot a glance at the balcony to see if Donna Amalia was there. She was.

"If you ask me, she has the housekeeper bring her a bedpan, so she doesn't have to give up her vantage point. I'd put her in jail, is what I'd do. God, I hate people who can't mind their own business."

They climbed up to the fifth floor. The real estate agency was closed. They went over to the other door. Romano rang the bell.

In the silence of the landing, they heard whispering on the other side of the door, then the sound of the peephole being opened. And the same woman's voice as before: "Who is it?"

"This is Di Nardo and Romano, from the police, signora. Open up, please. We have a warrant."

There was a brief silence, after which they heard a complicated bolt being twisted open.

The door opened just a crack, revealing an eye and the fingers of one hand.

"Could you show me your documents, please?"

Romano extended his ID and the faxed copy of the warrant. The hand took them and the door shut again. Di Nardo puffed out her cheeks, Romano threw his arms wide. The door opened up again.

"Please. Come in."

They walked into a sort of drawing room. The place looked comfortable, the furniture was new, it had recently been painted, and there were pictures hanging on the walls. Tidy, spotless. Still, Alex felt ill at ease, though at first she couldn't put her finger on why. Then, she understood. It was fake. Everything looked like what you'd expect to see in an interior decorating magazine. It could have been a showroom in a furniture store.

She thought all this in a second; then she looked at the woman who had opened the door.

She was little more than a girl. And she was stunningly beautiful.

Her face betrayed her age. Her skin was luminous and free of flaws, her cheeks just slightly plump; she had large hazel eyes, and a tense, almost fearful expression. But her body, sheathed in a pair of jeans and a white blouse, captured Alex's unalloyed admiration. She was glad she hadn't removed her sunglasses. The girl was tall, even though she wore flats, her breasts were ample and firm, her belly was taut and her legs were long; she tilted her head to one side with unconsidered grace, her lips were full and sensual, she had a tiny beauty mark at the corner of her mouth. She could easily have been an actress or a model.

The policewoman noticed that Romano too had been stunned at the sight. His mouth hung open, his gaze was vacant; understandable. Though certainly her partner wasn't imagining that Alex was thinking how she'd be able to make much better use of that wonderful body than he ever could.

At last, Romano snapped to.

"*Buongiorno*. Do you . . . ma'am, do you live here? With who . . . we've come to check some things out, so . . ."

The girl turned to Alex, clearly confused. The policewoman intervened: "*Buongiorno*, signorina. Could you identify yourself, please?"

Before the girl had a chance to speak, there was a discreet little cough behind them; the two policemen turned with a start and realized that a man had walked into the room.

"I apologize, I must have startled you. *Buongiorno*, officers. I'm Germano Brasco, an architect and the leaseholder of this apartment. Please, make yourselves comfortable. Nunzia, did you ask the officers if they wanted a cup of coffee?"

Romano looked him up and down. The name had rung a bell, though he couldn't remember any specifics. The gentleman looked about sixty, well dressed, tall, with a luxuriant head of white hair and a well-groomed mustache, also white. With an equally well-manicured hand he pointed toward the corner of the living room furnished with a sofa and two leather armchairs.

"Shall I bring espresso for you all, would you like that?" The girl's voice was thick with the accent of the local dialect. "I can bring it on a tray, with the sugar separate, will that be all right?"

Even though the questions were directed toward the two

guests, they were spoken with the girl's large eyes fixed on the architect's face; he nodded agreeably. The girl vanished toward the interior of the apartment.

"You'll have to forgive her, Nunzia is so young. She still isn't entirely comfortable playing the role of mistress of the house. Please, make yourselves comfortable: what can we do for you?"

Romano had remained standing, showing no strong inclination to get to know the man; but Alex understood that the longer they stayed, the more information they'd be likely to come away with: she felt certain that there was something strange about that mismatched couple, and she wanted to get to the bottom of it.

So she sat down, implicitly accepting the invitation and obliging Romano to follow suit.

The man, too, sat down. He was wearing a light gray suit, a matching striped tie, and a light blue shirt. On his lapel, he wore a pin indicating membership in an exclusive municipal association. He wore a pair of glasses with gold frames; they glittered in the sunlight pouring in from the balcony, where the curtains were wide open. As Romano sat down, he glanced outside and met the angry glare of Donna Amalia, keeping watch from her usual vantage point. He was tempted to wave hello.

"Now then, officers: what fair winds have blown you to our door? What crime have we committed?"

He was making a show of great self-confidence, wanted to appear friendly. Romano felt his hand start to itch: he jammed it in his pocket.

"We're just here checking out a report, architect. We received a complaint, probably based on an erroneous interpretation of entrances into and exits from this apartment, and decided to look into it. That's all."

"Too bad. This city, as usual, remains true to its nature. No respect for a person's privacy. I understand."

Alex broke in: "On the other hand, you should know how many crimes, large and small, come to light as a result of this failure to respect other people's privacy, architect. Now, just how long have you lived here?"

The man burst into a hearty laugh: "No, no, officer. I don't live here. I'm the leaseholder, I pay the rent, but I live in Posillipo. For heaven's sake, who could stand to live in the midst of all this chaos?"

Romano squinted to ward off the irritating glare that was reflecting off the man's gold glasses frames, and asked: "But if you live in Posillipo, pardon me, why would you rent an apartment in this neighborhood?"

Brasco assumed an air of innocence: "Well, you see, I like to have lots of different places at my disposal, where I can spend my spare time. Sometimes I just need a change of scene. I'm in charge of major urban renewal projects, my architecture firm works all over the world, we take part in international design competitions. Every so often I like to go into seclusion: it inspires me, helps me to come up with new ideas. Oh, here's our coffee! Nunzia is so good at making coffee. How many sugars?"

The girl had brought in a tray with demitasse cups and saucers, and, after carefully setting down the various objects on the side table, had remained standing, a forced smile on her face.

That smile gave Di Nardo the creeps. It looked like a mask. She asked her: "What about you, signorina, aren't you going to sit down?"

Nunzia turned to look at the architect, as if asking his permission. The man nodded, and the girl took a seat. Alex had the impression she was watching a well-trained pet.

The warrant officer went on: "So you come here only occasionally. How occasionally?"

Brasco's voice grew thick: "Hard to say. Occasionally, like

you say. But let me ask you again: is there something wrong? Something I ought to know about?"

Suddenly Alex butted in: "What about you, Signorina? Do you work with the architect?"

The question was met with silence. Nunzia's eyes were those of an animal caught in a trap. Brasco answered for her: "No, no. Nunzia is a friend of mine; actually, the daughter of friends of mine," the architect hastened to correct himself, as if to cover up some mistake. "She's a young woman, at her age, kids want a little freedom; I don't mind if she stays here whenever she likes. That's all."

Alex turned again to Nunzia: "So you stay here, signorina. And what is it that you do? Do you work, do you study?"

Romano, who had jotted something down in a notebook, asked: "And by the way, what's your name and where do you live?"

Once again, Brasco replied: "Her name is Annunziata Esposito, and her address is Vico Secondo all'Olivella, 22. She's a . . . she's thinking of enrolling in school to get her high school diploma. I think she finished middle school."

Di Nardo gave him a cold stare. "Does the young woman have trouble speaking? Some serious problem pronouncing words? Dyslexia? Does she stutter? We'd prefer she answer the questions herself, thanks."

The words, harsh in themselves, were buttressed by her dry tone. Romano looked up from the notebook and turned toward her. Brasco blinked repeatedly.

"No, no, of course not. It's just that she's very shy. Nunzia, answer the lady. Don't make me do all the talking."

"And what do you want me to say? I stay here. That's all."

Her deep, warm voice was trembling with fear. That girl was terrified; Alex was certain of it.

"Well, tell me, signorina: how long have you been here, that is, how long have you been the architect's . . . guest?"

The hesitation had been intentional, and Brasco had recognized the implicit accusation. The central point, the nature of the relationship between the established professional and the young girl, was now on the table. Nunzia once again tried to lock eyes with the man, but this time she was unsuccessful: the architect stared at Alex, putting on a show of self-confidence that he hardly felt inside.

"I . . . it's been seventeen days."

They waited, as if there was something more; but the girl had nothing to add.

"And what do you do? Do you go out, see the town, visit friends . . ."

Nunzia twisted her hands together in her lap and shot a mute plea for help in Brasco's direction. Then she answered: "No, I . . . I stay here. I don't want to go out. I don't go out. I stay home, and I like it here."

She sighed, satisfied with the effort she'd made. Brasco spoke up: "Nunzia had a little problem with her nerves. And her folks asked me if I could give her a place to stay for a while, so she could recover. And now you're recovering, aren't you, Nunzia?

The girl nodded forcefully. When she spoke or gesticulated, her youth was fully on display.

"I'd like to see the lease, please," Romano said. "As well as the IDs, both yours and the young lady's."

Brasco nodded, getting up from the couch.

"No problem, officer. Even though I don't really understand the reason for all these questions, as if there weren't already criminals enough to catch in this city."

Romano leapt to his feet, his expression suddenly grim. His voice was flat.

"Sometimes criminals don't look like criminals. Get me those documents now, and skip the commentary. Get moving."

Everyone stared at him in surprise. Alex, with a shiver, realized that her partner had taken offense at the architect's words and was starting to lose control of himself. She stood up in a hurry: "My partner asked you to do something, architect. I hope you're willing to cooperate."

The man handed over the IDs with a trembling hand, having gestured for the girl to do likewise. He tried to recover a shred of dignity: "I . . . I know a great many people, you know . . . If I was to ask for an inquiry into this absurd interrogation, perfectly respectable people, at home, bothering no one . . ."

While Alex was checking the IDs, Romano never once stopped staring at the architect, who was unable to hold his gaze. A muscle twitched in the policeman's jaw and his lips were pressed together in a white slit, pale with tension.

"Oh, you do? And exactly what would you tell all these people you know, architect? Would you tell them about your pied-à-terre, and the young girl you keep there? And are you perfectly sure you'd have their unwavering support?"

Di Nardo placed a hand on his arm and spoke to him in a firm voice: "That's enough, Romano. That'll do. The IDs are in order, and they confirm everything we've been told. We can write up a report."

By now the tension was so thick you could cut it with a knife. Nunzia had taken a step backward toward the wall, as if she wanted to disappear. Brasco was looking at the floor, breathing rapidly.

Alex set the IDs down on the side table and said: "Thanks for your cooperation, we won't inconvenience you any longer. If the young lady's stay should extend much longer, and if she were to choose to transfer her official residence to this address, you'd be required to file the appropriate forms. Have a good day."

When they were back out on the street, Romano pulled a cigarette out of a rumpled pack.

"I didn't know you smoked," Alex said to him.

"In fact, I don't. Not anymore, anyway. But there are times when I feel the need, and I stick a cigarette in my mouth without lighting it."

"They're an odd couple, eh?"

Romano snapped: "Couple? What the fuck are you talking about, couple? Did you see their IDs? Did you see how old he is? Sixty-three years old, the dirty old pig. And she's eighteen, turned eighteen last month. Eighteen! He's old enough to be her grandfather."

Alex tried to calm her partner down: "Maybe it's true, that he's a family friend. And that the girl had a nervous breakdown. You can't always think the worst of everyone, you know."

Romano looked up toward Signora Guardascione's balcony.

"Sure, why not, and I might be Maradona. He waited for the girl to turn eighteen, that way nobody can say a thing. Filthy pig. Well, at least the old lady will be happy. We checked everything out and we can wrap this case up."

As they were getting into the squad car, Alex thought to herself that maybe there were still a few other things they could check out.

XXXVI

The woman with gray hair walks along, dragging her feet. But no one notices.

She's fat. She's old. Arthritis has left her hips misshapen, every step is pure torture. The thunderclaps echo, the crowds hurry down the street. Not her. Haste is for those who know where they're going, for people who have a smile to share with someone, somewhere. The woman with gray hair has no more smiles, hasn't had for a long time.

She has a plastic bag in one hand, the woman with gray hair. She bought herself a couple of tomatoes, a box of individual cheese portions, and an apple. The grocer, without her having to ask, tossed in a sprig of basil and a tangerine. She didn't even notice.

She's wearing a heavy woolen jacket; the color is by now indefinable but it might once have been gray, like her hair; it's stained down the front. A shapeless dress covers a slip, which also serves as a nightdress and which she never takes off. She wears a necklace with a metal cross. Her hair is filthy, and for lack of a hairbrush, it has tangled into tiny insoluble knots.

She wears two men's socks, and a pair of slippers, tattered, with holes in the soles.

The woman with gray hair heads down the stairway of the subway, taking it one step at a time; she brings one foot down and places it next to the other, then repeats the motion. She braces herself on the railing, a tiny grimace of pain with every step.

No one sees her, as if she didn't exist.

On the escalator, a boy slams into her furiously; she almost drops her bag, but she manages to regain her balance just moments before tumbling to the ground.

The boy doesn't notice; no one notices.

The woman with gray hair doesn't change her expression. Her eyes remain glued to the floor.

The woman with gray hair lives alone, in a two-room apartment where she once lived with her mother. She stopped paying rent two months ago because her social security payments barely suffice to cover her one daily meal and the medications she needs to survive. In a day or ten or twenty, someone will come along to evict her, and then she won't know where to turn.

The woman with gray hair lacks the strength to cry, or even to complain. She has no phone numbers to call to ask for help, no friends who can assist her, no relatives to ask for shelter or a hot meal.

She doesn't even have the wherewithal to suffer, the woman with gray hair. She's lost all will, even the desire to see the sun come up in the morning. She goes on living because she doesn't know what else to do, and because she assumes that Someone Else's will counts more than her own.

In the midst of the crowd, she tries to win herself an advantageous position from which to board the train. Her aching hips, her weight, her years all conspire to make her the slowest animal in the jungle: unless she wants to be left behind, she'll have to push herself forward, very close to where the doors will open.

School has just let out. The worst time of day. Little bands of teenagers swarm the streets shouting, laughing, and shoving, indifferent to anyone around them.

A boy a few yards away performs a vulgar imitation of someone and the other kids all burst into laughter, playfully slapping and elbowing each other; a girl accidentally shoves the woman with gray hair, making her wobble frighteningly. The girl turns around, sees the woman with gray hair, and laughs right in her face; then she turns back to her friends, holding her nose and pantomiming the urge to vomit. They all laugh. This is the only time that anyone notices her.

The woman with gray hair doesn't lift her gaze from the small dark pit occupied by the subway's tracks.

Seen from behind, the woman with gray hair is the very picture of despair. Her slumped shoulders, her head, which hangs low, the filthy locks of hair that hang from her head like dead leaves. Who knows what memories pass through her mind. Who knows what thoughts.

Now the woman with gray hair sets her bag with its few items of food on the ground. Even though it weighs almost nothing, her fingers, pitiless, are radiating pain. The woman with gray hair lets out a faint moan.

But no one notices.

Pity, the woman with gray hair thinks as the tunnel fills with the buffeting wind of the oncoming train. What pity?

The kids laugh again, loudly, their young hair fluttering in the currents of air. The crowd braces for the arrival of the subway.

A shadow slides up behind the woman with gray hair.

No one notices.

The kids laugh at nothing in particular: they don't notice.

The two people in love, gazing into each other's eyes: they don't notice.

The young mother, arranging the blankets in her baby carriage: she doesn't notice.

The office worker, hurrying to finish the article in the free newspaper, so he can toss it in the trash before boarding the train: he doesn't notice.

The night watchman, struggling to keep his eyes open, fighting off exhaustion from the shift he's just finished: he doesn't notice.

The pickpocket, carefully monitoring the crowd for purses left open or wallets in back pockets: he doesn't notice.

The high school teacher, staring, hypnotized, at a female student's ass, sheathed in a pair of jeans so tight it's like a second skin: he doesn't notice.

The two nuns, chattering away in who knows what language about which of the two of them is going to be sent on a mission to Asia: they don't notice.

The ticket checkers, talking about soccer while waiting for someone with a friendly expression to accost, knowing that the ones most likely to lack a valid ticket are the ones with scowls on their faces, but knowing also that they're also the ones most likely to put up a fight: they don't notice.

The woman on her way back from grocery shopping, struggling not to drop any of the bags and parcels she's carrying: she doesn't notice.

Just before the train pulls into the station, just as the woman with gray hair is asking Whoever sits on high in heaven to please give her the strength, a hand touches her gently in the middle of the back and gives her a small shove.

The woman with gray hair falls without a peep into the small abyss of the tracks, at the very instant the train pulls in.

No one notices.

The one who does notice, with a scream, is a young woman just rushing down the stairs in a last-ditch attempt to catch the train; she misses the train but what she does arrive in time to see is the sad spectacle of all that's left of the woman with gray hair.

A gentle hand slips a note into the plastic bag still sitting on the platform.

With a farewell to the world that the woman with gray hair lacked the strength to utter.

But no one notices.

XXXVII

When they reached the entrance to the La Vela yacht club—that was the name spelled out in looping script on the large brass plaque—the wind had picked up again. It had been threatening to rain, and rain hard, nearly all morning and for the first part of the afternoon; thunderclaps had marched closer and closer, while lightning flashed out over the sea; but instead of rain, the winds had again started blowing violently, and the black clouds were once more scudding rapidly across the sky.

Aragona and Lojacono headed downhill toward the front door of the elegant villa surrounded by greenery; through the ornamental plants they glimpsed the club's dock, the masts of various sailboats bobbing in the breeze like so many trees. Pisanelli had told them that their meeting with the Baroness Ruffolo needed to be informal and confidential, and so they didn't show their police IDs at the door.

The doorman, who seemed to have wandered out of a movie from the Fifties, was outfitted in full regalia: livery, sideburns, and white gloves. He looked Aragona up and down with ill concealed distaste: the fake tan, the aviators, and the shirt, unbuttoned to reveal his chest. The police officer lifted his chin and glared back at the man over the rims of his glasses with a look of defiance. Two worlds, facing off. Then, with the demeanor of someone giving way only under extreme duress, the doorman led them into a small private room, where a waiter came to receive them. He could have been the doorman's twin brother.

As they followed him through a succession of drawing rooms, the walls crowded with silver cups, trophies, and plaques of all sorts, Aragona whispered to Lojacono: "Where the heck are we?"

They reached a large room furnished with twenty or so card tables and little else; crowds of people clustered around the tables, most of them women holding hands of cards, while all around hovered waiters, like bumblebees in springtime, carrying trays loaded down with cocktails and canapés. In defiance of the prohibitions posted on the walls, the air was heavy with clouds of cigarette smoke.

They crossed the room, following the strutting waiter. Here and there, eyes rose from the cards and fixed on the two guests. Lojacono, to his surprise, detected a couple of lascivious glances shot their way by decrepit old women well into their eighties, attracted by the sight of fresh meat. He shuddered.

One of the walls consisted of a series of plate-glass windows overlooking a veranda, deserted except for a small table where an elegantly appointed woman sat. The waiter took them directly to that table, bowed to the lady, and said: "Baroness, here are the guests you were expecting."

The woman was in every way identical to the other women crowding the room: her wrinkled, heavily made up face; her enormous dark glasses; her pearl necklace and gaudy, antique earrings. She was staring out over the veranda's spectacular panorama: an all-encompassing view of the bay and the mountain above it, the raging sea and the clouds scudding across the sky.

"*Grazie*, Amedeo. Please find out what the gentlemen would like; I'll have another margarita, please. Go ahead, make yourselves comfortable."

The voice sounded like a sheet of sandpaper being dragged over a nail file. Her tone was dry, typical of those who are accustomed to issuing orders.

They asked Amedeo for two coffees, and the waiter turned and vanished without a sound. They sat down.

The woman slowly turned to look at them, staring at them through the dark lenses. The fact that they couldn't see her eyes, along with the intricate network of wrinkles covering her skin, gave her face a fixed, reptilian quality that made them both uncomfortable. Aragona fidgeted in his chair, and in a bid to regain his dignity removed and replaced his glasses; that gesture, however, had no effect, and the woman went back to looking out over the sea.

"I'm Anna Ruffolo. Giorgio Pisanelli tells me that you may need to have a word with me. Giorgio is a friend, I certainly can't turn down any request from him: but one thing needs to be perfectly clear."

The croaking voice stopped, for no apparent reason. A moment later, the waiter shimmered into sight with a tray, set down on the table two espressos, a cocktail, a plate of finger pastries, and then turned and vanished.

Lojacono wondered how on earth the woman had known the waiter was about to arrive. As if he'd uttered that thought aloud, the baroness said: "In here, the waiters function like a series of relay stations. They're paid actual salaries by certain individuals to report all the gossip and news, the rarest of commodities in a world where nothing ever fucki—nothing ever happens, which is the world we live in. And right now, you're the news, as you can see."

Without bothering to turn around, she tilted her head backwards. Aragona looked into the room behind the plate-glass windows and realized that at least a couple dozen women with blue-rinsed hair and enormous earrings were covertly observing them.

The baroness resumed her speech: "I was just saying that one thing needs to be perfectly clear: this conversation never took place. You can't write a report on it, you can't tell anyone else about it, you can't make the slightest mention of it to anyone at all, you'll never be able to say you met me or talked to me. Otherwise, nothing doing, and you can both go your way after enjoying your coffee. I didn't ask your names, and I don't want to know them. Make up your minds, and let me know."

Lojacono said: "We understand, signora, and we thank you for your help. No one will ever know that we met, aside from the few colleagues with whom we're working this case. Outside of the police station, no one will ever find out about this meeting. And there will be no written record of it. I guarantee it."

Once again, the woman turned her head in his direction and stared at him, then went back to looking out at the sea.

"What is it you want to know?"

"Signora, you are aware of what happened to De Santis, Cecilia, wife of the notary Arturo Festa. Pisanelli told us that the victim was a friend of yours. We don't have much evidence: it appears to be a burglary gone wrong, but there are some things that just don't add up. We wanted to know a little more about this woman: did she have any worries, was there anything, or anyone, in her life that could have led to what happened. Whether she'd told you about anything that happened, or if she might have told anyone else who can help us head in the right direction."

The woman sat in silence, sipping her cocktail. Then she said: "De Santis, Cecilia. That's what you call her: De Santis, Cecilia. Last name first, first name last. That's all she's become, poor Cicia, a last name followed by a first name on a police report. To me, she was Cicia. That's who she's always been, since the first time I saw her, when she was a newborn. I was fifteen, and our mothers were friends. As were our grandmothers, for that matter. And probably our great-grandmothers, too. You see, that's the way our world is: small. There are only a few thousand of us, maybe three thousand; we all know each other, we never see anyone else. Every once in a great while, lately, we've accepted someone new into our midst, but only if they're good for a show: if they have a lot of money, or great artistic talent. They give us something to talk about, something new to say, but basically we never change."

A gust of wind shook the plate glass.

"Our world. Vacations in Cortina, on Capri. A trip every so often, nothing much; a place in New York or Paris, an office in London. Salons. Clubs. All of them without windows, because we don't want to know what else is happening in the world, or in the city: we need to convince ourselves that our lives are actually the whole universe. Look at them, behind that window. They're all wondering: who are these guests who've come to see Ruffolo? What are they saying to her? And what about her, what's she saying to them? None of them will ask me a godda . . . blessed thing, of course: but they'll talk about nothing else for weeks. Just as they'll talk about Cicia, and her murder, for years: that's our world. How dreary."

Aragona coughed softly.

"And De San . . . the victim, was she like that? Like all these other women?"

"Cicia? No. Not entirely, at any rate. Certainly, she belonged to the club, and she had a place on Capri and in Cortina, just like everyone else. But there was something different about Cicia. She was capable of love. Of real love, love that makes you sad, that makes you suffer, the way people out there love. And she took it upon herself, without making a show of it, to help other people. She did a great deal of charity work, did you know? Twice a week, with no fanfare, she went to teach in a nursery school, in a terribly poor part of the city, one of those places where no one would go, even in an armored car driven by the Italian army. I used to tell her: why don't you pay someone else to go for you, that way you can give work to some poor underpaid teacher; but she'd say: no, I have to go. Because I'm selfish, and I so love spending time with those little treasures of every race and color. That's how Cicia was."

The sea had kicked up again, and it was slapping at the wharf where all the boats were moored. The baroness went on: "Not that we don't know how to love, in our world. In fact, we can devote all the time we like to love: to love and to health. That's exactly what money is for, isn't it? So we can spend time on the finer things. And what could be finer than love? Except for canasta, of course." She sipped her cocktail. "But there was something unique about Cicia. She only fell in love once. You saw her in . . . a state I can't imagine, and pictures didn't do her justice. She was no beauty. But there was a kindness, a charm to her eyes that captivated people. She was lovely, magnificent: but in her soul. She had a thousand colors, Cicia did, in her soul. I used to make fun of her, I told her that she was in the running for sainthood, and she'd laugh, but the truth is that Cicia was different from everyone else."

Lojacono courteously tried to steer the conversation back to the investigation.

"Baroness, we have no doubts that the lady was an extraordinary person. For that very reason, though, we wonder who might have wanted to do her harm, and why. If you cared for her, and I'm certain that you did, I'd like to ask whether you might have any ideas in that direction."

The sea went on howling incessantly. A couple of the yacht club's sailors, dressed in yellow raincoats that flapped in the wind like flags gone mad, struggled on the wharf to reinforce the moorings of several boats.

Ruffolo thought it over.

"Cicia had just one weakness. Only one. Her husband, Arturo. A self-regarding asshole, a ridiculous peacock who never missed an opportunity to lunge at the first hen that clucked past. He was nothing, a nobody, until he had the enormous good luck to meet Cicia. He was a nobody. And she transformed him into one of this city's most important notaries, with a network of incredible contacts that allow him to work as if he were the only notary in town. In exchange, he cheated on her so many times, made her a complete laughing-stock, until, years ago, she simply stopped seeing people. I talked to her every day, begging her to tell him to go get fucked once and for all—which is what he was inclined to do any-way—but she just told me that she loved him all the same. Absurd, no?"

Lojacono agreed: "Yes, it's absurd, Baroness. But it happens quite often. Had anything in particular happened lately? Any disagreement, any argument or cause for special friction?"

"I'm afraid not. I'll say it again, in spite of my advice, Cicia refused to start any kind of discussion with that asshole husband of hers. And by now he'd lost all remaining restraint."

Aragona took off his glasses, underscoring his increased interest: "What do you mean, all restraint?"

The baroness snorted: "He even came here once, to a party, with his whore. Here, to the yacht club, where if he hadn't been Cicia's husband no one would have even considered hiring him as a waiter. And you should have seen her, the young miss: dressed like a harlot, with red hair and mile-high heels, greeting people right and left as if she were his lawfully wedded wife."

Lojacono asked: "Do you know the girl's name? Who she is?"

"Of course I know. Do you think anything happens in here that isn't immediately known and discussed, including the two of you? Her name is Iolanda, Iolanda Russo. She's an accountant, or a tax consultant, or who knows what other cover story for her true profession."

"Her true profession being?" asked Aragona before Lojacono could manage to wave him off.

"Hooker," Ruffolo specified, and then went on, as if nothing had happened: "A pathetic scene: everyone was trying to get away from them, mortified, while he chased after them to introduce her. A girl young enough to be his daughter, and he was presenting her as 'an extraordinary professional, whom you might find very useful'; let me tell *you* what she was useful for. Anyway, the new development, which was actually nothing new, is that he had started showing off his whores again. He'd stopped, or at least been more discreet, for a few years. But men like him can't help it, sooner or later they go back to being themselves."

Lojacono listened with interest. Then he asked: "Do you think, Baroness, that your friend felt insulted by her presence? That she could have demanded an explanation, and that someone might have . . ."

Ruffolo laughed. There was something rough and annoying about it, like a metal file being dragged through gravel.

"Who, Cicia? No. She suffered, but she never showed it. She thought her husband was perfect, a wonderful gift from God, and that he had the right to have his fun, now and then. That's what she called her husband's affairs: having his fun, now and then. He'd had lots and lots of affairs, so why would she have objected to this one in particular?"

Outside, the sailors went on battling the wind, the waves, and the moorings. Aragona watched them, fascinated. Then he asked: "But in your opinion, Barone', who could it have been? Who could have possibly wished to do such terrible harm to such a kind and gentle person?"

Ruffolo looked out to sea too: "I don't know. It might actually have been a robbery. And that would be a fine irony, that the most generous person I've ever known should have been killed for money or a handful of jewels. Certainly, the peacock would have had no motive: without her, he's done for. What matters to me is that I've lost my friend, the only one I could really talk to, instead of talking endless bullshit with those stringy old geese behind that glass. And even though she was younger than me, she could have been a thousand years old for how clearly she saw things. What matters to me is that I miss her. And when she died, a part of me died with her, the best part of me. The only part that was worth a damn."

They sat in silence for a while, until the two policemen realized that the woman was weeping, though she was crying no tears. Then the baroness said: "Now I'm going to stand up and say goodbye to you. I'll kiss the younger of you on the cheek, and I'll shake hands with the older one. I'll say that I saw a nephew of mine, who came to see me with a friend, to ask me for money. That's the sort of thing that happens to all the women here. If you need anything else, get in touch with me through Pisanelli. I want you to catch whoever did it, and I want you to throw him in prison. Unlike Cicia, I am a deeply vindictive person. All right?"

Lojacono nodded. Then, suddenly, he said: "Can I ask you something, Baroness? Why did your friend collect those objects, those spheres with the snow inside?"

Ruffolo turned slowly and aimed the lenses of her glasses at Lojacono's face. Then: "Why do you want to know? What is the meaning of this question?"

"I don't know. I believe that if someone devotes that much time to something, well, then, it must have some importance. Even if, looked at from outside, it might seem trivial."

The baroness went on staring at him, expressionless. Aragona shifted uncomfortably in his seat. There was something about that woman that made him uneasy. He focused on a sailor tightening a knot around a bollard, poised between the wharf and the surface of the sea.

The woman spoke, addressing Lojacono: "You're Sicilian, aren't you? You look Asian, but you're Sicilian. I can tell from the accent. Nice place, Sicily. Smart people there." She looked back out to sea, and said: "The snow globes. Cicia had been collecting them forever, since she first got married. During her honeymoon, I don't remember where, her husband bought her one. When she got back, we laughed about it, I told her it struck me as appropriate, given that gentleman's complete lack of taste; but she took that gift as if it were a precious diamond. After that, she scooped them up everywhere she went; who knows, perhaps she was trying to find a glint of the happiness she'd once experienced. Or else it was just something to fill her time, since her husband had basically deserted her. The fact is, whenever any of us went anywhere, she always asked us to remember to bring one back for her. I think I must have bought her a couple myself, may God forgive me."

They got to their feet and went through the little pantomime that the woman had requested, Aragona faking an affectionate farewell, Lojacono a formal one.

And once again they made their way through the smoke-filled room, the targets of a thousand darting, curious gazes.

Outside, the wind was outdoing itself.

XXXVIII

On the way back to the station house, they didn't have much to say. There weren't many people out on the street and most of them sought shelter from the rain and wind by sticking close to the walls.

Suddenly Aragona said: "And yet, at a certain point, I felt sorry for her. You might laugh, Loja', but I felt sorry for that old woman. I got the impression of loneliness, of a total state of despair. Even though she has more money than everyone I know put together. Go figure."

"You're not wrong, you know," Lojacono replied. "Better to starve to death and not know where your children's next meal is coming from. That way you get through the day a little faster and you don't become a slave to the canasta table."

His partner shot him an offended, sidelong glance: "That's not what I'm saying. Still, I wouldn't want to be her. In any case, our friend the notary doesn't come off particularly well from the description Pisanelli's friend gave us. By the way, how did she and Pisanelli become friends, do you think? They're both a hundred years old. Maybe they used to screw, back in the Paleolithic."

"That's their business. Still, I'd be grateful to our colleague. If it wasn't for him, we'd never have gotten the information. That was an interesting conversation; the notary's new girl-friend is becoming increasingly important. We should find a way to meet her, but in such a way that she doesn't decide to zip her lips and throw away the key, the way he did."

The atmosphere in the station house was as stormy as the weather outside; an argument was under way between Di Nardo and Romano about an inspection they'd conducted together.

". . . no doubt," Romano was saying, "that man is a real piece of shit, that we agree on. And I was the first to say that the girl isn't his friend at all, she's something quite different. Still, we checked their IDs. And everything checked out, right? So what can we do about it?"

Di Nardo, who'd taken off her sunglasses, revealing a face creased with weariness, replied in voice that was calm but hard: "We both got the same impression: it's not just a case of some old man keeping a young girl. The sense we both got was of abuse, of one person willfully controlling another. That girl definitely isn't happy. She's terrified, living in fear, riddled with anxiety. Are we supposed to pretend we can't see it? Or are we going to choose to turn our backs, are we going to take that guy's advice and worry about catching real criminals, are we going to be scared off by his threat to reach out to one of his highly placed contacts?"

Palma broke in: "Wait a second, what highly placed contacts? Did this architect try to threaten you two?"

Romano gave Di Nardo a nasty look: now Palma, like every commissario he'd ever known, would demand that the investigation be halted to avoid trouble.

He related what the architect had threatened to do and admitted that he'd been on the verge of losing his temper, and that if it hadn't been for Di Nardo, whom he gestured toward without looking in her direction, he'd probably have laid hands on the man.

Palma surprised everyone by saying: "Ah, you should have told me that right away. If that's the case, we have to keep investigating. Go drop by the girl's home and talk to her parents. See what they have to say about it. If something emerges, anything at all, that suggests we're not getting the whole story, we'll take this guy and question him seven ways to Sunday. All right?"

Everyone was stunned. Palma, Ottavia Calabrese decided, was the Perfect Man; she fantasized about kissing him.

Lojacono broke in, doffing his overcoat: "The two of us, on the other hand, spend our afternoons at the yacht club, sipping cocktails with elegantly dressed aristocrats. Anyone want to swap assignments?"

Palma spread his arms wide: "Someone has to do some work around here. Come on, tell us all about it."

The lieutenant summarized the day's events, including the visits to the concierge and to the forensic squad. Aragona threw in, bitterly: "I'm not even going to tell you the look on the face of that asshole from forensics the minute he heard where we were from. I'd have liked to slap him silly! If it hadn't have been for Lojacono who . . . who made a phone call, he wouldn't have told us a thing, not a goddamn thing."

Palma nodded: "I understand, yes. Still, next time, let me take care of it, through official channels. That way, they'll stop trying to get in our way."

"The incredible thing," Lojacono commented, "is that they blame us for what happened. That was all before we even got there; what do we have to do with any of those guys?"

From the far end of the room came Pisanelli's deep voice: "We knew those guys, as you call them. They were our colleagues, same as you and me and him and her. Men with a hard job and not much money, and sick children to take care of, and debts. Men who fell into temptation, when all their job gave them was a mountain of shit in each hand, same as it does us every day of the week."

Silence fell. Everyone was looking at the deputy captain.

"That doesn't mean they're not criminals, let me be perfectly clear. Especially because they didn't just skim some money off the top, they also sold nasty shit to innocent kids and fried their brains. And that's one thing no one will forgive them, and won't forgive those who decided to keep this place open: the fact that those guys could have been any of us."

Palma tried to shift the topic away from those bitter thoughts: "Anyway, they're going to have get used to the fact that we work hard here, and we do a good job. If they can't, too bad for them. As far as I'm concerned, this Bastards of Pizzofalcone thing just makes me laugh. Ottavia, do we have any news for Lojacono and Aragona?"

Calabrese tapped open a couple of files on her monitor. "A little something, yes. The autopsy report came in, and it confirms what the doctor says he mentioned to you at the scene: a fractured cranium was the woman's sole cause of death. Otherwise, she was in good health for a woman of her age. Practically speaking, the doctor tells me in this email, the woman would have lived to be a hundred if someone hadn't decided to bash the back of her head in with a blunt object."

Romano snickered: "Oh, that's rich, a perfect state of health can only be certified with an autopsy. Better than a CAT scan, eh? My compliments to the doctor, Calabre'."

Ottavia continued: "In fact, there's nothing like an autopsy to determine one's state of health: I may put you up for one, Romano; if you ask me, big and strong as you are, the results would be outstanding. In any case, that's not the only news we have for Lojacono. My friend the IT expert called, and he told me that the analysis of Festa's computer is almost done. And you want to know what?"

She fell silent, clearly enjoying the moment. Palma thought to himself that she was irresistible.

"Come on, don't leave us hanging! What did your friend find out?"

Ottavia couldn't believe she'd become the center of the commissario's attention.

"I had to threaten him, and remind him of just how much of my homework I let him copy when we were taking the same computer class, but he finally gave me the information. Now then, there's nothing special on the hard drive, just the usual things: deeds, basically, and legal texts and other things of that sort. So they decrypted the password for his email, and here too, except for some spam, it was all just work-related."

Aragona decided not to conceal his disappointment: "Because this old mummy still uses homing pigeons or something to send messages to his mistresses. Goddamn it."

Ottavia shook her finger no: "In fact, right at the very end, something interesting did emerge. Very interesting. Unfortunately, I couldn't talk him into sending me a copy, because it'll be submitted to the investigating magistrate once the overall exam is complete, but I did get him to read it to me over the phone."

She waved a sheet of paper in the air. Palma laughed: "There's no stopping her, if a woman gets something into her head, she'll do whatever it takes. Okay, so tell us what you found, don't keep us on pins and needles!"

Ottavia read from the sheet of paper: "It's an email sent to the online travel agency IlTuoViaggio.com, one of the most popular ones on the web. Basically, fifteen days ago the notary reserved a trip for two to Micronesia: three stopovers; the last leg via biplane. Departure scheduled in two days."

They all sat openmouthed. The first to come out of his trance was Aragona. "Where the fuck is that, Micronesia?"

"Oceania," Pisanelli replied. "More or less on the other side of the world."

Di Nardo asked: "But don't you have to provide names, when you make reservations for a trip like that? I don't know, IDs, passports . . ."

Calabrese nodded: "That's right, Di Nardo. That's exactly right: you have to provide IDs. And the notary did just that: he provided IDs, complete with first and last names and dates issued. A very thoroughly documented email; in fact, my friend tells me, he asked whether it might not be useful to scan the IDs."

Lojacono was expressionless, like a Buddhist monk trying to levitate.

"That means we know what names he made the reservations under, and that the departure was scheduled for four days after the death of his wife. What about the return trip?"

"No return trip," Ottavia replied. "They were one-way tickets."

Palma was confused: "Are you saying the notary planned to leave for Micronesia and never come back?"

Romano thought it over: "Not necessarily. Maybe they just wanted to leave the return date open, and decide later when to come back. Sometimes people do that, especially for long trips."

Aragona was baffled.

"Whatever the case, round-trip or one-way, it strikes me as pretty serious evidence, it substantiates some of our suspicions. The notary plans and arranges a trip overseas, one-way, with his lover, and, as chance would have it, four days before the happy couple is scheduled to fly away, the beloved wife, the sole obstacle to their dream of bliss, dies after having her head bashed in with one of those glass balls with the fake snow inside. All this must mean something."

Pisanelli scratched his head: "All things considered, our young colleague here isn't all wrong. After all, as Anna Ruffolo told us, lately our friend the notary had been going around showing off his redheaded girlfriend right and left."

Ottavia, however, still had a point to make: "Why don't any of you ask me whether I'm done, before you start leaping to conclusions? Doesn't it even occur to you that you ought to ask under what names the reservations were made?"

No one said a word; everyone was clearly disoriented. Ottavia went on: "Because the reservations were made for Arturo Festa, the notary; and for his wife, Cecilia De Santis. The victim."

The news fell into a well of bafflement and silence. Ottavia decided she'd kept them on tenterhooks long enough and added: "But in the email making the reservation, the notary explicitly requests confirmation of the clause in the contract that allows him to change one of the names up to twenty-four hours prior to departure. In case of serious impediment."

Aragona leapt out of his chair: "There you go, guys! We've got him! He made the reservation under his wife's name to keep from looking guilty, and then he was planning to substitute her name with his lover's at the very last minute! Death comes under the heading of serious impediments, doesn't it?"

"There's something strange about all this," the commissario said. "If you plan to kill your wife, you can't seriously think that four days later they're going to let you fly off to Micronesia in a Hawaiian shirt and a straw hat, hand in hand with your lover."

As if talking to himself, Lojacono concluded: "Without even taking into account the fact that, if you were going to make those reservations, the last place you'd do it is on the office computer, since it's the first place the police would go and look, which is in fact exactly what we did."

Alex Di Nardo wasn't convinced: "True enough. But it's also possible that they hadn't planned to kill her. Perhaps, and this is only a hypothesis, he went to see her to tell her that he was planning to leave her and go to Micronesia, she put up a fight, and he wound up killing her."

Romano nodded: "With the first thing he could lay hands on, the snow globe. And he was hoping it would shatter into bits, which meant he'd be rid of it, the same way he'd be rid of his wife."

"Though let's not entirely rule out," Pisanelli added, "the

theory that a burglar just might have murdered her when the poor notary was planning to make things up to his wife by taking her on a second honeymoon, after breaking up with his lover during one last, red-hot weekend together."

"Or else," Ottavia concluded, "he asked if he could change the name so he could pretend he had some other commitment at the very last minute, send his wife off to Micronesia with some girlfriend of hers, and stay here to fuck the redhead undisturbed, and then the signora was murdered during a burglary by someone who was in cahoots with the housekeeper, and who happened to find her at home when he expected her to be out."

"Jesus," Aragona exclaimed in amazement, "and you think I'm the one who's been watching too much TV, eh? Have the lot of you ever thought of becoming screenwriters instead of cops? You'd make buckets of money, you would. Well, so, we're back to square one, is that right?"

Lojacono threw open his arms: "Not necessarily. What we can say is that the field of hypotheses is narrowing considerably, which is what always happens the more evidence one acquires. For instance, we now know that, with or without his wife, the notary was planning a trip, and that doesn't seem at all insignificant."

"So now what are we supposed to do?" asked Aragona. "Festa won't talk to us, we can't go see the redhead because she's not officially connected with the case . . ."

Palma reassured him: "There's no reason to think we can't talk to the notary and the young lady. We're working with Dottoressa Piras. And in the meanwhile you have something else to check out, don't you, Lojacono?"

The lieutenant nodded.

"That's right. We need to go find out what the housekeeper has to tell us, Signorina . . ." and here he checked the Xerox of the young woman's ID, "Mayya Ivanova Nikolaeva. Who had the apartment keys, the keys to the door that wasn't forced open. Perhaps she has some explaining to do. Come on, Aragona, this time we can even take the car, which should make you happy. Let's see if we can finally crash head-on into the side of a building."

XXXIX

L isten, I don't trust what your lawyer is telling you. If you ask me, we're making a huge mistake."

"But if you decide to go to a professional, then you have to trust him. That's why we say you've 'entrusted' someone with your defense, right?"

"Don't try to palm that old saw off on me, I know all about entrusting yourself to a professional. I use that line at least four times a day. You do remember the line of work I'm in, don't you?"

"Of course, of course. But neither you nor I have enough experience in this specific branch of the law, right? We talked about that at some length, if I'm not mistaken."

"True enough. But it seems to me that the context has changed. Something has happened, hasn't it?"

". . ."

"And so, we need to rethink our position. And we need to rethink it in a hurry. When was the last time you talked to this goddamned lawyer of yours?"

"Half an hour ago, trust me, if I don't call him he calls me, if you ask me he's planning to make a fortune out of this case."

"And that's exactly what I wanted to talk to you about. Follow my reasoning here, please: when you're advising someone on the best path to follow in a given situation, I don't know, let's say it's a merger, or a purchase entailing fractional ownership, or the division of an inheritance, don't you also keep in mind how you can make the most money off the job?"

"Listen, I . . ."

"Do me a favor and don't lie to me, please. This is important, tell me the truth."

"Well . . ."

"Exactly. And I do the same thing. It's human nature, I think. And what would make this lawyer—what would make any lawyer we decided to entrust our case to—the most money?"

"Wait, listen to me, you aren't trying to tell me that . . ."

"If you, or I, or the both of us were indicted, that's what would make a lawyer the most money. If a long, burdensome, tortuous trial began at our expense. Which, in the meanwhile, but only incidentally, would ruin both our lives. And not just our lives, as you know very well."

"Are you kidding? Do you have any idea what you're saying? This is one of the most respected lawyers in one of the oldest and most celebrated courts in the country, and . . ."

". . . and he's exactly the same as all the others, just much, much more expensive. I wouldn't blindly trust my own cousin, in this particular situation."

"Well then? What do you suggest doing? Supposing, just supposing, we decide to go ahead and ignore my lawyer's advice, what would you propose?"

"Simple: we need to talk to them. We keep our cool and our equilibrium, make sure our versions match up perfectly, and tell them calmly and collectedly the things we need to say. Because no one can believe—or even think—that we had anything to do with what happened."

"You're crazy, you know. Completely out of your head. Believe me, the prisons are overflowing with people who went in to talk to the police, all calm and trusting. Just last week, I read about a man who served twenty-two years—twenty-two years, you understand that? And he was innocent, innocent as a baby. Some other guy turned up, facing charges on who knows what, and he confessed to the murder the first guy did the time for, and you know what they did? They released him, with their sincerest apologies. After twenty-two years! His life is ruined! Don't you get it?"

"You see? You're starting to lose your cool. Which is exactly what you can't do. Now, why don't you just listen to me, for once: which side has the burden of proof?"

"What?"

"Do we have to prove that we're innocent, or do they have to prove, if it ever goes to trial, that we're guilty?"

"What does that have to do with anything? What are you trying to say? Of course, they have the burden of proof. But still . . ."

"Exactly. And just who would you focus your investigation on, if you were the prosecuting attorney? On someone who came forward of his own free will, or on someone who told you that he wouldn't ever talk, not on his life?"

"My God, my God, this is ridiculous. If only it had never happened, if only I'd had a chance to talk to her . . ."

"There, now you're starting to snivel again. Stop and think, instead. And tell me: what would you do?"

"I . . . it's only natural, refusing to talk certainly encourages investigations, the lawyer himself admits it. On the other hand, there's no danger of being caught in a contradiction, which can happen very easily. Or do you think that they'd interview us together, maybe take us out for a pizza? You don't know them."

"Are you saying you do? Or that your greedy lawyer does? I'm telling you we need to talk to them, I'm sure of it. I can feel it. Let's show them that we're happy to collaborate and you'll see, it'll all go fine. After all, the silver is still missing, isn't it? For all I know they'll decide to focus on the housekeeper."

"I'll think it over. I don't know, but I promise I'll think it over."

"And remember: this isn't just our problem anymore. We have someone we have to think about. We can't make mistakes."

"No. We can't make mistakes. Not anymore."

XL

With the part of his mind that wasn't feverishly praying he wouldn't plow into a semi at an intersection, Lojacono thought about the city.

To see it like this, from the passenger seat of a compact car without police insignia, charging at breakneck speed down crowded streets and narrow alleys, with Aragona at the wheel, blissfully chatting the whole time as if he were sitting comfortably in the living room of his apartment, was a very odd experience.

Without his noticing it, the lieutenant had begun to change his mind about that very strange city. He'd stopped thinking of it as nothing more than a prison, a domestic exile to which he'd been sentenced because of a damned lying informant, a penalty imposed without trial or cross-examination. He was finally trying to get to know the place a little better, if only so he could work there; a policeman, he knew, has to breathe the air of the city he works in. He has to be able to savor its silences, its hesitations; he has to know the smell of its fear and suspicion, its indifference and arrogance, in order to be able to fight them. Otherwise it's over before it starts.

Certainly, it was no easy matter to interpret such a complicated place, he thought to himself, as Aragona, busy detailing the plot of a movie he'd just seen, missed plowing into a motor scooter carrying three people by a scant fraction of an inch. Ostentatiously elegant streets, lined with designer shops and luxury automobiles, alternated with steep, narrow alleys that ran uphill, crowded with miserable apartments and kids who could barely be called toddlers playing in the road, on stoops, inhaling exhaust fumes. Enormous piazzas, closed off to traffic and watched over by dozens of traffic cops, gave onto tangled networks of narrow lanes where anything and everything could be bought and sold, the stalls and carts loaded with merchandise blocking the way to cars. Broad boulevards, dotted with banks, up and down which professionals in dark suits moved hurriedly, carrying leather briefcases full to bursting, opened out into dark little piazzas fronted by wonderful deconsecrated churches where, indifferent to the howling winds, bare-chested boys surrounded by swarms of mopeds played endless soccer matches. It was as if the souk of Casablanca or the markets of Marrakesh had been transported into the center of Milan. Lojacono wondered what could be said of a place like this.

"An extraordinary actor, let me tell you. You should have seen him, long hair, dark glasses, all ragged and rumpled: a perfect policemen and yet his colleagues kept him at arm's length because they thought he was dirty cop. I watched that movie and I was thinking the whole time that in a certain sense, we're like that too, no?"

Lojacono had understood that today he'd need to give him free rein while he drove, otherwise it would be even worse: Aragona kept looking over at him and slapping him on the shoulder as if they were just chatting at the bar, never slowing for even a second. He wished he could do the driving himself, but he didn't know where to go: Mayya Nikolaeva, housekeeper to the late Signora De Santis, lived in a small alley off of who knew what street, over by the main train station.

The neighborhood, Lojacono soon realized, was for the most part inhabited by foreigners. Men and women of color exited and entered buildings carrying huge bags full of merchandise, making their way through cars double-, triple-, and quadruple-parked; Indians with crowds of children greeted each other as their paths crossed; the grocery stores carried signs in Italian and many other languages, often written in incomprehensible scripts.

Aragona turned down a tiny street, parking the car so that two wheels rested on the narrow sidewalk, blocking it completely.

"Well, this ought to be the place. I don't need to tell you that we can't count on the advantage of surprise, as you can see."

Nearly all the people who had been crowding the street when they arrived had in fact promptly dispersed, though there was absolutely no insignia identifying the car as belonging to the police.

"They can smell us coming, they can smell us. And immediately the missing visa virus spreads, even if their visa actually is perfectly valid, or their damned country has already joined the European Union and they don't even need one anymore."

Muttering under his breath, Aragona checked the street number of the building against the Xerox of the young woman's passport. Then he nodded, and walked into a dark, dank atrium.

An elderly woman was scrubbing the steps; they asked her where Mayya's apartment was and, without bothering to look up, the woman said, in a heavy eastern European accent: "Fourth floor, apartment with door."

They had some difficulty making their way upstairs, because it was getting dark and there were no lights. They could smell a heavy odor of spices and onions, and voices could be heard from a number of apartments, all speaking foreign languages. On the fourth floor there was in fact only one door; the entrance to the other apartment was wide open, and it was deserted.

They knocked on the door and Mayya opened it immediately, as if she'd been standing there waiting.

"*Buonasera*, please come in."

They found themselves in a place that looked nothing like the rest of the building. Two long-necked lamps cast a warm light onto the spotlessly clean room, which contained a table and chairs, a sofa and an armchair, a coffee table and a flat-screen television. Photographs hung on the wall, most depicting Mayya with her arms wrapped around a tall, dark-haired, powerfully built man, who wore a serious, vaguely embarrassed expression. The general impression was of a normal middle-class apartment whose inhabitants were neither filthy rich nor lacking in the essentials.

"Signorina," Lojacono said, "you remember us, don't you? We met . . . we saw each other a couple of days ago, in the notary's apartment."

The girl nodded, her expression pained. Seeing her now, the two policemen realized she looked less young; her face bore the marks of a sorrow that seemed sincere, shot through with faint worry. In that part of town, having two policemen in your home must not exactly be considered good luck.

"Certainly. Please, come right in. I make some coffee?"

The lieutenant shook his head no, while Aragona, rather rudely, wandered around the room studying the photographs.

"No, thank you. We'd like to ask you a few questions, if you don't mind. We preferred to come here, rather than sending for you. It should be quick, no more than a few minutes."

Mayya ran her hand through her hair—the gesture had to be instinctive because her hair was already perfectly groomed.

"I understand. Okay. Let's sit here."

She pointed to a sofa and an armchair, and settled herself in the armchair. Her hands were the only part of her that betrayed nervousness: she couldn't stop clenching them, separating them, and wringing them together. The rest of her body was still, stiff; no emotions filtered out through her even, somewhat nondescript features.

Aragona, who had stopped near a photo of the dark-haired

man, said: "And this gentleman, in this photograph, who is he? Does he live here with you?"

Lojacono noticed his partner's rude tone; the girl replied without turning around, her voice unflustered.

"That is my boyfriend, Adrian. He works, soon he is home."

Aragona smirked slyly and looked over at Lojacono, nodding as if he'd just found the guilty party. The lieutenant ignored him and turned to the woman.

"How long had you worked for the Festa family?"

"Two and half years, almost three. Do you want to see work papers?"

Lojacono raised one hand, made a vague gesture.

"No, maybe later. And how did you like it there, with them?"

"Notary was never there, I went nine in morning and then stay till five in afternoon, I only see notary a couple times. The signora is . . . was kind, courteous. I loved her. Very much."

For a moment, her lips quavered and her eyes filled with tears. Then she gave a short sharp cough and regained her self-control. Lojacono thought to himself that she really had cared for the victim. Or else she was a first-rate actress. Or perhaps she'd just experienced a moment of regret.

"When you got there, in the morning, did the signora let you in?"

"No, I have own keys. So if signora was out, or sleeping, I not wake her up."

Aragona, still standing behind the girl, asked: "And how long had you had these keys?"

The girl replied, still looking at Lojacono. Aragona's hostility was unmistakable, and she had chosen the interlocutor she preferred.

"After two weeks, the signora gave me keys. I've had ever since."

The lieutenant resumed: "And the other morning, then, you

didn't find anything strange, nothing out of place or anything like that . . ."

"No, everything like always. I not even notice about silver things, not looked on shelves, went in kitchen, made breakfast, went to look for signora, not there in bedroom, I . . ."

She stopped, gulped, and raised her hand toward her face but stopped, mid-gesture. Her bottom lip began to quiver again and a tear rolled down her cheek. She made a visible effort to regain her composure and then brought her eyes, reddened now, back to Lojacono: "Signora was good lady. Kind to me, kind to everyone. I never remember once hearing her yell, she never angry with me, with no one. I don't understand who it could be. I don't understand, how or why. I don't understand."

Aragona snorted. Lojacono glared at him and asked: "Did you ever hear Signora De Santis argue with anyone, say, on the telephone? Or did anyone ever come to the house, maybe even for just a few minutes? Did you ever see her argue with anyone, maybe with the notary?"

Mayya thought it over. Then: "When I was there, almost no one ever came. Sometimes girlfriend of signora, the baroness, lady a little bit old . . . And she talk to signora in loud voice, but signora laugh, they didn't fight. Only baroness got mad with signora, signora never got mad with baroness." After a short pause, she continued: "Notary, when home, didn't talk much. He stayed in his office, even when they ate he not talk much with signora. I never hear them arguing, no, not that."

Lojacono nodded. He could just imagine the baroness denigrating the victim's husband to her, and the way the woman must have let those criticisms slide off her back. It matched up with the information that they'd already gathered.

"And did she go out often, the signora, during the time you spent in the apartment?"

"No. Sometimes notary's office car would come get her, with driver, and she went out to buy something. She had passion for snow globes, you saw how many she had in that room. Sometimes she came back with new snow globes, and she'd look at me as if to say sorry. She couldn't resist."

At that very moment the door swung open and in came a slightly older version of the man from the photographs hanging on the wall.

He furrowed his brow and turned to Mayya: "What's going on? Who are these men?"

Aragona walked toward him: "Police. Who are you? Last name, first name."

Aragona came up to the man's chest, and the man's musculature made him look like a bodybuilder, to say nothing of the grim expression on his face, but Aragona's tone was nevertheless threatening.

The young man blinked rapidly and became cautious: "Florea, Adrian. I live here. Has something happened?"

Aragona looked up at him from his vantage point several inches below; didn't answer. Adrian shifted his weight from one foot to the other, clearly uneasy.

Lojacono reassured him: "No, nothing. We were just asking the young lady here a few questions about what happened the other day at the place she works. Do you know anything about it?"

Before the other man had a chance to reply, Aragona roared: "First I want to know where you're from, how long you've been here, and what you do for a living."

Lojacono started to tell him to calm down but, realizing that the information would come in handy anyway, he changed his mind. Florea shifted his gaze from one to the other and then, evidently accustomed to these kinds of questions, said: "I'm of Romanian nationality. I'm thirty years old, and I've been here since I was twenty. I have a small delivery truck, and I transport soft drinks for a company based in Poggioreale."

He spoke perfect, practically unaccented Italian, which

confirmed his story. Aragona stared at him, nodding, as if what the young man had told him was a confession that matched up exactly with what he'd expected. Then he said: "Well, we'll see about that. ID, please. Quickly."

The man pulled out his wallet. Lojacono sighed: he disliked Aragona's attitude, his unmistakable prejudice against the immigrant even though there was no reason to suspect him. But he wasn't the kind of cop who argued with his partner in front of outsiders. He made a mental note to give Aragona a stern talking-to once they left.

He spoke again to Mayya, who hadn't spoken up.

"Signorina, there's something I need to ask you: have the keys to the signora's and the notary's apartment always been in your possession? You didn't lose them, for instance, and then find them again, you didn't give them to someone, even if only for a few hours, a local deliveryman, the building's doorman, anyone. Please do your best to remember."

Adrian, who had walked over and was now taking off his jacket, commented sarcastically: "Of course, it's only natural. Whenever anything bad happens, if there's an immigrant nearby, well, then, it must be him. Even if all his documents check out, even if he's breaking his back to make ends meet, even if he's well liked. If there's an immigrant, then nothing could be easier: we know who did it."

Aragona took a step forward, removing his glasses with his usual flourish and raising his voice threateningly: "Listen up, you: we ask the questions and you answer them, understood? No one around here is saying that anyone did anything. What's the matter, you have a chip on your shoulder? Why don't you tell me where you were Sunday night, eh?"

Lojacono got up from the couch: "Oh, oh, now that's enough out of both of you! Florea, believe me, there's no prejudice against you. At least not on my part—" and here he gave Aragona a meaningful look; Aragona put his glasses back on.

"Let's try to gather the information we need as quickly as we can, so we can be on our way."

The man wrapped his arms around his chest, and said, slowly, articulating every word: "On Sunday night I was here, fast asleep. Because in the morning, I wake up at four, and by 4:30 I'm already out in the street, loading up cases of mineral water to transport from one end of the city to the other for pennies. And I thank God I have the work, because there are lots of people who, in order to eat, have had to do things I've never done and never would do. But they do it because they need to feed themselves and their children: and back home there's nothing to steal and no one to steal it from. And there's something else I want to say: Romanian isn't the same as gypsy. There are gypsies, and there are Romanians. I'm Romanian, and I work all day long. Doing honest work."

"Good for you, well done!" Aragona retorted sarcastically. "We have a regular statesman here, who the fuck are you, the president of Romania? All these excuses just make me laugh, that's what they do. I've seen plenty of others like you, and you all act like little lambs, I haven't done anything, I'm innocent, I'm the best person in the world, I'm a saint! Then, dig down a little, dig down a little deeper, and out comes enough shit to fill a truck twice as big as the one you drive. We'll check into it, you can count on that. And if it turns out that you or some friend of yours . . . because we know how it works with you people, one of you gets the job and another one pulls it off . . . had anything to do with what happened at the Festa home, I'll pound you black and blue. In person."

Lojacono decided that, sometime in the near future, if only in the interests of saving his life, he was going to have to force Aragona to stop going to the movies—unless it was to see cartoons or Italian comedies.

Florea blinked again, and from the height of his six feet three inches spoke down to Aragona's five feet seven inches in a suddenly halting voice: "But . . . I didn't do anything, I swear it. I went out early, because just to earn a little extra I work Sundays, too, and so I was dead tired . . . Mayya stayed home, she made me dinner . . . we were alone, just the two of us here, and . . ."

Mayya intervened, calmly. She hadn't stirred from her chair, she hadn't shifted, and she continued to stare straight ahead.

"I never let go of keys, always kept them in purse, never lost, never loaned. They are here, if you like I give them to you right now. Anyway, I'll never go back there. Never again. At night, I . . . every night I see poor signora on floor, with head in blood . . . Never again go there."

When they were alone again in the car, Lojacono turned to Aragona: "Do you mind if I ask what's come over you? You assaulted that young man as if you already knew he was guilty."

The officer shrugged: "If you only knew how many I've seen like him, down at headquarters. You have no idea the things they're capable of doing. They're a regular tribe, an assembly line: maybe he took the keys, and the girl went along with it, they made copies and then handed them off to someone else, who drove the car with two more in back, and they went over to the woman's apartment and did what they did."

Lojacono nodded: "Maybe. And maybe not. Maybe we take them and throw them in a cell, the way we always do, just because they have no one to corroborate their alibis; and then whoever actually killed the signora can relax in the warm sun, maybe on Capri or in Cortina, as the baroness says, with a cocktail in one hand, congratulating themselves for having pulled off a perfect crime, or simply for having gotten away with it. And special thanks to those two assholes Lojacono and Aragona, who were in a hurry so they picked up the first Romanian they bumped into and got him a thirty-year sentence."

Aragona thought it over: "Let's say you're right. I'm just saying theoretically, eh, because when I see these people I always ask myself where they get the money to buy a flat-screen TV, because when I bought mine I actually had to ask my dad for the cash. But let's just say you're right. These two have no alibi, in point of fact, because they say that they were alone together that night. And we don't know anything else: the notary refuses to talk to us, we can't go question his lover because we have no probable cause, and all we got out of the Baroness What-the-Fuck's-Her-Face is what a saint the signora was. Well then, can you tell me what we're supposed to do now?"

Lojacono sighed: "I don't know. We need to talk to the notary, somehow. But I don't know how. The fact is, we don't have anything else to do tonight. Let's just go home, okay, and we can sleep on it."

Aragona screeched out into traffic, without yielding or even bothering to turn his head.

XLI

On the landing, Giorgio Pisanelli ran into the Commendator Lapiana, his next-door neighbor. They exchanged a discreet *buonasera*, but Pisanelli didn't stop to chat because he was in something of a hurry; he gestured to the envelope he had tucked under his arm, as if that were a justification, and shut the door behind him.

He couldn't prevent a few drops of urine from staining his trousers. He sighed from the pain of urinating, doing his best to avoid seeing the streaks of blood in the toilet bowl. At last he flushed and watched as the swirling water carried away his worries, his anguish, and a hint of guilt.

He turned on the stereo, and Mozart's pure soul began to ring out through the dank air of the apartment. Pisanelli had a suspicion that ever since Lapiana's retirement, his neighbor had been eavesdropping on him. Pisanelli didn't want to give Lapiana the satisfaction of thinking that he was starting to talk to himself. He had things to tell Carmen that night, and he didn't want to be overheard.

He put the envelope on the table in the dining room and opened it, dumping out photographs and documents. He began putting them into order, whistling the Symphony No. 40 in G minor as he did so.

You see, darling, he said, a new one. Leonardo says that I have to rid myself of these ghosts; that I'm projecting, that I'm transferring my anxieties, the burdens weighing on my soul, onto other people. But you and I, my sweetest love, know that's not how it is.

Look at this one, for instance. Last week, well outside the boundaries of the precinct, at Piazza Dante. In the subway: she waited just a second before the train pulled in and then threw herself in front of it. It's pretty unbelievable, no one noticed a thing: a woman jumps onto the subway tracks at rush hour, thousands of people inside the train and hundreds more on the platform, because we all know very well that with trains running one every fifteen minutes you have to fight to board the cars, and no one notices a thing. Doesn't that strike you as absurd?

But there are plenty of absurd things, this time as well. Like I was saying: outside the boundaries of the precinct. In that case, you'll ask me, and I know you'll do it because you're so intelligent, how did you find out about it? And how does it fit in with the other "suicides" that are in the other room, the photographs and newspaper clippings pinned to the wall? Well, it's pretty simple. Signora Carmela Del Grosso, seventy-nine years old, lives, or better, lived on Vico Terzo Nocelle. She wouldn't have lived there much longer, because she'd received her eviction notice some time ago, and it was almost time for the marshals to come and physically eject her. Well? Is that a good reason to end it all? If everyone who received an eviction notice in this city were to jump in front of a subway, they'd definitely have to up the number of trains they run.

So, what people say to me is this: Pisane', admit it; the woman did it because she was poor, very poor, she couldn't pay her rent and she had nowhere else to go. But what I say to them, and you tell me if I'm wrong, my love: does a woman who wants to end it all, who wants to kill herself, take a train all the way to Piazza Dante? And does she take that train to go see a grocer she knows, who doesn't make her pay for the few morsels she eats, which by the way she had with her in a plastic bag that she left on the platform?

Yes, darling, you're right: exactly. A woman doesn't go all the way to Piazza Dante to jump in front of a train. She ends it all at home, and that way those assholes who want to evict her by force find themselves face-to-face with a corpse—and with their own consciences, for once. But instead Del Grosso walks miles and miles so she doesn't have to pay for . . . let's see, it's written on the report . . . two tomatoes, a bunch of basil, an apple, and a tangerine. And a box of individual cheese portions. How much, five or six euros? For a woman who wants to die?

And these idiots, just to avoid doing the paperwork, just to keep from having to ask around a little bit, file everything away in a hurry. Suicide, Pisane'. Admit it. Suicide. And why do they say that? Because there's a goddamned suicide note.

Well, take a look at it yourself, the famous suicide note: written in all caps as usual, with a firm hand (a woman, nearly eighty years old, who writes as if it came out of a computer printer!) and without misspellings, though she'd only finished fifth grade and had no books or newspapers in her home, nothing but an old TV. She wrote: "I can't take it anymore. I'm leaving this world on my own two feet. May God forgive me." But you tell me, darling, are those the words of someone who's about to kill herself?

They found the note in the grocery bag. With the cheeses. I think she leaves it at home, her suicide note. She sets it up nicely, perhaps at the center of the table. And if, on the other hand, she decides to make it all the way to Piazza Dante, she doesn't leave a note at all.

I continue to believe it, my love; in fact, I believe it more every day. There's someone, one person or several, who's killing people and making them look like suicides. It's easy for them to say—for Leonardo, Ottavia, Commissario Palma, all my colleagues, everyone who thinks I'm mental, that I'm an aging obsessive: you think I don't know that they think I'm crazy?

But I'm not crazy. You know it and I know it, my love, that I'm not crazy. And do you know how I know, that they aren't suicides? Do you know?

Of course you know, my love. You know. Because now you're where everything is known. But that's not the only reason. You know because you did it yourself. You know how it's possible to be so afraid of the mountain of pain you'll have to climb, you know how your heart can clench in your chest before a doctor's verdict.

You, my love, couldn't face it.

I saw it happen, the way your desire to go on living slowly dwindled in your eyes, little by little. I listened as your silences got longer, as your gaze lost its focus. I heard you stop talking, heard you stop listening to the vague, pointless chatter that I unleashed in your direction, in hopes of chasing off the phantom of death that was already clouding your soul.

You did want to leave this world, my love. And when you found the way and the opportunity, you didn't think about writing pointless notes as if this were a birthday party or some tearjerker. You did it and that was that. You took all the pills you could find and swallowed them one by one, methodically. I wonder how long it took you.

And you must have known from the beginning that you would suffer. That you'd wind up drowning in your own vomit, spasming in agony, my poor love, while I was who knows where, chasing some miserable crook, in search of a form of justice that doesn't exist, not on this earth.

You wanted to die, my love. You wanted me to let you go. And when, the night before it happened, you held my hand and gazed into my eyes, with all the love in the world, through your tears, I just thought you were in pain and tried to take your mind off it. Instead, with that gaze, you were simply writing your farewell note.

Signora Carmela Del Grosso, with her bag of tomatoes and cheese portions, didn't want to leave this world. You did. That's why I know, that's why I have to keep on searching, why I can't stop now, why I have to live: because, before I let this stupid cancer kill me, I have to find out who is killing these people, and why.

After all, we'll see each other afterward, my love.

And then we'll never be apart again.

XLII

Warrant Officer Francesco Romano didn't want to go back home. He had a nasty sense of foreboding.

All that day he'd tried to reach his wife, but Giorgia's phone seemed to be turned off. He wanted to tell her how sorry he was; that he wished he was dead when he remembered how violent he'd been with her; that he'd been on edge lately because of his work, because of the way he'd been kicked out of the Posillipo precinct, where he'd always hated working, come to think of it. He hated being around that crew of spineless ass-kissers, and now, to his surprise, his first few days in that strange new place were turning out to be not bad at all; he wanted to tell her how sure he was that now everything was going to turn around, that everything would go back to normal and they'd be able to laugh together the way they used to.

He'd have told her, if her damned phone hadn't been turned off, how much he still loved her. That life without her made no sense to him. That deep inside, under the brutal gorilla mask he knew he sometimes wore, there was still the same shy boy who had once surprised her by bringing her an immense bouquet of roses for her birthday, back when they were both at the university. He'd have also told her, if that fucking bitch of a recorded voice wasn't telling him every five minutes that the subscriber he wished to reach was unavailable, that not being able to have a baby wasn't the sort of thing that could break a love as strong as theirs, not a love that had lasted for so many years. That he really did wish to reach the subscriber in question, and he wanted it more than any other damned thing in the universe.

But the phone was still turned off. And now Warrant Officer Francesco Romano continued to drive around in circles like an idiot, just so he could put off going back home; he was terrified at his own fragility, at the sure knowledge that he'd go to pieces if, when he did get home, Giorgia wasn't there.

Nature, he thought to himself, is a nasty critter. Nature always surfaces, sooner or later. It surfaces when you least expect it, and it brings you face-to-face with all your worst nightmares.

In the end, he parked a little farther away, so he could stretch his legs before fetching up at his own front door. The wind didn't seem to give a damn that night had fallen, and it went on screeching the way it had been now, with rare breaks, for the past several days. Leaves, scraps of paper, plastic bags, twigs and branches: rubbish of all sorts pinwheeled through the air, serving as a kind of backdrop for Romano's darkest thoughts.

He'd thought about it a million times, about exactly what happened in moments like that: the way a red curtain seemed to descend over his eyes, about how he'd lose control of himself, as if someone or something next to him in the car were reaching over and grabbing the steering wheel, taking him wherever it wanted. In moments like that—Romano would have said if someone had managed to persuade him to discuss those matters freely—in moments like that everything seemed perfectly logical. It was the opposite of what you'd think. It wasn't absurd; instead it made perfect sense. It was terrifyingly natural to grab a man by the neck; it was the most obvious thing on earth to land a backhanded slap across his wife's face; it was normal to shake some guy back and forth until he practically passed out. It was the opposite that seemed unthinkable, in moments like that.

Romano would have asked this hypothetical interlocutor:

and do you really think you're telling it straight? Every time you tell yourself: I'd like to kill this guy, and instead you just smile? All the times you'd secretly like to take bloody bites out of the lovely face that tells you: you know, there are just times when I don't understand you, but instead you reply in a calm, gentlemanly voice, Here, let me explain. Do you think you're being honest, you fucking ass?

He found himself staring at the downstairs entrance. Then he pulled out his keys, opened it, and went in. He took the stairs, not the elevator, just to delay for a few extra minutes the likelihood of a discovery that would place him face-to-face with the consequences of being himself. He counted the steps, twenty, thirty, forty. He got his breathing under control and walked into his apartment.

Darkness. Not a sound. Outside, the wind rattled the shutters as it tried to get in. Romano, in the darkness of the front hall, listened and thought to himself that even if you stand perfectly still, in the darkness, the sound of a home changes. Now he was inside, but before there had been no one. No one at all. The apartment was empty. The subscriber he wished to reach was unavailable.

He took a deep breath and turned on the light. Nothing seemed different. Everything looked the same, the knick-knacks, the coatrack, the carpet. All the same. No smells of dinner, though. No background noise of a television left on. No clatter of pots and pans. No kiss.

He took off his overcoat and hung it up. He felt as if he were moving underwater; his movements were slow and measured. He could feel his heart pounding in his throat, in his ears; the roar was overwhelming.

The dining room. Just as he'd expected, the table wasn't set; no signs of love in the air, or anywhere else. Or actually, there *was* something: exactly what he'd imagined all day long, just below the level of his consciousness, where he'd built a detailed image frame by frame, item by item, with each unsuccessful phone call.

A sheet of paper.

Folded in half, at the center of the table. With a pen lying on top of it, a pen that had presumably been used to write something on the paper. But what? The policeman's mind started formulating theories, before the other one who lived inside him, the one who sometimes grabbed the steering wheel, started cackling madly: what the fuck are you imagining, asshole? You're imagining things because you're not brave enough to touch that sheet of paper, to pick it up and read it. And then use it to wipe your ass, maybe.

He reached out his hand and picked up the letter. A grimace, when he recognized his wife's handwriting, remembering how many times he'd made fun of her for her rounded script, like that of a teenage girl.

What if I just didn't read it? he thought. What if I crumpled it up and threw it away? Maybe everything would just go back to the way it used to be . . .

Instead, he started reading.

And he read to the very end.

Dear Francesco,

You knew it. You always knew it, that someday we'd come to this point. Because you wanted us to end up here, right at rock bottom. And last night, we finally touched it.

I've always loved you; I always thought that you'd be the man of my life, my husband, the father of my children. That we'd grow old together, hand in hand. We were kids, you know, and every time I thought about the word love, I thought of you. I knew it, that deep down inside you there was something terrible, that your nature wasn't just that of the man who knew how to be so gentle and sweet that he could move me to tears. That sometimes there was something in your eyes that scared me.

You know, a woman takes a man because she picks him over all the others. She sees his shortcomings, and she thinks she can change them, but men don't change; and a man picks a woman hoping that she'll never change, but women do change, they always do.

I've changed, and you've stayed the same. We've taken different paths, even though we stayed together.

Until last night.

You'd never hit me before. I know that you'd been tempted to do it, more than once; I saw your hands gripping the armrests of your chair, your muscles straining under your shirt, your jaw clenching. Your eyes staring into space and losing all expression. But you'd never hit me.

But last night you did.

The hand across the face is nothing. The swollen lip is nothing. The black eye is nothing.

But the fear I feel when I'm around you, now, that is something. I could never, I will never be able to live with a man I'm afraid of.

I don't know what happened, or when. Maybe it was not being able to have a child, for me. Or what happened with your job, for you. But I can clearly sense that something is broken, and there's no way to fix it.

I'm leaving you. Please don't try to find me. It would be too painful to have to say these things to your face, for you even more than for me. I don't believe that after last night we should ever see each other alone: I'm afraid of you. I don't want to erase all the wonderful memories we share, and replace them with fear.

Sorrowfully, tenderly,

Giorgia

*

Like a robot, Romano set the sheet of paper down on the table: slowly, gently, as if it were the dead body of a tiny bird that had, once and for all, stopped singing.

Then, still moving slowly, he went into the bedroom.

The bed was carefully made, the two pillows perfectly lined up, the bedspread immaculate. He lifted one corner: the sheets were freshly washed. She'd made sure to take even her smell with her.

Dear Francesco, she'd written. Dear Francesco. Not Fra', what she usually called him. Not *my love*, not *sweetheart*, the things she called him when they were alone together. No. Dear Francesco. Like a stranger, like a fucking acquaintance. Like a goddamned friend, a coworker. Dear Francesco.

And at the end, he thought, as his heart turned up the volume in his ears as he walked over to the armoire: sorrowfully and tenderly. What the fuck is that supposed to mean? You feel tenderness for a dog, for a child; and sorrow is something you feel when someone dies, isn't it? And there are no dogs here, and no one's died. We're still alive, Giorgia: so it's still possible to fix things, don't you see? That is, we could.

If we wanted to.

A glance at the top of the armoire confirmed what he suspected: the big suitcase was gone. The note, the sheets, the suitcase: three pieces of evidence add up to proof, Warrant Officer Francesco Romano.

He opened the armoire. Empty. In a corner was a little sack full of lavender, to keep away moths. He remembered the day they'd bought it, a whole day spent at Ikea: how terrible that had been.

You see, Giorgia, he thought as he shut the door to the armoire. I even spent a whole day at Ikea, just to make you happy. Doesn't that count for something? It doesn't count for shit, does it? Nothing counts for shit. The subscriber you wish to reach is unavailable, Warrant Officer Francesco Romano. Forever.

With a swift thrust of his arm he delivered a punch to the door of the armoire, demolishing it.

And finally, he began to cry.

XLIII

N*ight. Another night. The third.*
The third night after the air was full of the sea, after all that water was suspended in midair, driving into your eyes, your hair, your lungs. The night of wind and blood, of pain in the heart.

The third sleepless night, spent jerking upright at the thought of you, at the memory of your voice speaking that last word to me.

No.

The night of that sound. That absurd sound, the sound of wood cracking, that little snap, a strange wet sound. Like when you step on a big bug. And then the globe rolling away, having done its work. I wonder where the globe rolled. Maybe it was just horrified at what it had done, and it hurried to conceal itself.

Your back, and the noise. You were wrong, to turn your back on me. You shouldn't have turned your back. That was it, your fatal mistake. You died because you turned your back on me.

I read somewhere that after the first seventy-two hours, the chances of catching a murderer drop by 60 percent. They don't drop to zero, of course; but they diminish sharply.

I wonder if they'll figure it out. I wonder if they'll come for me in the end. In any case, I'll remember that snap till the end of my days, that much is certain.

No regrets. You shouldn't have turned your back on me, you shouldn't have said that word.

No.

No one turns their back. Not on me. And another thing, you don't block the path of true love. The path of true love, and someone like you who's read lots of books ought to know this, can't be blocked. Love can only be seconded, encouraged, applauded. Love is a prima donna, the star of the show: love doesn't like to be belittled, to be hidden backstage and told to wait.

And above all, you don't turn your back on love.

And then the sea. I walked, you know, after the snap. I walked and walked. I was invisible, in the midst of all that wind that turned into sea in the air.

I had some thinking to do, and I needed to be alone. If I think when I'm alone, I find the solution. I always find it.

This is the third night. I don't need to walk, tonight. Tonight I'm staying home, in peace and quiet.

And I remember the word, that no, *the word that you said to me. And your face, sad and weary. And your back.*

Who knows, maybe you wanted me to do it. Maybe you even expected it.

The third night: starting today, according to statistics, a 60 percent drop.

The third night.

Snap.

If only I could get some sleep.

XLIV

Ottavia got to the office very early. She had told Gaetano that her presence at that predawn hour was required, but the truth is that she was simply trying to spend as little time at home as possible.

Since the incident at the swimming pool, which she had in any case managed to keep her husband from finding out about, Riccardo had become more oppressive than ever. He never let her get so much as an inch away from him, he followed her everywhere, he hung on her arm, even keeping her from cooking or doing housework. When she went to the bathroom, the boy sat outside the door and slowly began banging his head against the wooden door, bong, bong, bong, one blow a second like a grandfather clock. It drove her crazy. By leaving for work hours before her son woke up, she'd spared herself the need to push him away, in his mute efforts to keep her from leaving at least for that day. And, a hidden part of her reminded her with annoyance, it had spared her Gaetano's umpteenth attempt to make love.

She said good morning to a sleepy but impeccable Guida on duty at the front door; the police officer's metamorphosis was so unmistakable that she couldn't help but ask herself once again what had turned him into a model policeman. She walked into the large group office, and the half-darkness of the ongoing battle between night and dawn was broken only by a faint glow coming from the partially closed door of the commissario's office.

She thought of some official intrusion, an unannounced inspection. When that horrible mess had happened with the confiscated drugs and her coworkers who turned out to be dealers, the inspections, from various agencies and offices, from magistrates, the police, even secret organizations accredited solely with anonymous faxes, had come thick and fast. But that was over, wasn't it?

She peered through the gap in the door. She could just glimpse a bit of desk, with a lit table lamp; a number of documents scattered across the desktop; a pen and a highlighter; three fingers resting on a sheet of paper. Not moving.

Ottavia felt her heart surge in her chest.

When she was sixteen years old, she had walked into the office of her father, a lawyer, to show him a portrait, a cartoon of him that she had drawn herself. She was good at drawing, and she had a special relationship with her father. She was the last of four children and the only girl; she and her father adored each other.

She had stopped cold in the office door, cartoon in hand, mouth frozen in a smile that would never be the same. She'd stopped cold in the door of the office, staring at the corpse of her father, cut down by a heart attack, his head sprawled over the papers on the desk, one hand lying on the desktop. She'd never drawn anything again.

She felt that twenty-five-year-old horror suddenly bloom afresh in her heart, as new as if it had been born in that instant. She let out a dry sound, something halfway between a scream and a groan, her hand over her mouth, eyes staring wide at Palma, who lay sprawled out in the exact, identical position as her father had the last time she'd seen his body, except for when she and her mother had dressed it for his final journey.

But when she let out that brief shout, the supposed corpse of the late Commissario Luigi Palma, known to his friends as Gigi, sat up with a start and gazed around in bewilderment, his eyes bloodshot and his appearance even more rumpled than usual. Draped over his forehead was a shock of hair, the mark left by the edge of his desk cut across his face like a knife wound, two days' worth of scruff on his face, a deeply wrinkled shirt. Ottavia thought that she'd never seen anything so beautiful in her life.

"I . . . what . . . who . . . oh, Ottavia, *ciao*. I'm afraid I fell asleep. What time is it, anyway?"

The woman struggled to calm her breathing and checked her watch.

"*Buongiorno*, commissario. I'm sorry to have frightened you, it's very early, it's . . . a quarter to six. You must have fallen asleep, when a person comes in to work too early . . ."

Palma yawned, rubbed his eyes, and slowly came to. Then he said: "No, I'm afraid not. Yesterday I just never went home. Luckily, since I know myself, I keep a change of clothes here in the office, underwear and a clean shirt. And everything I need to shower and shave. Sad, isn't it? This is what becomes of you, when you let your work become more important than the rest of your life."

Ottavia moved away, hesitantly.

"Well, I'll leave you to your things. I'll head back to my desk and start up the computers."

Palma stopped her with a wave of his hand: "No, no, wait a minute. Keep me company. Let me send down for something from the café across the way, the one that never closes, even at night. What'll you have, a cappuccino, a pastry?"

He already had the phone in his hand; Ottavia felt uneasy, but she took a step forward into the office.

"Just an espresso, thanks. In the morning I just drink a glass of milk at home, I'm trying to . . . well, I'm paying attention to what I eat."

Palma switched the order around, asking for a *caffe latte*, a sweet roll, and a glass of orange juice for himself.

"That's a mistake, breakfast is the most important meal of the day. And another thing, I don't mean to speak out of turn, but you don't need to lose so much as an ounce! I think you're perfect exactly as you are. Sit down, sit down right here."

Ottavia blushed at the compliment and, hating herself for it, sat down primly across the desk from him.

"Thanks, but I'm afraid that's not the case, I need to lose a few pounds. But, if you don't mind my asking, why on earth . . . that is, is there some problem, some reason that you had to stay in the office overnight?"

She didn't know what to say to him. It seemed to her that the fantasies, the thoughts she'd been entertaining for the past few days were no longer a form of escape from her unsatisfactory life, but an explicit message, branded in fire on her face; she hastened to assume a serious, professional expression.

Palma seemed happy for the chance to engage in a little conversation, and he cleared his desk of documents, restoring at least the appearance of order to his workspace.

"No, no. That is, you understand, there's always so much to do, four-fifths of the work we do is bureaucracy, and someone has to take care of it. And after all, these first weeks are crucial if we're going to persuade the police chief not to close down the precinct."

Ottavia was astonished: "But . . . I thought the danger had passed. Four new employees have been assigned, and we're now fully staffed . . ."

"I'm afraid not, at least not yet. The police chief was very clear: unless we manage to regain lost ground, especially in terms of winning back the neighborhood's trust, they'll do away with us. There are still some, both at police headquarters and in the prefecture, who would be only too happy to cannibalize this precinct's resources and redistribute them. And after all, as you no doubt know, there's a carabinieri barracks quite nearby, and so . . ."

Calabrese felt a stab of anxiety in her gut.

"What about us, is there nothing we can do?"

Palma looked up at her. With his hair still unkempt, his shirt rumpled, and the mark on his face, he looked like a little boy who had just come home from an afternoon of playing soccer in the street. The woman felt a wave of tenderness sweep over her.

"You're all doing great work, and that's the most I can ask. The guys working the field are doing fine, and you and Pisanelli are providing the kind of support I'd been hoping for. Sure, if we're able to get our hands on whoever murdered the notary's wife in a hurry, that would be a tremendous help. But I'm afraid that, unless we're able to make some significant progress by next week at the very latest, they're likely to take the case out of our hands. There are too many important people breathing down our necks on this thing."

The woman tried to offer some words of encouragement: "But the Chinaman seems—at least to me—like a good detective. Maybe what happened with the Crocodile was more than just dumb luck, in spite of what the usual gossips like to say."

Palma laughed: "The Chinaman, eh? I've heard him called that myself, old Lojacono. Truth be told, he does look Asian, with that face of his. No, no question, he really is good at what he does. I saw him work on that case, you know: all the rest of us kept looking in the wrong direction, and he was the only one who'd understood it all. If only we'd listened to him earlier . . . Oh well, we can only keep our fingers crossed and our hopes up. What about you, though? What are you doing here so early?"

Ottavia looked down at the tips of her shoes, embarrassed.

"I . . . oh, I don't know, I just couldn't sleep and instead of tossing and turning in bed, I thought I'd come in and get a few things done. I'm doing a little research for Di Nardo and

Romano on that architect, Germano Brasco. He's very power-ful, he gives work to lots of companies, he has projects all over, and I . . ."

Palma looked at her with greater interest. He'd sensed that the woman had just tried to change the topic of conversation, and that triggered his curiosity.

"Why are you having trouble sleeping? You aren't having problems with your son, by any chance?"

Ottavia raised her head, abruptly, furrowing her brow: "No, certainly not. And wait a minute . . . what do you know about my son, sir?"

The commissario raised both hands: "Forgive me. I . . . I read the personnel files, and . . . but it's none of my business, that was intrusive, I apologize."

Ottavia sighed, sadly.

"No, no. I should be the one apologizing. It's just that . . . it's really hard, you know. Sometimes other people's pity is even harder to take, that's all."

"I understand, I really do. I had a brother, older than me by a year, who had Down syndrome. He hasn't been around for a long time now, he died when he was twenty; my folks had a hard time handling him, they may have been ashamed of him. But I loved him and I spent lots and lots of time with him. When he died I was still just a kid, but it was the biggest tragedy of my life. Certainly, I wasn't his mother, so a lot of the ramifications are probably beyond me; but it's hard, and I can understand better than most."

Impulsively, Ottavia asked: "But what about you, sir, don't you have children?"

"You don't seem able to use my first name, do you? But just you watch, I'll bring you around. I'm stubborn. But no, I don't have any children. And as you can see, I don't have a wife either to worry about what's become of me if I don't come home at night. I'm divorced."

Now it was Ottavia's turn to feel awkward: "Oh, forgive me, commissario. I had no way of knowing . . ."

Palma laughed and ran a hand through his tousled hair.

"Oh, don't mention it, it's been three years. By now I'm used to it. And honestly I remember my divorce as a genuine liberation, the final months were pure hell! Being married can be worse than prison, you know."

Worse than prison, thought Ottavia. Much worse. At least there's an end date on a prison sentence, and you can count the days off on your calendar. Then she added: "No question, though, if all you do with your liberty is take advantage of it to sleep in the office, it might have been better not to get it in the first place, don't you think?"

Palma thought it over: "You know, Ottavia, a person can spend a lot of time at the office for one of two reasons: either because he doesn't have a lot else to do outside, or else because he likes being there. Likes being there more than he likes being anywhere else. Don't you think?"

Just then, in the nick of time, a very sleepy waiter from the bar appeared, carrying a tray precariously perched in one hand. He excused himself as he walked into the room.

"Oh, at last, here's our breakfast! But now I expect you to split this pastry with me. Otherwise I'll have to assume that you find me so disgusting, just having woken up, that you're trying to get out of my office as quick as you can."

And he shot her a wink.

Ottavia laughed. Well, good morning, she thought to herself.

Well, good morning, Palma thought to himself.

XLV

The bomb went off midmorning, and just at the right time.

Inside the precinct house, optimism was certainly not reigning supreme.

Ottavia hadn't looked away from her computer screen once, the tip of her tongue sticking out of her mouth between pinched lips, her brow furrowed; she was working nonstop to keep from having to think, to avoid having to reckon with herself.

Pisanelli, aside from his frequent bathroom breaks, which in any case went unremarked by the others, leafed through old case files comparing Xeroxes of the suicide notes in which a dozen or so different people had bid the world adieu.

Di Nardo and Romano were getting ready to check things out at the home of Annunziata Esposito, in Vico Secondo all'Olivella, 22. Alex watched her partner's face, which seemed carved in granite; it was devoid of all expression and had the grayish complexion of someone who hadn't got a wink of sleep. Romano hadn't uttered a single word since he'd gotten to the office at 7:30 that morning.

Aragona and Lojacono were drafting reports on the interrogations they'd conducted yesterday: the housekeeper and the doorman of the victim's apartment building. They'd reached a dead end, and they knew it. They hadn't even succeeded in ruling out any of the original conjectures: the theory that this had simply been a burglary gone wrong still held water, as did others—that the murder had been a crime of passion or property. "If only the door had been forced, at least," Aragona had said. "I'm tempted to force it myself, after the fact. That way at least," he'd added, "I could throw that Romanian clown, the housekeeper's boyfriend, in jail."

For his part, Lojacono was also distracted by worries of a more personal nature. The night before, while he was eating dinner at Letizia's trattoria and telling her how lucky he was to still be alive, having barely survived being driven around town at breakneck speed by that lunatic partner of his, he'd received a phone call from Marinella, much later at night than usual.

The girl, in tears, had told him all about a furious fight she'd had with her mother.

"That bitch," she'd said to him through her sobs, "that stupid bitch, after doing exactly as she fucking pleases, now she thinks she can lock me up, can you believe it?"

Lojacono had tried to calm her down: "Honey, don't talk like that, she's your mother. And the things she's telling you are for your own good, aren't they?"

He found it paradoxical that he of all people was being forced to defend Sonia from their daughter's accusations, which he actually endorsed wholeheartedly; but from where he was there was really nothing else he could do.

"I'm telling you, she's a bitch! I was in my bedroom, with a girlfriend of mine, and she, SHE!, was smoking a cigarette. *She* was, I wasn't! And she came busting in like a maniac, shouting at the top of her lungs, and she embarrassed me; my girlfriend was staring at me, she almost started laughing! Fuck it, I'm not a little girl anymore. You understand it and you're miles away, but she doesn't and she lives with me!"

It took Lojacono a solid fifteen minutes to get her to stop sobbing and shouting. And he'd also gotten her to promise that she would stay at home that night, though with her bedroom door closed, rather than go out and sleep at one of her friends' houses just to stick it to her mother.

When he walked back into the trattoria, Letizia had arranged for him to be served a new bowl of rigatoni; the one he'd been eating earlier had gone cold. He'd told her about the phone call, and she had tried to console him, doing her best to minimize the gravity of the situation: "From a distance, things always seem more serious than they are," she'd told him, "especially fights between two women. And as far as that goes, Marinella is right, she's a woman now, not a child anymore; parents are always the last ones to realize it."

She was wearing a light-blue angora pullover with a plunging neckline that showed off her magnificent breasts; that sweater had caused more than one quarrel among the couples dining there that night. Unconsciously, or at least less than fully consciously, she was trying to put her best qualities on display in order to capture the policeman's interest. That night, though, he seemed so caught up in his own problems that he probably wouldn't have noticed her even if she'd danced naked on his table.

Lojacono had added, disconsolately: "At least she'll talk to me. That's something, anyway. If this had happened, I don't know, six months ago, she would have had to get over it on her own, and who knows what might have happened. I'm really worried about all this."

Letizia had laughed; and then she'd said: "You know, right by here there's a high school, and sometimes groups of kids come here for lunch; I give them special deals so they can enjoy a nice hot meal when they have somewhere to be in the afternoon and don't have time to get home to eat. I watch them, and I listen to them talk. They're better than we think they are. Sweeter, more caring, real idealists. They might seem cynical to us, apathetic. But they know what they want, and they want to live good lives in a better world. With a few exceptions—fewer exceptions than among us adults—they're not criminals, they're just kids. They're just the way we were when we were their age. If I were you I wouldn't worry so much, it's perfectly normal for a young girl to fight with her mother. The stories I could tell you about what I was like when I was her age."

She had caressed his hand, on the tabletop. And he had smiled at her.

But now, after a sleepless night, the thought of Marinella, who had no one to talk to, who walked to school with a heavy heart, still filled him with sadness; and that wasn't helping him do his job. Nor was the atmosphere, which was once again grim, doing much to encourage a sense of optimism.

But, in fact, the bomb was about to explode.

The bomb stepped out of a dark-blue official car that had rolled silently into the courtyard of the precinct house.

Dressed in a dark and somewhat severe skirt suit that was, however, incapable of entirely concealing her shapely curves, she was, as usual, out of the door before the driver could hurry back to open it for her. She headed off, striding briskly, toward the front door. Guida half rose to ask her who she was but she sped past him and headed straight up the stairs, attacking the steps with urgency.

She burst into the detectives' open-plan office. Though she was petite, as always, she immediately filled the room with her presence, catching the attention of everyone there. Her dark eyes rested ever so briefly on the women, Ottavia and Alex; Alex returned her glance, with unmistakable appreciation for the fine physique of this new arrival. At last, she spotted Lojacono and said, with a strong Sardinian accent: "There you are, Lojacono. Let's go, come with me to the commissario's office, we need to talk to him."

When he saw her, Palma stood up cheerfully from his seat,

but his eyes betrayed his worry: "Dottoressa Piras, what a surprise! We talked just yesterday, I hardly expected . . ."

Laura asked him to take a seat, and sat down herself. Lojacono remained standing.

"Hi there, Palma. I thought it was best to come in person; I have news. It's safe to talk in here, right?"

"Certainly, Dottoressa. Go ahead, tell me all about it."

"I asked Lojacono to be here, because as we know he's working on the Cecilia De Santis murder case, isn't he?"

Palma nodded. "Yes, that's right, along with Corporal Aragona. Shall I ask him to come in, too?"

Piras raised one hand in warning: "Oh, good lord, no. If necessary, Lojacono can brief him. Well, where are we?"

Palma gestured to Lojacono, who began to explain: "At a dead end, I'm afraid. We've talked to everyone, the housekeeper, the doorman, the employees at the notary's firm, even a close personal friend of the victim, on an informal basis, thanks to the good offices of our colleague Pisanelli. Aside from the hypothesis of a burglary gone wrong, which can't be ruled out despite the discovery of the loot, the theory that it might all hinge on something to do with her husband's behavior, with the fact that he cheated on her constantly, still strikes me as the most plausible. But, given the fact that we can't talk to him or to the young lady . . ."

Piras nodded. "Right. All this lines up with the impression I'd developed. Well, half an hour ago I received a phone call. It was from the notary's lawyer, an old criminal specialist with quite a reputation here in town, one of the most persnickety, troublemaking, hypocritical sons of bitches I've ever had the misfortune to deal with."

Palma sighed; rich people always have the best defense lawyers. But Piras had a bomb and she was there to detonate it: "In short: the notary is willing to be questioned."

Lojacono and Palma couldn't believe their ears. What

could this mean? Laura continued, pleased with the effect her news had had on the two men.

"He unspooled a long tale of woe, and told me how he'd tried to talk his client out of it; how he'd implored him right up until the very end, for the usual reasons: the possible misunderstandings that might arise, our well-known ability to put the worst spin on things, etc. But it seems that the notary wouldn't budge: he says that he has nothing to hide, that he's innocent, that he has nothing to fear, and so on. That's not all: on a completely confidential basis, with the proviso that it doesn't constitute an admission of any kind, it seems that the guy also discussed it with his girlfriend, and she also thinks they should talk."

Lojacono was surprised: "What do you think this means, Laura? Why this sudden reversal?"

Palma replied: "It might mean that they really don't have anything to hide, but that they can't prove it. So they're hoping that, if they help us in our investigation, we can somehow prove their innocence for them."

Piras smirked: "Or else, maybe, in the past few days they've managed to arrange things so that in fact they *can* prove the two of them had nothing to do with it. It wouldn't be the first time that's happened."

Lojacono put his hands in his pockets.

"Well, still, at least we can talk to them. And we can finally lay eyes on this notorious redhead, the one our friend the notary even dared to take to the yacht club, making himself the talk of the town for a few days."

Before Piras had time to reply, Ottavia stuck her head in the door: "Commissario, Di Nardo and Romano are on their way to check out that one thing. Do you want me to tell them anything?"

"No, thanks, Ottavia. Just tell them to let me know as soon as they have something."

The magistrate caught the glance that the two of them exchanged. The woman was pretty and clearly infatuated with the commissario, and the attraction seemed to run both ways. Fun, and better that way. She wondered why she felt relieved and decided not to answer her own question. Instead, she went on: "The lawyer asked that his client not be forced to come into police headquarters or to the district attorney's office, to avoid giving the press, which is on his trail, an opportunity to embellish. And, with great sadness, he informed me that the notary doesn't want him, the lawyer, to accompany him; and I believe it, I can't even imagine how much the guy charges to be present for a police interrogation."

"Well then, Dottoressa," Palma asked, "would you prefer to question him here in the station house? Or do you want to go call on him at home?"

"No, that's exactly why I came here directly. I believe that the best thing, at this point, is for Lojacono and Aragona to go to the notary's office, and alone. My presence would seem too official and our friend might very well go back on the defensive. Instead, if he's in his own office, with the same two men who came to see him the first time, he might feel safer and decide to open up. And after all, there's still this other matter."

Lojacono and Palma exchanged a quizzical glance. Piras sighed: "You know very well that the future of this precinct is still up in the air. If there are results to be achieved, better for them to be the work of the staff of Pizzofalcone. If I'm there, it's not the same thing."

Palma answered her gratefully: "Dottoressa, that's very, very kind of you. I only hope that . . ."

Laura waved her hand dismissively: "Let's forget about that, and in any case I have the utmost faith in Lojacono, we've already discussed the matter; I'm sure that he'll pursue this case with the necessary expertise. No, if anything, try to keep Aragona from making a mess, as he seems all too inclined to do."

Lojacono walked Laura to her car, in the courtyard. As they went past, Guida snapped to attention, shooting the lieutenant a frightened glance. Piras stifled a laugh.

"I have to admit, the place has changed pretty drastically since I was last here. Are you liking it?"

Lojacono shrugged: "You know, work is work. All things considered, everyone seems pretty sharp, and they all want to do their best. But it hasn't even been a week yet."

"Same old Lojacono, optimism itself. You could at least show a little gratitude, no? But the important thing is, let's hope we can manage to keep the place open. That's still not a given, at this point."

It occurred to the lieutenant that the way she emphasized her consonants and the dimple in her chin were causing him to think thoughts that were hardly in keeping with the respect due to a prosecuting magistrate.

"We'll do our best, I promise you that. As always."

She looked up at him, her eyes dark and piercing.

"As always. And try to remember to live a little, every now and then."

She climbed into the car and waved for the driver to go. Leaving Lojacono to wonder what the hell that was supposed to mean.

XLVI

It was certainly no simple matter, to get to Vico Secondo all'Olivella, 22.

It lay at the center of a maze of narrow lanes, all identical, one perpendicular to the next, uphill and downhill; and the walk was made all the more challenging thanks to the Innocenti scaffoldings and buttresses that had proliferated in an attempt to shore up precarious buildings, though no one ever seemed to be working on them, and to the shops selling seafood and fruit and vegetables presumptuously invading the already narrow roadway, and to the chairs set out in the street to discourage cars from parking. And to the endless parade of motor scooters zipping past, expelling clouds of exhaust in the faces of children scampering from one *basso* to the next, the stray dogs sleeping in the middle of the street, and the delivery vans loading and unloading, indifferent to the growing lines of honking cars behind them.

It was like a constantly flowing eruption of molten chaos, like a huge cauldron where a dark foul-smelling liquid was bubbling incessantly away. Alex wondered how anyone could live in that place.

And she also wondered what the hell had come over Romano, who was even more taciturn, even grumpier than usual. Sitting next to him, she could detect a dull roar, like the sound of distant thunder, warning of a storm about to burst.

They were making their way down the street, checking the very infrequent numbers impressed into the walls of the

ancient apartment buildings. It was ludicrous to think of getting there by car. Every so often, like a shaft of light cutting
across the darkness, through ramshackle street doors hanging
open, they could glimpse magnificent gardens and tall plants
swaying in the wind.

When they finally came to what ought to have been number 22, they found themselves before a delivery van blocking
the entrance to a crumbling *basso* apartment at ground level.
Two men were loading the van with household belongings,
boxes, and badly dinged-up furniture. A fat, middle-aged
woman, her hair gathered up atop her head and fastened with
a large plastic clip, was watching the work and issuing instructions in dialect in a hoarse voice.

They walked over and attracted her attention. "Excuse me,
signo'," Romano asked, "is this number 22?"

The woman turned around, glaring: "That depends. Who
are you looking for?"

There could be no doubt that the woman had understood
at a glance exactly who she was dealing with. At those lati-
tudes, Alex thought, people recognized cops from a distance,
they could sniff them out. Though it was equally probable that
a team of street kids had taken off at a dead run the minute
they entered the neighborhood, shouting to all who cared to
listen: look out, here come the cops.

Romano, however, was in no mood for idle chitchat:
"Signo', it doesn't matter who we're looking for; either this is
number 22 or it isn't. And if you ask me, this *is* number 22, and
you are Signora Esposito."

Alex appreciated her partner's straight talk, and as she took
a closer look she realized that it was possible to discern, in the
woman's porcine features, buried under the literal weight of
poor nutrition and early aging, a certain resemblance to the
beautiful girl they'd met in the shuttered apartment.

The woman erupted into coarse laughter. "So what, around

here practically everyone's named Esposito. What would I
know about who you're looking for? Anyway, yes, I'm Assunta
Esposito. Who are you?"

The two men had stopped loading the truck and, though
they remained at a certain distance, they were following the
conversation. Two other individuals, a man and a woman, had
appeared at a window across the way.

The air was growing thick with hostility. Though the pocket
of her overcoat, Alex placed a hand on the bulge beneath her
belt, and the touch immediately restored her confidence.

Romano hadn't taken his eyes off the woman's face. A muscle
had started to twitch in his jaw, and Alex knew that promised
nothing good.

"Your daughter is also named Esposito, first name
Annunziata, eighteen years of age, isn't that right? If so, we need
to speak with you and your husband."

The woman's eye came to rest on the couple looking out the
window.

"Come inside."

She turned and headed indoors, displaying an enormous,
swaying backside to the two policemen. Alex wondered
whether the magical creature she'd admired just the day before
was genetically destined to turn into this, or whether it was
merely a matter of whether one took care of oneself.

Inside the ground-floor *basso*, there was all the characteris-
tic chaos of moving house. The virago let herself flop down
onto a wobbly chair that groaned beneath her weight. Romano
and Di Nardo looked around for a place to sit, but found none
and remained standing.

"What has my daughter done? Why are you looking for her?"

Di Nardo replied: "Who told you that we're looking for
her? We're looking for you, actually. My name is Di Nardo,
this is my partner Romano, and we're from the Pizzofalcone
precinct."

The woman snickered as she lit a cigarette.

"You're out of your jurisdiction, commissa'. We're in the Montecalvario precinct here."

Romano nodded.

"My, my, aren't we well informed about police jurisdictions; well, then, you must have regular interactions with the various precincts, no?"

One of the two men loading things onto the van broke in: "And what is that supposed to mean?"

Di Nardo stepped to one side, so she could keep an eye on both the woman and the two men. The men were young, overgrown boys, and one of them clearly resembled both the woman and the girl.

Without bothering to turn around, Romano asked: "Who are these two gentlemen? Why don't you introduce us, signo'? Otherwise we're liable to think they're a couple of rude oafs."

The one who had spoken took a step forward, but the woman raised a hand to stop him.

"These are my sons, commissa'. Pietro and Costanzo. Forgive them, they're cranky because I'm making them work and they aren't used to it. We're moving, as you can see."

"I'm not a commissario and neither is my partner. And where exactly are you moving?"

The woman put on a ridiculously supercilious air: "We've rented a slightly superior apartment."

Romano waved his hand to take in the surroundings.

"Hard to imagine, it's so delightful right here. And just where would that be?"

"Corso Vittorio Emanuele," the woman replied. "A building that was recently renovated."

"And I can just guess who owns the building and the company that renovated it," Di Nardo commented. "Your two boys, here, do they have jobs?"

The second man, a hulking youth with a grim expression,

replied: "Of course we have jobs. We work for the same building contractor that . . ."

The mother broke in brusquely: "Shut your trap, you idiot. Speak when you're spoken to, didn't you hear the commissario? Don't be an oaf."

Romano assumed a tense expression, which resembled a grimace of disgust: "A new job, and now you're moving to a new apartment. So many new things. Just what's going on in your family, signo'? And what about your husband, if I'm not prying, where would he be?"

The woman stared at him, eyes narrowed in the cigarette smoke.

"My husband is at work. He's an executive assistant. He goes to deposit money in the bank; he takes the wife and children of a very important man around the city, as their driver. He makes good money."

Romano lowered his voice a little: "In other words, you're making ends meet. Everyone's fine, with nice legitimate jobs, all aboveboard, you pay your taxes and everything. An apartment, plenty of money. Prosperity. And all thanks to that poor little girl. All you've had to give in exchange is your daughter."

The young man standing behind Romano muttered: "*Omm' 'e mmerda!* You piece of shit," and lunged at him. Di Nardo started to grab her gun, but Romano, without even turning around, jabbed backwards with his elbow, striking the man square in the solar plexus. He dropped to the floor, writhing and wretching; as the second young man, moving cautiously, stepped forward, Romano half turned and said: "I wouldn't try that if I were you."

The man froze, uncertain what to do next. The mother hadn't moved a muscle. She started speaking softly: "My daughter is doing fine. She's doing better than she ever has before, my daughter. She lives in a fine, beautiful apartment. She has plenty to eat, nice clothes, a television. Furniture, a kitchen, a fridge full of things to eat, that's what my daughter has. And who's ever seen so much food in the fridge? My daughter's doing fine, better than fine."

Di Nardo had pulled out her pistol, and she held it with the barrel pointing down toward the floor. Out of the corner of her eye she was watching the two young men: one was coughing and getting to his feet, rubbing his gut; the other one was standing stock-still, frozen to the spot by Romano's threat. Di Nardo had gotten the distinct impression that her partner had smiled in satisfaction after elbowing the man; she was forced to admit to herself that Romano was climbing the ranks of the very few men she respected.

He spoke to the woman, without looking in her direction: "She's doing fine, signo'? Locked in an apartment, without ever going out for a breath of fresh air, an eighteen-year-old girl? In the hands of man old enough to be her grandfather? You say she's doing fine?"

There was a moment of silence. A moped buzzed past, honking its horn in the narrow *vicolo* and drawing angry curses from a man on foot.

The woman whispered: "Well, why don't you just ask her? You'll see what my daughter has to say. It's not as if beauty lasts forever, you know. And after all, all those sluts on TV who shake their asses on command, what do you think they're doing, don't you think they date men three times their age? Children are supposed to do their bit to help out their families. Every one of them doing what they can, the best they know how. You can rest assured, my daughter is happy. And now, if you want to tell me what you need, we need to get back to moving."

Romano took a step forward and pulled his hands out of the pockets of his overcoat. Di Nardo noticed that he was clenching and unclenching his hands as if they'd gone to sleep on him.

"Why, of course, I understand. You need to get back to

moving. When are you going to get a chance like this again? In fact, I'd suggest you get as much out of this situation as you can, signo', because you're right, it's not as if beauty lasts forever. And it's hard times after that. Brutally hard times. No, we don't need anything from you. You're the one who needs to watch out. Because I swear to you, on my word of honor, signo', the minute you cross the line by so much as an inch, I'll kick your ass so hard it'll be twice the size it is now."

He'd spoken in a voice that was little more than a whisper, but every word he'd said had carried. The young man who'd gotten up from the ground had finally caught his breath; now he roared like a wild animal. Slipping his hand into his pocket he yanked out a switchblade and lunged wildly at Romano.

Alex assumed a crouch and held her pistol out at arm's length, gripping it with both hands; she aimed at the other brother, who had moved to pick a metal bar up off the ground: "Freeze! Don't you move!"

Romano whipped around with lightning speed and grabbed the first young man's hand in midair, clenching his wrist with tremendous force. The blade fell to the ground with a clatter. The entire scene had lasted less than a second. With his other hand, the policeman grabbed the young man by the throat and started to squeeze. The mother started to moan softly, like a dog whimpering. The larger of the two young men dropped the metal bar, staring at Alex's pistol as if it were the lone eye of some animal.

Alex noticed a strange light gleaming in her partner's gaze. The young man, choking, had turned faintly blue and his breath came in rattles.

Alex said, softly: "Francesco. Francesco, that's enough. That's enough."

As if awakening from a dream, Romano suddenly dropped the young man, who collapsed to the ground, desperately gulping mouthfuls of air. Romano took a deep breath; then he turned again to speak to the woman: "This one's on the house, signo'. This time I'm not going to run your boys in. It seems a pity to have all three children in prison. Even though, as far as your daughter's prison goes, you're the one who put her there. But you remember what I told you. Remember it, and remember it always. Because *I'll* remember."

And he walked out of the *basso*, followed by Alex, who still had her gun in her hand, though concealed beneath her coat.

By now, there was no one looking out of the window across the way.

They sat in silence, until Romano started the car. Then he spoke to his partner: "Listen, I should thank you. If you hadn't stopped me, I . . . You know, times have been hard for me lately, and . . ."

Alex interrupted him: "Forget about it. I didn't see a thing. And anyway, it was self-defense, that asshole attacked you twice."

Romano drove for a while in silence. Then he said: "There's nothing we can do, and you know it, right? Nothing at all. If the girl is there of her own free will, there's no way we can haul her out. She's an adult."

Di Nardo nodded.

"I know that. Still, I'd like to swing by that apartment one last time. Alone, if you don't mind; with you there, the girl might not talk. With me, seeing as I'm a woman, she just might open up."

Romano thought it over. Then he said: "Sure. Go ahead. But be careful, don't go overboard. This has to be unofficial; if the girl files a complaint, you'll be in serious trouble. Remember: you have a record, same as all of us."

"Right. Same as all of us. But I want her to tell me to my face, that she wants to live there, locked in like that. Otherwise, I can't accept it."

They sat a little while longer in silence, while outside the car the city and the wind howled dissonantly. Then Romano said: "Di Nardo, you're all right. It's an honor to work with you."

Alex smiled, without turning around.

XLVII

When they got to the notary's office, they immediately noticed the atmosphere had changed since the last time they'd been there.

At the front door there were six or seven people lined up with various notifications in hand, awaiting their respective turns; behind a bulletproof glass teller window sat Imma Arace; she was handling promissory notes, counting money, and stamping the documents to indicate they'd been paid. Beyond the glass door a great many other customers could be seen, moving from one desk to the next, while the employees worked busily. The notary was nowhere in sight.

The young woman behind the glass teller window looked up and met the two policemen's gazes; she furrowed her brow, looked back into the inner office, then pursed her lips and told the customer she was serving that he'd have to wait a moment. She stepped out of the booth, closing the door behind her with a bunch of keys that she carried with her, and walked over to the two men: "Hello, we were expecting you. We'd been told you were coming. Come with me, the notary is busy but he'll see you as soon as he can."

She led them to the small room where they'd earlier interviewed the office employees. They had to go through the large open-plan office to get there, and noticed the vaguely hostile glances of the other three employees, all of whom were busy with clients. Suddenly Aragona elbowed Lojacono and whispered: "Get *her*."

He was referring to Rea, the senior employee, who had undergone a genuine metamorphosis: the person she had once been, her hair streaked with gray, lips pursed, wrinkles, and tiny eyes behind Coke-bottle lenses, had been replaced by a very different woman, her hair, fresh from the hairdresser's, tinted a deep mahogany red, her lips expertly redesigned with lipstick, a thick layer of foundation covering up her wrinkles. She had, presumably, replaced her eyeglasses with contact lenses. Aragona took off his own glasses with his usual studied slowness and met the woman's malevolent gaze; then he observed to Lojacono, loud enough to be overheard: "She's convinced she's all hot now, but she's more of a double-bagger than she used to be."

The phrase was immediately followed by a smile and a wink in Marina's direction; the cute blonde was registering a document on the computer, and she returned the smile with some embarrassment.

Lojacono waved hello to De Lucia, the employee who had occasionally worked as the victim's driver.

It occurred to him that, while they were waiting, they could use the time to ask a couple more questions that he'd thought of during the earlier sessions; so he asked Arace if she could arrange for them to talk to Rea and De Lucia as soon as they were free.

The young woman nodded, and hurried away: she must have been given instructions to that effect.

The first person to come see them was in fact De Lucia; he was unmistakably upset. Lojacono decided that the notary and his lawyer must have warned his employees not to reveal any information, and so he was forceful, right from the start: "Listen, De Lucia, while we're waiting to see the notary, we're going to ask you a few things, you and your coworker. You understand, I'm sure, that we'd rather do it this way than have you picked up and brought in to the station house. In a way, it's better for you, too, isn't it?"

The little man adjusted his comb-over, with a trembling hand: "Better for us, too, certainly, lieutenant. Ask away."

Aragona rolled his eyes; he'd forgotten about the man's unfortunate habit of starting his reply by repeating the last few words uttered by his questioner.

"You sometimes worked as a driver for the signora, is that right?"

"I sometimes worked as a driver for the signora, yes. With the notary's car; when she asked to be driven somewhere, he'd always send me to take her where she wanted to go."

"Do you remember, recently, whether you took her somewhere in particular, somewhere different from usual? I don't know, a clothing store she'd never been to, a doctor's office . . ."

The man searched his memory: "A clothing store, a doctor's office? No, I really don't think so. The signora always went to the same places, she was a creature of habit. The various charitable agencies, the store that sold snow globes on Via Duomo, occasionally to visit her friend, the Baroness Ruffolo. A couple of times to the yacht club, but she hadn't gone there in months. So just those few places, really."

Lojacono nodded.

"And the last time you took her somewhere, when was that?"

"When was that? About ten days ago, I think. In the last week, the notary never sent me to pick up the signora."

"And did she ever seem nervous or tense? Worried about anything?"

The man responded in the negative: "Worried about anything, no, she was always cheerful and courteous. The signora, as I told you last time, was a saint. She never lost her temper, she was always in a good mood. I never saw her angry. Poor signora."

Lojacono sighed: all he needed was for the man to burst into tears right in front of him. He thanked him, told him he could go, and asked him to send his colleague in next.

The woman's metamorphosis wasn't limited to her face; as the two policemen had noticed when they'd first entered the office, Rea had tried everything imaginable and then some with the rest of her body. A tight-fitting dress, sexy in its intentions and ridiculous in its effects, put a number of stomach rolls on brutal display and jammed her thighs together as if in a vise, forcing the woman to walk like a geisha, a gait that was only aggravated by a pair of vertiginous stilettos. The overall effect really was grotesque.

Lojacono did his best to keep a straight face, while Aragona covered up an involuntary burst of laughter with a fake cough that fooled no one. The woman shot him a venomous glare and said: "You can just spare me the commentary, I've already got my colleagues laughing at me behind my back all day long. But I don't give a damn about what you all think; I've been concealing my femininity for too long. The time has come to flaunt it."

Lojacono threw open his arms: "Madam, you are certainly free to do whatever you think best. I just wanted to ask a few simple questions about your position in the office."

Rea stiffened with pride: "I'm the senior employee here, and the notary's most trusted collaborator. My professional standing here is above all suspicion, and I won't allow you to . . ."

The lieutenant held up a hand: "Good lord, no! No one is here to dispute that. It's just that, as the notary's closest collaborator, I thought you might be able to tell me something about the work he does here in the office and elsewhere. For example . . ."

The woman hissed back: "Do you really think that I'd be so unprofessional as to tell you things about the workings of this office without the notary's knowledge? As far as I'm concerned, the notary's best interests come before anything else, even my own reputation!"

Lojacono tried to calm her down: "No, signora, there must be some misunderstanding. I was just wondering whether, for instance, you had access to the notary's computer, if his work ever takes him outside his office, and, if so, who, if anyone, might accompany him. That's all."

Rea looked at him, narrowing her eyes still more. She was the very picture of suspicion.

"Obviously De Lucia and I, since we've been here the longest, have full access to all the office's files, both digital and hard copy. Lanza, the most recent hire, is in charge of what's kept online. She's not very bright, all she understands is the Web; the office's important work happens elsewhere and she has no access to it."

Aragona, hearing a woman who'd shown signs of finding him charming described as not very bright, took offense.

"Oh, is that so? And just what would the office's important work be, if I might ask?"

The woman replied with distaste, not even bothering to turn to look at him: "Probate cases are our important work; these involve documents drawn up by hand and recorded in a special ledger, accompanied by the year, date, and time at which they've been received. Mostly wills, but that's not all, and they must all be drawn up in the notary's presence. I'm in charge of them, the only one; and that's because I'm the most trusted employee in this office."

Lojacono looked interested: "And how does that work? Does the notary meet with the clients and then call you to transcribe the document or deed?"

Rea snorted: "That's not all, of course. Sometimes he goes out to see them; some of them are terminally ill, terribly old people. And I'm the employee he takes with him when he does. Just the two of us, me and him."

The last phrase was uttered in a saccharine tone. Aragona shot Lojacono a nauseated glare. The lieutenant added:

"Which means that this ledger is really just a sort of notebook that contains a chronological list of these documents, is that correct?"

The woman nodded gravely, making the large, showy earrings she wore clink.

"That's right. Now, if you don't mind, I need to get back to my work before they manage to screw things up in there. I'll make arrangements for someone to call you, as soon as the notary is free."

Aragona watched her leave the room. Then he said to Lojacono: "Loja', believe me, that woman would be truly evil if she weren't such an idiot. Believe me, now that his wife is dead, she's convinced that the notary is going to take her as a replacement. *Mamma mia*, she's ugly as sin!"

The lieutenant nodded in agreement: "That is exactly what she seems to believe. She might have some information that could prove useful to us, but I doubt she'd ever hand it over if she thought that it might harm her beloved notary."

A few minutes later, De Lucia stuck his head in the door: "The notary is ready to see you now, if you'd like to come with me."

XLVIII

How different he looked, the notary Arturo Festa. How radically he had changed, in just a few hours.

The cheerful, athletic, youthful, suntanned, optimistic gentleman they'd seen enter his office at the end of an obviously enjoyable weekend had been replaced by an old man, wounded and heartbroken, whose spirit seemed to have been shattered. When he walked into the large office where the professional was waiting to speak to them, Lojacono had the impression that nothing would ever be the same for that man.

Not that that kept Lojacono from suspecting the notary of being the killer; in his professional experience he'd had plenty, indeed far too many, opportunities to see how murderers could sometimes be enormously damaged by the crimes they themselves had committed; and to see the way in which the victims, as they ventured into the darkness from which there was no return, often took with them a piece of the soul of the person who had sent them there, a person who was then left to struggle through life with a burden of remorse.

Festa was a wreck. His face had a grayish complexion and was marked by dark circles under his eyes; a network of wrinkles creased his features in a way that hadn't been evident just a few days earlier. Or they might very well have just appeared. His hair was tousled, his shirt collar hung open over a loosely knotted necktie; his jacket was rumpled, as if he'd picked it at random from the closet and then worn it uninterruptedly for days at a time.

When his eyes met Lojacono's, the notary grimaced sadly.

"Hello, lieutenant. Please, make yourself comfortable, and thank you for agreeing to come here, for the sake of my reputation. I certainly appreciate the kindness of Dottoressa Piras, who spared me a disagreeable trip to police headquarters. Those buzzards in the press are trying to crucify me; they can't wait to name me as the 'prime suspect.'" He ran a trembling hand over his face: "Please forgive me, I haven't slept in three days. I just can't get to sleep. I'm afraid . . . I'm afraid of the dreams that will come, so I just don't sleep. And I'm especially afraid of that moment, you know, the moment when you wake up and you can't remember what's happened. And then everything rushes back into your mind. The awareness overwhelms you, and you feel all the grief, the same sensations all over again."

Aragona took off his glasses, in what was perhaps meant as a show of solidarity. Lojacono asked: "Why did you ask to meet us, Notary Festa? Why did you change your mind?"

Festa stared at him, as if he hadn't understood the question. Then he picked up the phone on his desk and asked: "Would you like some coffee? I need some coffee. For the past three days I've been living on coffee."

Lojacono and Aragona nodded, and he whispered the order into the receiver. Then he answered: "It occurred to me, quite simply, that it wasn't me. That I . . . I didn't do it, this terrible thing. And that, unfortunately, I don't have any way to prove that fact and so, if I told you the way things really are, you yourselves might be able to help me out of this absurd situation. And then . . ."

Aragona leaned in: "And then?"

"And then, I spoke to . . . to the person who was with me, the person that at first I didn't want to involve in this matter. And she told me that I should, in fact, that I *had* to speak with you. And tell you her name. Because, as I told you, we were together, she and I; we were together the whole time."

Rea came in, carrying a tray with three demitasse cups and a bowl of sugar. She was perched precariously on a pair of ultra-high heels, and turned a smile that was meant to be seductive on the notary; he didn't even bother to glance in her direction. The notary said to her: "*Grazie*, Lina, we'll add the sugar. You can go."

The woman left the room, with a vaguely offended air. Aragona watched her go, in disgust. Lojacono asked: "So that means you confirm the version of events you furnished Monday morning, is that right?"

The notary nodded, with conviction: "Of course I do, because it's the truth. I left for Sorrento Saturday morning, after telling poor Cecilia that I was going to Capri for a conference, knowing perfectly well that she'd never come with me, given her peculiar abhorrence of that sort of, shall we say, formal occasion. I swung by and picked up this person and then we went to the villa made available to me by my friends, who gave me the keys. They're wealthy Canadian businessmen, and they come here very rarely. We didn't leave the place until Monday morning, when we came back to town."

Aragona, who was taking copious notes, asked: "Later, perhaps you can give us the names of these friends of yours and the address of the villa. Now, what is the name of this person?"

They'd come to a crucial point. The notary hesitated again, took a sip of his coffee, sighed, and said: "Iolanda Russo."

Lojacono nodded: "And that would be the person who you've been seeing regularly, isn't that right, Notary Festa? The one who also recently accompanied you to a public event at a well-known yacht club in this city, correct?"

A glint of anger showed in Festa's eyes, but only for a moment. Sadness soon replaced it: "Baroness Ruffolo, eh? That witch must be having the time of her life thanks to this mess. She's always hated me, as have all the other self-satisfied degenerates who constitute the upper crust of this city. Well, at least she never concealed her feelings; I have to give her that."

Lojacono neither confirmed nor denied: "In any case, she was the young lady you took to the yacht club on that occasion, is that correct?"

Festa nodded, in despair.

"Yes. It was her. Lieutenant, I was born poor. My family comes from Basilicata, from the countryside; my parents were farmers. They broke their backs to send me to school, and there was never an instant, never a single instant, when it wasn't crystal clear to me that study and a profession were my only shot at not winding up like my father, who died of a heart attack one night, out in the rain. And my chances were bound up with Cecilia."

Aragona had stopped writing, his pen in midair, uncertain whether he should take this down. Lojacono gestured imperceptibly for him to go on writing.

"She wasn't beautiful. But she gave me everything I needed, and I don't mean money or connections, though she certainly had those: she gave me a sense of serenity. With her, I could focus on improving myself, on becoming the best. I know very well the kind of thing that Anna Ruffolo, or whoever it was that said it in her stead, must have told you: that my career is based on Cecilia's friendships. But that's not true, or it was only true at the beginning. My career is based on the fact that I'm good at what I do. Very good. And in this profession, you get work only if you're very good and very discreet."

Lojacono reflected for a moment: "Do you think you have enemies, Notary Festa? Someone who might . . ."

Festa interrupted him.

"No. I've thought it over, you know. I've thought it over thoroughly, in part because of this thing with the doors . . . Cecilia would never have opened the door to a stranger. But no one, no one I work with, would have had any reason to do such a thing. People entrust themselves to a notary and I safeguard their interests. I'm not a magistrate, I'm not even a lawyer. I never clash with my clients or with anyone else's. I can't use my job to hurt anyone."

Aragona asked: "You just said: Cecilia would never have opened the door to a stranger. In that case, what is that you think happened? Did someone else have the keys?"

Lojacono thought to himself that his partner couldn't seem to abandon Mayya's boyfriend, the Romanian who could so easily have taken the young woman's keys, as a lead. The notary replied: "Certainly, that's a possibility. All I know is that Cecilia was in a peaceful state of mind that night. I spoke to her around ten o'clock, and . . . oh, my God . . ."

His voice had dwindled away, and the two policemen both thought he was about to burst into tears; instead, the notary put his face in his hands and managed to compose himself: "I lied to her. It's what I always did, it had become a habit. I just lied to her. And she pretended to believe me, or maybe she actually did believe me, who can say. She was intelligent, you know; very intelligent. She may have decided to accept the fact that I was lying to her; maybe she knew, or she hoped, that I'd never leave her. And she listened to my lies as if they were the truth." He turned his weary gaze to Lojacono: "I told her that I was on Capri, that everything was fine. That she was right not to come, and that I was bored out of my mind."

"And what did the signora say to you?"

"That she was all right, that she'd go to bed soon, that she was already in her dressing gown. That a storm was blowing, and so she'd shut all the windows and blinds; that was something she didn't normally do, but the wind frightened her. That the concierge had repaired one of the shutters, I don't remember which. Lord forgive me, I was in a hurry and I didn't want to chitchat; if I'd known . . . if I'd only been able to imagine . . . but I wanted to break off the conversation, in part because the person who was with me . . . Iolanda . . . didn't like it when I spent much time doing anything that took me away from her. Anyway, she was about to go to bed; if she'd been expecting someone she certainly would have told me so."

"And so?" asked Aragona.

"And so, it was either someone she knew so well that she was willing to open the door to them in a dressing gown, something that she would never have done for just anybody, or else it was someone who had a set of keys and opened the door himself, and she happened upon him. One of the two, I'm sure of it."

Lojacono broke in: "Notary Festa, I'm sorry to have to ask you this question, but it's necessary. What is the nature of your relationship with Signorina Russo? Do you two have any . . . plans, any thoughts for the future? And if so, was your wife aware of them, in your opinion?"

Lojacono's question was met with silence. The notary gazed at his fingertips, pensively chewing on his lower lip. He was quiet for so long that the lieutenant began to doubt that Festa ever actually intended to answer. But then he said: "Many times, in the past, I've had . . . I've had affairs, I guess you'd say. Including with some of Cecilia's girlfriends, which I'm not proud of. I just can't seem to control myself. But this time things are different. Iolanda . . . is a very unusual woman, she refuses to be hidden, she wants to have it all. And once this became clear to me, it was already too late. And anyway, things between us . . . Lieutenant, our relationship can longer be undone, I can't leave her. I'd have told Cecilia eventually. Iolanda kept pushing me, and I was about to settle things."

"And you were never apart, in those two days? The young lady never left you alone?"

Festa blinked rapidly, as if an absurd theory had suddenly formed in his mind for the very first time.

"Who, Iolanda? But . . . but what on earth are you thinking, no! No! We were together the whole time, we didn't even go out to eat, we brought everything we would need with us."

Lojacono and Aragona exchanged a glance. The situation was clear, and they knew that it was based on words that couldn't be corroborated. And that the notary therefore remained the prime suspect, together with Signorina Iolanda Russo: the only ones who had any reason to want to ensure that Signora Cecilia De Santis, married name Festa, would leave the notary in question a free and very wealthy man.

Following that train of thought, Lojacono asked: "Notary Festa, your financial situation . . . the signora, in other words . . ."

"I expected that question. Everything was in her name. For tax purposes, everything we owned was in my wife's name."

This only confirmed what Lojacono had already guessed.

There remained one more thing to clear up; but he needed to proceed cautiously, because he still hadn't received the official report from the IT office and he didn't want to risk putting the notary on the defensive.

"We've heard mention of a trip that you were planning to take with your wife. A trip to a distant destination, about which you inquired from an online travel agency. What can you tell me about that?"

The notary's expression grew baffled: "My wife had asked me, some time ago, if we could take a trip. Maybe to reestablish some kind of equilibrium between us. But I had told her that right now, with a couple of major work issues to be settled, I couldn't think of going anywhere. I might have made some inquiries, but I don't remember ever even considering actually leaving."

It was clear to Aragona and Lojacono that they wouldn't get any more information from the notary about that matter. Once they had the official report, if it seemed worthwhile, they'd dig deeper.

They asked the notary for details on his mistress, including the young lady's address and phone number so they could make an appointment to speak to her. And they asked the notary also to aid them in obtaining all the information necessary for pursuing their investigation.

"Why, of course, anything at all," Festa replied, without hesitation. "Do you think I haven't figured it out by now? You're my only hope."

XLIX

A lex Di Nardo was concealed in a corner, hidden behind an entranceway.

In spite of the wind, whose fury had in any case subsided, the collar of her coat turned up and wearing a pair of dark sunglasses—which made her look something like a secret agent or private eye in a B movie, the kind her colleague Aragona was surely obsessed with—she stood there patiently, waiting, her eyes turned upward.

Thus decked out, she was keeping an eye on that grim old woman who sat sentinel at her window, missing nothing that moved along the stretch of street she could see from her vantage point.

Certainly, she could have just thrown caution to the winds and walked in, ignoring Guardascione perched up there in her armchair tatting away, one eye on her work, finishing one last doily that, as far as she know, might very well be destined for the toilet seat—if, that is, there wasn't one there already; she was probably tormenting her caregiver as well, calling her "slut" and observing her as well, with that unfriendly eye.

But, for some unknown reason, Alex didn't want to give the old woman the satisfaction of having identified a crime in progress, and knowing that she'd seen more clearly than most; it would have struck her as tantamount to rewarding behavior that, in some way, she saw as sleazy. And then, ever since she'd first seen Nunzia Esposito's eyes, those desperate eyes, the eyes of a terrified animal, eyes that clashed so sharply with her plastic

smile, and since she'd sensed on her skin how filthy the architect was, how miserably petty the mother of this alleged prisoner was, she'd developed a very clear idea of who the good
guys and the bad guys in this case really were.

As she was looking up and wondering, for the umpteenth
time, when the damned old hag would be forced to give in to
any conceivable physical need, her mind wandered to
Francesco Romano. She'd heard from a colleague in the
Posillipo precinct that he was someone who couldn't control
his rage; and that was why the commissario had gotten rid of
him the moment he had the chance. And yet, in the situation
she'd just witnessed, she hardly felt she could blame him. She
herself had felt a certain itch in her trigger finger: but that was
nothing new. Certainly, she thought, snickering inwardly, the
two of them made a fine pair, though better suited to a movie
like *Lethal Weapon* than to the streets of a city like this one.

Still, she was grateful to him for having understood her
request to go talk to the girl alone. To try to understand something more, to fully grasp the situation. She felt certain that the
girl was being held in that apartment against her will. If Alex
managed to discover the nature of that captivity, if she
received the slightest appeal for help, she would free her.
She'd find a way.

At last, Guardascione was gone; the event was so long-
awaited that in the end it was unexpected, and Alex very nearly
missed her brief absence entirely; still, she managed to slip rapidly through the front door of Nunzia's building. She'd made
it past the first obstacle.

She climbed the stairs and knocked at the door. After a few
seconds, she heard the girl's voice: "Who is it?"

"It's me. Al . . . Officer Di Nardo. But I'm not here on official business. Can I come in?"

There was a long silence. Alex shot an nervous glance at the
door of the real estate agency, standing just ajar; she wouldn't

have any way of justifying her visit in the face of the employee's inevitable curiosity.

From behind the door the girl asked: "Well, what do you want? Did you forget something last time you were here?"

As expected, Nunzia was stalling. She probably couldn't open the door because she had no key. But Alex had to make sure of it.

"No, I haven't forgotten anything. I just wanted to talk to you for a moment."

Another pause. Then the girl's voice, trembling with uncertainty: "I'd . . . I'd prefer not to let you in, really. Can't you tell me whatever you want from there?"

Alex felt pity for Nunzia.

"You're locked in, aren't you? You're locked in. You couldn't let me in even if you wanted to. I know. I know your situation. We've been to see your folks, we saw everything. You're locked in, I know it. And if that's the case, I can help you, you understand?"

The policewoman heard what she thought was a sigh, or perhaps a sob. When she was quite certain she'd get no reply, she heard the voice again: "Are you alone? The other one, the man, is he with you now, out there?"

Alex answered in haste: "No, no. I'm alone. I told you, this isn't an official visit. I want to understand. I just want to understand."

"I just want to understand . . ." — under her breath, as if trying to justify something to herself.

Then, to the policewoman's immense surprise, she heard the bolt moving and the door swung open.

The place looked different that it had the last time; it was clear that she wasn't expecting visitors. A gossip and fashion magazine lay open on the sofa, a bag of potato chips sat on the coffee table, with a few crumbs sprinkling the floor, as did a glass half-full of some dark liquid, possibly Coca-Cola; soothing jazz from the Sixties floated out over the apartment from loud-speakers concealed in the drop ceiling.

The girl wore a light dressing gown tied with a sash at the waist. She was barefoot, her hair was ruffled, and she had no makeup on. And she was stunning. She looked exactly as old as she was. Alex was appalled at the resemblance to her mother, and at the same time, the incredible gap that separated the girl from the horrible creature she'd met that morning.

The two women eyed each other up close. Even without shoes, Nunzia was taller than Alex. Now that she was face-to-face with her, the policewoman discovered that she'd been so positive the girl would never open the door that she had no idea what to say.

"Forgive me for coming to see you. I didn't mean to intrude. It's just that . . . I thought that . . ."

The girl waved a hand in the air.

"That's his music. I don't get it, I like Tiziano Ferro. But all he has is this music here, so it's this or nothing."

She took a few steps, moving with the melody, and grace-fully sat down on the couch, tucking her legs up beneath her and reaching out for a potato chip.

Alex, on the other hand, felt uncomfortable. She felt as if she'd been caught off-balance, and she wondered what she was doing there. The person sitting in front of her was certainly no prisoner.

"Forgive me. I shouldn't have come. I'm sorry. I really thought . . ."

Nunzia gave her a serious look.

"I know exactly what you thought. What, did you assume that I wouldn't know? That's what I told him, when I called him. And he told me that he'd make sure to be here. You thought I wasn't allowed out of here. That I was in some sort of prison. Isn't that right?"

Alex nodded. Nunzia went on: "You know it better than me,

284 · MAURIZIO DE GIOVANNI

signo'. Sometimes things seem to work one way, but instead they work in a different way. But then there are times when they're exactly what they seem. It's true, you know: I can't go out."

Di Nardo didn't understand: was the girl pulling her leg? She looked at the door, and said: "But . . . you just opened the door and let me in!"

Instead of answering, Nunzia stood up and peeped out through the curtain.

"There she is. She's always there, motionless by the window. It's just me and her, the old woman. We look at each other, she looks at me and I look at her. Sometimes she falls asleep with her mouth wide open, and her dentures fall out. She's disgusting, inside and out."

She turned to look at Alex: "He's out of his mind, you know. One time, a few months ago, he drove past the *basso* where we live. An enormous car, he was going to take a look at an old building he'd bought in the neighborhood, he says he wants to turn it into a residential hotel, very deluxe. If you ask me, it's idiotic; who would come to stay in a fine hotel in that shitty part of town?"

She sat back down and ate another potato chip.

"I have to be careful with these, otherwise I'll wind up worse than my mother; you've seen her, haven't you?"

She giggled, one hand over her mouth. Alex thought to herself that this was the most beautiful woman she'd ever seen.

"Anyway, he was lost, he didn't know his way around. He stops, he leans out the window to ask directions. I was standing outside our downstairs door, waiting for a girlfriend of mine. He says that from the minute he saw me, he lost it. He went completely crazy. After that, he came back every day: once on foot, once by taxi, once he had someone else drive him."

Alex had sat down in an armchair.

"What about you? What did you think of him?"

"What was I supposed to think about him, men had been

doing the same thing to me for two years already. My brothers too, for that matter. But he was kind: he brought gifts, to me and to my family. Lots and lots of gifts. One time a pair of earrings, another time a bracelet. Then, one day, he asked my father if I could travel with him, for a couple of days, he had to go up north to visit a construction site. And my father said: fine, go ahead."

Alex listened, entranced. The girl's tone of voice was nonchalant, as if she were talking about the weather.

"I thought he was going to have a heart attack, he's old. But he didn't. Still, the first time he saw me without my clothes, his eyes came that close to bugging right out of his head."

She giggled again, as if she'd just told a funny joke. Then, as if an odd idea had occurred to her, she stood up, lithe and quick, and pulled open her dressing gown. Underneath, she was naked.

"Now, you're a woman, you tell me the truth: how do I look to you?"

Di Nardo snapped her mouth shut and gulped. Nunzia's body was perfect, with firm but full breasts, a flat belly, long thighs, and a triangle of Venus that was just barely visible.

"You're stunning. Stunning."

The girl laughed, and refastened her dressing gown with a pirouette.

"I know. He tells me so all the time. That's why he doesn't want me to go out. He's jealous. He doesn't want anyone else to see me, because then men will start buzzing around here worse than horseflies around shit. He asked me, and I made him a promise. If you ask me, he's afraid someone will go tell his wife about me. I saw her one time, I went over to where he lives because I was curious: *mamma mia!* She's three years younger than he is, but she looks way older."

"But if you know that he's married . . . why are you with him?"

Nunzia turned serious. Her voice dropped to just over a whisper.

"Have you looked around at this place? And did you see where I used to live? Have you seen my mother? And the *vicolo*, did you see that? What kind of question is that?"

"But he's old, and you're . . . you're so . . . I mean, you're young!"

"So what? All I care about is the apartment and the way he treats me. What, do you think I'd be better off with a young man who'll slap me around from dawn till dusk, who'll knock me up ten times and make me live in a rat-infested ground-floor hovel? He's kind, he's courteous, and he gives me presents all the time. And he even helped out my family; I'm happy for them. And then, as far as that other thing goes, it lasts a couple of minutes and then he falls asleep. I hardly even notice it's happening, I just try to think about something else. It strikes me as a pretty fair price for all this, no?"

Alex couldn't believe her ears.

"But what about freedom? Staying locked up in here all the time, not being able to go out. Don't you miss fresh air?"

Nunzia thought it over: "Sometimes, actually, yes I do. But it's just a matter of time. You know what I want to do? What my mother recommended."

"What's that?"

"I want him to put this apartment in my name. For now it's a rental, but I want to get him to buy it and put it in my name. Then I'll open a checking account, and I'll tell him to put some money in it for me. And then, as we say where I come from, the pig's in my hands. In the meantime, though, I need to keep him happy, I have to give him what he wants. And if he wants me to stay home because he's jealous and he's afraid of his wife, that's fine with me, because in here I have a TV, a radio, and plenty of food. What else do I need?"

"I understand now. Sorry, I didn't get it the first time I

came, but now I do. The other time, when I was here with my partner, it seemed to us that you were afraid. I mean, there was terror in your eyes. And we thought you needed help. That's all."

"And you were right, no doubt about it, I was afraid, sure I was. I was afraid that he might decide that the whole thing was too risky, the police had even come thanks to that old bag of shit who can't mind her own business. And that he'd decide to take me back to that hovel of a *basso*, back to the horrible life I was living before. That's what I was afraid of. You should have seen him, the way he was trembling after you left, that partner of yours really scared him. But then I talked him out of it. I know exactly how to change his mind."

She giggled with one hand in front of her mouth, once more the young girl she actually was.

Alex stood up suddenly. All she wanted now was to get out of there.

"Well, good, then, I'd better get going. I'll leave you my card, in case you . . . well, if you need anything, just reach out. My cell number's on it too."

Nunzia stood up from the sofa with a graceful motion, went over to Alex, and placed a gentle kiss on her lips.

"Come see me sometime, if you feel like it. He's hardly ever here, and only ever during the daytime. Maybe bring me a pizza when you come; I love pizza."

L

Something.

Something was rattling around in Lojacono's mind, like an item not lashed down on the deck of a ship in open waters. It lay too far beneath the surface of his consciousness to be glimpsed, but it was still close enough to give him a sense of disorder, of irritation.

Something he'd heard? Something he'd seen? Something someone had said to him, or failed to say?

He did his best to focus as he pushed the pasta around in the bowl in front of him. Aragona looked at him from time to time but went on chatting. They'd stopped at a trattoria to have lunch before their appointment with the mysterious CPA Iolanda Russo, the notary's lover and a possible further source of information about the murder of Signora Cecilia.

The corporal was saying: ". . . so if they really want to organize a nice little robbery, they know how, you know. They're not just muggers, sometimes they can pull off capers that would make Italian professionals blush, I can assure you. So it's entirely possible that they went there with copies of the keys, they started scooping up silver from the first two rooms, then the signora showed up and everything went to hell in a handbasket."

Lojacono shot back promptly: "So you're saying they organize a job so well, with copies of the keys and so on, but it never occurs to them that on a Sunday night she'd be at home and getting ready to go to bed? And that they'd pick a time like that, late evening, when they could just as easily have used the keys to get in in the middle of the night, when they'd have no trouble sneaking around, no one to see or hear them, with the storm that was raging? No, I can't see it."

Aragona, who was truly fond of the idea of a burglary, was clearly annoyed by the lieutenant's objections, to which he had no good response: "Oh well, yeah, probably they were druggies, weirdos, or drunks. Those guys get tanked up before going out on a job, and then they can't even see straight. They saw the woman, grabbed the first thing that came to hand, one of those glass balls, and killed her with it. And after all, the stolen silver is the only concrete piece of evidence that we have, isn't it?"

That, Lojacono was forced to admit, was true. Aside from the something that kept rattling around in his head, the something he couldn't quite grasp.

At least, not yet.

Russo's office was in the town's business district, the only part of the city, and it was a small one, that hinted at the fact that it was still a major financial hub. It was a large building, with an immense lobby that was, in the early afternoon, more or less empty.

In the absence of a doorman, a bronze plaque, lined up alongside a dozen others just like it, told them the floor and room number of their destination.

The woman answered the door herself: "*Buonasera*. Please, come this way. I asked you to come by at this time of day because my employees are on their lunch break; better to be discreet."

Aragona admired the woman's derriere as she walked ahead of them toward an inside office.

She was quite a piece of work, Dottoressa Russo was: a luxuriant head of tawny hair, a pair of piercing green eyes, a tall, lithe body; she wore a short skirt that revealed a serious pair of legs. She was good-looking, knew it, and made no secret of the fact. But she was also rather aggressive, and this too she was happy to flaunt.

"Now then, I know that you've spoken to Arturo. That he told you where we were, last weekend, and what we were doing. Which means you know that we weren't in contact with anyone, and that we therefore have no witnesses."

Aragona struck a pose, placing one elbow on the armrest of his chair and dropping his voice a few octaves: "And just why weren't you in contact with anyone?"

"Maybe I failed to make the situation clear. If a woman goes away for the weekend with a very prominent married man, who happens to have told his wife that he's going to be at an extremely boring conference on Capri, then she's not about to go for a stroll downtown while enjoying a gelato. I realize it's not the sort of thing that happens to you very often, officer, but still, that's the way it works."

Aragona blinked repeatedly as if he'd just been slapped in the face. Lojacono asked: "How long have you known the notary Festa?"

"I first met him five years ago, but we've been seeing each other for a year and a few months. By which I mean, we've been a couple."

The lieutenant appreciated the frank talk. The woman was willing to level with them, and at least she'd spare them pointless hypocrisies that would just be a waste of time.

"Did you know Signora Cecilia De Santis?"

"I've met her once or twice, in a social setting. Once at the Teatro San Carlo, and another time at a charity auction she organized, last Christmas. Arturo begged me not to go, he was terrified at the thought. I told him not to worry, that I wouldn't so much as peek in; but instead, at the last minute, I changed my mind and went. I have to have to say that she showed a readiness of spirit that I never would have expected."

Aragona asked: "But wait, are you saying that the signora knew about the fact . . . about you and the notary?"

Once again, Russo gazed at him with an entomologist's detachment.

"Of course she knew about us. The whole city knew about us, it was and remains the number one topic of discussion for all the gossips that enliven the upper crust; do you think that she of all people wouldn't have heard? She'd known for months, oh, she knew. No doubt about it."

Aragona was fascinated: "And did anything happen? Did the signora confront you, did you have a squabble, a fight?"

The woman threw her head back and laughed, displaying a perfect, healthy set of teeth, worthy of the beast of prey that she was: "Oh, please. She was smart enough to know that anything of the sort would have spelled her final defeat. It was precisely what I was hoping for, and it would have been wonderful. But she did no such thing. Instead, she thanked me graciously when I bought one of her horrible glass balls, at an exorbitant price."

Lojacono listened attentively: "So the signora knew. And you and the notary knew that she knew. How does one resolve a situation like that? What were you waiting for?"

Russo stood up and walked toward the window. Outside, the clouds were gathering, dark and menacing.

"Lieutenant, do you know this city? It's three cities, really. One city, the one that really matters, is just a small town with a population of a few thousand. A second city consists of everyone with a job and a salary, who live from the 27th of one month to the 27th of the next, hoping they'll be able to afford a beach vacation. The third city, with a million or so inhabitants, gets by and tries to survive as best it can."

A fat drop of rain hit the pane of glass and started sliding down it.

"Getting into the first city is no simple matter. Not because it's inhabited by a better sort of people than the others are, let's be clear on that: they're almost all idiots, inane, shallow individuals who haven't faced a real problem in generations and wouldn't know how to if they did. But they have money. Lots and lots of money. And they won't let go of a cent, not for any reason."

Lojacono and Aragona noticed that the description matched the one that the Baroness Ruffolo had provided of her milieu at the yacht club; though they were coming at it from opposite directions, the two women were in complete agreement.

"Arturo and I weren't born into that world. We didn't get in by birthright, we don't have any institutional role or position. But we're better than them, far better. We've had problems, we know our way around them, we know how to evaluate them, and we've overcome them. So we know how to solve their problems too, and in fact we do solve them." Here she turned to look at the two policemen, keeping her arms wrapped tight around her chest. "So they use us. They can't do without us. But there's a big difference between needing us and welcoming us. Cecilia, Arturo's wife, knew that she was in a position of strength and made the most of it. She pretended not to know about me and her husband, and thought that she could hold onto her position. But there was one thing she hadn't, shall we say, taken into account."

She paused. Aragona asked: "Namely?"

"I'm pregnant. I'm going to have Arturo's baby."

The words exploded into the silence like a gunshot. "Did the signora know that?" Lojacono asked.

"No, that's something I found out very recently myself, just a couple of weeks ago. I have very regular periods, I took the pregnancy test the second day after I missed mine. Arturo and I are the only ones who know; I went to tell him in person, at his office. I wanted to see the look on his face when I told him."

"And what look was there on his face when you told him?"
Russo walked back around the desk and sat down.

"At first, he was happy, overjoyed. He comes from a family
of farmers, he's accustomed to thinking of children as blessings
from heaven and she couldn't give him any. She couldn't have
children. Then, and this is what I expected, he started to bring
up a series of problems."

"What kind of problems?"

"Problems like: how will I tell her, now what'll happen,
how can I work around the fact that all of our property is in
her name, what's going to become of the clients that are friends
of hers, and so on. All problems having to do with her."

More drops fell on the pane of glass, in the silence.

The woman leveled her green eyes at Lojacono's:
"Lieutenant, let's not beat around the bush: that woman was
the only real obstacle standing between me and the thing I
wanted. I saw this man and took him for myself before he even
realized who I was. Women, real women, women who know
what they want—that's what they do. He and I are of the same
breed: we're both good at what we do and we both have claws.
Her social position was useful to him, at first, but now he can
walk on his own two feet. We both can. I just needed to bring
him around and now, thanks in part to this baby, I'd succeeded. It was just a matter of time."

Aragona asked: "A matter of what time?"

Russo went on talking while looking in Lojacono's direction: "The time to talk to her, and he was going to do it. Just a
little more time, and he'd have done it."

The lieutenant stared at her, expressionless: "But he hadn't
done it yet. And in the meantime the signora is dead.
Murdered, to be exact."

"Yes. And I can understand that, from your point of view,
the conclusion is obvious. But that's not what happened, you
know: it wasn't us. We were together, at the villa in Sorrento,

doing our usual pale imitation of normal life: a woman cooking for her man, a man chatting with his woman, laughing as if
the outside world didn't exist. We didn't do it. But we have no
way to prove it."

Lojacono asked her, just as he'd asked the notary: "Why did
you agree to talk to us, Dottoressa? What drove you to do that?"

"You're trying to catch the murderer, no? If we hadn't
talked to you, you'd have been convinced that we had something to hide. And Arturo's lawyer was afraid that we might
somehow contradict each other or ourselves. But how can we
contradict ourselves if we tell you the truth?"

Lojacono nodded.

"I understand. But you have no proof. And the only sure
thing is that the signora is dead."

"It's true, her death is one sure thing. And I won't deny
that, as far as the future goes, that solves a few problems for
me; but only if you succeed in tracking down whoever really
did it. Right now, it's worse for me: it isn't going to be easy for
Arturo to rid himself of memories, images, and souvenirs of a
life spent together. It's one thing to think back on a tear-
streaked face screaming at you, railing against your betrayal,
quite another to remember a gentle smile and the memory of a
caress. How can you compete with a photograph?"

Lojacono nodded again.

"Dottoressa, who do you think did it? Do you have any suspicions, any ideas?"

The woman thought it over at length and then said: "No, I
couldn't say. Maybe just some thugs, this city is scary and the
police can't do much, no offense. But I actually don't know
much about the life she led. I have to admit, though, that I've
never heard anyone say anything bad about her, and believe
me, that's a rare thing in certain circles; people would have
been especially happy to offer me any gossip they could come
by. Instead, never a word. Her only passion, an innocent one,

was for those glass balls; I wonder if she could read the future in them. She was a good woman, and I certainly never had it in for her. Things happen, people meet. That's all."

When they got outside it was raining, really starting to come down. They ran flat out until they reached the car and got in, just managing to avoid getting drenched.

Aragona cleaned his eyeglasses with a paper tissue, taking an almost priestly care.

"You go in to question someone with one set of beliefs, and pretty soon, you realize you have to throw them all away. I expected someone completely different; this is an ordinary woman who got herself knocked up by the first guy who came along; hardly some dark lady who drove a mature professional to commit murder. So we're back to square one."

Lojacono ran a hand through his wet hair: "Still, she leveled with us, and she openly admitted that De Santis was an obstacle in her way, keeping her from the man she wanted. And we shouldn't underestimate the importance of the fact that she's pregnant: women in that state often start to look at the world differently."

Aragona thought about what his partner had just said: "Maybe so; but to me she just seemed like she was worrying about the future. I can't see her confronting De Santis and killing her; and I can't picture her maneuvering the notary into killing his wife either, as far as that goes. But I'll tell you one thing, I wish I'd been there when she went into the notary's office and told him about the baby, and he started muttering about how he couldn't, that his friends, that his clients, and what people would think, and so on. I can just imagine how that signorina yelled; they probably heard it a mile away, that's what I'd bet."

He chuckled, and went on wiping the lenses. And he failed to notice, at first, that beside him Lojacono was sitting wide-eyed, and had turned to stare at him.

When he saw him, he stopped short, glasses and tissue still in hand: "Well? What is it? What did I say?"

His partner started to laugh, softly. The laughter spread, until it had taken over his face.

"You know something, Arago'? I'd underestimated you. In fact, you're a genius, a goddamned genius. A fucking genius is what you are, Arago'!"

Aragona didn't have the slightest idea of what Lojacono was talking about.

Outside, the rain was turning into hail, and large pellets were rattling against the windshield.

But nothing was rattling loose inside Lojacono's head now: everything was where it belonged.

LI

It was like a fever. From that moment, time seemed to accelerate, as if someone had pushed the "fast-forward" button on their day.

Lojacono explained his theory to Aragona, discovering as he put it into words that all the tiles of the mosaic were fitting into place, every element now had an explanation, each individual incongruence had been ironed out.

The young man was delighted, as if he'd just been given a priceless gift.

"Fantastic. Fantastic. And it was all right in front of our noses. Well, what are we waiting for? Let's wrap this case up!"

Lojacono shook his head: "No. Not yet. We still have a few things to check out first. Let's get to work."

And they split up, each going his own way.

Lojacono went back to the barracks where the forensic squad was headquartered.

He was drying off in a waiting room when he was greeted by an out-of-breath Bistrocchi, who—the memory of the brutal humiliation he'd been subjected to last time still fresh—didn't hesitate to put himself at the detective's complete and entire disposal.

Lojacono immediately asked after the information that interested him. The man in the white lab coat threw his arms out wide: "Unfortunately, lieutenant, there too we have no prints. Clearly someone was wearing a pair of gloves there too.

It's also true that only rarely do we find clear prints on that type of item; there's almost never a direct contact with the fingertips . . ."

Lojacono interrupted him; he didn't have time to sit through a lesson on the detection of fingerprints.

"Listen, sir, all I want is to examine the object. Would that be possible?"

Disappointed, Bistrocchi left the room and returned with a transparent plastic bag. He put on a pair of latex gloves and carefully extracted its contents.

Another plastic bag. A shopping bag

"Here you are, the stolen silver was found in this. As you can see, there's a rip in the side, possibly caused by one of the objects either while they were being transported, or when they were tossed into the dumpster."

But that's not what Lojacono was interested in. On one side of the plastic bag there was a logo of some kind. He spoke to Bistrocchi: "Excuse me, but could you turn it toward me, so that I can get a better look at what's written on it?"

He leaned forward and read.

The first confirmation.

Aragona, heading over to the notary's offices and, as usual, driving at breakneck speed, was hosing pedestrians down, sending tidal waves of rainwater onto the sidewalks as he fiddled with his cell phone: he needed to get in touch with Ottavia Calabrese immediately.

Luckily, she was the one who answered: "Ah, *ciao*, Aragona. I would have called you later: you remember the report you asked me to do on Adrian Florea, the notary's housekeeper's boyfriend? Well, he's clean. No priors, no evidence of any contact with ex-convicts, or . . ."

Aragona sighed loudly: "Of course, just what I expected. I only wanted to run the check to make sure, I saw when I met him that he was a stand-up guy. And after all, we have to stop assuming every immigrant is necessarily a criminal! Tell me something else, though: by any chance did the official report come in from the IT department?"

Ottavia chuckled: "Not yet, they're taking their time. What is it you need, though?"

"I need the date and time that the email reserving the trip to Whatchamacallit was sent from the notary's office. Can you help me out?"

By the time he reached the firm, he had the information. He asked to see the notary, who immediately led him into his private office. Aragona had to force himself not to lock eyes with any of the employees, which Lojacono had so often warned him against.

Once inside, after making sure that the door was securely shut, he asked the notary for what he needed.

The legal professional was baffled: "That's very, very confidential information. It's not the sort of thing I can share with just anybody, we have fiduciary responsibilities to safeguard the secrecy . . ."

Lieutenant Lojacono had warned him of this possible, last-ditch evasion, but time was running out; he wasn't about to be thwarted by propriety. So Aragona said exactly what he and his partner had agreed on: "Notary Festa, if you want to get out of this situation in one piece, there's no alternative. If you can't do it for your wife's memory, do it for yourself."

And, after thinking it over briefly, the notary picked up his phone and, in a brusque and decisive voice, summoned the signora Lina Rea to his office.

Lojacono caught a taxi, and was refreshed by the experience of crossing the city while not gripped by the horrifying certainty that either he or a dozen innocent citizens were about to die.

The rain was falling incessantly and the traffic, already tangled, was only getting worse; the streets were starting to flood.

The lieutenant asked the taxi driver how long he thought it would take, and received an eloquent shrug in reply. At that point he tried to call Marinella; he hadn't heard from her since their last, stormy conversation, in the aftermath of her screaming fight with her mother. The girl's cell phone, however, seemed to be off.

Then he called Laura Piras, to bring her up-to-date on the case. The woman answered on the second ring: "Hey, *ciao*! What's going on, do you have news?"

"I believe I do. If you ask me, we've cracked it."

"Really? Tell me everything. Spare me no detail."

Lojacono told her the whole story, starting with his visit to the notary's office, and then moving on to his meeting with Russo. And he told her, specifically, how it had been Aragona's chance phrase that had torn the veil from his eyes, showing him a new theory that he was now in the process of checking out.

Piras listened intently, breaking in now and then with brief questions and monosyllabic sounds of confirmation. Then she said: "Incredible. Really incredible. The thing that surprises me most is that Aragona actually seems to have justified his existence. And just what do you intend to do now?"

Lojacono told her about the things that were still being checked out, by Aragona at the notary's office and by him, after his recent trip to forensics.

She asked: "And now you're heading over to the store, is that right? To check out the logo on the bag. You know, it really does add up. And I won't lie to you, it would be a blessing, a spectacular success to throw in everyone's face, everyone who said that Pizzofalcone should be shut down immediately. But if I were you, I'd move cautiously: you need to obtain a full and complete confession; otherwise, any two-bit lawyer will be able to dismantle your whole theory in seconds. You have a series of clues, but not a single piece of solid evidence."

Lojacono objected: "What do you mean, clues? I explained

everything to you clearly, that's the only way it could have happened! We've got it, we know who it was, and we presumably have the motive as well."

"Sure, but I could never authorize you to make an arrest on this basis. You can't just work by a process of elimination, and you know that: we need proof, certainty, and right now you have no solid evidence. And no certainty either, believe me. Which means you have just one option: you need to obtain a full confession, which is, as you know, the hardest thing. And I can't help you get that from here."

Lojacono reached the store filled with a new anxiety; in the space of just a few yards, walking from the taxi to the front door, he got thoroughly drenched. He asked the shop clerk a few questions, and she directed him to the section he was interested in, which was downstairs. In a corner, at the end of an aisle that boasted a wide selection of dishes and glasses adorned with wedding announcements, there was a display case that looked exactly like the shelves at the scene of the crime.

He walked over to it, hands in his pockets, rivulets of water dripping off his raincoat, creating a small puddle on the gleaming floor. Behind two layers of glass, a dancer with a ukulele looked up at him, smiling sweetly. He didn't smile back.

A few minutes later, he was leaving the store with a bag in hand that was in every detail identical—except for the rip on the side—to the one now being held in the forensic squad's laboratory.

At the same time, his cell phone buzzed in his pocket: it was Aragona. His partner, jubilant, told him that he'd just found the confirmation that they needed at the notary's office.

Now they just needed to wrap the case up, as Aragona had put it.

Which was the hardest thing, as Piras had told him.

LII

Once they'd checked everything out, they'd headed back to the station house.

The meeting, which Palma had insisted that everyone attend, had been short but intense: it was clear that the choice of strategy and its success or failure would not only determine how the case would be resolved, but also whether or not the precinct would survive.

Lojacono and Aragona had revealed the identity of Cecilia De Santis's murderer and explained how they had figured it out. The confirmation had come from assembling various observations—from forensics, from the notary's office, from the luxury housewares store. When they'd finished talking, there had been a moment of intent silence.

Romano and Di Nardo had agreed with Aragona: he wanted to make an immediate arrest, convinced they had all the elements necessary to construct a successful prosecution. Palma and Pisanelli, in light of their more extensive experience, had instead counseled a more cautious approach: they'd seen more than a few criminals walk free because someone had been in a hurry to wrap up an investigation.

Ottavia had nodded: "That's true. But it's also true that if we submit all our evidence to the magistrate, someone else will have the privilege of completing the investigation; and if we—and I mean all of us—are convinced that we know who committed this murder, it's not fair for those guys to get to wrap up the case. Especially if this might determine our future as a precinct. As far as I'm concerned, I'm for trusting Lojacono and Aragona: I bet they'll get a confession. I'd let them try."

Pisanelli, noncommittally, had said they certainly risked putting the guilty party on notice, and giving the murderer time and opportunity to prepare a stronger defense; but he also had to agree that, if there was a way to save Pizzofalcone, this was it.

And so now Lojacono and Aragona found themselves standing under a narrow overhang, seeking shelter from the driving rain, the scene dimly illuminated by a streetlight that hung from an overhead cable in the middle of the street and was swaying in the wind. They were waiting for the person who had murdered Signora Cecilia De Santis to be so good as to exit the building across the street.

The tension was palpable, and for the past several minutes neither man had said a word. Every so often Aragona took off his glasses and tried to wipe them off with a handkerchief that was already soaked; Lojacono wondered how the hell he could even see through those preposterous blue-tinted lenses now streaked with rain.

At last, the person who had murdered Signora Cecilia De Santis emerged from the front door. The person stopped at the threshold, looked out at the pouring rain, trying to gauge the distance that needed to be covered in order to reach the expensive sedan that was waiting to be driven to the dry shelter of a garage. The person sighed, and pulled out a pair of black leather gloves.

Lojacono and Aragona emerged from the shadows and briskly crossed the street, indifferent to the puddles they splashed through on the way; they approached the person who had murdered Signora Cecilia De Santis, one man on each side. "Let's get in the car," Lojacono said. "That way we can have a little chat."

Once they were inside, Aragona in the middle of the back-seat and Lojacono in front, in the passenger seat, the murderer said: "That way we can have a little chat. And just what are we supposed to chat about, lieutenant? I've already told you everything I know."

Lojacono said: "No, De Lucia. You haven't told us everything. We know that, because the first time we talked, you said that the poor signora stayed shut up in her apartment with all the windows and shutters fastened tight, but you couldn't have known that, because the notary told us that during their phone call his wife had told him that she had just closed the windows and blinds, including the one that the concierge had just fixed, but also that she didn't usually do that. We know because only you and Rea had the passwords to the notary's computer, and Rea doesn't know how to use computers at all; and from that computer, reservations were made for a trip, reservations made with a specific request, that it be possible to change one of the names up to one day before departure, and the name that was to be changed was the notary's, because the people who would be going on that trip were you and the signora. We know it because that email was sent at 10:13 A.M. on March 5th, and at that exact time, as we know from the probate ledger, the notary was in fact with Signora Rea drawing up a last will and testament on Via Posillipo. We know it because the shopping bag used to carry away the silver that was stolen as a cover and then discarded in a dumpster was the same bag used to bring the snow globe, the murder weapon, into the apartment, because it had in fact just arrived; and you are the one who purchased it, in the store where you regularly accompanied the signora, and where they remember very well who purchased the snow globe, claiming that it was a purchase being made on the signora's behalf. We know, because the absence of fingerprints at the scene of the crime is due to the fact that you were wearing these gloves, the gloves you use to drive the notary's sedan, to make sure you don't smear the briarwood steering wheel with the ink from the promissory notes you handle all day. And we know it because you've known and worked for the notary all these years, which makes it plausible that the signora would have opened the door to you at that time on a Sunday night, in a dressing gown. We know everything. The only thing we don't know is why you did it."

There ensued a silence that, to the two policemen, seemed to last for a thousand years.

The chubby little man sat there with his head bowed, his wet comb-over plastered dismally to his cranium, his thick glasses lenses fogged up, his gloved hands cradled in his lap, motionless. Outside, a gust of rain lashed the windshield.

At last, he looked up, lost in thoughts and memories. And he spoke, repeating as usual the last few words uttered to him.

The only thing you don't know is why I did it.

Do you think I haven't asked myself the same thing?

Do you think I haven't been wondering it every minute, since it happened right up until this very second?

Who even knows why I did it.

All I know is that I did it, and that my life ended at that very instant, along with hers.

He didn't deserve her, you know. That man didn't deserve her. He's a bastard, an arrogant, shallow bastard. He likes women, he doesn't let even one of them get by him: if you only knew how many young women, mature matrons, even barely legal girls I've seen pass through his hands over the years. And I know it, because the bastard used me to cover his tracks. Oh, the lies I've had to tell, to everyone, when, instead of working or going home, he was acting the playboy around town.

And he owed everything he had to her; she had even given him the money that allowed him to study for his civil service exam. And his clients, the highly placed friends he was so proud of, they all came from her. He owed her everything.

My position, you understand, is like a front row seat. From where I sit you see lots of things, you understand lots of things. Over the years I've seen what kind of a man he is, and I've seen what a wonderful woman she is. She was. Because now she's dead, isn't she? She's dead. And I killed her.

He'd tell me: Rino, do me a favor, she wants to be taken here or there, you take the long way round, or pretend the car isn't working right, stall, give me time to get back, you already know what we're talking about, right? And he'd laugh, and shoot me a wink. How that wink disgusted me. And he'd say: we understand each other, man to man, eh? What was I supposed to understand, man to man, sitting in my little furnished room, reading a book or watching a movie on TV, while he's staying in the finest five-star hotels with beautiful women, spending the money he earned thanks to her?

Still, I was happy. I was happy because I got to spend time with her. She was a wonderful woman, you know that? She suffered, she suffered terribly. He thought he was pulling the wool over her eyes, but she understood it all, she knew everything. She kept her pain to herself, and she avoided other people because every friend she saw, male or female, couldn't wait to tell her all about her husband's latest exploits. Shitheads, you know: they like to see other people suffer. Sometimes even here in the car, while I was driving, they'd say to her: Don't you know, can't you see? I hear that what's-her-name ran into him on Capri with this woman, and so-and-so saw him in Sorrento with some other woman. But she'd just smile and reply: I don't care, and she'd change the subject; but I knew how it tore her up inside.

But she'd talk to me about it. She was the only one who'd talk to me. I don't talk with anyone; that office is a nest of vipers, just put three women together and forget about the Gaza Strip, there's your intractable war zone. Better to have nothing to do with them. I live a private life, I'm not the kind of guy who's out and about at night. She was the only person who talked to me.

What else were we going to do? She in her luxury, me in my poverty, we were two lonely people. At least we could comfort each other. And we did.

We got into the habit of going off to Bagnoli, down by the water. There's a place there, a miserable dive bar, really a kiosk more than anything else: two or three tables. It's quiet, and no one who knew her would have been caught dead there. She'd send for me, tell her husband that she needed to go shopping for something or other, and right away, he'd say: Rino, go pick up my wife, and take as long as you can. And he'd shoot me a wink. She used to laugh about it, she said it was the only time it was her pulling the wool over his eyes.

We'd sit there and we'd talk and talk. She'd order a tea, hot in the winter, iced in the summer. I'd pay. That was important to me. A man pays for his woman's drinks, doesn't he? Even if she's wealthy, and you're just a penniless wretch.

He's rich, charming, handsome; but he's made of plastic. He always took her for all she was worth, and I wouldn't even let her pay for her tea. We'd hold hands. I remember the first time, she took my hand; I never would have had the nerve.

I would ask her why she put up with it. She'd answer sadly: he's my husband. I think she actually felt guilty, the bastard made her feel guilty; because she hadn't been able to give him children, because she didn't think she was pretty, even though she was, she was beautiful, you know. The two of you never met her, you never saw her when she looked out to sea, or when she suddenly broke into laughter. She was beautiful.

The last year had been pure hell for her. Because now there was this new girlfriend, the redhead. This one wasn't like all the others, the whores he'd pick up, play around with for a couple of days, and then discard; lunch, an expensive dinner, a hotel, and a bouquet of roses the morning after, roses that he'd send me to buy, slipping the money and a note into my pocket, shooting me that fucking wink. This one was different.

I noticed it the very first time, when she came to the office for some work-related matter. A tough one, no-nonsense, aggressive. He gave her the usual melting glance, and she smiled the way all the others usually smiled, but in her smile I could see the wild animal that had spotted its prey. I wasn't surprised when they became a couple.

She found out about it immediately, of course none of her friends could wait to tell her. Poor Cecilia. She tried to tell herself it would end, but it didn't.

I think she clung to the idea that she was still, in spite of everything, his wife; that he might have his flings, but he'd always come home to her in the end. That with the other women he was killing time, enjoying himself, trying to forget the fact that he was getting old; but she, she was his safe haven, where he could show his weaknesses and curl up in Mama's arms. Maybe he was actually the son they'd never been able to have. Maybe she felt like the mother; and after all, you never abandon your mother.

But that one, the redhead, wasn't about to let herself be treated the way he treated all the others. The redhead wanted him, she wanted him all for herself. She needed him: prestige, money, connections. In the end, he'd found himself a woman who was just like him. Even worse.

She's intelligent, the redhead. She's cunning. Little by little, she even forced him to show her off in public, she didn't care how it made him look, how it made his poor wife look. When a woman like her makes up her mind, she doesn't let anyone stand in her way.

One day, she asked to have me pick her up, and I found her puffy-eyed from crying, wearing a pair of oversized sunglasses. He hadn't come home that night, and he hadn't even bothered to call; she'd called him herself, and he'd told her, Quit bothering me. And on the phone she could hear a woman laughing in the background. She told me the story, in despair, at our little place down by the water. I did my best to comfort her. She said to me: I should have found a man like you, I really should have. I looked for a man who wasn't part of the world I grew up in, because that world disgusts me: but I should have found a man like you.

It was then, only then, that I started to think. Before then I hadn't even dreamed that a woman like her, a queen, a goddess, would do so much as look twice at someone like me. But she'd said it, right? She'd said it herself, that should have found a man like me. So?

She always used to say that, one fine day, she was the one who'd run away. Far away, someplace by the sea, with white sand and palm trees. She'd laugh and say she knew that was the dream of every shopgirl and shampooist, and she'd say that maybe deep down she really was a shampooist. And I'd say that maybe I'd take her there, me of all people, and she'd laugh and laugh. She'd say that to get there we'd have to stow away in the hold of a ship, like African slaves in America. She was so pretty when she laughed, you can't even imagine.

Then one day the thing with the redhead took place, the day she walked into the firm, went into his office, closed the door, and started screaming like a lunatic, everyone in the firm could hear her. Rea got a look on her face, you've seen her, she's obviously head over heels in love with the notary, as if someone like him is going to even notice someone like her; she came that close to storming in there to defend him. So anyway, the redhead was screaming that now, with a baby on the way, she'd no longer tolerate being hidden in the shadows. That she was giving him a son, something that poor old woman never did for him, and so she wanted the position she deserved. Those were her exact words: that poor old woman. When they heard that, Imma and Marina, those two idiots, looked at each other and burst out laughing. Intolerable: two silly geese laughing at the best woman in the world, all because that bastard couldn't manage to keep his pants zipped.

Then, that's when I made up my mind. I had the money, little

*by little I'd set it aside; but not enough for the trip. For that I'd
have to use the firm's money, the account we use for the promissory notes, where we keep the cash that comes in. The notes are
for a lot of money, there's always a sizable overage, it would have
taken them at least a month before they realized it was missing
and by then it would be too late, by then she and I would already
be on the beach. Happy. At last. Because if we could be happy at
Bagnoli, sitting at a rusty table next to a polluted beach, in that
magical spot we'd be in paradise.*

*I made the reservations in his name, but I asked how late I
could change the name of one of the travelers. I had all the time
I needed. Now I only needed to tell her.*

*I waited for the right moment, when the bastard was organ-
izing his usual nice weekend with the redhead. I had driven
them myself; I knew they wouldn't be back before Monday. I
prepared carefully, I'd have to tell her gently, but also firmly. It
would be a difficult decision, I knew that well. But it was necessary, don't you see? The only way for us to find a little happiness,
too; and after all we had a right to happiness, no? Didn't we have
the right to a little happiness of our own?*

*So I decided to take her an apt little gift, to show her that she
could count on me. I went to the shop on Via Duomo, the one
where she was a regular customer. We went there often, she so
loved those snow globes, the* boules de neige, *as she called them in
a perfect accent. One time I asked her why she liked them so much:
and she said that when she looked into them she could dream of a
future that didn't exist, and it would all seem real. She was beautiful when she smiled; but I told you that already, didn't I?*

*And so I went to the store, and I looked for a glass ball that
would tell her about the place I wanted to take her. That's how I
wanted to tell her. Now she had to stop lying to herself, she
couldn't go on pretending to ignore reality: the redhead was about
to have a baby, and he was going to leave her. That was clear.*

In that case, we might as well beat them to the punch and run

*away together. Let him keep all the money, I'd take care of her,
I'd do something, I'd find a way.*

*She opened the door immediately, and there was fear in her
eyes. Outside, the storm was raging, the sea was in the air, even
up on the fifth floor, and she'd shut herself in. But she opened
the door immediately when she heard it was me, and the first
thing she wanted to know was if something had happened to
him. To that bastard. Not much of a beginning, eh? Maybe I
should have understood from that question alone, and stopped
right there. At least she'd still be alive. And I'd be a free man.
But free to do what?*

*I told her no, he was fine, doing much better than she and I
put together, in fact. That as usual he was holed up in some villa
in Sorrento, naked, drinking champagne with the redhead,
thinking of the future that awaited them, a future as a happy
family: him, her, their child, and Cecilia's money. I was harsh: it
seemed to me that the time had come for her to open her eyes
and understand what was already clear to me. Blindingly clear.*

*She listened to me. She looked at me without speaking. I had
to raise my voice, outside the wind and the sea were pounding
on the windows as if they wanted to get in. It was like being in
a movie.*

*I told her that we should run away together, that we, too, had
a right to be happy. I told her that I'd already made reservations,
that she didn't need to bring anything, just herself, that I'd take
care of everything. She ran her eyes over all those snow globes,
you've seen them yourselves, no? Hundreds of heavy glass snow
globes, organized by country, each full of an imaginary future
like a gypsy fortune-teller's crystal ball at the carnival.*

*At last, she spoke. And she told me that in her heart, in her
future, there was no room for happiness without him. That she
loved him, that she had always loved him. That he would come
back, that he had always come back. That she'd take him back,
even with another woman's child. That in the end money would*

take care of everything, the way it always had in the past. That she was very sorry for me, very; but that she had no intention of going anywhere.

And she turned her back on me.

I don't know whether it was her words—that she was sorry for me—or because she turned to go. I felt I'd been erased, expelled. And mocked. How dare she turn and walk away? Was I nothing, no one? Didn't I deserve, I don't know, at least a caress, a tear? A sign of regret?

I remember the rage of that moment. I don't remember what I thought, I don't remember doing it. But I did do it. I was standing there, in the middle of the room, still wearing the gloves I use when I drive this car, the bag in one hand and the glass ball with the hula dancer in the other. And she turned around and walked away.

Maybe I wanted to stop her. Maybe I just wanted to get rid of the glass ball, which represented all my illusions. Who knows. The fact remains that I threw it. At her, as she was heading for her bedroom, to sob into her pillow like she did every night.

After I don't know how long, I saw her lying there on the floor, no longer breathing. So I tried to think fast, I was afraid. I took some silver, just the first few things I could get my hands on, I tossed them into the bag, and I left. Then I found a dumpster and I tossed it all in. And then I sat down on a low wall, hoping that the waves would be big enough to sweep me away. Maybe all the way to that island.

Maybe I'd find her there, on the beach, waiting for me with a smile.

She was pretty when she smiled. Beautiful.

Did I tell you, how beautiful she was?

LIII

Brother Leonardo, the parish priest of Santissima Annunziata, heaved a theatrical sigh: "Teodo', would you get it into your head once and for all that we're monks? You can't come to me every day asking what we want to have for lunch, suggesting dishes you can't even find in a restaurant. You do what you think best, but try to economize because we're short on cash, as you know all too well."

Brother Teodoro scratched his bald head: "What are you trying to tell me, because we're monks we can't eat? I respect all the precepts, Leonardo, and you know it. I know what we can eat and what we can't, I know we're supposed to avoid meat when we can, and I spend as little as humanly possible. But what's wrong with trying to spruce up even a bowl of lentils? It's still God's bounty, isn't it?"

Leonardo stood as tall as his four foot eleven would allow and struck a pose of heartbroken chagrin. He knew that getting in an argument with the monastery's cook was the worst thing he could do, especially when there were worshippers outside the sacristy waiting to say confession.

"All right, do as you think best, Teodo'. I have to go and hear confession, and by the way it wouldn't be bad if every so often you tried to help me out with that, too, instead of hiding behind your responsibilities in the garden and the kitchen; otherwise our congregation will start to change their minds, and instead of confessing their old sins, they'll go commit new ones."

Teodoro, who, unlike Leonardo, was a big, strapping man, with a sizable belly, blushed: "You know very well, Leona', that if I can, I like to . . . avoid hearing confession. It embarrasses me, I couldn't say why, but it does, and we've talked about it a number of times. I feel like I'm peeking into people's homes, into their darkest rooms."

The minuscule monk stopped midway through the process of donning his vestments and turned to stare at his brother: "Teodo', I hope you're just pulling my leg, because that would be a very grave sin. It's a vow, a sacred duty for any priest, to hear confession. I know it isn't easy, in fact, it's our most burdensome obligation, but can you imagine if we didn't do it? Who would comfort all those tormented souls? Who would help them to find peace? I don't want to hear you say anything like that again!"

Teodoro looked down at the floor in embarrassment: "You're right, I know it. But if it's possible, I'd like a dispensation; I can take care of all the other things that need doing, and after all you have Pietro, Roberto, and Samuele, no? That is, if it's necessary I'm always here, but if it's possible to avoid it . . ."

Leonardo felt sorry for that enormous man with such a fragile heart. He walked over and gave him a pat on the back.

"Don't worry, Teodo', it's all right. I know you don't like it, and if I can keep from asking you, I do. Now let me go, though; and for lunch, as usual, do as you think best: I'm certain that it will be as delicious as ever, and we'll all think to ourselves that we made the right choice when we decided to become monks, for our bellies as well as for our souls."

He walked out into the cool, welcoming church. The angry sound of pouring rain was muffled here, and the large stained glass windows let in a grayish light. His expert gaze roamed over the pews: aside from the three little old ladies who came in every night to kill time by reciting rosaries, there was a small group of young people with a couple of guitars, rehearsing songs for Sunday, and several people waiting by the confessional farthest from the altar.

The monk shot a quick wink at an old woman, her head covered with a handkerchief, and stopped to talk to the young people, praising them for their hard work on the countermelody to *Laudato si'*; at last, he went over to those who were waiting to confess.

He sighed. Teodoro hadn't been completely wrong: sometimes it was an ordeal to take on the grief and shadows that ordinary people carried within them. Luckily, many of those who sought confession were familiar to the parish priest, as fully three of the four waiting that day were: a widow getting on in years who still had impure thoughts that engendered equally risqué dreams, dreams that she inevitably found herself regretting guiltily the instant she woke up; a pious teenage boy going through a difficult puberty, who sometimes gave in to the impulse to torture small animals and spray-paint walls; a wife who cheated on her unsuspecting husband with the next-door neighbor, the real father of her son. Serial sinners, who cleansed their souls with a few prayers before going back to stain them again, always with the same petty sins.

The fourth individual, though, was new to him. As he hurried toward the confessional, his oversized vestments flapping all around him, looking just like a little boy wearing one of his mother's dresses, Brother Leonardo thought of Giorgio Pisanelli. Something about the man's posture as he knelt in prayer, or perhaps his pained countenance, reminded him of his friend.

As he was listening to the confessions of the widow and the boy, Leonardo thought back to the policeman; after his wife's suicide his desire to go on living had slowly drifted away, as had all his ties to the world. Even Giorgio's phone calls with his son were increasingly infrequent and brief; Giorgio himself had confided that he sometimes felt uneasy asking for news about the life of someone who had become a distant acquaintance, even in his memories. And then there was the illness for which, in spite of Leonardo's nagging, the deputy captain refused to seek treatment.

Leonardo loved Giorgio. It pained him to know that his friend took no comfort in his faith, but he knew that he could hardly force it upon him; he wished that he could make up his mind either to rededicate himself to life, or else to let go of it entirely. This partial despair, this obsession with the suicides he was investigating, were evidence only of negative courage, of an obstinate kind of survival that was somewhat perverse.

The man Leonardo had never seen before took the sacrament, kneeling with a sigh. "Father, forgive me for I have sinned," he said.

The old man told Brother Leonardo that he was newly retired, that he'd been alone for years, that until just a few weeks ago he'd lived for his work alone, and now he saw no one, neither friends nor relatives; Leonardo was reminded even more strongly of Giorgio, and the monk felt a stab of sorrow. The man spoke of the relationship he'd had for many years with a coworker, a married woman: a long and tragic love affair. He told the priest about her unexpected death, and the immense void that it had left in his heart.

He told him that he had committed no grave sins, at least not in the conventional sense, anyway: but that for some time now he'd yearned intensely for death. He was a religious man, and he knew that toying with the idea of death was a sin, and a grave one. He lacked the courage to put an end to his life, and in any case his life was not his own, as he knew very well: but to wish for it so devoutly, Father, and to ask God for death in every prayer, every blessed day, wasn't that in itself a turning of his back on the Lord's will?

Gas, thought Leonardo. This is a case for gas. He lives all

alone, without anyone else; no one goes to see him, no courtesy visits, no phone calls. It'll be too late by the time he's found, if the windows are tightly shut.

Giorgio, Giorgio, Leonardo thought, my poor friend. Don't you see what a great grace it is—for those who want to escape from a life of pain, an existence made up of silence and shadows, where every memory is a knife to the heart—to find someone to take up that burden? Don't you see how hard it is to help these poor wretches, without letting them stain their souls with the most horrible sin of all? Don't you see that the one who performs this act of extreme charity is delivering them to Paradise?

The old man interrupted his confession to weep over his own loneliness and Leonardo, as he waited for him to recover, mused about the chorus of angels that would sing as the man entered the Kingdom of Heaven, angels that Leonardo's own kindly hands would accompany on that final step, the step that even the angels lacked the courage to take; he thought about how each angel would be able to tell the Holy Father what a blessed man Leonardo had actually been.

He whispered the man's absolution. And, pulling a pen and a piece of paper out of his cassock, he said: "My son, tell me where you live. I'll come call on you myself, now and then, to keep you company. And to bring you spiritual comfort."

LIV

T he idea came to Ottavia as a chaotic morning drew to a close.

The phone hadn't stopped ringing for a second; the national TV networks had pulled their news vans up early and parked outside the front entrance, blocking traffic so that cars honked endlessly and irritatedly in the steady rain; Guida, at the door, was directing traffic, sending TV journalists and camera operators brandishing large shoulder-mounted television cameras this way and that.

What's more, Palma had been asked by police headquarters to take part in a press conference that would lay out exactly how the suspected murderer had been identified and captured. The commissario told them all in the large open-plan office that he'd done his best to fend off the request, saying that the case's successful resolution was all due to the more than competent professionals who had come to work for him; that they should ask someone who was used to holding press conferences to do it instead, since none of them was interested in the spotlight. They were policemen.

They had agreed not to identify, except in internal reports, Lojacono and Aragona as the investigators in this specific case: it was to be considered a shared success, and it was useful to attribute it to the structure as a whole. Now let's see if they decide to shut us down, Aragona had quipped sharply, though he admitted to himself that, deep down, he really would have enjoyed going in front of the cameras. For that matter, if it hadn't been for Aragona's mention of the fact that Russo had shouted that she was pregnant within earshot of the notary's employees, it would never have occurred to Lojacono just what effect the news might have had on De Lucia who, at that point, had felt entitled to organize an elopement with the victim.

The killer, who had signed his own confession, hadn't asked for a lawyer, and so the court had appointed one. He seemed to have lost interest in his own fate. Palma had arranged to inform the notary, who was incredulous; the commissario suspected that he, too, felt a certain amount of guilt over what had happened.

Around one o'clock in the afternoon, glancing in dismay at the phone that simply wouldn't stop ringing, Ottavia said: "What do you say we all go out for a pizza tonight, someplace without a landline and where there's no cell phone coverage?"

Palma, standing by the rain-streaked window, exclaimed: "Why, of course, what a magnificent idea! And of course, the dinner's on me!"

Romano nodded, as did Pisanelli, and Di Nardo said: "I'm in."

Lojacono spoke up: "I know the perfect place. I'll call ahead and make a reservation."

Aragona burst out laughing: "Oh, now that's too much. The only out-of-towner is the one who knows the perfect place! How does make the rest of us look?"

Letizia had reserved a private dining room in the back for them. Palma had told them to bring whomever they wanted, but they'd all showed up alone.

Aragona joked that they might as well just have ordered in pizza at the station house, and that this confirmed that cops are sad and solitary individuals: the quote came from who knows what American TV show, and it earned him a chorus of *fuck yous* from his colleagues. Palma asked Ottavia why she hadn't asked her husband to come. She blushed and said that

Gaetano preferred to stay home with their son; she couldn't bring herself to confess that she hadn't even invited him.

Letizia was an attentive and magnificent hostess. She brought her guitar and sang a number of songs in dialect for them, songs that were greeted with rounds of delighted applause. Lojacono's colleagues made jocular and repeated reference to the way she looked at him, and he in turn told them how he and Letizia had just become good friends, since he went there for dinner every night.

"So how come you don't weigh 350 pounds?" asked Pisanelli, dipping another chunk of bread in the bowl of ragù.

"Forget about that, why don't you take her to bed?" asked Aragona, eyeing Letizia's generous breasts dreamily as she served tables in the other room, which earned him an elbow in the ribs from Romano. "Why, what did I say wrong? What's the matter with that? She's nice, she's a great cook, she's a real hottie, and she's clearly crazy about Lojacono. He's a cop, not a priest!"

"Friendship is a beautiful thing, Arago'," Lojacono retorted. "I don't want to ruin it."

"Why not," Di Nardo said under her breath, "it's not as if sex necessarily ruins a friendship. It's just another way of communicating, that's all."

Lojacono thought about this, and Laura Piras popped into his head. Just another way of communicating. In the meanwhile, Marinella had stopped answering his phone calls; tomorrow he'd have to call her mother to find out if his daughter was okay. He hoped with all his heart that nothing had happened to her.

The excellent food, the fine wine, the music, and the general euphoria made that night a great success, in spite of the grim misgivings they'd all had.

Aragona, decidedly tipsy, got to his feet: "I'd like to see them call us the Bastards of Pizzofalcone now. Actually, now that I think about it, let them! It's our moniker, no? And really, we ought to give each other nicknames. That'd be fun, don't you think? Tough cops. You, Lojacono, can be the Chinaman, and Romano, here," and he slapped his colleague on the back, "can be the Hulk!"

Romano glared at him grimly: "Not a good idea, because you'd definitely wind up being the Asshole."

As they were all laughing, Laura Piras walked in, magnetically attracting the notice of every man in the room. She wore a pair of light blue jeans, boots, and a navy blue raincoat over a white blouse; her informal attire made her look even younger, an impression further accentuated by her hair, which she'd pulled back and tied in a ponytail.

"Hi all, I hope I'm not intruding."

Palma leapt up to greet her: "Dottoressa, what an unexpected pleasure! Please, come sit with us, we'll order something for you to eat."

"No, thanks, I've already had dinner. Perhaps just a glass of wine."

Letizia, as if possessed of a kind of radar, had suddenly materialized in the little room. The two women found themselves face-to-face: the tall and shapely restaurateur; the petite and provocative Sardinian magistrate. Only Ottavia perceived the smidgeon of tension in the smiles they exchanged. Though they were meeting for the first time, each had heard Lojacono speak of the other.

"What can I bring you, signora?" Letizia asked.

"Nothing, thanks," Piras replied. "I'm only staying for a minute." She turned to address the table full of people: "I just came by to inform you that, in light of the results of your investigation, there was a high-level, closed-door meeting at police headquarters this afternoon. And it was decided that the Pizzofalcone precinct house will remain operational, effective immediately, and that the current allocation of resources will now become permanent. Palma, you'll receive an official communiqué in the next few days. I hope you're all happy about the news: I know I am."

Those words were greeted by a burst of applause; in the main dining room, a few curious diners turned to try to get a peek at what was going on.

The party was over; they exchanged goodnights, saying they'd see each other in the morning. They weren't friends, and who knew if they ever would be; but they were a team, and there could be no doubt about that.

Just outside of the restaurant, Piras went over to Lojacono: "I drove," she said. "You want a ride home?"

Letizia, who was pretending to pay attention to a table of lingering diners, was trying to figure out what they were talking about; the lieutenant had given her a tender goodnight kiss on the cheek, and that had made her happy, but now she saw him with that little short job with the big tits and the large, limpid eyes, and suddenly she was worried.

Lojacono made sure that his colleagues had all left: he knew that he'd catch endless hell, especially from Aragona, if he was seen leaving at night in the company of the famous, unapproachable, and widely courted Dottoressa Piras. He accepted her offer and walked off with her, unaware that he was breaking Letizia's heart; Letizia watched them grow smaller in the distance and thought to herself that if Piras wanted war, then she'd get it.

The drive through the rain wasn't a particularly talkative one. Piras drove fast and sure, respecting lights and road signs, a happy novelty to Lojacono, who had spent the last three days in the car with Aragona. Every time she shifted, the magistrate's hand brushed against the policeman's thigh.

From time to time, Lojacono looked over at her profile, illuminated by the streetlamps that shone through the rain. She struck him as exotic and yet in some way familiar, as if he'd recovered her from some forgotten past.

She looked over at him, taking her eyes off the road for a moment: "What's wrong? Why are you looking at me?"

Lojacono said nothing. Part of him wondered what would happen once they got to his apartment; whether he'd invite her to come upstairs, whether she'd accept or not. Whether they'd kiss. He also thought, with a touch of anxiety, of the state of his bachelor apartment—the leftover food in the fridge; the dirty laundry scattered everywhere—but then he remembered that at least he had a cold bottle of white wine, and felt reassured.

At last they arrived, just as the rain began to fall harder. Laura said: "I'll walk you to the front door, you don't have an umbrella," putting off for a few seconds Lojacono's worries. They crossed the street together, laughing and jumping over puddles.

They walked through the street door, still laughing for no good reason; they failed to notice a dark figure standing in the atrium.

The figure stepped out of the shadows and took a step forward, finally illuminated by the fluorescent light.

The girl leveled her almond-shaped eyes at Lojacono's own, sniffed loudly, and said: "*Ciao*, Papi."

Acknowledgments

Certain stories have many eyes; it is by bringing all these eyes together that it is possible to build and so tell the story. The eyes of this story are all here.

Ed McBain, unparalleled master.

The angels of the city, Fabiola Mancone, Valeria Moffa, Luigi Bonagura, and Luigi Merolla, who told me about good and evil.

Giulio Di Mizio, who told me about death.

Dino Falconio, my brother, who told me about a firm, and what happens there. And Anna Giulia, she knows why.

Laura Pace and Annamaria Torroncelli, who told me about autism.

Eliana and Chiara, who told me about love.

My Roberto, who told me about grief.

Francesco Colombo, who met my words halfway.

Severino Cesari, who recognized my story out of all the others.

Paolo Repetti, who believed in it and defended it against everything and everyone.

Maria Paola Romeo, who brings it out into the world.

The Corpi Freddi, who were there at its birth, and who will keep it safe for me.

My eyes, my encounter, and every word of mine for my Paola.

ABOUT THE AUTHOR

Maurizio de Giovanni is the author of the "Commissario Ricciardi" books, hardboiled historical noirs set in 1930s Naples whose sales exceed one million copies. He is also the author of the contemporary Neapolitan thriller, *The Crocodile*. He lives in Naples with his family.